—the—

SUGAR THORNS

Kayla Rose

Cover design by Kayla Rose
Cover art by Boyan Dimitrov/Shutterstock

ISBN 978-1-7336165-7-7 (paperback)
ISBN 978-1-7336165-6-0 (ebook)

BOOKS BY KAYLA ROSE

The Apple Tree

The Rain in Sapphire

The Hallowed Hideaway

The Sugar Thorns

Part One

Tangle Beach, Oregon

1

Blair

Let's get one thing straight. Otherwise, I'll go crazy.

Blair is not just a girl's name. It's not. The name's completely, absolutely unisex. Boy or girl—doesn't matter—it is as neutral as a plain, white wall. As uncommitted as Nolan's views on whatever business shenanigans my dad is currently fixated on. (That probably makes more sense if you know who Nolan is. And my dad. I'll get to them later.)

Yes, okay, *most* of the time, you'll find the name attached to a female. And sure, maybe my parents should've considered this before attaching it to me nearly twenty years ago. But it is the name they selected for me, and I'm not here to complain. I just want to get this out of the way, before we move on to anything else.

Blair. You can look it up. It's Scottish. And *unisex.*

Got it?

Okay. Cool.

2

Roxie

Every morning, I start my day the same way. My alarm goes off at 5 a.m., just as the sun is coming up. I slide open the window in my bedroom, leaving the gauzy, yellow curtain drawn. I let fresh air waft in, feel it suffuse the room with its blend of salt and sugar. It sweeps over the sheets of my bed, tumbles down the hair over my back. I would pull the curtain open, too, but there are other houses out there, and I don't like that. I can see three of them from my window, all closing in around me, and what can I say? I'm a girl who likes her privacy. Or at least the illusion of it.

Before leaving my room, I change into an old T-shirt and pair of stretchy shorts. I slip something out from underneath my bed: a small journal, a birthday gift from what feels like eons ago. I have a pen tucked inside. Today, I scribble down the three words extra carefully, extra slowly: *I miss you.*

It's no surprise when I discover Christine already occupying the bathroom down the hall. Of course. She's an early riser, too, but for totally different reasons. For her, waking up bright and early is a matter of giving herself enough time to glamorize with mascara and hairspray (or whatever it is she uses so religiously in there), and to energize herself with exactly two and a half mugs of coffee.

But not me. I don't wear makeup, and I don't drink coffee. And I never plan to. I have no interest in those things. I'm only fifteen years old. Although, being fifteen doesn't seem to hinder the other girls I go to school with. They wear plenty of makeup, consume plenty of caffeine. I really might be the only one who isn't trotting around as a contoured, latté-wielding specimen.

After whacking on the bathroom door with my fist, I get Christine to begrudgingly swap places with me so I can pee and tie my hair into a ponytail. And then I am out of there: down the stairs, a quick pulling-on of my worn sneakers, out the front door. Onto the final and most important stage of my morning ritual.

As soon as my feet touch the gravel road, I am running.

∞

My name is Roxie Morah. I'm a girl who loves fresh air, sweet food, having things be quiet. That's partly why I wake up when I do and set out into the world while the sunlight is new, while there is still a layer of misty fog suspended from the trees. It's as quiet as it gets. As the day wears on, though, that will change.

I live in a place called Tangle Beach, and this time of year, *quiet* is not a word you could correctly use to describe it. Tangle Beach—one of many little coastal towns sprinkled up and down the edge of Oregon—totally changes in the summer, filling up with scads of tourists, the beach itself noisily swarming with them every weekend.

And right now, it is June. June first, to be exact, and that means tourist season is undeniably upon us. It didn't always used to be this way. This crowded. At least, that's what I've been told. No one cared about Tangle Beach for years and years, decades and decades—no one cared much about Oregon in general. But they care now. They really, *really* care.

Now, you'll meet people not just from Portland and Eugene and Seattle, but people from all over the country, sometimes people from different parts of the world. There are all sorts of differing opinions on this phenomenon, depending on who you ask. The residents' opinions, I mean. Christine, for example, totally loves all the activity, because of the huge boost in business for her. And, because she loves the idea of living in such a trendy, desirable hotspot. Of course, I couldn't care less about that kind of thing.

But, anyway. Tangle Beach, for right now, at 5 a.m., is quiet. There is just the background susurration of birds, the roaring ocean, the sound of my feet colliding with the rocky ground. I run and I run, and I push myself into a full sprint, flying by the short, wooden fences that line Seawood Lane. I feel my lungs burn, the cool air stinging them, but I keep going as fast as I can. This is my version of coffee. This is what helps me wake up. This is what helps me with more things than I can say.

∞

There are different routes I take to get where I'm going. Sometimes I head for the ocean and sprint along the beach. Sometimes I go through town. Today, I'm using back roads, even though this route takes the longest. That's not what it's really about, though — getting there as fast as I can. It's about the running, and then of course, the place itself.

By the time I make it there, my chest is on fire and my calves are on the verge of cramping. There is an unused parcel of land here, one of the only spots in town that hasn't been developed yet. It is forested pretty densely, and I am always happy to let it swallow me up, to slip inside between the friendly, moss-patched trees. I go toward the heart of the parcel and then sit down in my place, my destination, finally giving my pounding heart a break.

Blackberries. They grow everywhere here. You can find them on just about every corner of town, brambles spreading and stretching, twisting and tangling. That's why they call it Tangle Beach. A lot of people find them a nuisance — the blackberries. They'll just keep growing if you let them: they'll take over your yard, your driveway, your fences and gates. They'll thrive in our humid soil and snag your skin and never develop the tamed-look people seem to want.

But for me, it's different. They could never be a nuisance to me. Never ever.

The brambles right here in this spot are my favorite in town. I didn't actually grow up in Tangle Beach; I was born twenty minutes east of here, in an area called Shoshone. And these blackberry bushes remind me of home, because this wooded lot is totally quiet, just the way I like. No houses in sight. No people. I perch on a stump and study these vines. Sometimes I even talk to them. I'm not a crazy person, I promise, but there's something about it that makes me feel less alone.

So, I sit. I see my favorite plants around me, their thorns and trusses. I talk, and I listen.

And then, it's time to leave. Time to return to the real world. On the way back to Christine's house, I make sure not to run. Slowly, slowly, I walk.

3

Blair

Now that we've gotten the whole name situation out of the way, there are really only three things you need to know about me:

1. I wish I'd grown up in the sixties. Maybe the seventies. Even the eighties would have been passable.

2. I love—*love*—music. I'm talking the kind of love a pudgy kid has for cherry cheesecake, the kind of love a vampire possesses for ripe, supple necks, the kind of love salty peanut butter has for sweet strawberry jam. You get the idea.

3. And I can't stress this last one enough: I do not—*ever*—want to end up like my parents.

I guess there's probably other stuff you might want to know, beyond those core basics, so I might as well elaborate. I hail from the greatest city on earth: The bustling, the invigorating, the ever-alluring and never-disappointing New York City. (Cue Billy Joel's "New York State of Mind." That saxophone solo—Billy just gets me.)

There's simply nowhere else like my insomnious New York, New York. And I should know; I've been around.

My family is what you might call *well-off* (okay, we're a few steps beyond well-off), and each summer of my life, we've absconded from my beloved home for a three-month-long vacation. One year it was Spain, another it was Miami. Last year was New Zealand. And I'm not trying to brag, believe me. I just want to make my point, which is that I'm very serious about my infatuation with New York. For me, all those other places just can't compare. I only wish I had gotten my way and were attending college in Manhattan, amidst all my skyscrapers and lively sidewalks. But we can talk more about that later.

There's another reason I wanted to mention my family's summer vacations. Like I said, last year was New Zealand. But this year, we're not on the other side of the world. Just the other side of the continent. At the end of May, I wrapped up my first year of college, traveled back home to meet up with my parents, and away we went. Goodbye yet again, New York—hello, this year's temporary digs. We just got in the other day. And this is how my story really starts. The interesting part, anyway.

My mother, my father, Nolan, and I are kicking off summer on the coastline of Oregon, in a funny little ocean town by the name of Tangle Beach.

4

Roxie

B eing fifteen is stupid.
It's a super annoying age. I'm not a child anymore, but I'm not an adult, either. I'm stuck in the middle, in some kind of no man's land where people treat me in whatever way is most convenient for them. Of course, by *people*, what I really mean is *Christine*.

Christine Lambert—my legal guardian, my supposed relative—has a special knack for driving me crazy. To be fair, she would probably say the same thing about me. She thinks I'm immature because I'm different than her, because I don't dress like her and talk like her and care what other people think of me. I think *she's* immature, because she's in her early thirties and actually believes those are the kinds of things that make you "grown-up."

When I get back from my run this morning, Christine is finishing her last bit of coffee in the kitchen. I hurry upstairs to throw on one of the few outfits I own that I know she will find just barely acceptable. Back downstairs, she's waiting for me at the front door, her Dooney & Bourke tote bag over her shoulder, keys jingling in her fingers.

"Roxie . . ." She eyes me over: my simple, cream tank top and chambray shorts. "Could you at least wear your hair down? Ponytails aren't professional."

"Whatever you say, boss." I pull my scrunchie out but leave it on my wrist, because I know that will annoy her.

"Honestly, would it kill you to wear a skirt one of these days? I'd even settle for a skort."

"I'm fatally allergic to impractical clothing. So, yes, it would kill me."

Christine sighs. "Okay, whatever. Let's get going. We have a long day ahead of us."

∞

"My bride really had her heart set on English ivy."

We're at a floral shop in town. We've been here for over two hours (kill me). Even though I like flowers, I don't really like the ones in here, the way they are all trimmed and refined and refrigerated. I like the flowers that grow on the sides of the roads, the big bushes of rhododendrons, the wild roses and the blue hydrangeas.

"I'm sure she'll be just as happy with our substitute. Again, we're just not able to get ivy this time of year. But I can assure you, this substitute greenery looks nearly identical."

It's been the same kind of back-and-forth between Christine and the florist, over and over, a totally mind-numbing ordeal. This is Christine's job, and this year, I've found myself along for the ride.

Between the months of May and September, Christine Lambert runs a small wedding planning business: Lace & Tide. And because I don't have anything else to do, and because I wouldn't mind making a little money, I've agreed to help her out for the summer. When wedding season's over, I will be back in school, starting my sophomore year of high school. Christine will go back to working full-time as a receptionist at a dermatology office in town. During these summer months, though, they let her work part-time, allowing her to plan a decent number of coastal, destination weddings.

I'm like her scribe. That's my job. There's a different booklet for each engaged couple, and it's my job to take notes in the appropriate sections of the appropriate booklet while Christine does all the talking at these appointments. Right now, the booklet I have spread open on the counter is labeled, *Woodruff-DeMarco.* I'm in the *Floral* section and am busy scribbling down the words, *Ivy substitute: nearly identical.*

"Could you make sure to include that in a sample bouquet for next week? My bride will be in town that Wednesday, and I know she'll want to see it for herself."

The florist, a very sweet, older lady named Vera, gives Christine a polite smile. "Of course. Next Wednesday. If you can stop by in the afternoon, I'll have that ready for her."

Christine shoots a sudden look my way.

"Roxie. Did you write that down? Wednesday afternoon."

"Yes, Christine." I try my best not to sound agitated.

"Wonderful. Thanks, Vera. I'll see you then, if not sooner."

We head out of the floral shop, *finally*, into the day that's turned sunny and mild. Then, it's straight into the convertible Volkswagen Beetle, onto our next appointment. We're going to a bakery now, which is a reality that happens to make me want to clench up my fists into tight balls until my fingernails make me bleed.

See, the thing is, I wanted to work with Christine, for Lace & Tide, this summer. I really did. It's just that being a scribe wasn't what I had in mind. What I wanted to do was something totally different.

I wanted to bake. It's what I love most: whipping up sweet concoctions in the kitchen, perfecting them, decorating them so they're almost too pretty to eat. Getting caught up in the simple tasks of folding a silky cake batter or crimping the edges of a buttery pie crust.

It's a skill that was handed down to me—it's in my genetic code—and I treat it as seriously as I do my daily morning runs. It's another one of those scarce things in my life that makes me feel not-so alone.

So, anyway. I wanted to bake this summer, to create all of the wedding cakes and treats for Lace & Tide's clients. Sometimes I fantasize about it at night, before I fall asleep. A tiered, vanilla bean beauty topped with wild strawberries and roses. A tower of lemon cupcakes swirled with honey buttercream and a finish of white chocolate shavings.

Christine and I got into a pretty nasty argument about it back in April. She knows I'm a top-notch baker—no one can deny that. But she told me that I'm not *"responsible enough."* That fifteen is *"too young"* to take on that level of obligation. I told her she was being closed-minded, and when that didn't work, I might have possibly slipped in the word *moronic* . . . to which she responded by stomping into her bedroom and slamming the door shut.

So, next thing I knew, we somehow reached this lame compromise of me tagging along to the florist, the rental places, the venues, and of course, the bakeries.

The most popular bakery in Tangle Beach is called Pacific Pastries. That's where Christine and I have wound up after our two hours spent at Vera's Floral Design. We're still focused on the Woodruff-DeMarco wedding, which will be held later this month: a sunset ceremony on the beach, and a reception at a fancy-pants event space in the middle of town.

"So," Christine gets started with the baker across the counter. I'm secretly amused right now, because the guy looks terrified of her. "My bride wanted a champagne cake with raspberry filling and a vanilla buttercream. Could you have samples ready for Wednesday of next week?"

The baker confirms he can, and Christine peers over her shoulder at me to make sure I'm jotting this down.

"Actually, I made a small test-batch today." The baker fiddles his fingers together, trying not to make eye contact with the living Barbie doll before him. "Do you maybe want to taste it while you're here?"

"Might as well. If you can be quick about it."

When he returns, he has two small square-cuts of cake on their own little plates. He hands one to Christine, and one to me—which catches me off guard. Usually I am like a ghost to these people. To everyone, really.

Christine makes an obnoxious *mmmm* sound after her first bite. "Wonderful. My bride will love this."

Popping some of the cake into my mouth, I consider the flavors, the textures. I have to keep myself from shaking my head in disapproval. Blatantly, I glare in Christine's direction. She can see me from the corner of her eye. I know she can. Now she's the one avoiding eye contact.

It isn't until four hours later that we're done for the day, back home in the dolled-up house on Seawood Lane. And I'm not exactly a happy camper. After changing back into my running outfit and restoring my hair back into its ponytail, I go into the kitchen. It is a white and sterile kitchen, and I don't like it, but it's all I've had over these last three years.

Sifting. Measuring. Beating, stirring, pouring. I let myself escape into it all. I feel my anger dissolving. I feel my connection to this art form. I even feel myself smile a little.

The end-result makes me smile full-on, pride blooming inside me. It is a three-tiered, naked cake, allowing me to admire each layer of fluffy champagne sponge and bright-red raspberry filling. There is the smooth, vanilla frosting, too, and I've arranged fresh raspberries on the very top with a light dusting of powdered sugar.

I cut myself a piece, and it is every bit as good as it looks. A *million-billion* times better than that bland, uninspired sample at Pacific Pastries. With perfect timing, Christine happens to saunter downstairs. She sees me in the kitchen, sees the cake on the countertop, sees the way I am arching an eyebrow her way.

"Want to try some?" I ask. "It's really good."

She hesitates.

"I don't need the extra calories. I'm running out to the market. Be back in a flash."

As she strides away, every ounce of my anger comes flooding back in an instant. This is the effect Christine Lambert has on me. Whether I like it or not (small hint: I don't), this is my life.

5

Blair

Do you ever have one of those days when you just feel torn? Like you just can't make up your mind? That's how my Friday is kicking off, as I'm gazing out this new window of mine, checking out my view of the Pacific Ocean.

I just can't decide: Creedence Clearwater Revival? Or Paul Simon?

This is a *must*: every day of my life has to begin with one of my favorite songs. Of which I have many, naturally. I'm not ashamed to disclose this morning practice of mine. Not even a little. I get some groovy auditory vibes going via my phone and Bluetooth speakers, and I proceed to dance around like a madman whilst singing along and throwing on some clothes.

So, the question is, CCR or Paul Simon? "Have You Ever Seen the Rain?" seems a bit too dreary for the fun-in-the-sun, beachy day I'm about to drink in. On the other hand, "Me and Julio Down by the Schoolyard" just reminds me too much of New York City.

Then, it hits me. And it's so obvious. Why didn't I think of it sooner? I completely change course, and about a minute later, Don Henley's "The Boys of Summer" is ricocheting around the walls of the room. Picture a nearly-twenty-year-old college student sliding around on the floor, waving his arms around in the air, rummaging through a suitcase, pretending his fist is a microphone while straining his voice into a high pitch. Yep. That's me. Blair Porter.

So, I have my own guest house here for these next three months. Which is pretty nifty. The main rental house is just across the driveway, and that's where I'm heading after my musical ceremony has been completed.

The breeze is strong outside as I cross over to the main house, and it carries a briny scent I'm not used to. We're as "beachfront" as you can get in Tangle Beach. I'm guessing it's about a five-minute walk to get down our road, across the walking path, over a mound of grassy sand and all the way to the crashing waves.

"Blair."

My dad hears me enter the main house, tossing a very quick glance my way. It figures that, despite this place providing a variety of ocean views, my dad has his eyes firmly glued to the television. Glued to the news, to be specific.

"Dad. How's the morning?"

I grab myself a glass of O.J. in the kitchen while my dad mumbles something about the stock market in response to my question. This house has one of those open concept designs that makes it so you can hear everyone and anyone no matter where they are. Nevertheless, I opt to join my dad in the living room and plop down on the arm of a chair.

"Where's Mom?"

It takes a minute for him to reply.

"Sleeping."

"Still? It's getting pretty late."

"Yeah, well. You know Rita."

Rita and Philip Porter. These are my parents, the humans who brought me into this world, for reasons I've never really been privy to. And that's not me saying I wish I hadn't been born—I'm *all* about existence. It's some good stuff. Without existence, I wouldn't get to experience Carole King and James Taylor, now would I?

Anyway. I'm just trying to say that Rita and Philip Porter aren't exactly the most . . . *parental* parents that ever were. So it's even more perplexing that I have an older brother. But that's a topic for another time.

"Sooo . . ." I gulp down the rest of my tangy O.J. and drum my hands on my thighs. "Where's Nolan?"

"Huh? Oh, I think he's sleeping, too."

"Oh. Alrighty. So, we're all the way here on the Oregon Coast and no one wants to go check it out?"

The talking head on the big screen states something that is, apparently, highly offensive to my dad. He reacts accordingly and spits out, "No-spin news, my ass."

"Okay, then. I guess I'll head out as a lone explorer. I'll come back later for Nolan."

The delayed response: "Yeah, okay, Blair."

None of this is unusual, by the way. It's always been this way. But that is A-okay with me. Really—it is. I don't much care for chilling out with Rita and Philip Porter. I'd much rather chill out with people who actually possess souls. You know, people like the aforementioned Carole King, to whom I am now listening on my wireless earbuds. "I Feel the Earth Move" is my current soundtrack as I set out into Tangle Beach.

It's a cute little town, if I do say so myself. It's very clean, with all these quaint buildings covered in brown shingles. It doesn't matter if it's the Post Office, a café, a spa—they all have those beachy, brown shingles and look almost indistinguishable from one another.

While cruising around past all these shops and restaurants and art galleries, I think about New York. I just can't help myself. I wonder how hot it's gotten there. I imagine a green, sunny Central Park and my busy, humming sidewalks (although, to be honest, the sidewalks in Tangle Beach are busier than I anticipated). I would've liked to stay in New York for the summer, since I was away in Ithaca for nine, sad months. But I didn't want my parents to have a wild freak-out, didn't want to trigger any unnecessary friction. Ever since what happened with Graham, my brother, they've become all kinds of sensitive to any signs of me going against the grain.

I decide not to think about Graham, or even New York. Just go with the flow. That's what I strive for. That's how I keep the peace, and keep my sanity. And I happen to be a pretty big fan of sanity.

Fast forward to later in the day: I return to the main house to get some food. My mom has finally emerged from her slumber. I find her in the same spot my dad was on the sectional, Nolan at her side and a mimosa in her grip.

"Oh, Blair. Could you get me a refill?"

She extends her flute in my direction, and I oblige. Kind of. I pour in a hefty amount of O.J. and just the tiniest splash of champagne.

"Thank you," she says when I hand it to her. "God, that jet lag nearly put me in a coma."

"Right. Jet lag. Hey, where'd Dad disappear to?"

"I think he went to Starbucks to get some work done."

Again, none of this is unusual. When one appears, the other vanishes. It's a super-fun magic trick they've perfected over the years. (That's me being sarcastic, if you couldn't tell.)

"Hey, buddy." I give Nolan a generous scratching behind the ears. He is technically my parents' golden retriever, but I love him like my own. "Wanna come to the beach with me?"

Thank goodness for Nolan. The only truly sane one in my family. He leaps off the couch, making my mom nearly spill her drink. Now, I'm finally about to have some real fun. It's time for me and my best friend to introduce ourselves to the Oregon Coast, up-close and personal.

6

Roxie

Another morning, my same routine. The open window, the fluttering of my curtains, the journal underneath my bed. The words: *I miss you.* Another run, another conversation with the blackberry brambles. And another long day of wedding planning annoyances, until at long last, I am once again free to do what I want.

Well, except that last part isn't really true. I'm in the mood for baking something warm and comforting, like cinnamon rolls with a cream cheese icing, or a pan of dark chocolate brownies with melted marshmallows on top. It doesn't always have to be fancy.

But, it looks like I won't be baking anything tonight. Christine has taken over the kitchen for the evening. She's running around in there like a crazed rabbit, attempting to put together some kind of salad for dinner.

I leave her to it. I'll figure out my own dinner later. I don't like Christine Lambert's cooking, something I've made perfectly clear to her over the last three years. I know that sounds rude, but I'm just not willing to lie the way everyone else seems to be. When she gives me a plate of undercooked salmon and burned quinoa (how do you burn quinoa?), I'm not going to smile and say, *Wow, this tastes great,* like other people probably would.

Honestly, it's better for both of us if I just fend for myself. So I slip on a pair of flip-flops and go outside, even though my stomach is a little grumbly. I walk twenty minutes to the beach and sit down in the sand to watch the sun descend into the blue ocean. I squint my eyes, let the wind whip hair around my face. There are a lot of people populating the shoreline this evening, clusters and pairs of them.

I, like always, am by myself.

I know it's not normal for a girl my age to have no friends. I'm really not kidding when I call myself a lone wolf. It's my own fault—I don't put in the effort to make friends—because, well, there just isn't anyone I want to be friends with. The girls at Tangle Beach High are not like me. I am not like them. And, anyway, relationships never truly last, do they? It all fades away if you give it enough time.

I only ever had one friend in my life. She was perfect, and I think about her every second of every day.

$$\infty$$

Maryanne Morah. My beautiful, sweet, matchless Mama. She named me Roxanne so our names would be linked, but called me Roxie so I could feel like my own person: a tomboy who liked romping around outside, examining snails and bugs, napping in the long, weedy grass behind our home.

Our home was in Shoshone. I mentioned it before—Shoshone, I mean. Just twenty minutes inland, a woodsy area with its own school district and a microscopic town center. No one really cares about the place or pays it much thought. Except for me.

My mind goes there, when I'm feeling down or lost or just plain bored. In my head, I retreat to that place, to my old home. I try to remember every little detail, try to bring it all back to life.

The house was small and green. Inside were wallpapered rooms. A garden window in the kitchen. Dried flowers that Mama hung from hooks on the ceiling. I picture myself walking down the hallway: the walls lined with her art, charcoal drawings of animals and plants, her simple signature in the bottom corner each time. *Maryanne.*

I glide past the old, upright piano in the sitting room, and I step outside. Five acres—true privacy. No neighbors, no traffic sounds, no streetlights or people or other houses. Just trees, a tiny creek, and of course, the blackberry bushes.

They were her favorite. The blackberries. I can see her standing in front of those huge, wild brambles, plucking off soft, dark berries, dropping them into a tin can. I can see her long, brown hair, like mine, her tall, slender frame in a white, floral dress. We stuffed ourselves with those berries every summer, struggling to save leftovers for her baking.

Yes, Maryanne Morah baked. It was what she was known for, not just in Shoshone, but in Tangle Beach, as well as the other neighboring towns. She sold her desserts and treats to a number of different businesses (cafés, restaurants, inns). She provided catering for events here and there (family reunions, parties). It earned her a reputation, and most everyone knew her name.

There were people who liked to say Maryanne Morah had her fair share of secrets. And that was certainly true when it came to her baking. No one knew how she made her pies so perfectly balanced between sweet and tart, her cakes somehow moist and fluffy at the same time.

I would watch her in the kitchen when I was little. It was my version of watching television, and I was always captivated by her skills. The effortless way she could crack, open, and discard an egg all with one hand. The magical way she could taste-test a batch of cookie dough and know exactly what was needed to take it to the next level.

As I got older, I helped her. I learned everything from her. How to brown butter over the stove. How to coat berries in flour before folding them into a muffin batter. How to trust my hands and my taste buds more than measurements and instructions in a recipe. Mama didn't even use recipes—she was an intuitive baker, and I believe that's what made all the difference.

As you could probably predict, her very favorite desserts to bake were always the ones with blackberries. A simple, warm blackberry pie. Blackberry upside down cake. Blackberry Danishes with mascarpone and lemon curd. Blackberry tarts and muffins, cobblers and frostings, and just about anything else you can think of.

In my imagination right now, I am back in that kitchen. Mama's at my side, and we are baking up a storm. The garden window is cracked open to let the fresh air swirl around us and keep us cool. There are dried wildflowers above me. The walls are yellow like butter, and the backsplash tiles box in little, blue rabbits that always made me laugh when I was little.

I can smell the berries. Just for one, brief moment. Then, I'm hit by a blast of ocean wind, and I'm sitting there in the sand while the sun melts away, while the beachgoers head back to their hotels and homes and families, and I am alone.

7

Blair

A whole week has gone by, and this has got to be *the* most boring summer vacation of my life. I wish Graham were here with me, instead of in Uganda or wherever he's roaming around nowadays, free-spiritedly and all that.

Okay—enough whining. That's no way to roll through life, is it? And besides, I've got Nolan, and I've got my music.

I woke up crazy early this morning. I don't know why; my eyes just snapped open and I couldn't fall back asleep. So eventually I gave up, jived around to my song of the day (King Harvest's "Dancing in the Moonlight"), and abducted Nolan from the main house so we could go to the beach.

That's where I am now. The beach here is a long, straight stretch of sand and sea. It's perfect for throwing a frisbee as hard as I can and letting Nolan go bounding after it like it's the canine holy grail. The water looks dark right now with it being so early in the day, and, let me tell you, that is the coldest water I think I've ever felt. The kind that chills you 'til your bones turn blue. The kind you *don't* want to go swimming in. It's also really windy today, so there's no chance I'm taking off my T-shirt and getting a nice tan.

For a while, it's just me and Nolan and the bellowing tide. It's kind of peaceful, I guess, but my preference is to be surrounded by other humans. I like to people-watch, and I like to feel as though stuff is really happening around me.

And then, something does happen. Suddenly, it's not just me and my furry golden on the beach, and I find myself an opportunity to people-watch. *Person*-watch, to be more accurate. There's a girl sitting in the sand, a ways down the shoreline. I don't know where she came from. It's just like, out of nowhere, there she is. Her knees are drawn up to her chest, her arms wrapped around them. She's a brunette, and her hair is going crazy all around her face.

Girls . . . Should we talk about girls? Perhaps we should.

To be completely honest, for me, girls are not the most interesting part of life. I mean, I've had some girlfriends before, but it was always casual, and truthfully, just not worth it to me in the end. My friends feel differently. Every college party last year was a chance to survey the flocks of females, maybe even to be as bold as to make contact with them. My friends were always wanting to tell me about the latest noteworthy girls on their radar—a redhead Jonah met on campus, a pre-med student Wesley met in Biology.

And then there's me. And I'm just not like that. I hung out with some nice girls here and there throughout the semesters, but I couldn't think of a reason to ever take things further than just hanging out. I guess there's something wrong with me, and if so, I fully blame my parents.

This girl on the beach . . . I wonder why she's all alone, why she's here so early in the morning, why she's just sitting there, staring at the water. Nolan gallops back to me with the frisbee in his mouth. I take it from him and reward him with a good scratch behind the ears. He's breathing hard and is nothing but dog-smiles and unearthly energy, which makes me laugh.

The wind suddenly picks up even harder, just about knocking me over. I regain my balance and give the yellow frisbee another good, strong fling out into the distance. Nolan takes off at full speed.

What happens next is not so good.

Actually, it's pretty dang bad.

At least, that's what I think at first.

8

Roxie

Pain cracks into my skull, a sharp flash and hammer, and I hear myself gasp. I feel my body teeter to the side, mostly from the shock of it, and I press my hand to the side of my head. Next, there's noisy panting sounds, and a dog is jumping all over me, toffee-colored and shaggy and obviously wanting to be my friend.

I'm too disoriented to really do anything, so I just stay there in the sand and give the dog a little rub on the neck. I was on my way back to Christine's house. I just finished visiting the blackberry bushes and decided to take the beach route back home. I ended up stopping to watch the ocean, because, well, I'm never too eager to get back to Seawood Lane. I got to thinking about my old home again and had totally receded into my own little world.

"Nolan! Nolan! Hey, buddy!"

I look up, and I'm faced with some guy looming over me. The dog's owner, so it seems. He's wearing a T-shirt and red-and-blue swim trunks that make me think of snow cones.

"Nolan, come on, give her some room to breathe." The guy grabs the dog by his collar and tugs him away. "Hey, are you okay? I'm so sorry, God, I feel horrible."

He's talking to me. But I'm still pretty out of it. My eyes are darting all around. There's the dog. There's the sand—and a yellow frisbee right beside me—it must have been what hit me. And there's the guy, his hair blonde and styled kind of funny. It's a few inches long but combed around this way and that, parted on the side but sticking up in some places. Groomed, yet messy, and a lot more volume than my own hair has ever enjoyed.

"Are you all right?" He's kneeling down now, and I get a better look at him. Faint, blonde stubble around his jaw. Eyes like blue fire. "Are you bleeding or anything?"

"I'm fine," I finally speak up. "I'm okay."

"I'm such an idiot. The wind got all crazy and I didn't think my frisbee would go so far. Are you positive you're all right?"

"I'm fine," I repeat. "Really."

"Can I make it up to you somehow? Do you want to hit me in the head to even things out? I don't mind. I mean, I deserve it."

"That's . . . not necessary."

But this guy isn't giving up. He keeps blabbering away:

"There's gotta be something we can do. I really want to make it up to you. Nolan does, too. This is Nolan, by the way."

The toffee-colored retriever has his tongue sticking out and his dark eyes glued on me, just like his owner does. The eyes part, I mean. Not the tongue part.

"Hi, Nolan." I reach out and rub his head.

"And I'm Blair, in case you were wondering. But—'You Can Call Me Al.'"

I stare at the blonde guy. I squint my eyes at him. "Al?"

"Yeah, you know. 'You Can Call Me Al.' Paul Simon."

I continue squinting at him in total confusion.

"Paul Simon?" he says, his voice getting pitchy. I shrug. "You don't know who Paul Simon is? Okay, never mind, we'll clear that up later."

"Wait." I shift around in the sand. "Did you say your name's Blair?"

"Yep. That's me."

"Isn't that a girl's name?"

He laughs, and it's a pleasant sound, the way Mama used to laugh. Easy and goodhearted.

"It's unisex, actually."

"Is it? I don't know . . ."

"You'll just have to take my word for it. But, anyway. Care to introduce yourself?"

I feel put on the spot all of a sudden. My muscles tighten up.

"I'm Roxie."

I leave it at that. I'm not one to blabber or try to charm others, make a good first impression. I'm not a shy person, I just don't care about that stuff. I'd rather stay guarded and observant.

"Roxie. Cool. Well, listen. I'm serious about wanting to even things out. I whacked you in the head with my frisbee—not cool. Let me at least get you some ice and make sure you're okay. My place is just over there if you want to come over for a quick sec. And I promise I'm not a serial killer or anything."

He points inland, in the direction of all the fancy vacation homes that always fill up this time of year. So, he's a tourist.

"I don't know . . ." I mumble.

"Please?" he says to me, and those burning-bright eyes of his really are pleading with me to say yes.

He extends his hand my way, offering to help me up. And I don't know why, but I take it.

It was the laugh. I realize this once I'm stepping foot into the brown-shingled house adorned with red petunias that cascade from window boxes. I find myself in a space that has high ceilings, shiplap walls, a small kitchen, huge windows facing the ocean. And I realize that's why I agreed to come here, agreed to follow this blonde stranger back to his vacation rental. It was because of his laugh.

"Why don't you take a seat, anywhere you like. I'll get the ice."

The golden retriever trots over to a dog bed that's set up beside a showy fireplace. Blair makes his way to the kitchen, so I trail him and sit down at a counter stool. This is definitely weird. I've never done anything like this before. I have my routines that I follow every day, and popping into some guy's house for ice is just not one of them.

"Okay, let's see. Can I take a look?" Blair approaches me at the counter with an icepack in his hand.

"Sure."

It's the only word I've uttered since entering his house. I'm feeling much more reticent than usual. But Blair doesn't seem to mind.

"Oh, hey, do you want some gum?" He slips a pack of Trident out of his pocket, offering me a stick.

"That's okay."

"Alrighty. I'm kind of hardcore addicted to this stuff."

After popping a piece in his mouth, he gets closer to me and gingerly places his hand against my temple. I feel his fingers brush my hair out of the way. I hear him go, *Hmmm.*

I can smell the Trident on his breath. Crisp and sweet. I make sideways glances, attempting to study this tourist better. His eyes are round, with half-moon creases below them. His hair is a warm caramel kind of blonde, like the drizzle I always make with apple pie. He's clearly not a high school student. He's older, which makes me feel even stranger for being here right now, having his hand grazing my skin.

"Well, you're not bleeding. Which is kind of nice. It looks swollen, though. I think you're going to end up with a gnarly bump tomorrow. All because of silly ole me."

He applies the icepack to my head and keeps his hand on top of it.

"Maybe I should get you some Advil," he notes.

"That's okay. You really don't have to worry about me. I'm fine."

His eyes linger on me. Thoughtful. Animated. Everything about him is animated. His colorful clothes. His funny hair. The way he talks, the way he smiles.

"How about this. If there's anything you can think of so I can make this up to you—you let me know, okay?"

"Okay." I hear a clock ticking somewhere in the house. I see a baby grand piano positioned in front of the windows. There was a larger house across the driveway outside, and I wonder who else this Blair guy is vacationing with.

"Where are you from?" I ask. He's still standing close to me, so I keep my voice on the quiet side.

"New York City. Ever been?"

"No. Never. I don't think I'm much of a city person."

He grins, recoiling the slightest bit. "Ah, no, don't say that. No one should say that until they've been to New York. You seriously need to go. It'll convert you into a city person. Guaranteed."

I laugh a little. "I don't know. I'm pretty set in my ways."

Blair smiles right at me while chewing his gum. Something about it makes me feel warm. Could it be that I like the attention I'm getting from him right now? I swear, I'm normally the type of girl who dislikes even the subtlest hint of attention.

"So, what about you, Roxie? Where are you from?"

"Oh. Nowhere."

"Nowhere?"

"I mean," I say, "I'm from here. I live here. In Tangle Beach."

He nods his head in consideration. "Nice. Are you going to college in the area? I didn't realize there *were* any colleges out here."

The question catches me off guard. I look him directly in the eyes.

"No, um. I'm in high school."

He stops chewing his gum.

"Oh. Yeah, of course you are. Senior?"

"Sophomore. I'll be a sophomore this Fall. I'm fifteen."

"Sophomore," he repeats. "Nice." Then I hear him clear his throat, and he pulls the icepack off my head. "Well, sorry again about this whole frisbee fiasco. Looks like the swelling's gone down some. Nolan and I both offer our sincerest apologies for derailing your morning."

My morning. The ticking clock. Suddenly, it's like I'm back in the real world, the universe where I live on Seawood Lane, where Christine Lambert is waiting for me to get back so we can attend to Lace & Tide affairs.

I spring up from my stool, and Blair takes a hefty step back.

"I have to get going. Like, right now."

"Yeah, sure." He looks frazzled. "Sorry again."

And he laughs. As I head out the door and sprint southward past all the extravagant houses, that laugh sticks in my head. I know that I want to hear it again.

9

Blair

Okay, well. That was interesting. I'm still standing at the counter, trying to process what just happened. The icepack is melting in my hand, and my gum is getting tough and bland.

I mosey over to the fireplace and take a seat on the hearth, close to Nolan. I keep working my jaw with the gum, prop my chin in my hand, moderately impersonating Rodin's *The Thinker*. (Side note: I once got to see the most famous version of that sculpture in Paris. Good stuff.)

I know I basically just got done rambling about how girls aren't my biggest focus in life, how I'm not all that interested in women and dating and girlfriends. But . . . when I jogged up to this girl on the beach, when I saved her from my drooling canine . . . it was peculiar. The whole event ended up being massively peculiar.

It was something about her eyes. Or maybe her hair. They were both brown, her hair long and sleek. Her eyes were catlike, the kind that tempt you to ogle like an idiot. And her skin—it was so golden, healthy-looking, like sunshine was about to burst from it. But, you know, in a pretty way.

Anyway. I have to admit, there was something about her that was on the verge of bewitching. That's why I asked her to come to my place. I mean, other than the fact that I *did* whack her in the head with my frisbee.

Here's the truth: I thought she was around eighteen years old. Maybe seventeen. She was tall. Almost as tall as me. And she seemed so damn mature. But when she said she was in high school—that she's a *sophomore* this fall—it felt like a frisbee had just whacked *me* in the head. An illusion crumbled right before my eyes.

It was so obvious, then. Of course she was only fifteen years old. Suddenly, I could see it: the youth in her face, something about the roundness and fullness of it, the glow of it. The way she was dressed: a purple shirt with a heart on it, loose shorts, dirty sneakers. The way she was fiddling her fingers together in her lap and being so shy.

The spell was broken. Man, I really am an idiot. I didn't know what to do at that point, but thankfully she took off like a bat out of hell. Leaving me to sit here with Nolan and curse myself for asking a fifteen-year-old to stop into my house so I could nurse her back to health. I'll be twenty in September. I feel like the world's biggest creep right now.

Honestly, though, it felt nice to interact with someone who wasn't Rita or Philip Porter. And Nolan seemed to like the girl. But that's just Nolan; he likes everyone.

Roxie. Roxie of Tangle Beach, Oregon. With the cat eyes and the dirty shoes.

I guess I better go see what Rita and Philip are up to next-door, speaking of those two. But first, I'm suddenly and urgently in the mood to hear one of the greatest songs in all existence, America's "Sister Golden Hair."

10

Roxie

"**I** wish you'd let me teach you how to put on makeup sometime, Roxie."

It's Saturday morning, and I've been running around the house, helping Christine get everything all sparkly and lemon-fresh. A client is coming over later in the afternoon, a bride named Shelby Frasier, of the Frasier-Isaac wedding. Hers will be an August wedding with a sunset beach ceremony and a reception held in a hotel ballroom. Did I mention that every Tangle Beach wedding is basically the same?

"I don't need you to teach me to how to use makeup, Christine." We're finishing up the dusting in the living room. Christine likes to have meetings here with her clients every so often, because she feels it gives Lace & Tide a *"personal"* touch. "I have no desire to look like a wannabe contestant from The Bachelor."

"It's just about looking put together," Christine retorts. "Like you didn't just roll out of bed. You're not a tween anymore, you know. You should stop parting your hair down the middle. Start wearing real bras. Don't you want a boyfriend one day?"

A boyfriend. How could I ever have a boyfriend when I can't even make regular friends? How could I ever get that close to someone? It's totally dumb, but I think about the blonde New York City guy from yesterday. I rub my hand over the goose egg up by my hairline. It's tender. Suddenly I'm smelling Trident and hearing that laugh.

"Okay. Sure, Christine. I'll start wearing makeup and *real* bras and parting my hair on the side . . ."

Christine looks at me, intrigue coloring her slightly wideset eyes.

". . . *if* you let me start making all the wedding desserts from here on out."

She breaks eye contact, spritzes Pledge on her coffee table, rubs a rag around maniacally. Says, "Never mind. I don't know why I try with you."

"Funny. I was just thinking the same thing."

"Okay." Christine stands up and assesses our work. "Nice and clean. I have to run out for my hair appointment, but I should be back just in time for Shelby."

"Touching up your highlights?" I tilt my head at her with a smile. She hates it when I call them highlights. Which, of course, is why I always do it.

"It's balayage, Roxie. I stopped getting highlights in 2003."

She stomps over to the front door, grabs her keys, shoulder bag, sunglasses. "You know, the kitchen isn't quite as tidy as I'd like. Would you please put away all your little experiments over there? Maybe hide them in the fridge. I don't want Shelby to get confused."

She leaves before I can respond, but I guess that's probably for the best. I wouldn't have had the nicest things to say in return. I look over to the kitchen and see the so-called *little experiments* I crafted last night. Mini rustic tarts, made with the plums I found in the back of the fridge. To be fair, they're not the prettiest desserts I've ever made, but I know what Christine is really up to. She's just being her usual, rude, controlling self. Putting me in my place.

I go over to the round, nautical-rope-lined mirror that rests on the fireplace mantel. I examine my bare eyelashes, cheeks, lips. I look at the middle part in my chocolaty hair. I snap the strap of my cotton bralette. And I think about the fact that Christine will be gone for the next few hours, and how Shelby Frasier will be here just after that.

It comes to me rapidly: an idea, a scheme. One I'll have to get going on pronto for it to work. Before leaving the mirror, I can't help but grin at myself. Knowingly. Maybe even a teensy bit diabolically.

∞

The Frasier-Isaac wedding binder isn't very thick. I remember Shelby being a sweet and simple girl, and that's part of why I think this plan might work. I flip to the *Catering* section and see what Shelby had in mind for dessert.

She wants cupcakes, according to my notes. Christine was planning on ordering them from Pacific Pastries, as usual. I refresh my memory: Last time we saw Shelby, she was undecided on the flavor of the cupcakes. She was torn between red velvet and cherry.

Next, I take a peek at the *Florals* section. Shelby's flowers are very much decided. She wants wildflower bouquets and centerpieces—daisies and violets and trillium. I can feel the wheels turning in my mind, can see the vision forming, more and more detailed, more and more perfect.

I know just what to do.

∞

Just barely, I seem to pull it off. I set the last cupcake on the tiered cake stand and take a step back to see how it looks. I already know how it tastes, because I scarfed one down as fast as I could. And as far as I'm concerned, it did not disappoint.

"It's wonderful to see you two again. Come on in."

The front door swings open, and it's Christine in her freshened blonde locks. Plus Shelby Frasier and her mother, Heidi.

It's like magic. It's like destiny. Shelby steps into the house, smiling and taking off her shoes, even though Christine didn't ask her to. And then—she sees me in the kitchen.

"Hey, Roxie. How've you been?"

I open my mouth to reply, but Shelby's eyes alight on the display of little cakes in between us.

"Oh, wow," she breathes. She comes right up to the counter and examines them up-close. I know I'm biased or whatever, but they really are beautiful. You can see the scarlet cake, a mildly-chocolate red velvet. Inside, I cored out the centers of the cupcakes, filling them with a bit of cream cheese frosting and a cherry reduction. On top, there are swirls of that same frosting, painted with the same cherry reduction. To finish it all off, one black cherry sits proudly at each peak.

I had to literally sprint to the market to buy the cherries and cream cheese. On the way back home, I plucked tiny wild daisies from the side of the road. Now, they are sprinkled daintily around the perimeter of the cake stand.

"These look incredible. Can I try one?"

Shelby glances at me for permission, and I urge her forward.

"Go for it."

Sending me a smile, she cautiously takes hold of one of the desserts. Shelby is ten years older than me, twenty-five, and she's one of those people who always seems content. I'm not the type of girl to have lots of role models, but if I were, Shelby Frasier would be a good candidate.

Her eyes widen as she savors her bite. Heidi has wandered over, now, too, but Christine is lingering behind them.

"Is it good?" Heidi inquires of her daughter.

"It's unbelievable. Mom, you have to try one."

So she does, and it's the same reaction, the same widening of the eyes. I'm beaming right now, and I'm focusing on the mom and daughter before me—not on Christine.

Heidi looks as pleased as her daughter. "Wow. They really nailed it." She twists around to address Christine. "Pacific Pastries made these? I wasn't expecting samples so soon. Were you, Shelby?"

Christine and Shelby both begin stammering, and I know what I have to do now. The last step. I have to speak up, raise my voice.

"I made them."

That makes the chatter go quiet. Quickly, I clock Christine's facial expression. Not the happiest look I've ever seen. But then Shelby is speaking.

"You made these, Roxie?"

There's that smile of hers. I smile back. "Yeah. Red velvet cherry cupcakes. I combined your two ideas. And I know that daisies are in your bouquet."

Shelby addresses the wedding planner now, who I can tell is hastening to process all of this.

"These are exactly what I want," Shelby says to Christine. "Can Roxie make them for the wedding reception?" Then she turns back to me. "Would you be comfortable with that?"

"More than comfortable," I respond.

Almost there—almost there. Now, we are all waiting to hear what Christine has to say.

She fastens on her fakest smile and sweeps a hand through her *highlights*.

"Whatever the bride wants! Roxie can definitely make your dessert. What a wonderful idea."

I know there will be hell to pay later, but for now, I don't care one bit. I'm soaring up in the clouds, so happy, I feel could go on a five-mile sprint, I could do something crazy and impulsive—and an impulsive idea does pop into my head. Something that, for some reason, sounds exactly like what I want to do.

I tell Shelby and Heidi that I won't let them down, and then I excuse myself, because my presence at this meeting is no longer necessary. I dust flour off my T-shirt and grab my running shoes on my way out.

11

Blair

Possibly the hardest task known to man: Choosing one's favorite Electric Light Orchestra song. It's damn near impossible. ELO is a treasure trove of vibrant, quirky, classical-pop-rock-disco fusion, and narrowing it down to just one song? It's taken me years to decide.

A lot of people would probably go with "Mr. Blue Sky" or "Evil Woman," which are both fantastic, don't get me wrong. But I always find myself coming back to "Livin' Thing" (I'm a sucker for those back-up vocals and strings—thanks, Jeff Lynne). So that's what I dance around to this Saturday morning, before I bum around town by myself for several hours and then wind up in the main house with Rita and Nolan.

My dad is AWOL, and my mom has Nolan on her lap, a book in her hand. It's a novel from Penguin Random House, which would drive my dad up the wall if he knew about it.

"Why didn't Philip get this author?" she says to me while flipping to the next page. "He seems good. I like his . . . *motifs.*"

There's a fifty-fifty chance Rita knows what the word *motif* even means.

"Well, you know," I pipe up, "Dad doesn't make all those decisions."

"Yes, but I'm just saying, Blair. Sometimes I think he could do a better job with the company. There's always room for improvement."

"Right. Sure. Always room." I slump into the sectional. "Do we have any plans for next week? Anything remotely interesting?"

"I might get your father to take me wine tasting. There are some fantastic vineyards east of here. So I've heard."

I groan. "Perfect. A nineteen-year-old guy's dream. Vineyards and forbidden drinks."

"Come on, now, honey. You know I'd let you sip some wine when no one's looking."

"Gee. Thanks, Mom."

I'm sitting there, thinking about how severely bored I am, when I notice that Nolan has perked up in my mom's lap. He jumps to the floor, his tail swishing back and forth as he trots to the front door of the house.

The door is mostly made of glass, and so I see who's there before I open it. I run up behind Nolan and greet this surprise of a visitor.

"Well, hey, there."

"Hi," she states.

She is breathing heavily and looks particularly—*alive*. Her cheeks are peachy from plenty of blood flow. Her cat eyes shine.

"I knocked next-door, but no one answered. I thought I would try here. Do you remember me?" She points to the bump on her temple.

"Yeah. 'Course. Roxie, right? How's the head?"

She ignores my question, like she doesn't have time for small-talk. Or maybe she just doesn't *like* small-talk.

"Do you want to go to the beach with me?"

I let her query sink in. Nolan clearly wants to go with her. Rita is absorbed in her book.

"Oh. I guess—I could go to the beach. With you. Yeah. Why not?" I laugh awkwardly, and she's already pivoting in a circle to get going. But then she stops. She turns around, points a finger at me.

"Just no frisbees this time. Okay?"

I hold my hands up in the air and hear myself chuckling again.

"You got it. No frisbees."

∞

It's me, Nolan-on-a-leash, and this girl. We're all walking in a horizontal line on the shore. The sun is still high in the sky. There are sunbathers and beachcombers and kids building sandcastles. The water looks like glass to me, it's so bright. I shield my eyes while stepping over washed-up strands of seaweed.

"So. Blair."

The girl raises her voice over the sound of the waves. I look at her, and I still can't believe I thought she was a college student yesterday. Her hair is in a ponytail, and she walks with a childlike bounce in her step.

"So. Roxie."

She grins. "What's your last name?"

"Porter. Yours?"

"Morah."

"Morah," I test it out, see how it sounds in my own voice. "Roxie Morah. Cool name."

"Roxanne Morah, actually. But no one calls me Roxanne." She makes a face. "Too *stiff*."

"Hold up." I stop walking. Nolan and the girl stop, too. "'Roxanne'? Like, The Police?"

She is looking at me as though I'm an alien. I'm used to it—I've gotten that look plenty of times throughout my life.

"Okay," I say, "I could maybe, possibly understand not knowing Paul Simon's stuff. But do you seriously *not* know 'Roxanne'?"

Her laughter is light and quick, almost a scoff. She seems different today. Not so shy. I wonder why she's here, why she came back to see me. I wonder why I'm here with her.

"You're really into music, aren't you?" Roxie Morah utters it as though it is an odd fact, an unusual phenomenon.

"You could say that, yeah. And you're really a clueless shut-in when it comes to music, aren't you?"

The teasing push she gives my arm surprises me, as does the smile that pulls at my mouth.

"Maybe you could help me with that," she says. "How long are you staying in Tangle Beach? When do you go back to New York?"

"Oh, uhhh, I'm not totally sure. Sometime in August. Late August."

I can see her brain working with that information, chewing on something.

"That's perfect," she suddenly declares. "I have an idea."

"An idea?"

Color me confused. This girl, this situation, has got me all kinds of puzzled.

Roxie clarifies for me: "You said I should let you know how you could make things up to me. You know, for hitting me with your frisbee. You said if I thought of something . . . you wanted to even things out between us. So. I thought of something. Maybe."

"Oh, right. Okay, then. I like to think I'm a man of my word. What is it?"

"It's something I saw at your house yesterday. Can we go back there?"

This request makes my stomach squeeze, my eyes flicker down to the beige sand. "Back to my house. Well, yeah, okay. If that's what it takes. To my house, we go."

∞

It's the piano. We're in my guest house, and while I'm stooping to unhook Nolan's leash, Roxie Morah heads right for the shiny, black instrument. That's part of why I told myself this summer vacation would be okay—I saw there was this baby grand here and knew, if nothing else, it would help keep me company.

"Do you play?" Roxie grazes her long fingers across the keys. She definitely has one of those lengthy body types, the kind people say will *fill out* eventually, but maybe never does. Not that I'm unduly fixated on her body. I'm not. It's just one of those things you can't help but notice.

"Yeah," I finally answer her question. "I play. For sure."

"Are you good?"

The bluntness makes me laugh. I come up to the piano myself. "I mean, I'm not the bragging type, but I *did* have lessons most of my life. I'm not too shabby."

"Play something for me."

"Yes, ma'am."

I tilt my head side to side as I sit on the bench, trying to think up what precisely to play. I feel like a peacock right now, so eager to display my brilliant tailfeathers. I admit it, I can be a bit of a show-off.

I go for some Mozart. Specifically, Sonata No. 11. The 1st Movement. It's my personal favorite of his Sonatas. And in case the choice of Mozart surprises you: I truly am all about the oldies.

I jump right into a later variation of the Sonata, Variation IV. It's the most impressive part, in my mind, with wild-looking *main gauche*—my left hand hopping back and forth from bass to treble clefts. One second, it's doing its thing at the lower end of the keys, and the next, it's jumping over my right hand to hit some of the higher notes.

"No, no, no," Roxie suddenly chirps over my performance, waving her hands around. "No. Stop."

I come to an abrupt halt. This is a first for me. Being interrupted mid-performance.

Roxie's brows have gotten all scrunched-up. "That's way too complicated. What the heck?"

"You don't like it?" Slight woundedness bleeds through my tone.

"I like it," she says. "But I can't play something that hard."

I stare at her, waiting for further clarification. Yet, it doesn't come.

I rub my hands against my thighs. "Can you play anything? Do you want to give it a try?"

Roxie suddenly lowers herself to the edge of the bench. Quickly, I slide toward the left to make room for her. As much room as I can. Roxie depresses a key, a high A note, and lets the sound linger a while.

"I had a few lessons when I was little," she answers me. Her gaze seems faraway, but only for a moment. "Not like you, though. Not like professional lessons. What's your deal, anyway, Blair Porter?"

"What's my deal?" I ask. I scoot a bit more to the left. Roxie has her eyes on me, and they're eyes that feel very scrutinizing.

"Yeah. Like, why are you in Tangle Beach? What do you do when you're home in New York? Who was the lady in the other house—the one reading a book? What's your *deal?*"

"Oh. Gotchya, my deal. Well. That lady was my mom. Rita Porter. Um, my family goes on vacations every summer, and for some reason, we ended up on the Oregon Coast this year. Lovely little place you've got here, by the way. And I wish I could say I'm returning to the City at the end of August. But tragically, I'm a college student in Ithaca. I go to Cornell. Just finished my first year there."

Roxie absorbs this information.

"So your family is, like, really rich or something?"

I can't help but laugh. "Boy, you don't have much of a filter, do you, Roxie?"

She looks away, down to the black-and-white keys. "Sorry. You're not the only one who's said that. Queen Christine is always nagging me to think before I speak."

"Queen Who, now?"

"Never mind." She sits up straighter and caresses the pristine faux-ivory before us. "I want you to teach me a song, Blair. On the piano. That's how you can make things up to me. It has to be pretty simple, not like what you just played a second ago. And not very long either. No more than three minutes."

49

"Oh. Roxie, I don't know—"

"I want you to give me a lesson every week, to make sure I can play it perfectly by August."

"Every week? Jeez, I'm not like a teacher or anything. I've never given lessons before." I'm scratching at my neck and feeling just a hair uneasy.

"I'm sure you can do it. You don't seem like an idiot. And I'm a quick learner. It's not like I'm a complete beginner."

"Are you sure you have time for that? You said you're fifteen. Don't you have to study for your driver's permit, or do . . . other . . . . fifteen-year-old activities?"

She gives me a serious look. Not a drop of humor in it.

"Blair. This is what you can do for me. It's really important. And then, we'll be even. For the rest of our lives."

For the rest of our lives. This girl isn't messing around. I can tell she means it when she says this is important to her. Plus, I *did* injure her . . . And also, it's not like I have anything else going on during these next few months.

"So? Blair?"

Her brows are arrowed in lessening patience. I notice a freckle just behind her ear. The lack of piercings in her earlobes. I think to myself: What's the harm in it, really?

What could go wrong?

12

Roxie

My first piano lesson ever was when I was six years old. It was early September. I had just gotten home from school, darting out of the bus, down the rural road, up the gravel driveway. Tears burned in my eyes, which was why I was running so fast, trying to make sure not a soul would see.

I never liked school. Not then, and not now. I never seemed to fit in or make friends. I never felt comfortable—only when I was home with Mama could I relax and just feel okay, away from judgmental eyes. Away from judgmental comments.

I found Maryanne Morah in the backyard, on her knees before the blackberry bushes. The berries were so healthy there at our home, so full of life and water and sun, they lasted longer than anywhere else I've ever seen. Mama spotted me right away as I approached her. She saw the tears pooling in my eyes, and she patted the ground beside her.

"What's wrong, baby? What happened?"

I knelt right next to her, and she set her hand before me, palm-up, for me to wrap my fingers around. Her fingers were what she called *berry-bruised*: purple stains from the warm juices, small pricks from the thorns.

"Roxie? What is it, my rabbit? Talk to me."

Although I had made it to my sanctuary, my safe place, I still refused to let the tears roll down my face. I have always been stubborn, have always hated feeling weak.

"It was Penny Bledsoe. She said something to me on the bus."

"What did she say?" Mama's voice was soothing and low, like the fuzzy bumblebees floating and humming in the bushes around us.

"She said I'm weird, 'cause I don't have any brothers or sisters." I kept my fingers squeezed around Mama's hand. I kept my gaze right there, too, and nowhere else. "She said that's not normal. But if I *did* have brothers or sisters, they would . . ."

Mama waited for me to finish. Her hair was in a low braid today. Her dress was pale like the sky. The tin can in front of her was two-thirds full.

"She said they would be weirdos like me."

Kids at school always found me odd. During recess, I liked to try to plant flowers in the dirt and see how many little, lime-green frogs I could find in the ferns. I didn't play on the swings or the monkey bars like everyone else. I didn't join clubs or whisper about who had crushes on whom.

Mama set her other purple hand on top of mine, sandwiching my small wrist. "Oh, Roxie. You can't let them get to you."

"What am I supposed to say, Mama? When Penny calls me names. When she calls me a weirdo."

"There's only one thing to say to that."

Finally, I glanced up to meet her hazel eyes. She had the most beautiful face, Maryanne. Not a drop of makeup. The faintest freckles on her cheeks.

She smiled at me, a hint of sadness in it. "You say, *Thank you.*"

We went into the house, then. Mama brought her can of berries with us, and I watched her in the kitchen as she transformed them into a simple loaf of sweet bread. I loved the way she baked, something graceful in it, like its own kind of dance. I loved the way she folded the batter, pinched sea salt from a bowl and sprinkled it around in snowy circles. *Every bit of sweetness needs its salt,* she used to tell me. *It's all about the balance.*

After getting the loaf in the oven, she washed her hands at the garden window—though that purple stain never quite seemed to come off.

"Come with me," she said, drying her hands on a red towel and starting for the sitting room. "I want to teach you something."

We went to the upright piano. Wooden, old. Chipped, stained keys. Out of tune. A creaky bench. There were never any picture frames or knick-knacks on top of the instrument. Mama said it wasn't a shelf for décor. And I agreed with her—because I always agreed with her, always trusted her, every second of every day.

We sat on the bench together, and I listened as she played a little melody, her skinny fingers squiggling around like daddy long legs.

"I'll show you how to play it," she said when she was done.

"Why?" It was a silly question, but I'd never been a musically inclined child.

"Because, my little weirdo. Music helps us feel better."

I surrendered the smallest of grins, and my first piano lesson unfolded right then and there. It was a simple song: just the right hand, just the white keys. After thirty minutes, I had mostly mastered it, and Mama told me that was good for today. She was about to slide off the bench and float away. But I stopped her.

"Why *don't* I have brothers and sisters?"

My question filled the room like a discordant set of notes. Mama stayed beside me, and she combed a hand through my long hair.

"I think I'd like it," I went on, "if I had some. Wouldn't you like that, too, Mama?"

"Yes, baby. I would."

"So, why not? Why don't I have any?"

Her pause felt long and heavy. "Sometimes—it just doesn't work out that way. Sometimes life just gives you what you have."

I thought about this. I sat there on the bench and tried to get my six-year-old brain to accept this answer.

"But you wish life gave you more?" I asked. "You wish it worked out different?"

She wrapped me into her arms, then, and she held me tight.

"Oh, no. No, that's not what I meant. I could never feel that way, Roxie. Not for one second."

My voice came out muffled, into her dress that smelled of thyme: "How come?"

"Because, I have everything I could ever want and more. I have you."

∞

After three years of no piano music in my life, I'm suddenly having another lesson. Only this time, it is at a sparkly, black piano. And with a very different teacher.

A week has gone by since I last saw Blair, since I convinced him to teach me a song. I have my reasons for these lessons, believe me. I really do need to learn something. The songs Mama taught me are too simple, too short. And so I persuaded Blair Porter to grant my request, and we agreed to meet back up at his vacation house in seven days. He said he wanted some time to decide on a good song, make sure he knew it like the back of his hand, and feel confident in showing me how to play it.

I'm so exhilarated when I show up to his house, my arms and legs are tingling, jittery. I'm like a little Chihuahua—ever since I tricked Christine into giving me the baking gig for Shelby Frasier's wedding, I've been in this jittery-excited-Chihuahua kind of mood. And now, with these Blair Porter developments, I'm starting to think this summer might actually be kind of, sort of nice. Something different. A change of pace.

Blair has a stick of gum in his mouth when he opens the door and ushers me in. He goes to the piano straight away, taking a seat and rubbing his hands together. I sit beside him, try to keep myself calm and steady. It's interesting being so close to a boy like this. A college boy, no less. There's that smallest bit of blonde stubble around his jaw—his jaw that works the minty-smelling gum. His jaw that opens into a smile, aimed right at me, and I take him in like he is some other lifeform.

"Alrighty, so. Ready for Lesson #1?"

He's all business today. No beating around the bush.

"I'm ready if you are, Blair."

Then, his fingers, hands and wrists: they begin.

It's a slow song.

It has a careful pace.

The whole thing feels careful, like the piano's keys are made of thin glass.

Yet the song is tender. Warm.

As I continue listening, I close my eyes, and I can see the song in my mind. Two people dancing after a rainstorm. Their shoes are getting wet from the puddles. Their hands are clasped, arms holding one another, and they step and spin slowly, carefully, savoring each moment.

"What do you think?"

Blair consults me after the song comes to its final, tender notes. I open my eyes, see him looking down at me. I think of blue flames, how they are hotter than the orange.

"It's perfect," I say. "What is it?"

He looks pleased to hear I'm on board.

"Good ole Mozart. It's the fifth variation of Sonata No. 11. I thought it would be easy enough and about the right length to meet your requirements. So you think you can learn it by August?"

"I know I can. As long as you're not a crappy teacher."

He laughs, and then we embark on the first lesson. We start with the right hand. Blair demonstrates on the lower part of the keyboard, while I try to copy him in the higher section. It turns out it really is pretty simple, and after ten minutes or so, he's showing me a little of what the left hand does.

I can't help but think of Mama during all of this. She never taught me any Mozart, nothing fancy like what this funny blonde boy is now teaching me. But I know she would have liked this song, which is what makes it so perfect.

"I guess we can stop there for the day."

Blair rises from the bench after about forty minutes, resting an elbow atop the angled lid. "Do you have a piano at home you can practice on?"

I picture Christine's house, all decked out in knick-knacks and beachy décor. Throw pillows that read, *Beach House*, and, *On Ocean Time*. Vases filled with sand dollars and white starfish. The round mirror on the mantel lined in nautical rope.

"No, actually," I say. "Christine doesn't have any instruments in the house. Would it be all right if I came here to practice every now and then? I don't know anywhere else there's a piano I could use."

Blair's eyebrows do a funny thing, arching and then furrowing a couple times in a row. He's leaning against the piano and tapping a hand against his leg.

"Oh. Well. Sure. I guess you'll need to practice sometimes, won't you? Yeah, just stop by whenever. I'll probably be here or next-door. Actually—what's your number? We can text to coordinate our lessons and whatnot."

"I don't have a phone."

Blair stares at me. "Seriously? A teenager without a phone? I thought such creatures didn't exist."

I give a shrug. "Christine tried to get me one, but I refused. I can't stand the thought of her being able to contact me wherever and whenever. Plus, it's not like I have anyone I want to talk to."

He seems to consider this, nodding his head. Then: "I have two questions for you, Roxie Morah. One: Why do you need to learn this song? And two: Who's this Christine I keep hearing you mention?"

Christine Lambert. The person I got stuck with, out of all the billions of humans in this world. God or Fate or Whoever has a very different way of doing things compared to if I were in charge.

"Christine is my guardian. She's a relative of mine. She's in her thirties." I try to keep myself from sighing. "It's just the two of us. Plus all the neighbors squished around the house."

Totally on purpose, I ignore his first question about why I requested these lessons of him. It's not something I want to talk about. To anyone.

Blair is studying me, absorbing both what I said and what I didn't say.

"If I may be so blunt, Roxie, you don't sound all that fond of her. *Queen Christine*. Isn't that what you called her?"

"Well . . . She's not the devil incarnate or anything. She's just . . . not what I expected. Not what I'm used to."

"How long have you lived with her? You grew up in Tangle Beach, right?"

I can tell he wants to ask about my parents. The curiosity is there, just below the surface.

"No. I grew up a little of east of here. I've been in Tangle Beach under Queen Christine's reign just a few years."

"Oh. Nifty."

"What about you?" I ask. "What are your parents like? And why are you guys so rich?"

Blair laughs and surprises me when he sits back down on the piano bench. Our legs are almost touching, but not quite.

"Ever heard of Porter Publishing House?"

I consider it. "Sounds familiar. I think."

"That's my family's book publishing company. My dad's. We're definitely not as big as Penguin or Hachette. But we're respectable. Based out of the great New York City, of course. We do all kinds of genres, work with all kinds of authors."

"Hmm. Porter Publishing House. I'm not the biggest reader, honestly. I guess you probably are, though?"

Blair grimaces. "Don't tell anyone, but . . . I'm not much of a reader myself."

"Oh, right, let me guess." I move just a little bit closer to him, but he doesn't seem to notice. "You'd rather be listening to your music. Mozart and Simon Paul. Right?"

In that moment, his laughter comes out in a quick burst. He starts shaking his head side to side. I think it must be the most becoming sound in the world, that laugh.

"Simon Paul, oh jeez. Roxie. It's *Paul Simon*. You know what?" He slides a phone out of his pocket and starts poking around on it. "I think you're in need of another music lesson today. Sit tight, Miss Music Hermit."

What an odd feeling all of this is. I've never just sat down and had a conversation with any of the kids from my school. I've never *wanted* to. But being with Blair feels different. All I want is to do is sit tight, as he's instructed, see what he has in store for me. I feel a weirdly intense desire to know as much about him as I possibly can.

"Okay, listen up." He sets his phone on the sheet music stand. "This is Paul Simon. Also known to some coast-dwellers as *Simon Paul*."

The song that starts blaring from his phone is bright, upbeat, a kind of song that isn't wasting any time. And neither is Blair; right away, he starts wriggling around with the rhythm and singing along with the lyrics. I can't make any sense out of those lyrics, but in some way, I like that. The smile on my face is so long it almost hurts. Blair turns to me, saying, "What do you think?" over those bright, bursting horns.

All I do is laugh and shrug while he keeps angling his shoulders and bobbing his head. Before the song is finished, Blair jumps off the bench and starts tapping his fingers against his phone again.

"It's all about the oldies, Roxie," he proclaims. "I'm going to change your world with this stuff. See what you think of this one."

I lean forward to check what he's queuing up next for me. Something called "Build Me Up, Buttercup." The Foundations.

"You gotta get off your butt for this one. No sitting allowed."

To my surprise, Blair suddenly takes my hands in his and pulls me off the bench. A janky piano gets started, and a male singer is borderline screaming through the speakers of the phone. Next thing I know, Blair has me dancing around with him on the shiny

58

wood floors. It reminds me of the way little kids dance with each other: hands clutched together, arms swinging up and down, loose and floppy. Nothing even a little remotely refined about it. Blair is lip syncing to the song as we bounce around, and I don't know if I've ever laughed so hard before. At least, it's been a very long time.

"You do the back-up!" he shouts to me, and I find myself lip syncing along the best I can through my laughter and through our totally-silly dance moves.

When the song begins fading out, Blair releases my hands. He goes to his phone again and rubs his fingers along his chin in contemplation.

"One more for today. How about . . . some Elton John? I mean, when can a guy ever go wrong with Elton? Let's do . . . 'I Guess That's Why They Call It the Blues.'"

It's another piano-based song, but slower than the other ones Blair's shared with me today. The rhythm of it stands out to me, an infectious, simple beat. The sound of the music falls somewhere in between almost-happy and almost-sad.

Blair sits on the piano bench and smiles at me while the song goes on. I'm still standing on the wood floors, and I curl my arms around my chest. Part of me wishes he would take my hands in his again. But another part of me is okay that this isn't happening, that he's keeping his distance. I'm not used to all this interaction. All this attention. It feels as if all these newfound doors are suddenly opening up to me. New portals I might be able, might be willing, to step foot into.

The song has an expected ending: satisfying, complete.

"So." Blair sends a questioning face my way. "Music Hermit. Does your world feel any different now? Now that I've expanded your harmonic horizons?"

I smile, roll my eyes. But, of course, I know the truth. There's no way I'm going to say it to this crazy, electric Blair Porter of New York City. It's something I'm just going to keep to myself, for now.

The truth is that my world does feel different. Totally different. And something tells me it's only the start.

13

Blair

Roxie Morah of Tangle Beach. The fifteen-year-old girl who's a quick learner, it turns out, on the piano. How could it be that someone who picks up on Mozart so quickly, simultaneously believes Paul Simon's name is *Simon Paul?* I mean, it's not Paul & Garfunkel, is it? No. It's *Simon* & Garfunkel. But I suppose she's probably never heard of that heavenly musical pairing before, anyway.

It's funny, though—she's not a lost cause. I can tell. She just needs a little help, someone to enlighten her, to show her *the way.* I will be her teacher, her Shaman. I have this sense I'm going to be seeing a lot more of her over these next few months. And my feelings on that are mixed.

"Blair, can you pass me the limes?"

I'm having dinner with my parents now. *Both* of them, at the same time, in the same place. Imagine that. We're on the front deck with the view of the ocean. Tourists keep pedaling bicycles down the road and checking out our family of four (counting Nolan, of course) on their way by. I return the favor and ogle the tourists right back, happy for the people-watching opportunity.

The bowl of lime wedges gets passed down to my mother as requested—always the good, obsequious son am I. My dad sits at the head of the table, cutting into some of the filet mignon he's grilled tonight. Once in a blue moon, we wind up having dinner together as a family, because, well, honestly, it's just hard to completely avoid it.

"That's your third gin and tonic, Rita."

My dad doesn't look at her when he speaks. He looks at his steak. A stranger could easily presume that the steak's name is Rita.

"It's my second, Philip. There's more tonic in it than gin, anyway."

Oh, yes. Dinnertime with my parents is a blast. Aren't you jealous? It was better with Graham. More tolerable, I should say. Until he went all hippie-style rebellion on them.

"Second, my ass," my dad not-so-quietly mutters with food in his mouth.

"Do I need to start keeping a tally? I will. Blair, tell your father to relax."

"Blair doesn't need you to tell him what to say, Rita."

So, these are my parents, when they're in close vicinity of one another. Their story is a depressing one, in my keen estimation. I don't know how anyone could view it as anything other than depressing.

They met in college. Well, no, they met when my *mom* was in college. She was eighteen, a freshman. My dad was twenty-seven at the time. Nine years her senior. He'd finished college a long time ago and had been working at the Publishing House ever since. His father was the one who started the company, in case you were wondering, and he'd been preparing my dad to take it over when the time came (which, it did, faster than anyone expected).

Anyway. My mom was a college student. My dad was just visiting Cornell to see a friend of his, an old business professor he liked to run ideas by. It may be true that Philip was simply handed Porter Publishing House, born into his wealth, status, and career. But, it's also true that he is legitimately a business-savvy guy. No matter what my mom says, he *is* good at his job. Maybe too good. He lives and breathes that company stuff.

So, back to the story: he was chatting up his professor buddy in the guy's campus office, and that's when Rita Evers came waltzing in. Cue Gary Wright's "Dream Weaver" (you know, like in *Wayne's World*?). Except not really—it wasn't some grand, romantic moment. Rita was there to ask the professor an exam-related question, and Philip ended up injecting himself into the conversation, ultimately asking her on a date. Which she readily accepted.

He liked her because she was attractive. The same blonde hair color that I have. Same pale eyes. Plus some other features my dad is too egocentric to realize I *don't* want to hear about. The worst part is that he liked her because she was young. Excuse me while I gag up some of my filet mignon.

Similarly, my mom liked *him* because he was older. Accomplished. Established. You know, all the stereotypical stuff. They started sleeping together right out of the gate (and yes, I hate that I have this information stored deeply, permanently within the folds of my brain matter, traumatizing me from now until eternity. My mother has shared bits and pieces of this tale with me after too many drinks. My father has shared bits and pieces seemingly for no reason other than to disturb me).

Graham came into existence pretty damn fast. Poor little Graham Fetus. There was a lot of uproar and yelling and crying while he was just chilling, doing his thing all floaty-like in utero. And the result of all the uproar was a shotgun wedding. A lifelong commitment. A beautiful marriage between two wonderful human beings. My sarcasm overflows, if you can't tell.

"You should really try some of the risotto, Philip. It's good, isn't it, Blair?"

I've already eaten up everything on my plate, except for the radishes that were in the salad. And the cucumbers. Nolan is lying on the deck down by my feet. I've been slipping him some bites of filet throughout our meal.

"Pretty good," I confirm. "Kind of tangy."

Philip is picking at his teeth with the steak knife. "I don't like risotto. You know that."

"Blair. Who's that girl I've seen coming around lately?" My mother switches the topic, turning her focus to me. "The tall brunette girl, with the ponytail?"

That gets my dad's full attention.

"A girl? What girl?"

"She's just a girl," I say, shrugging. "A local. She's in high school."

I don't want to talk about this. Not with Rita and Philip. I'm trying to go for nonchalant, unruffled, as I speak. I rub a napkin over my mouth and gaze out to the ocean. "She just wants to, uh — play the piano in the guest house. Doesn't have one at home."

Part of the truth. That works.

"She's cute," my mom remarks. It makes me tremendously uncomfortable.

My dad's equally uncomfortable contribution: "Brunette, huh?"

I fear I'm starting to sound less . . . unruffled:

"It's just a little agreement we have. It's nothing. All about the piano. I mean, can you blame her? That thing's a beauty. Yamaha's underrated, don't you think? Everyone's into Steinways these days, but what about all the pristine Yamahas of the world?"

It doesn't matter what Rita and Philip say in response. Because I've started tuning them out. I let my hand dangle down in front of Nolan's snout. He licks my fingers, and I let my mind wander.

Without even meaning to, I start brainstorming up other songs I need to introduce to Roxie Morah, next time I see her. These tunes need to be in her life. I need to prescribe them to her, like medicine. It's as simple as that. This is my duty. Shaman Blair. Sensei Blair. While my parents prattle on without me, I am forming a mental, *must-hear* playlist.

14

Roxie

I'm back at my blackberry bushes in the fresh, early morning, after writing, *I miss you*, in my journal, after opening my bedroom window, after practically tearing Christine out of the bathroom so I could relieve my bladder and get ahold of my hair scrunchie.

When I'm here in this spot, it doesn't really matter what is going on in my life, in the world, in the whole universe. I feel my heart rate coming down while sitting on the stump. I feel a peacefulness while checking up on the brambles, seeing how some of the berries are reddening. The sight of it makes my tongue prickle. I can taste how sour they must be right now. They need more time, more sun and water and clean air.

It's Wednesday, one of Christine's workdays at the dermatology office. I love workdays at the dermatology office. Especially in the summer. Christine will be gone almost all day, and that means no wedding planning, no bossing me around, no criticizing every little thing about me.

I can do whatever I want today. Anything at all that strikes my fancy. I can sit here in my private blackberry haven as long as I want. I can splash around on the beach on my way back to the house. I can spend hours in the kitchen, baking up a storm, two cakes, three pies, four dozen pastries.

And something else occurs to me: If I want, I can even run over to Blair Porter's house and see what he's up to, get some practice in on his piano. He *did* say I could stop by whenever.

I spring up off the stump and feel energy surging back into my blood. My heart rate is picking back up. I tell the brambles goodbye, that I'll be back again tomorrow. Hopefully Blair meant what he said. Hopefully he wasn't planning on sleeping in today.

∞

I rap my knuckles on the door, set my hands on my hips. Wait to see if Blair comes to greet me or not. The fog is lingering in the air today, a salty mist that's making me even more thirsty than I already am from the sprinting.

I know that Blair's awake. There's music coming from inside the house. *His* kind of music. But he's not coming to the door, so I give a stronger knock and peek in through the windows.

Oh, he's awake, all right. There's a flash of him grooving around, hands in the air. And shirtless. Another flash goes by, and this time I see him attempting to pull on a T-shirt while flailing around in his own, personal Blair-style. The next time he's in view, his eyes finally find me, and the look on his face is priceless.

His breathing is labored when he opens the door and regards me face-to-face.

"Oh. Hey, Roxie."

His music is fading away, and I'm trying not to laugh. Blair's totally flustered right now.

"Were you dancing by yourself in there? While getting dressed?" I ask.

"No. Maybe. Yes. I do that sometimes."

"Do you, now?"

"All the time, actually."

"Interesting," I note.

"Well, what about you?" He looks me up and down. "You look a little sweaty there yourself."

I shove at his arm, hear him chuckle as I squeeze past him, into the house.

"Oh, sure. Please, come right on in. Has anyone ever told you your manners aren't the sharpest or shiniest?"

"Manners are dumb," I respond, and I get positioned at the piano, try to remember where my fingers are supposed to begin.

"That's beautiful. *Manners are dumb.* Quote from Roxie Morah."

I stick my tongue out at him. He's still over by the door. Cherry-red shirt. Jeans. He doesn't really look like a rich kid to me. Aren't rich kids supposed to wear polos or something?

"So, you're here to practice, I take it?" Blair tugs a jacket off a hook on the wall. "I guess I'll see if Nolan wants to go on a little stroll with me. But you knock yourself out. Make me and Amadeus proud. Take as long as you want."

And I do. Take as long as I want, I mean. That's my whole idea. I'm not just here to practice Mozart. I can't tell if Blair's aware of that or not. How oblivious are boys?

When he gets back with Nolan a whole fifty minutes later, I'm still right here where he left me, on the piano bench. I've repeated the first bit of the Sonata about a hundred times.

"Still at it, huh?"

Blair is chewing on his bottom lip as he unzips his coat. I don't know about Blair, but Nolan is certainly happy to see me—I scratch him behind his ears when he greets me at the piano.

"That's a bummer you don't have a piano at your house."

"Kind of, yeah," I say. "Except I don't like being in that Seawood Lane house, anyway."

"Where *do* you like being?"

I meet his gaze, my hands still submerged in golden fur. I shrug. "I don't know. Only a few places, really."

"Do you go out running every single morning?"

"Yep."

"And where do you go when you run?"

My eyes flash back down to Nolan's shiny black ones.

"Nowhere."

"Huh." Blair pushes off the door, wanders into the kitchen area. "Nowhere. Sounds like a nice place."

His grin induces one of my own. "You're weird, Blair."

"You know, I'm tempted to say the same about you."

Something tightens in my stomach. I think of Mama. *Thank you.* I don't say it out loud, but I think it.

Blair examines me from the kitchen, leaning his elbows atop the bar. Meanwhile, I start examining his kitchen more closely. It's a lot nicer than Christine's. Not so sterile and lifeless. The cabinets look like pine. The counters are a deep green color. A skylight in the ceiling lets in a natural, gray glow. That fog is still coating everything outside in its ghostlike veil. It hasn't lifted one bit. Not great for a day at the beach.

But it is great for something else: a day in the kitchen.

"Do you want to hang out today?"

My question makes Blair stand up straight. I hop off the bench and go to the kitchen bar, opposite him.

"Roxie. You really want to hang out with *me*? I'm sure there are tons of other people you'd rather be chilling out with."

"*Chilling out* with?" I smirk. "No. There aren't."

"Girl friends?"

"Nope."

"High school . . . acquaintances?"

I shake my head.

"Queen Christine?"

Even he gets a dubious look on his face after suggesting it.

"Okay, Blair. Look." I bow over the countertop to get closer to him. "I'm not the social butterfly you seem to think I am. I don't have girl friends or high school acquaintances. And it seems like you don't have anyone here either, except for Nolan."

He hangs his head. "You're not wrong."

"Well, then. Maybe we could be kinda-sorta friends? You and me. For the summer. We could hang out sometimes, here and there. Or *chill out* sometimes. Like today."

Blair is on the verge of accepting my proposal. I can tell.

"Just a matter of passing the time," I go in for the close. "Together."

He inhales, puts on a smile like he's being a good sport.

"What exactly did you have in mind for today, Roxie?"

A little bird seems to flutter its wings inside my chest.

"I was thinking something with butterscotch."

We're at the market, Blair and I. I found a few supplies in his kitchen (flour, sugar, baking soda, and salt), but we'll need more than that to mix up a nice, proper dough.

"Why are we baking cookies again?"

The eggs I'm assessing are all intact, so I set the carton in our basket. We've already located the butterscotch chips, the cinnamon, the graham crackers, and now it's just a few items in the dairy aisle.

"I mean," Blair continues, "don't get me wrong. I like cookies. Cookies are great. There are these ones at a bakery in the East Village, *huge*, like the size of your face. And they're rad as hell. I mean, heck."

He looks at me askance, grimacing. "Rad as *heck*."

I roll my eyes, move on to the butter.

"You don't have to censor yourself in front of me, Blair. I've heard swear words before. I go to public high school. And my cookies are better than your precious New York City's."

"That's quite the claim. I'd love nothing more than to press you on it, but I feel I have to ask—have you noticed the dude over there that keeps looking at you?"

My head snaps up from the shelves of butter, swivels around, and I see him, at the other end of the aisle.

Something in me sinks a little. He's not a *dude* so much as he is a boy. A boy from my school. It's as though my uttering the words *public school* have magically summoned him. And now that we've made eye contact, he's coming this way.

"Hey, Roxie."

"Oh. Hey, Tim."

Tim Redding. He stops just in front of me, right next to all the boxes and tubs of butter. He looks rightfully tan in his white Riptide shirt. I've heard girls at school describe his looks as something along the lines of a *"young, beachy Mark Ruffalo."* Whatever that means. To me, he always looks half-asleep, half-confused.

"Man, I haven't seen you around at all since school ended. How's your summer been?"

"Nothing to write home about," I respond. He's waiting for me to elaborate. I don't.

"Cool. Who's your friend?" Tim turns to regard Blair. "Hey, man. I'm Tim."

"Blair Porter. Good to meet you."

A handshake is exchanged, and this whole scenario makes me wish we hadn't come to the market at all.

"Blair," Tim echoes. "I didn't know that name was—"

"Unisex." Now Blair's really perked up. "Yeah, it's unisex. One of those things that can go both ways, you know what I'm saying?"

Blair laughs. Tim doesn't. Neither do I. Awkwardness abounds.

Tim asks: "You're an out-of-towner, then?"

"Ah, you got me. Yeah. My family's here for the summer. Roxie here is just . . ."

I look over at Blair, suddenly very curious as to how he's going to finish his sentence.

"She's just showing me around Tangle Beach. Getting me acquainted, you know. Nifty place. Tangles and all."

Tim appears mildly amused. I, on the other hand, visibly wince in Blair's direction.

"Cool." Tim gives a nod of his head. "Well, hey. Roxie. I'll see you around?"

"Probably. Small town." I turn back to focus on the butter before Tim leaves the scene.

A *tsk-tsk* sound issues from behind me.

Blair says, "Didn't we already chat about those manners of yours, Miss Morah?"

"Sorry, *Mom*. Let's go check out before I run into anybody else from school."

In the checkout line, Blair's not letting me off so easy. "I thought you said you didn't have any high school acquaintances."

"I don't."

"Then who was this *Tim*? He seemed . . . friendly. Enlighten me, if you will."

I sigh. "Tim Redding goes to my school. We're in the same grade. We *know* each other, but that doesn't make us *friends*. Or anything like that."

"Okay, all right. That's all fine and good. But why so cold to the guy?"

"No reason."

I'm lying. There's kind of a reason. But it doesn't matter.

"Well, I'm just saying." Blair pays for all the food while I bag it up myself. "You could have at least given a halfhearted smile to the poor kid."

Kid. Now, that's interesting. I never thought Tim Redding looked young. But today, I could see the physical difference between a high school boy and a college one. The difference between Tim and Blair.

"I treat everyone that way, Blair."

"Hmmm."

We're out the doors, bagged groceries in hand, walking back to the guest house.

"You're not that cold with me," Blair remarks on the sidewalk. "If you treated other people the way you treat me, maybe . . ."

"Maybe what?"

I'm getting agitated. I want this discussion to end, to move on to another topic. Any other topic.

"Maybe you'd have more friends? Just food for thought. Merely throwing it out there."

I start walking faster. My agitation has morphed into anger.

"I don't think you get it," I snip. "I don't want friends."

Blair speeds up to stay at my side. "Aren't I your friend, though? Isn't that what you said back at the house? We could be friends."

"No." I stop in my tracks and turn to face him. My chest is burning. "I said *kinda-sorta* friends." Then I take the two plastic bags in my hands and thrust them into Blair's.

"I'm going home," I state.

"What! Why? What about the cookies? What just happened? You're giving me whiplash here."

"I'm not in the mood for cookies anymore."

A spin of my heels, I start heading my way.

15

Blair

"Rich Girl" by my good buddies Hall & Oates. I know as soon as I wake up—which has been getting earlier and earlier these days—this is the tune to start my day.

On the surface, "Rich Girl" may strike you as upbeat, soulful, lighthearted, and entirely dance-worthy. But personally, I've always interpreted this song as giving off some doleful, down-in-the-dumps vibes. I can still dance around to it while getting dressed, but my classic moves aren't so sharp, aren't so heartfelt today.

I know something went wrong yesterday, with Roxie. And it's been just about driving me bananas. I can't stop thinking about it and just feeling *off*. Yet again, I wish Graham were here. He could help me figure this out. He was always better with this stuff than I was. Stuff that pertained to girls.

I was just trying to be helpful yesterday. I really was. We ran into that Tim kid at the market, and something about it made me feel weird. I know I pushed too hard on the whole *friends* subject. That seems obvious now, hindsight being so 20/20 and all. The problem is, I'm just not sure where to go from here.

What would Graham say? What would he advise?

He'd say to just talk to her, probably. *Girls are talkers.* I swear I heard him say that once. Graham would always hand out his advice like it was so obvious, which maybe it was. And maybe it's obvious now:

Find her, and talk to her.

So, off I go. Step one: find her. To start, I wander over to the beach. Maybe she'll be out here, like she was that first time, the day of the frisbee debacle. There's no sign of her out in the sand, though. I consider heading into town next, to test my luck there. But something else pops up in my brain. She said the name of where she lives. Yesterday, when she was at my place. She called it *that Seawood Lane house.*

Ten minutes later, I'm there. I used my phone for directions and walked myself through previously unexplored parts of Tangle Beach to get here. Seawood Lane is holiday-gingerbread-house quaint. It's a narrow, gravel road with lots of vibrant foliage, quirky little fences, happy-looking homes. I wonder why Roxie doesn't like living here. If I get a chance, I'll have to ask her.

What happens next is just a matter of luck. I see her. She comes out the door of a blue, two-story house and runs to a convertible Volkswagen sitting in the driveway. Without much forethought, I jog that way, managing to catch her attention before she gets in the car.

"Blair?" Roxie's oblique eyes reveal her surprise. "What are you doing here?"

"Hey. Sorry to show up out of the blue. I was hoping I'd find you somewhere on this road. Do you think we could chat for just a quick sec?"

Then comes a sound—a clearing of the throat.

I failed to notice earlier that there was a woman sitting in the Volkswagen, behind the wheel. I take a glance at her. It must be Christine, the royal one herself. She's even tanner than Roxie. Her hair is yellow-blonde. Sunglasses shield her eyes, but she's definitely looking my way.

"I can't right now," Roxie says to me. "I'm working today. I have to get going."

"Oh, you work?"

That would explain why she looks different today. Her hair's down, and her clothes look less casual than I've seen.

"Yeah," she says, "with Christine. I really have to go."

Christine cranks on the engine to drive the point home.

"Okay, but—just real fast." I rub my hands together, think on my feet. "I just wanted to tell you I'm sorry about yesterday. About the crap I said. Annnddd . . . I was really looking forward to your cookies that allegedly surpass my all-time favorites. The ingredients are still untouched at my place . . . If you wanted to come by when you're done with work, I'll help you make them?"

Roxie stares at me blankly. Just for a beat. Then she brushes some hair out of her face, and there's a curling of her lips.

"Okay, weirdo. I'll be there."

∞

And she is. She shows up later than I was expecting, almost seven o'clock. And she's back in her normal attire: comfortable, practical shorts and T-shirt.

"Hey, stranger."

Roxie groans. "Don't say that. I hate when people say that."

So, we're back to normal. Back to being okay. Just like that.

"You want to get some of your music playing?" she asks once we're in the kitchen. She's already searching for bowls and the mixer and measuring cups.

"Oh? Does that mean it's growing on you? Are my lessons working?"

Roxie counters, "I wouldn't say that. I just thought you could have your favorite thing going while I have mine."

It takes me a minute to make sense of this. I watch the way she moves about the kitchen, the way she fluffs the flour and levels it in the measuring cup. I see the look on her face. Focused. But not a stressed-out kind of focused. A simple, happy kind.

"So. This is your favorite thing?" I come up beside her while she whisks powdery ingredients together in a bowl.

"Yeah," Roxie replies. "This is it."

"Baking."

"Yep. Baking."

"Not running?" I angle an eyebrow. "I thought maybe running was your thing."

"Running is—it's a different kind of thing. I do it for different reasons. I bake because that's my real thing. And it always will be."

I nod my head, meditate on her words for a moment. She's starting to open up to me. For some reason, I like the way it feels.

"Sounds serious. How'd you learn to bake?"

Roxie brushes past me, over to the fridge to fetch some sticks of butter. Then she locates a pan, lights a burner on the stove, gets the butter melting.

"My mother. She was a baker, too. She was amazing. She taught me everything I know. But it's more than just that. It's in my blood."

"Wow, so your mom is—she *was*—um—what was her name?"

Suddenly, Roxie whirls around and looks right at me.

"Blair. Are you going to just stand there being the world's most worthless sous-chef? Get your stupid music going, crack two eggs into that bowl, and show me where the food processor is."

"Yes, ma'am."

So, we bake, and I provide some mellow Carole King that permeates the kitchen. Roxie orders me around, and not long later, a sweet and homey aroma is permeating the kitchen along with the music. It's a perfect combination, if you ask me: Ms. King and a batch of homemade butterscotch cookies.

"New York can't beat me on this. No way."

We've gotten settled on the couch with a plate of Roxie's creations. The sun is just starting to go down over the ocean, casting the living room in a snazzy, golden glow. I take a cookie specimen in my hand, hold it up into the warm light.

"Let's find out, shall we?"

Roxie takes a cookie for herself. "You *have* to be honest with me, Blair. Promise? No sympathy lies."

"No sympathy lies," I concur. And I try a bite. I can taste the graham crackers that we pulsed up into a powder—but they're not too sweet, like I thought they might be. And they give an interesting texture, a fine crunch. Then there's the melted butterscotch chips, completely harmonious with the caramelly dough, the touch of salt, the somehow dense *and* light crumb.

It's like a good piece of music, really, with all the right notes coming together to create something bigger and better and new.

"Well? Blair?"

"Roxie. You may very well be the Mozart of cookies."

The smile that lights up her face is brilliant, contagious. Then, she throws a soft punch at my arm.

"Ouch. What was that for? I just gave you an amazing compliment."

"You can't just say it to make me feel good. Do you really mean it?"

Rubbing my arm, I munch down the rest of the cookie and enjoy the experience once again. "I swear to you, I'm not just blowing smoke up your ass. I mean, *butt*. These are better than the ginormous ones from back home."

She grins. "Swear on Paul Simon?"

"Even better: I swear on Sir Paul McCartney himself."

"Why is that better?"

"It just is."

Roxie laughs and shifts around so she's *right* next to me on the couch, our legs touching. I think I can smell her shampoo or soap or something. Like wild fruit.

"Ugh. I'm exhausted. Christine wore me out today."

Her next move startles me. Alarms me. She maneuvers around so she's lying across my lap, her head on the armrest of the couch, her back settled atop my legs. She closes her eyes and lets out a breath. Carole King is still crooning at a very low volume from the kitchen.

"Oh, yeah. Work." I try to distract my mind, delve into conversation. "What kind of work is this exactly?"

Roxie tells me about something called Lace & Tide, how Christine's a wedding planner, how Roxie works as her quasi-assistant. She mentions there's a wedding coming up this weekend that she'll have to help out with. And she says she managed to attain the dessert-catering role for a wedding at the end of summer, something she is clearly proud of.

I'm listening, but all the while that this conversation plays out, there's Roxie right below me. She has her eyes closed the whole time; she really is exhausted. It's hard to focus on what's being said when I feel her body pressing into my thighs each time she inhales. When I can *really* study her in this moment.

There's the freckle behind her ear, but also the honeyed smoothness of her skin. I never noticed the way her nostrils flare just a little. Or the way her lower lip is so full. I won't let my eyes wander below her neck.

"Blair?"

"Yeah?" I chirp. Roxie sits up, moves off my lap, and I feel my muscles loosen up.

"I better get home before the sun's gone."

"Right. Of course. Let's get you on your way. Shall we?"

She tells me to keep the cookies for myself when I ask if she wants to take some home. I walk her to the door, and I'm trying to think of something lighthearted to say to put a close to our evening.

Instead, something else spurts out my mouth:

"Did you know I'm turning twenty in September?"

Roxie stands there, arrowing her eyebrows, beholding me as though I'm the epitome of awkwardness. Maybe I am.

"Okay," she says. "That's nice."

"Yeah, yeah. It'll be cool. And, when's your birthday?"

"February. Why?"

"Just wondering. February. That sounds . . . wintery. So, I guess that makes us five years apart. Basically."

"Right. Okay. Are you going to start asking me what it's like being an Aquarius, or can I get going now?"

I let out a breathy, dismissive laugh and throw a gesture in the air. "Sorry. Get going. See you at our next piano lesson."

"I'm glad you came and found me this morning, Blair."

Then, she hugs me. It seems innocent enough, like she's merely saying goodbye to a friend. I smell the wild fruit again in her hair, and I hold her against me for just a quick moment.

"Night, Blair," Roxie says.

"Night. Have a safe . . . walk."

I shut the door behind her.

Five years.

It's not *nine* years, like my parents, but. Still.

Still.

16

Roxie

Every summer, Mama and I went to the farmers' markets. Not just the one in Shoshone. We also went to the markets in other neighboring towns, including the biggest one in Tangle Beach. And we weren't there as shoppers, we weren't there for fun—we were there to sell Mama's desserts.

Her pies were her bestsellers. Blackberry pies, of course. She also had mason jars of berry jam for sale, and every once in a while she'd make batches of berry muffins, or even just bring crates of fresh-picked blackberries themselves. But it was really the pies that were the star of the show.

One day, when I was eight, we were at the big Tangle Beach market, right in the middle of town. It was cooler there than it was in Shoshone, the ocean wind stronger than I was used to. Mama let me wear her fuzzy cream cardigan, oversized and baggy on my frame, making me look like a polar bear. People would look at me funny, but I didn't care. I would look at them funny back.

Maryanne treated everyone as though they were special. All the passersby and customers. She would ask them where they were from and actually seem interested in their answers, even if they said they were from Salem. My job was to hand out samples, little paper cups containing a generous bite of that scrumptious pie. Every time someone took a sample, it was the same reaction. Like with the man in the lavender, short sleeve button-up that morning.

"I've never tasted anything like this."

He stood at our booth with bright eyes, sunglasses on his head, a charmed gaze directed at Mama. I liked his gaze. It seemed real and kind.

"That's some great pie," he said.

"Thank you." Maryanne beamed. "Where are you from? Here on vacation?"

"Actually. I just moved here. Yesterday." He laughed, and I thought his eyes might be permanently stuck on my mother's.

"That's wonderful. Welcome to your new home, then. What brought you this way?"

Their light conversation went on while shoppers kept moseying by in a lazy-river stream. At the end of their small talk, the man purchased the largest-sized pie Mama had. I helped package it up with the ribbons and dried flowers tied around the case, a business card slipped in between, and the Lavender Man sent his kind gaze my way.

"I'm sure you'll love it here," Maryanne said before he went on his way.

But he only got a few steps down the road. Next thing I knew, he had backtracked and was standing before us again.

"I don't suppose . . ." he uttered, then paused.

I didn't quite understand it then, but the look on his face was a smitten one. He was completely taken. And why wouldn't he be? Maryanne was like a small-town angel. Her long hair, pure face, her airy, floral dresses. A small-town angel who could bake.

The Lavender Man cleared his throat. "I don't really know anyone in town. And now I have this huge pie. Maybe you'd like to share it with me sometime. Maybe I could see you again."

Maryanne laughed. Not in a rude way. Not a drop of malice in it.

"I'm sorry." The wind blew her billowy sleeves around her shoulders. I watched the scene play out before me as if I were sitting in a theater. "I can't."

The man's hopefulness was dashed.

"Oh, God. I don't know why I just assumed—that you weren't married. I'm so sorry."

"No, don't be sorry. I'm not married. But you should find someone else to share that pie with."

Confused, but ever as smitten, Lavender Man really did go on his way that time. Later in the day, we were back home in Shoshone, in the backyard. Mama had spread out a blanket for us, and we were lying on our stomachs, drawing on pads of white paper, letting the sun's rays pulse into us. Over on her side of the blanket, Maryanne was using charcoal to create a robust, lifelike robin. Never much of an artist myself, I was scribbling with crayons to draw simple, bulky flowers.

"What happened with that man today at the market?" I asked. "Why couldn't you have pie with him?"

Maryanne kept drawing, so I did the same.

"He didn't really want to have pie with me. He meant something else."

"What did he mean?"

"It's hard to explain, baby."

But I wanted to understand. I could feel myself scowling and crinkling my forehead. Mama must have noticed.

"Roxie. Have you ever liked a boy at your school? Thought someone was cute?"

I turned this over in my mind, over and over.

"Not really. But last year I heard some girls saying stuff like that. Girls in my class. Miranda thought Joey was cute. Joey thought some other girl was cute."

"Okay. Well, adults are that same way."

I said, "So, the man at the market thought you were cute."

She chuckled as she shaded her robin's beak.

"I guess he did."

"So, why wouldn't you eat pie with him?"

"Sometimes," she replied, "for some people, sharing pie isn't in the cards."

I could feel my frustration building as I wrestled with her words, replayed the scene from the market. Lavender Man seemed so nice. If he thought Mama was cute, what could be wrong with that? Really, there was something else at the heart of my frustration and confoundment. It chewed and chewed at me, and suddenly, it just flew out of my mouth:

"Mama. Where's my dad?"

Her drawing and shading came to a stop. She peered at me, and I didn't like that look on her face. Something sad and worried.

I continued, "I know everyone has a dad. That's how it works."

She set a hand on my back, rubbed circles into it.

"I don't know where your dad is. I'm sorry, baby. Even back when you were born, I didn't know where he was. He's just never been part of our story."

Our story.

We went on drawing. I didn't have any more questions for the day. I didn't need any more answers on that subject. The truth was, I was only mildly curious about my father. As I grew older, as the years went on, it was never really something that nagged at me, certainly never tormented me. I had my Maryanne, and she was more than enough for me.

That afternoon in the sun, on the blanket in our yard, I gazed over at Mama. I saw her simple, beautiful robin on the white paper. I felt myself smile, and I forgot all about Lavender Man.

17

Roxie

Christine is not happy today.

It's Saturday, the end of June. Day of the Woodruff-DeMarco union. Our very first wedding of the season.

Christine always gets uptight on wedding days. And I can't really blame her for that. As far as I can tell, weddings are inherently chaotic and stressful messes, and it's Christine's job to make them play out the least chaotic and stressful as possible.

But today, there's more than that contributing to Christine Lambert's uptightness. I can tell there's something else going on. It's three in the afternoon, and she and I are both at the fancy event space in town, supervising the set-up process.

Christine orders everyone around—the venue people, the rental people, Vera's floral delivery people—and makes and takes phone calls every fifteen minutes. I follow her wherever she goes, a perfect shadow. I have the dense Woodruff-DeMarco binder in my arms, full of all the notes I've taken throughout their wedding planning process.

Christine finishes up a phone call, and then she turns to me. We're standing by the long table where the bridal party will sit. Above us are wooden, vaulted ceilings and crystal chandeliers, an interesting mashup of coastal and cosmopolitan.

Christine stares at me, unusually silent after hours of nonstop jabbering.

"Yes?" I say. "Something wrong? Do we need to go back to the beach yet?"

"I'm just really surprised."

"By what? The ivy substitute? I think Vera was right. I can't tell the difference."

Christine smooths a wrinkle in her sleeveless, mauve dress. She forced me to wear a dress myself today, a simple black one she bought for me when I refused to go shopping with her.

"I didn't realize you had a boyfriend, Roxie."

"Wait, what?"

"I guess I shouldn't be surprised you didn't tell me. I would've *liked* you to tell me, but . . . What really surprises me is the age difference."

I'm frazzled. Flummoxed. The DJ is doing a sound check in the opposite corner. The caterers are tinkering with china and champagne flutes at the tables around us.

Christine goes on: "The boy who came to our house the other morning. Do you think I'm oblivious? I was right there in the car, Roxie. How old *is* he? He didn't look like a high schooler."

"Oh my gosh, Blair?" My cheeks flush with a fiery discomfort. "Blair's not my *boyfriend*. Are you kidding?"

My guardian is skeptical.

"Then what is he? And *who* is he?"

"Blair—he's just a tourist. We're friends. Kind of. He's giving me piano lessons."

"Piano lessons. Why?"

The way she says *why*—it's like she can't even begin to fathom a potential reason why anyone would want to get acquainted with a musical instrument. I certainly have my reasons, but there's no way I'm telling her.

"I just wanted to learn a little Mozart. Why do you care?"

"Roxie. You didn't answer my question. How old is he?"

I fiddle with the Woodruff-DeMarco binder, repeat the information Blair blurted out the other night:

"Twenty in September."

Suddenly, by total luck, Christine's phone starts ringing. But she doesn't answer right away like she normally does.

"You might feel really cool hanging out with an almost-twenty-year-old tourist, Roxie. But it's not smart. Don't even think about crossing into boyfriend territory with this guy."

"Seriously? Christine. I'm not thinking about crossing into any *territory*. Blair's not my boyfriend."

"Right. Sure."

Before finally answering her call, she adds, "Blair. Isn't that supposed to be a girl's name?"

∞

This is the longest day of my life.

It just won't end. It's five o'clock now, which means the ceremony will be starting in an hour. Christine and I are back at the beach to make sure no last-minute fiascos have cropped up.

Everything looks good to me. The white chairs, the tall lanterns lining the aisle, the big arch with flowy voile draped around it. Guests are already starting to filter in, so I hurry over to the little table standing behind the last row of seats. My job right now is to hand out wedding programs and ask people to sign the couple's guest book. It seems easy enough.

Then, a couple different things happen. One of them is good. The other, not so much.

I see Blair. And Blair sees me. He's on the beach with Nolan, tossing some driftwood around for the golden to fetch. When Blair spots me, a smile lights up his face, and he jogs over this way, bringing his furry friend along with him.

"Roxie, hey. Looks like I get to see you in action."

"Hey." I'm happy to see him. *Really* happy, to be honest, but I'm not in a position to chat and hang out. I'm about to point this out to him, but then the other thing happens. The not so good one.

Christine pops up next to me and announces, "I just got off the phone with Martha." Then she notices Blair. "What's he doing here?"

Blair and I both look to each other. Nolan yawns. Before either of us can answer Christine, she's speaking again: "Martha had a question for us."

Martha DeMarco. The mother of the bride. People are always warning you to watch out for bridezillas, but I think they've got it wrong. In my brief experience in this industry, it's the mothers of the bride you have to watch out for.

"Everything okay?" I ask, even though I can tell it's not. An elderly couple ambles up to the table, so I put on a quick smile as they get their program and sign the guest book. Christine, Blair, and Nolan all smile, too, until they're gone.

"She's wondering about the shell ceremony," Christine finally shares.

"The what?"

Her normally even skin tone has gotten blotchy, her eyes extra big. Her words come out hectic and fast:

"Martha's saying they wanted to have a special seashell ceremony with the guests. Just before the vows. She says we all talked about it weeks ago." Then her huge eyes flicker over to the binder I have tucked on top my lap. "You wrote that down, didn't you, Roxie? The seashells are around here somewhere, right?"

"Seashells?" I start flipping through the binder madly, a frantic feeling rising in my gut. "I don't remember anything about that. I would've written that down."

I look up to Christine, and now I'm sure my eyes are just as big as hers. But I realize what's going on. I can see it in Christine's blotchy face. *She* doesn't remember anything about a seashell ceremony, either. It's something Martha DeMarco has suddenly pulled out of thin air. Only, Christine's not about to admit that.

"I can't believe you didn't make a note of that," she jeers. "Roxie, that's your *job*. And you wonder why I won't trust you with more responsibilities."

"That's so unfair." I have to keep myself from standing up and raising my voice. "I've been taking notes of *everything*. If Martha DeMarco sneezed, I took a damn note of it."

"Don't swear at me. Can you just be professional for one second?"

I'm a millisecond away from exploding, throwing the binder into the sand, and storming away. But then Blair speaks up. He's still standing there, watching this whole mess take place.

"Sorry to interrupt," he starts, and Christine and I shoot daggers his way, "but what exactly is this *seashell ceremony*?"

He's trying to get us back on track, to help address the actual problem. And it works.

Christine crosses her arms over her chest. "Martha wants all the guests to be given a seashell when they arrive. Then, before the bride and groom exchange vows, a hurricane vase will be handed around while the officiant prays, and the guests will all put their shells in the vase as a blessing for the couple. They want to keep the vase in their house as a memento."

I let this sink in.

"That's the dumbest thing I've ever heard."

"Well, I don't care what your take on it is, Roxie. This is your mess-up. I need you to make sure everyone gets a seashell before the wedding starts. And find a hurricane vase."

"How am I supposed to do that, Christine? I need to stay here to greet everyone. Can't you make some phone calls or—"

Just then, her phone goes off jangling. She glowers at me, and I hate her right now. I never should've agreed to be her scribe, or assistant, or whatever I am. I never should've ended up under this woman's roof.

She says: "I've got too much on my plate. Just figure something out. Otherwise, we'll have to rethink you making Shelby Frasier's cupcakes in August."

The reigning witch flees the scene, leaving me rattled and *fuming* and completely at a loss.

"So," Blair intones. He has one eyebrow raised, and I realize he's chewing his Trident gum. "That's Christine."

"That's Christine. And *I* am totally screwed. I swear, this is the first I've ever heard of a stupid seashell ceremony. I *would've* written it down."

"I believe you."

"I don't know what to do. I'm kind of freaking out here."

Blair works his jaw with the gum, starts tapping his hand against his swim trunks.

"You look nice, by the way," he says. "The dress."

"Blair. How am I supposed to get ninety-five seashells before six o'clock? While also greeting guests as they show up?"

He goes quiet for a minute. I can hear Nolan breathing. Another guest appears, and I try not to show my panic while he signs the guest book.

Suddenly, Blair states, "I'll be right back."

I give him a crazed look. "Any chance you could stay here and brainstorm with me? Do you have a cell phone I could borrow or something?"

"Don't worry," he says. "I'm going to fix this."

Then, he jogs away with Nolan.

∞

Twenty-five minutes go by. And I'm freaking out more and more with every second. Like, seriously freaking out. Verging-on-a-panic-attack kind of freaking out. I'm sweaty, my heart is pounding, my stomach is in a million nasty knots. Christine's going to kill me. She'll hold this over me forever. I'll never get to do wedding cakes for Lace & Tide. I'll never have any true solace or joy while I'm living in the Seawood Lane house.

Another five minutes speed by, and there's still no sign of Blair. Christine's vanished, too, but for that, I'm grateful. I just can't understand what Blair's up to. Is he really coming back? I've been unsure from the start, and now I'm really beginning to question him.

I barely know Blair Porter. And as far as he's concerned, I'm just some random, little teenager in a tiny, nothing town. He's stuck in Tangle Beach for the summer, and I'm just a girl who's glommed onto him while he's here.

My thoughts continue spiraling out of control. And then ten more minutes go by. That means that in just another ten minutes, the ceremony is going to begin, the groom will be standing under the arch, the bridal party will be making its way down the sandy aisle. Almost all the seats are filled up now, the guests all chattering amidst the sound of the ocean.

There's no way a wacky seashell ceremony is taking place tonight.

"Hey."

I twist to the right, and there's Blair. He's back. He's sweatier than I am. His chest rises and falls in quick succession. There's something almost enticing about seeing him in this state, but I'm way too upset to dwell on that.

"Hey," I practically wheeze. "Where've you been? What's going on? We're pretty much out of time here."

Like a magic trick, Blair moves his arm from around his back. And in his hand is the most beautiful thing I've ever seen: a large, gorgeous, blue-tinted vase. Filled to the very brim with a random assortment of seashells.

Proudly, he sets it down on the table before me. I let out the biggest sigh ever, a sigh that signals the rest of my body to relax. I can feel my adrenaline tapering down.

"How did you do it?"

"The vase was in one of the bathrooms at my parents' house. There were shells used as décor in different rooms around the place, so I snatched all those up. Got about forty. Then I ran into town and hit up two different gift shops to buy bags of shells they had for sale. After that, I was still a little shy, so I went to the north part of the beach where I've noticed a lot of debris collects. Most of what I found there was broken stuff, but I figured that would have to do. So I got your ninety-five seashells. I'm pretty awesome, right?"

I leap from my seat and throw my arms around Blair's neck. He laughs and curls his firm arms around me. Yep—he's definitely sweatier than me right now, but I don't care.

"I have to hand these out before it's too late," I suddenly realize, stepping away from Blair.

"I'll help."

And then it's done. Every attendee has their silly little seashell for the silly-blessing-whatever-memento thing. I give the elegant vase to the officiant and quickly explain what it's for. The fiasco has been neutralized. The rest of the wedding will go exactly as planned, no bumps in the road. Christine will not eat me alive when it's all over. My cupcake gig is no longer in jeopardy. It's done.

Blair and I go back to the little table. He has to take off; the wedding's about to start, the sappy processional music playing.

He leans in, electrically close to my face. He sets a hand on my back and whispers to me with his minty breath, "I'll catch you later, okay? Get some good sleep tonight. You deserve it."

I go to whisper, *Thank you,* but he's already stepping away through the sand. I watch him go, and I feel something in my chest. Something raw and warm. A twinge. A prick. Almost like a little thorn in my heart, but it's sweet somehow, and I want it stay there. I want the feeling to last forever.

18

Blair

Who knew I would be such a great piano teacher? All those stuffy lessons Rita and Philip forced me to sit through as a kid are paying off.

Roxie and I are sitting at the Yamaha, and she can already play the first chunk of Variation V with near flawlessness. She is more on the robotic side of flawlessness, and I'm trying to get her to treat the staccato notes with the separation and *pop* they deserve.

But other than that, she's just flying along, nice and easy. I can't believe it's July already. Another month or so at the baby grand, and Roxie should be good to go with the piano song she's bartered out of me.

The next bit I show her involves a touch of classic-Mozart trills. I remember struggling with them back in the day, so I take my time explaining my tips and tricks.

"Make sense?" I check with her.

"I think so. Yes."

"Yes, *Sensei*."

"Yeah . . . For the hundredth time, I'm not calling you that, Blair."

Upon trying a trill out for herself, Roxie's face scrunches up unhappily. She tries again, her fingers seeming to trip over themselves. Like I said, Mozart trills are no piece of cake.

"This is just ridiculous," she says after giving it another try. "Is this part even necessary? It seems a bit much."

"Take it up with Mozart."

We work for another ten-ish minutes, and then I can tell Roxie's ready to call it quits for the day, her piano stamina having worn off. Which means we get to move on to my favorite part of our music lessons.

Today, I've got a few different songs lined up that I need to present to Roxie Morah. I kick it off with David Bowie's "Starman," which Roxie laughs at and pronounces *weird*. She calls a lot of my music weird, though, so that's not saying much.

George Harrison's cover of "If Not For You" is labeled as *boring*, so I switch it up to his more energetic tune, "What Is Life." That one gets a stronger approval from my naïve Music Hermit. It seems that little by little, I am winning her over, showing her The Way of the Oldies.

There's just one more song I have in mind for now, so I get it queued up and hit *play*. It's Cass Elliot. "Make Your Own Kind of Music." Short and sweet, as the saying goes. Whatever happened to short songs, anyway? Why does everything nowadays have to be a five-minute affair? I know I sound like an eighty-year-old when I say that, but you know what? Maybe eighty-year-olds have a point or two to be made.

"Oh." Roxie's spine lengthens as the soft, sunny music begins, as Mama Cass' voice flows around us. "Oh!" she says again, looking at me that way Nolan does when I ask him if he wants to play fetch with his favorite stuffed animal.

"I know this song," Roxie breathes.

"You do?"

She listens attentively as the energy swells in the chorus. "Mama sang this song."

"Yeah, you're right. Mama Cass. I can't believe we found a song you already know."

"No," Roxie says. "*My* Mama. She used to sing this song. Around the house, when she was baking or folding clothes. Or outside, when we picked berries."

I'm not sure what to say in response to that, but Roxie doesn't seem to be looking for a reply. She's receding into the music, and so I let her. I let her recede more and more until the song fades away.

Roxie looks contemplative, faraway, lost in thought.

"I forgot about that song. I forgot she used to sing it."

I remain quiet.

"I hate that I'm forgetting things." She stares at the black-and-white keys. "That's part of the reason I run every morning, why I go to my spot."

"Your spot?" I finally voice.

She pivots toward me on the bench and reaches a hand to my shoulder. Slowly, deep in thought, she smooths out a wrinkle in the sleeve of my shirt. The warmth in her hand transfers through to my skin.

"Blair. What would you think if we got to know each other even better?"

I swallow hard. "What . . . exactly would that entail?"

She stands up. "Going on a walk. Come on. There's something I want to show you."

$$\infty$$

We don't walk. We run. It starts out as walking, but I just don't think this girl was born to shuffle her feet, leisurely stroll, lightly meander.

As her pace picks up on the beach, so does mine, trying to keep up, and next thing I know, the pair of us are dashing up the shore. We fly north, past town, then cut inland, winding through quiet roads, and by the time we stop, I can feel my heart spasming up in my throat.

Now, we head deep into a forested section of land, deeper and deeper. There's moss and ferns, so much more moisture here than back home, water saturated in every cubic inch of the air and ground. It's cool in its own way, but I miss the Hudson River, my ferries and cabs, my Manhattan skyline.

"This is it."

Roxie comes to a halt where there's an ivy-covered stump in the ground. I thought Tangle Beach was quiet, but this is next-level hushed. I hear some light twittering of birds, but other than that, it's like I'm up in space. A very green version of space.

"Do you want to sit?" Roxie settles on the stump, so I follow suit.

"I want to sit for the rest of my life." I'm still trying to catch my breath. Blood rockets through the arteries in my neck. "So, this is your spot?"

"I come here every morning," she confirms, "to check on the blackberries."

I didn't notice them earlier, but now I do. Right before us is a whole labyrinth of the messy vines. I like the way they look, the way they bend and twist, the way some of the vines are thicker than my two thumbs put together.

"Are they ready yet?" I ask, which causes Roxie to shoot me an incredulous look.

"No, city boy. See how they're still red?"

"Hey, it's not my fault stuff like this doesn't grow around Manhattan. I've never even been berry-picking before. Of any kind."

"That's stupid." She shakes her head. "You should pick some with me this summer. *Later* this summer, when they're not as red as your face is right now."

I give a long huff and puff. "Guess I'm out of shape. I blame college."

Roxie turns toward me, rests her elbows on her knees. She's wearing a yellow tank top today with something sort of frilly at the neckline. Different than her normal thing.

"College. Tell me, Blair. What's college like? What are you majoring in, anyway?"

"I'm getting a B.S. in B.S. A Bachelor's of Science in Boring Shi—crap. Boring Crap."

She rolls her eyes at me, and I go on:

"Business school. That's my stale destiny, set in stone. Right now, these first couple years, it's just all the general education stuff.

94

And to answer your other question, college is different than high school, for sure. A lot more freedom. A lot more work, too."

"Do you go to parties?"

"Eh, here and there."

"Do you drink?" Her interrogation persists.

"Here and there."

"Do you hook up with people?"

"Roxie," I laugh, but I shift around uncomfortably. "Come on."

"Well?" she presses me. "Do you?"

I look to the ground. "No. Honestly. I don't really do that."

She seems satisfied by this. I glance at her, and she's biting into her lower lip.

"Why business school? Why is your destiny set in stone?"

"Oh. Well . . ." She wasn't kidding when she said we were going to get to know each other better. "My parents want me to work in the family business. Porter Publishing. So I have to get a business degree at Cornell, like my dad did, then an M.B.A, and then get some boring job in the company. I'm supposed to take over one day, also like my dad. They wanted Graham to do it, but all of that backfired."

"Who's Graham?"

Her query surprises me. I guess I've never mentioned him to her before.

"Graham's my older brother. They were grooming him for the Publishing House. It was always expected that he'd take it over when the time came. Then, one day, he just snapped. He was at Cornell, getting really close to finishing his undergrad degree. But he never did, because suddenly he ran off to Africa and joined a nonprofit over there. My parents didn't take the news so swell."

"Wow," Roxie says. I can see her digesting the story. The reality is, I'm still digesting it myself. It happened just last year, and I can't get over the fact that Graham just bailed on *all* of us like that. On me.

Roxie's voice brings me back to the moment: "So, your parents are, like, wound super tight? Or what's their deal?"

"You could say that. My word of preference is *dysfunctional*. My dad's all business and politics. No off-switch. My mom likes to get drunk and dance to 'Billie Jean.'"

My answer is met with a blank stare.

"'Billie Jean?'" Roxie echoes.

"Oh, no. Not again. You can't *not* know that song. Roxie. Tell me you know that song."

She pushes me on the arm and breaks into a smile. "Relax, Blair. I'm just messing with you. Even *I* know Michael Jackson. You could use a chill pill sometimes, you know."

I throw my hands in the air defensively. "I never know with you. I'm still in shock you knew the Cass Elliot song."

Then, she goes quiet. She gazes at the vast blackberry bushes before us. She stares into them long and hard.

"My mom died three years ago."

Birds chirp. A subtle breeze moves through, carrying ocean brine. There is a hardness in Roxie's eyes. It makes me feel as if layers of my heart are being peeled away.

"We had a little home together in Shoshone, east of here. A green house on Wild Road. It was private like this, no one else around. There were huge brambles behind our house, like these ones. That was my favorite thing in the world, picking berries together every August."

She appears to recede again, like when we listened to Mama Cass. Water clings tight to her brown eyes. I don't know what to do, what I'm supposed to say in response to something like this. I've never known the adversity and heartache that this fifteen-year-old girl is far too acquainted with.

"How can it be," Roxie's words tremble, "that my favorite thing in the world could be taken away from me, just like that? Just gone? Never again."

Tentatively, I reach out for her hand. She looks at me when I touch her. She looks down at our hands as I cup my palm around hers.

"That shouldn't have happened to you," I speak. "It shouldn't be that way."

She nods her head and some minutes go by, her hand still in mine.

"Christine is Mama's cousin. They were never close growing up, not like some cousins are. I'd never even met Christine before . . . But when it happened, there was no one else for me to go to. It was either Seawood Lane or foster care. I guess Christine must have some form of conscience living inside her. To have kept me out of the system like she did. I always felt like she resented me, though, like I screwed up her life plans. She probably wishes she were married by now, with a kid of her own."

I simply listen. Now's not the time to inject my own thoughts, or even ask questions. It's just the time to listen.

Roxie says, "It never stops hurting. I miss her every day." She fixes her eyes on mine. "It always hurts, Blair."

In an impulsive move, I take my hand out of hers, and I wind my arms around her shoulders. I pull her into me, and her hands find my back, my hands stroke down her hair. We sit like that on the stump, and somewhere outside the wooded lot, the ocean's waves go on breaking against the shore, people go on bustling about, the world goes on spinning.

19

Roxie

Tangle Beach is packed today. There's a big sandcastle competition this weekend, and people are here a day early, swarming the beach and sidewalks.

I'm in town on Lace & Tide business with Christine. We barely managed to find a spot to park on the street (I *told* Christine we should just walk), and then we had to squeeze around the masses of tourists to get to the Village Square. It's like this courtyard place surrounded by two stories of businesses: there's an ice cream joint, an art gallery, and the large pizza parlor that takes up most of the lower level.

We're here to go talk to a salon upstairs for the Bentley-Turner wedding, which is taking place in two weeks. Sunset ceremony on the beach. A boozy reception at the town hall venue. No surprise, right?

"Oh, God." Christine pauses on the wooden steps leading up to the salon. She's eyeing the long line that trails out the door of the ice cream joint. "I'm having the worst cravings this week."

She presses a hand over her lower stomach, so I know what that means. I started getting periods two years ago, and those menstrual cravings can be something fierce.

"Perfect day for ice cream," I badger her. It's over eighty degrees out. That's hot for Tangle Beach.

"I shouldn't." But she keeps gazing downward, longingly. "I already had Starbucks for breakfast."

"Rocky road . . ." I croon. "Mudslide . . . Double fudge brownie . . ."

Chocolate is her favorite. I grin as I see her resistance breaking down.

"Dang it, Roxie. Here, give me the Bentley-Turner binder."

"Why?"

"So you can go get a spot in line for a scoop of mudslide while I handle the salon business myself."

I surrender the binder.

"Works for me. As long as you're sure you can handle that big, heavy binder all by your lonesome."

"Just go. Here's my card. Get a scoop for yourself, too, if you want. *A* scoop. Singular."

Feeling triumphant, I hop down the stairs two at a time and get at the end of the teeming line. I'm pleased with myself: I've managed to get out of a wedding planning appointment *and* score some ice cream. Today's turning out to be all right.

Every day's been pretty nice lately, since the Woodruff-DeMarco wedding wrapped up, since I took Blair to my secret blackberry spot. We're planning on hanging out again tonight. We're going to bake mini raspberry cupcakes and watch some old movie Blair swears upon. I don't think I'll care for it too much myself. The movie, I mean. But that's okay.

"I said I'd see you around, didn't I?"

My eyes fly to the right, and I'm confronted with the sight of that same person I ran into at the market last month. That same boy. Tim Redding.

"Tim. Hi. Again."

He's not in the ice cream line. It seems he's been hanging out in the Square with some friends from school. I can see the group behind him, taking up one of the outdoor tables.

"Are you just out by yourself today?" Tim asks. I take note of his Quicksilver clothing. To my knowledge, he doesn't actually surf. "Or is that out-of-town guy hiding around here somewhere?"

I clear my throat. "Nope. Just me."

"Oh. Cool. Are you guys, like, together or something? I couldn't tell."

"Nope. Not together."

As soon as I give the answer, I wish I had lied and said we were. A crooked smile pulls at Tim's mouth.

He says, "Ah, okay. That's cool."

Here's the thing about Tim Redding. The thing I didn't want to share with Blair back when we ran into him last month. Tim and I have been going to school together for a few years now, but then suddenly, at the onset of our freshman year of high school, he started treating me differently. For some reason totally beyond me, Tim Redding decided he was "*into*" me.

It began with chatting me up at my locker (I cut the conversations short as often as I could).

Then, he invited me to one of his basketball games (I didn't go).

At the end of the year, he tried to offhandedly ask me if I were interested in going to the spring formal (I told him I thought school dances were stupid, to which he then replied, *Oh, yeah, totally, same here*).

"Well, hey, look." Tim steps forward with me as the line inches closer to the door. I have my arms folded over my stomach, Christine's credit card in a hawk-like grip. "There's this thing on Sunday night."

Uh-oh. A thing.

"A bonfire. Just some people from school. Pretty mellow."

I know where this is going. I stare straight ahead, trying to get a look at the ice cream menu beyond the open doorway.

"If you're not doing anything that night, if you wanted to stop by—we're gonna be at that spot around Ocean and Pine Avenue."

Tim lingers, waiting for my acknowledgment. I'm forced to look his way if I want him to leave. Which I do. Want him to leave, I mean.

"Right," I say. "Bonfire, Sunday night. Copy that."

"You think you can make it?"

I *can*, but . . .

"I'm not sure, Tim. Maybe. Maybe not."

Thankfully, at long last, I've made it to the doorway of the ice cream place. I'm almost inside.

"Well, hopefully I'll see you there," Tim says. And he heads back to his posse, leaving me in peace.

When I get up to the counter, I order a scoop of Christine's super-rich mudslide in a cup. I've always preferred fruity flavors myself, so I go for the seasonal berry cobbler swirl.

Remembering Christine's demands, I make sure to order myself two scoops.

$$\infty$$

I love making frosting.

I love mixing up cake batter, too, and everything that's involved in baking, of course (other than the dirty dishes at the end). But there's something about whipping up a fresh bowl of frosting. I think it's because it's one of the final steps, and there's all this anticipation building inside me, this eagerness to see my finished product.

"Berries," I order Blair, and he hands me the bowl of fresh raspberries I instructed him to crush for me earlier.

"Zest."

He transfers the bowl of lemon zest my way.

"You remind me of a surgeon sometimes," Blair comments while watching me gingerly fold the berries and zest into the vanilla buttercream. "And I'm your nurse. The cupcakes are your patients. And the spatula is your scalpel."

"Surgery's too technical." I scoop the pink frosting into a piping bag and twist up the end. "Baking is an art."

"Like music?" Blair makes a clever flick of his eyebrow.

"Sure," I concede. "Baking is more like music than surgery. I'll give you that. Do you want to try icing some of these?"

"I could give it a shot."

"It's pretty easy with the star tip. Just start with a small dollop in the center, then swirl around it."

Blair's face morphs into a look of pure concentration. He grasps the piping bag awkwardly, the way a toddler might. This is going to be good. I prop myself up on the counter and observe as

101

Blair readies himself, stretching his neck side-to-side and uttering, "Here we go."

He gives the bag a forceful squeeze over one of our mini cakes—and I can't contain myself when the frosting comes spurting out in huge, messy blobs, drowning the cupcake, dribbling over the corner of the baking tin, even running down Blair's hand.

Blair takes in the sight of the pink chaos he's created, then looks at me.

"So. I'm basically a pro."

I'm just about snorting from my laughter. Blair looks so stupefied, bewildered. And the mess he's made: it's like a fairy fluttered by and vomited all over the place.

"You think this is funny, do you?"

"How did you manage to get frosting on your shirt?" I notice the glob on his shoulder, and my laughter is rekindled. "You're such a mess, Blair."

"Well, aren't you so high and mighty up on your countertop? All clean and stain-free? Maybe you'd like a taste of your own frosting."

Blair comes right up to where I'm sitting on the counter, and I screech when he comes at my face with his icing-smeared hand. I push on his chest and lean back to keep him away. "Blair! Stop!"

The struggle goes on, and now we're both cackling and giggling like full-moon lunatics. I squeeze away from him, hop to the floor and go to make my escape out of the kitchen. But he catches me by the refrigerator and pins me against it.

"Blair Porter—" I go to make a threat, but it's too late. I gasp as he swipes his hand across my cheek, leaving a residue of the velvety-berry buttercream on my skin.

All our laughter and anarchy is defused, then. Blair is grinning, hovering over me, one hand pressed against the fridge by my shoulder. The kind of stance I've seen boys take with girls at the school lockers.

"Oops." Blair grins wider. "Roxie, you've got something on your face."

He uses his finger to draw a line of frosting down my other cheek. The fridge is cool, humming against my back. Blair smells like mint and raspberry, and his finger is warm on my face. His body, his face, are poised close to mine. I let him draw another line over my chin.

"You suck, Blair."

I look up to see his blue eyes, and there's a change in his gaze. He's not smiling anymore. His focus is where his finger touches my chin, just under my mouth.

I can't mistake the fluttering feeling in my stomach. A sudden yearning trickles over me. Blair and his fire eyes, the creases just below them, his blonde hair, the barely-there stubble around his jaw. He's handsome, in his city-boy way, and our closeness right now pricks at my chest.

Taking hold of his wrist, and I tilt my head down just an inch, so that Blair's finger slides onto my mouth. It feels perfect. Surreal. I turn my head to the left just a little, to the right, feel his warm, rough finger graze over my lips, the tingle it sparks. I check Blair's reaction, and his eyes are still locked where his finger is, tracking the movement. His brows scrunch together. His breathing has changed. He is so close to me, his head hanging down toward mine. I tilt my head so his finger is positioned in the very center of my lips, and I start to open them.

Then—the spell breaks. Or something breaks. Blair tugs his entire arm away from me as though he's just laid hand on a piping hot stovetop.

"God, Roxie."

His tone is crisp. Biting. I've never heard him sound like this before.

"What?"

He backs away to the other side of the kitchen, and he won't make eye contact with me.

He lashes out: "You can't do stuff like that."

"Like what? I was just messing around, Blair."

I'm angry, and I'm not trying to hide it. I match his harsh tone and feel my fingernails dig into my palms.

"Maybe you're too young to understand." He speaks to the floor. "But you can't *mess around* like that."

Now I'm seething.

"I understand just fine," I quip. "I'm not a kid."

"You're fifteen."

His words slice into me. Funny how two simple words can hurt so much.

"Yeah, I'm fifteen, and you know what? I might be the most mature fifteen-year-old to walk the planet. My teachers all say it at school. *Roxie's so mature for her age.* Christine's clients say it, too, even though she won't acknowledge it." I let out a sharp breath. "And there's a reason I ended up this way. It wasn't just by chance. I've been through a hell of a lot more than your average teenager has to go through. I've been through more than *you've* been through in your cozy, elitist world. So, no. I'm not a kid. I'm not *too young* to understand."

Blair is quiet after my rant.

I feel my anger dwindling the longer he stays silent.

Maybe I went too far there at the end. I didn't mean to go as far as to insult him, point a finger back at him. He can't help the life he was born into, just like I can't help the one I've been appointed.

Blair keeps his head to the floor a few minutes longer. Eventually, he speaks.

"I'm sorry."

He meets my gaze. His whole presence has softened, and it makes me soften in turn.

I sigh. "I'm sorry, too."

We both stand there, tarnished in raspberries. I use my hand to wipe some of the sugary cream off my face.

"I lost my cool," Blair says. "Which isn't very cool of me. I shouldn't have snapped at you like that."

"Can we just—" I wipe more frosting from my face, "—forget any of that happened?"

"Sure. Clean slate. It's been erased."

"Okay. Good."

The fridge hums in the background. A window is open in the living room, and the ocean booms beyond it.

"I ran into Tim today," I blurt. I'm not sure why I share this particular bit of information at this particular point in time.

"Oh," says Blair. "That kid from the market. Tim Bedding."

"Redding. Yeah. He wants me to go to some bonfire thing Sunday night."

Blair nods his head.

"Maybe you should go."

"Maybe I should."

But I don't really mean it. I guess I'm just trying to gauge him in some way, get a read on his current state.

"Maybe it'd be fun for you to socialize with some . . . same-aged peers. I think you should try it out. Give it a chance."

I think about this. At first, I had no intentions of actually going to the bonfire. But maybe I *would* make an appearance if . . .

"Tell you what." I move away from the cold fridge and toward the cupcakes that still need to be finalized. "If you really want, I'll give it a chance."

Blair eyes me, inquisitive.

"If," I say, "you come with me."

20

Blair

This might have been a bad idea.

It's dark and cold out, crystal clear skies up above, a freezing ocean slashing and bashing into the shore behind me. And, I'm sitting on a log, surrounded by a dozen or so high school kids.

Marshmallows are being roasted for s'mores. Smoke from the fire keeps blowing straight into my eyes. I opted to wear my desert chukkas tonight, and now the insides are coated in pesky sand.

Let's just say I don't fancy myself much of a bonfire guy.

But I'm here. This is what I agreed to do tonight. My reason for doing so is sitting right beside me. Roxie is dressed in a purple pullover and jeans. She's trying to show me how to toast my marshmallow without burning it; meanwhile, the other teenagers murmur and laugh around the embers. I feel so out of place here. I feel like an intruder.

"Roxie. You came."

Roxie and I both look up. The Tim Bedding kid from the market has made his way around the circle to where we are. He steps over the log and takes a seat next to Roxie. A rather close seat.

Tim is visibly surprised by Roxie Morah's presence. He says, "I wasn't sure if you'd make it tonight. But you're here."

"Here I am," Roxie confirms with that indifferent tone she defaults to around this kid.

Tim grins. "I'm glad."

Roxie flashes an odd glance my way before she angles herself more in Tim's direction. "Me too."

He smiles wider, and there's that obvious surprise written all over his tan face again.

"Hey, man. Blair, right? It's cool you could make it, too." Tim leans forward to nod my way. "Your marshmallow's burning."

I snap my head down to see that the marshmallow has, in fact, transformed into a flaming, charcoaled glob on the end of my stick. Whoops. I was so captivated by the goings-on to my right that I forgot all about the orange flames straight in front of me.

I pull the burnt marshmallow out of the fire and give it a frown.

"Another one bites the dust. I'm a newbie to the s'mores game, if you couldn't tell."

"For real?" Tim looks perplexed. "You've never made s'mores before?"

"Classic Blair Porter." Roxie rolls her eyes. "Such a city boy."

Tim asks, "Where are you from again?"

I won't lie, this is probably my all-time favorite question to be asked. Answering it never gets old.

"Only the greatest place on earth."

"Costco?" A kid a couple spots down pipes up, apparently eavesdropping on our conversation.

"Don't mind him," Tim says. "That's just Ethan. Ethan loves Costco."

"You know it, Redding. I'd live in Costco if they'd let me."

"I know, buddy. That's the dream."

"I'm from New York City," I cut in, and this information seems to resonate with Tim on some level.

"New York City," he repeats. "I've always wanted to go there."

"You have?" Now Roxie's the one who appears surprised.

"For sure. You can really make something of yourself in a place like that. Have you ever run into any celebrities?"

I tap my chin, trying to think who the most impressive person might have been over the years. Sadly, I've never encountered any of my most beloved musicians in or around the City. But there was . . .

"Bon Jovi."

Roxie, Tim, and Ethan all react accordingly. Yes, even Roxie, my little Music Hermit, finds this impressive. Tim, though, is by far the most fascinated.

"That's seriously cool. Can you imagine being that famous?"

Ethan says: "One time, I swear to God, I might have seen Maya Rudolph in a California Costco."

"That's cool, Ethan." Tim shakes his head and looks between me and Roxie. "Ethan's full of shit."

"Hey, guys." A girl across the fire raises her voice, and everyone listens.

"Chelsea Bradshaw," Roxie mutters to me, undertones of bitterness cutting through.

"Do we like Chelsea Bradshaw?" I whisper back, and Roxie simply glares at me.

"How about some truth or dare?" the girl suggests, but it comes off as a command more than anything else. Everyone's immediately on board, and I suddenly feel ten times more uncomfortable than I already was. Checking on Roxie's reaction to my right, I see it's not just me. This is out of her comfort zone, as well.

"Everybody has to go at least one turn," Chelsea dictates. "Once you choose either truth or dare, you can't switch. You pick your poison, and you stick to it."

Mumbles of consent oscillate around the fire. And so, the game begins.

A girl named Emily chooses truth and is asked how many guys she's made out with in their school. The number makes her face redden; guys snicker, and girls exclaim, "Em, why?"

A guy named Jason is dared to run into the ocean up to his chest. He doesn't appear to mind one iota and returns to us proud and soaked and shivering. It reminds me of Nolan.

It goes on this way, a predictable affair: one girl has to give the guy next to her a hickey; Ethan has to admit his Maya Rudolph story is fabricated; Tim has to surrender his phone to Chelsea and let her send a flirty text to a random girl on the cheer squad.

Then, it's Roxie's turn. I feel her anxiety. She's not showing it—she's got a hell of a poker face on tonight—but I know it's there. It's like her heart is hammering inside me. My stomach twists and turns just like hers.

"Roxie. I didn't realize you came out to join us tonight." Chelsea looks at her the way a vulture might scrutinize roadkill. No, we certainly *don't* like Chelsea Bradshaw. "So. Truth or dare?"

Roxie hesitates, pulls at the hem of her sweatshirt.

"Truth."

We all wait. Chelsea has taken some suggestions here and there throughout the night, but when it comes down to it, she is the arbiter of this game.

"Truth," the girl repeats. "Okay, Roxie. The truth it is." She narrows her eyes as she simpers. Her question is decided, yet she's dragging out the anticipation, Roxie's dread, as long as she sees fit.

"Tell us, then. Are you, or aren't you, a lesbian?"

The snickering flutters back around the fire, an obnoxious medley of high school immaturity and amusement. Roxie is stone cold.

"It's what everyone's wondering, anyway. Right?" Chelsea says, and I envision myself kicking sand in her eyes. "You've never dated any boys, so naturally, people draw, you know, *conclusions*."

Taking a peek over at Tim, I find that he's not grinning and chortling like the other kids. He is waiting for Roxie's answer.

Roxie doesn't give Chelsea the satisfaction of visible embarrassment. She doesn't blush, shift around, or even bat an eye. She stares at the auburn-haired teenage girl through the flickering fire.

Roxie says: "I know this comes as a major disappointment to you. But no. I'm not a lesbian." Then, she adds, "Sorry if you got your hopes up, Chelsea."

The boys in the circle, Tim included, eat that up, and I realize I never should've been nervous for Roxie. She knows how to take care of herself.

"Who are you?"

Chelsea's question turns all the attention onto me. Oh, great. It's my turn. Why did I agree to come to this gathering again? Something about wanting Roxie to socialize with same-aged peers. Something about our weird episode by the refrigerator, when the rational part of my brain nearly ran off on me—the part that is meant to remind me of the facts. And the facts are as follows: Roxie is five years younger than me; she's in high school; I'm in college. The facts are that my parents have a significant age gap between them, and their partnership has been less than blissful. They are a miserable pair to be around. I never want to end up like Rita and Philip Porter.

"I'm Blair," I announce before my curious audience.

"Blair," Chelsea iterates. The wheels turn in her mind. "How old are you, Blair?"

"Twenty in September."

"Really . . ." She finds this much too interesting. "Okay, then. Blair. Truth or dare?"

I regret my decision as soon as it comes out:

"Dare."

It was always my go-to back when I played this game at my high school parties. The word erupted from my mouth out of pure habit. Now I'm just hoping I get off easy and am ordered to go into the frigid sea like Jason was—or maybe even be commanded to char the ends of my hair over the fire? Something along those lines.

"I dare you to kiss one of the girls here. Any girl of your choice."

A sinking feeling pulls, yanks, at my guts. I assess Chelsea and hear E.L.O.'s "Evil Woman" playing in my head.

The nasty, sinking feeling is only getting worse. I actually feel myself gulp. To my right, Roxie's not bothering with a poker face any longer. I see the concern in her dark eyes, like she wants to save me. Like she, too, regrets coming here tonight.

"Who's it gonna be, Blair?" Chelsea presses.

"Ummm, well, see, the thing is . . ." I laugh while rubbing my sweaty hands together. "I can't . . ."

"You have to pick someone. It shouldn't be *that* hard. Just look around. See who appeals to you."

"Well, but . . ." I fumble and laugh again, despite not finding this at all humorous.

"I'll take his turn," Roxie suddenly calls out. All eyes flicker over to her, mine included.

"That's not the rules," Chelsea states. Yet, she appears intrigued.

Roxie makes her case: "I know, but. I'll take a dare in Blair's place. Any dare you want. As wild as your twisted brain can come up with. So, you can get both a truth *and* a dare out of me tonight. Which will probably never happen again for the rest of high school."

Chelsea's intrigue escalates.

"Okay. Fine."

Relief floods my entire body.

However, it only lasts a brief moment.

Chelsea says, "All right, Roxie. Now that we've cleared up the whole sexual-orientation thing . . . I'll give you a similar dare to Blair's."

The manipulative mastermind studies Roxie, then glances between me and Tim. "But since you *are* breaking the rules . . . your options will be a little more limited. So. I dare you to kiss one of the boys you're sandwiched between right now. Righty, or lefty? Blonde, or brunette?"

I'm never playing this game again. I'm never going to another bonfire again. I make these firm vows in my head while watching Roxie get put on the spot for the second time tonight. She turns her head my way, and I know what that means. I know her choice. She looks up at me. Something weird resounds in my mind, an odd little thought: *Not like this . . .*

And then, right before my eyes—

—Roxie turns the other way.

She takes Tim's face in her hands, and she plants a kiss on his cheek.

21

Roxie

"I meant on the *lips*, Roxie. Obviously."

"Well, then you should have specified that, Chelsea. Obviously."

And just like that, it's over. I've won. Chelsea Bradshaw scoffs a, *Whatever*, and moves onto her next victim in the circle. I'm finally off her radar and finished with this truth-or-dare nonsense, having spared Blair in the process.

Tim can't take his eyes off me since I kissed his face. It's like all these lights have flickered on inside him, like I reached out and found a switch he's been waiting for me to find all night.

"Sorry about that," I whisper to him as the game goes on around us.

"Don't be."

For the first time since the kiss happened, I twist to the left, wondering what Blair must be thinking about all this. I'm dying to know, honestly. Did it stir any reaction in him—at all?

Blair's looking right at me. His mouth hangs open a little. All of a sudden, he blinks rapidly and shoots his attention up to the starry sky, as if he's just located some totally captivating constellation up there.

So, a reaction *was* stirred. The realization bolsters me—it pushes me to keep going this way—and by this way, I mean to my right. I turn back to Tim. I whisper back and forth with him while the remainder of the group endures torment at the hands of Chelsea Bradshaw.

When the game's finished, Tim asks if I want to walk by the ocean with him. And so, that's what I do. For the first time since I've known Tim Redding, I'm saying yes to his advances.

When I stand up with Tim, Blair says, "Where are you going?"

"I'll be back in a bit," is all I tell him.

The conversation with Tim by the ocean isn't anything extraordinary. Actually, it's the most ordinary conversation you could probably have with someone. We don't stray very far from the bonfire. Tim asks me about my summer, and I ask about his. I keep checking up the shore where Blair is, and each time, I find that he's keeping tabs on me, too. Finally, he stands up and walks over to where Tim and I are lingering.

"Sheesh, it's getting chilly, isn't it?" Blair rubs his hands up and down his shoulders to make his point. "And late? Maybe we should get going, Roxie. I'll walk you home?"

I smile Tim's way. "I really should go. But thanks for the invite tonight."

"Yeah. For sure." Tim beams right back. "I'm really glad you came."

Blair and I leave. Thank God. We're out of there. As soon as we get off the beach and onto Ocean Avenue, I release a long, pent-up exhale. It's just me and Blair now, walking on the dark, quiet roads toward Christine's house. It's getting windy out, and when I look up at the moon, I feel dizzy. The silver clouds are billowing past it madly, like the universe is whirling out of control around me.

"What a night."

Blair's voice cuts through the darkness. I can't tell what mood he's in right now.

"That's actually a great song," he keeps talking. "Frankie Valli & The Four Seasons."

I stay quiet. I wonder if Blair's going to bring up the kissing conundrum Chelsea put us through.

"I don't know about that Tim kid," Blair finally says.

We turn onto Driftwood Lane, where there are some streetlights dimly illuminating the dark road here and there.

"You don't know about him? What does that mean, Blair?"

"I just—I don't know. Never mind."

Our shoes make dull, rhythmic patting sounds. The air feels cool and almost wet around us.

"That Chelsea character, though. Wow. What a gal."

I sneer. "She's great, isn't she? Three more years I have to deal with her. And everyone else at that place."

"My condolences. You'll get through it, though. Everyone does. And then life after high school can be whatever you want."

"Unless your name's Blair Porter," I say, "and you just do whatever your parents want you to do."

Blair jolts the smallest bit at my remark.

"Touché."

We're quiet again. We get to the end of Driftwood and go left on Beeker.

"I want to open a bakery. One day. That's what I want for life after high school."

I'm not sure why I share this piece of myself right now, with Blair, in the middle of the night. Especially after all the weirdness we just went through at the beach. But Blair looks over at me, his eyes shadowy, and I can see him weigh my dream in his mind.

"You should do that," he says. "Really. That'd be perfect."

I smile. It feels strangely wonderful to have my hopes validated. Seawood Lane is to our right, so we wander down the gravel, closer and closer to our destination.

"Thank you, by the way. For saving me from truth or dare tonight."

So, he's finally brought it up.

"I don't know what I would've done otherwise," he adds.

"You don't?" I ask.

"I mean . . . I would've had to kiss you. Just because . . . well, you know."

There's the thorny prick at my heart. I look up at Blair. "Because why?"

"Well. I'm not going to be a total creep and kiss a random high schooler." He laughs.

The feeling in my chest dies down. "Right."

We've made it to the house. We walk up to the front door. I think I like Seawood Lane more at nighttime. There aren't any streetlights on this road; it is simply a velvety darkness right now, giving it an illusion of privacy, tranquility. Leaves and branches rustle against each other as the wind careens by. Heard but unseen.

"I'm *really* not sure about that Tim Bedding, though."

"Redding."

We're lingering on the doorstep. It's probably around eleven o'clock by now. Christine has never given me a curfew, because I've never been the type of girl who needed one before.

"Redding, yeah. Do you know him very well?" Blair persists. And I'm glad he does.

"Not super well. Why?"

I get the house key out of my pocket and unlock the door.

"It's just—the way he looks at you. Or something. I don't know if I like the way he looks at you. Did you notice that tonight?"

I twist the handle and crack the door open.

"You might want to get used to it, Blair."

"Why's that?"

"Because . . . he asked me on a date tonight." I take a step inside the hushed house. "And I said yes."

22

Roxie

Today's the big day. My first-ever date. It sounds *so* weird; I can't get over it.

I, Roxie Morah—the girl who's never been boy crazy, never cared for romance movies, never been the slightest bit interested in having a boyfriend—will be going on a date this very afternoon.

And, what makes it even weirder is that it's with Tim Redding. Never in a million years did I think I'd be going on a date with *Tim*. I always envisioned myself turning him down again and again, over and over, until he finally left me alone.

I know my reasoning for saying yes to this date is kind of questionable. I don't *want* to lead Tim on. I don't want him to be my boyfriend. But I keep telling myself it's just one little date. It'll be harmless. Maybe even good. Maybe it'll satisfy whatever curiosity he has, and he'll simply move on to some other girl. Someone who makes way more sense for him than I do.

After going through my morning routine—the open window, the journal entry and the running—it's still so early in the day. I need to pass the time somehow and not go crazy in the process. Christine is at the dermatology office today, so I have the house to myself. That means it's the perfect opportunity to head into the kitchen and get lost in some baking.

We're well stocked on eggs in the fridge, and I spot some heavy cream tucked away in the back. The first thing that jumps into my mind is pavlova: a delicious, beautiful meringue topped with whipped cream and fruit.

I crack several egg whites into a bowl and beat them on their own before adding the sugar and going at it again. I love the glossy look of this mixture. I love the pillowy smoothness of the meringue, the way it stiffens up like magic as I add the remaining ingredients.

I let myself ebb away into my tasks, and at the end of it all, I'm really pleased with what I've created. The pavlova looks perfect, adorned in fresh whipped cream and slices of peaches and strawberries. It tastes just as it's supposed to: the crisp outer crust, the soft and light middle. My mind feels more at ease now, and the time has flown by pretty fast.

It's time to start getting ready for my date.

∞

First things first is a shower, which is simple enough. But then things get complicated.

Upon sliding open Christine's makeup drawers, it hits me that I don't even know what half of these products are for. A million creams and powders, tubes and palettes and brushes are staring me down, intimidating me fiercely. It's totally overwhelming. But I need to figure this out.

My skin feels all warm and glowy from the shower. I test out a dab of foundation cream over my chin, but the color isn't right. It holds a pink tinge, like the towel I have wrapped around me. Starfish isn't the look I'm going for, so I wash off the cream and decide I'll just focus on my eyes. That should be good enough.

For some reason, liquid eyeliner sounds like a safe choice. I attempt swiping some over my lids the way Christine always does, with the neat wings at the corners. But when I do it, it just looks ridiculous. Thick and messy. Scary even, like one of those haunted clowns. I wash my face once again, scrubbing the black liquid away.

After an hour of experimenting and cursing at the mirror, I finally manage to find a few products that work for me. My lashes are now coated in mascara, making my eyes look even more angled than they really are. I have a bit of espresso eyeshadow blended into the outer corners of my lids. I even brushed a little smidge of bronzer into my cheeks. To finish it all off, I discover that Christine owns a tube of soft, natural lipstick that doesn't make me look like I'm trying too hard. At least, I don't think it does.

The only thing I can think to do to my hair is spritz some volumizing spray into my roots and let it air dry. After the frustrating experiences I just had with applying makeup, I'm not about to tackle a curling iron for the first time in my life.

Now is where things get really bizarre. I made up my mind to do this last night, because I know for a fact that I don't have the right clothes for today. *Date* kind of clothes.

So, I cross over enemy lines, right into Christine's bedroom. It's a nice, spacious room with the same beach-themed décor as the rest of the house. I slip over the wood floors to get to the closet and tall dresser. Hopefully I can borrow the perfect outfit from *Le Boutique de Christine.*

She would hate it if she knew what I was doing right now. There's no way she'd be on board. I'm rifling around in her lingerie drawer, the very top one of the dresser. I *know* this is weird. Super weird. I swear this is not typical behavior for me. But all I own are sports bras and cotton bralettes. I try to shield my eyes from all the lacy panties tucked in here, and I locate a nude bra that doesn't seem horrible.

When I try it on, I'm surprised to learn two things. One is that the bra fits just right. The second is that apparently, this is a push-up bra. It feels funny having all that padding down at the bottom, but I decide to just go with it. Evidently, Christine does all the time.

For the outfit itself, I unearth a top that seems like a good balance for what I want. The straps are thick and smooth; the color is a burnt orange that complements my skin tone. It buttons up in the middle, and the neckline is just low enough, but not crazy low. I find a cream maxi skirt dangling in the very back of Christine's closet. I pull it up over my hips, and then I take in a deep breath before examining my reflection in Christine's full-length mirror.

Well. This is kind of funny: I look like the pavlova I created earlier today. The skirt is the meringue and cream—the vibrant top is the display of peaches and berries. My hair has dried with extra volume, as the spray promised.

I part my hair off to the side like Christine always says I should. Makeup, a real bra, and a side-part: maybe Christine actually would be proud of me today. I wipe off a bit of excess eye shadow at the corner of my eye.

I look pretty nice, really. Surprisingly nice.

Even though I *feel* totally, completely weird.

But there's no time to dwell on that. I have to get going before it's too late. I have a little stop I need to make before I meet up with Tim.

A quick, pre-date visit.

∞

Blair isn't answering his door.

I'm starting to get antsy and frustrated. This skirt is making me feel warmer than I'm used to. The wind keeps messing with my hair, blowing strands into my eyes. I'm running out of time.

I knock again, as hard as I can, stinging my knuckles. *Come on, Blair. Come to your door.* I need him to come to the door. He needs to come see me. It's the whole point of this madness I'm putting myself through.

I go to knock again when I hear a voice resound from behind me.

"Are you the piano lesson girl?"

Whirling around, I find a blonde-haired woman standing in the driveway, holding Nolan by his leash. It must be Blair's mom. The caramel-blonde hair is a dead giveaway, but she also has those same undereye creases.

"Hi," I chirp. Normally I'm not one to feel awkward, but I do right now. "Yes. Sorry, I was just wanting to tell Blair something."

"Roxie, isn't it?"

She knows my name. Blair's mom knows my name.

"Yes, I—"

"You're quite beautiful."

"Am I?"

Mama was beautiful. But I've never thought of myself that way.

"Blair's in here. Follow me, if you'd like. We can go find him together."

By *in here*, she means the main house. So I trail Nolan and the woman wearing the crisp capris and magenta blouse. Time keeps ticking down, closer and closer to when I'm supposed to meet Tim, but it looks like I'll just have to be fashionably late.

The main house is a lot more impressive than Blair's little guest house. Everything's bigger and grander. The ocean view is wider. We head into a large sitting room, where a man is watching the news. He looks like the type of person who never relaxes—he's hunched over his thighs, elbows digging into them, hands clenched under his chin. It's Blair's dad. The shape of his face is like Blair's, but other than that, I don't see much commonality.

"Philip. What'd you do with Blair?" His mom looks around the room. "He was in here just a minute ago."

"It's not like I lost our adult son, Rita. He went to find a phone charger or something."

Then, he perceives my presence. I can see him processing me like a computer processes strings of ones and zeros.

"You must be Roxie." He stands up, comes over to shake my hand.

Blair's mom *and* dad both know my name? So, he's talked about me. He's told them about me, at least once. This feels meaningful somehow.

Before I can respond to Blair's father, Blair himself finally makes an appearance. He comes around a corner, a phone charger dangling in his hand, and he freezes when he sees me.

"Oh. Hey, there. Everyone."

He looks among the three of us: his mom, his dad, me.

"Blair, your friend showed up looking for you." Rita says the word *friend* in a way that makes me feel confused and a little uncomfortable.

"Why haven't you introduced her to us sooner?" Now Philip is chipping in. "She's lovely. Just look at her."

I might be blushing. I hope I'm not. I have no idea what to say right now, and it seems Blair doesn't either. I can't get a read on the room. Subtext floats around beneath all these glances. But is it good subtext, or bad? It's lost on me.

Blair claps his hands together. "So sorry about that, Dad. Rita, Philip—this is Roxie Morah. And I'm sure she'd love to stay and chat, but we've got to head out."

"Already?" Rita questions, but Blair has got ahold of my arm and is rushing me out of the house, all the way out to the driveway.

"What was that about?" I ask.

Blair glances over his shoulder at the main house.

"You'd thank me for getting you out of there if you knew Rita and Philip better. But, looks like you're still in one piece."

He looks at me, and that's when it finally seems to hit him. Because, he's *really* looking at me. I feel his eyes go up and down the skirt, the orange top. He searches my face and settles on my eyes.

"Wow. You look—" He falters. "Different."

Something twists in my stomach. Different. Different wasn't exactly what I was going for.

"Well," I say, happy to explain my *different* appearance. "I'm on my way to meet Tim at the pizza parlor in town. For lunch."

Blair stares at me.

"For our date," I clarify.

"Oh. Right."

"I just wanted to stop by really fast to let you know . . ." What was my excuse again? I rack my brain as fast as I can. "To let you know that I can't make it to our lesson tomorrow. Christine's keeping me busy with some Lace & Tide stuff."

"Oh. Right," Blair says again.

"So. I better get going. I'm running late." I stand there a brief moment longer before spinning around in my sandals. And then— I feel Blair take hold of my upper arm, his fingers curling around my skin.

"Roxie. You're really sure this Tim kid is okay?"

I stifle the victorious smile pulling at my lips. Blair's eyes are running up and down my outfit again.

"What do you mean *okay*?"

"Like, he's not bad news, is he? He's not going to pull anything?"

"We're just getting pizza, Blair." I pause. "If that's okay with you."

Blair squints one eye. He releases his grip on me, slips his hands in his pockets. And he shrugs. That's it—one little shrug. It's the most infuriating shrug I've ever witnessed in my life.

"Of course," he says. "Sorry. Go get your pizza. You kids have fun." He winks.

My insides are as tangled as all the blackberry brambles around town. There's a burning sensation along with it. But what else was I expecting? What did I think was going to happen?

"Okay, then. Bye, Blair."

I don't give him the chance to say goodbye back.

23

Blair

There's nothing wrong with a guy taking his dog on an innocent little walk through the middle of town, is there? People do it all the time. They take their dogs on walks while other people are out on lunch dates. I'm sure it must happen constantly. And sometimes, the dog-walkers just happen to be going through the same part of town where the date-goers are having their pizza. Right?

I tried to stay put in my guest house after Roxie left. I really did. I made it about forty minutes, tinkering around on the piano and compulsively checking the time.

Alas, lo and behold, my restlessness grew to be too much, and now, here I am, moseying down Tangle Beach's main drag with Nolan in tow. Or maybe it's the other way around. My mom did *just* take him on a walk not too long ago, but he's always willing to go out and about if one of his human companions is.

This is fine, what I'm doing right now. It's good. No problem. There's nothing wrong with this. That's what I keep telling myself: I'm not doing anything that I shouldn't be. I'm just letting Nolan lead the way, and funnily enough, he seems to be heading for the Village Square, where I believe there may possibly be a sprawling pizza parlor by the name of Gino's Flying Pies.

What can I say? My dog loves the smell of pepperoni.

By now, it's probably been an hour since I saw Roxie at my place. And I can feel myself acting irrationally, ever since she stopped by. This whole date thing with Tim Bedding is what really set it off. Not to mention the way Roxie was all dressed up. What's the deal with that? Why does she think she needs to do that for some boring, small-town, messy-haired high schooler?

Nolan and I have made it to the Village Square. I slow down as I tread over the pavers. Then I stop in my tracks.

I wasn't really expecting to find her. I don't know what I was expecting. But I have found her. Right away. In plain view. Nolan plops down at my side, and I behold the scene I've just stumbled upon.

Roxie's at the other end of the Square, standing outside the shingled building of Gino's Flying Pies. With him. Tim. Boring, simple Tim. And there's ice cream. And *proximity.*

Tim's just about hovering over her, holding a cone of mint ice cream between them. He offers her some. And she accepts. She samples some with her mouth, and he takes the opportunity to step closer, even to let his gaze flicker down to her chest while she's preoccupied with the ice cream.

There's a sudden, white-hot festering inside me. A deep confusion. I shouldn't feel like my blood is beginning to boil, or like a creature is screaming and hollering within me. But I do. Apparently, there is.

It gets worse. After the ice cream has successfully been shared (which, by the way, *cliché* much?), I realize what's going to happen next. Tim is too close to her. He settles his hand on her nearly-bare shoulder. She looks up at him. He looks down at her.

Boring, simple Tim wants to kiss Roxie. He's *going* to kiss Roxie.

Without using any real thought, I pull Nolan's ball out of my shorts pocket, and I send it hurling to the other end of the Square while simultaneously releasing my grip on Nolan's leash.

Then, a second later: Roxie and Tim jump apart from each other as my amazing sidekick gets right in their way. Dogs can sure be useful. Nolan recognizes Roxie and starts jumping up on her legs to say hello. It's a beautiful thing, and I feel a grin take over my face—until Roxie's head snaps around and her sharp stare is aiming right at me.

Okay. Deep breath. Time to act like this is all one big coincidence.

"Nolan! Buddy! Take it down a notch!" I jog over and do my very best to look surprised upon greeting Tim and Roxie. "Hey, guys. Fancy running into you here. Sorry about Nolan. I really lost control of him there for a second."

Tim appears dazed by the sudden turn of events. The mint ice cream is melting in his grip.

"Hey, Blair. How's it going?"

Roxie has a question of her own: "What are you doing here?"

"Oh, you know. Nolan and I were just out for a little walk."

"A walk to the pizza parlor?" Roxie is fixated on me. I wish I knew what she was thinking right now. She doesn't look mad exactly . . . Maybe verging on mad?

"Yeah, well, I thought I might stop into the—" I go with the first business I see that's not Gino's, "—the Pirate's Grave Tattoo Shop."

Roxie tilts her chin to the sky. "Really. The tattoo shop."

"Yeah. Totally. I've been thinking about getting inked up. I mean, why not? I'm nineteen, so I can. And it's a form of art, right? But on your skin and whatnot."

"That's cool," Tim says. "What do you want to get?"

"Yeah, Blair. What *do* you want to get?" Roxie keeps her eyes perfectly steady on me.

"Oh, let's see. Probably a . . . dragon. Or—a turtle. Or maybe both?"

"Huh." Tim calculates this while we all stand there awkwardly in the sunshine. "Okay. Whatever floats your boat, man."

"I have to leave."

It's Roxie who says it, all abruptness, no segues. She studies me a moment longer, her chocolaty eyebrows knitting together. "Thanks for the pizza, Tim."

"Yeah, it was fun. I can walk you ho—"

But she already is brushing past him, past me and Nolan.

"Peace out, Tim. Your ice cream's melting, by the way."

I leave the poor, confused kid behind and go after Roxie.

∞

She's moving through town quickly. Nolan and I have to jog to catch up to her.

"Roxie. Wait up."

She doesn't. She keeps speed-walking past all the little shops, around the slug-like tourists.

"I'm sorry about all that back there," I try again. I feel weak when I say it, because I'm not really sorry. If I could go back in time, I'd do the very same thing.

Roxie must be reading my mind. She finally comes to a halt and faces me, saying, "Are you sorry?"

Again, I'm having a hell of a time reading her right now. She still has that verging-on-but-not-quite-mad look in her angled eyes.

"Okay, honestly," I start, "that wasn't all just happenstance. I was trying to keep an eye on you, because . . ."

She waits for me to finish.

"Because I guess I feel a little protective of you."

Roxie uncrosses her arms from around her chest. Her tone softens. "You do?"

"Yeah. Sure." My mind is scrambling. "You know, like, in an older brother kind of way."

Any softness that was there is now gone for good.

"Right. Older brother." Roxie turns back around, about to resume her speed-walking.

"Wait. Hold up. Please. I know I could have handled things better back there. Are you mad at me?"

She doesn't answer me right away. Actually, she doesn't really answer my question at all.

"Blair. You've kissed people before, right?"

My grip on Nolan's leash tenses. In my mind's eye, I see two girls from my high school. A third from Cornell, at the start of Fall Term.

"Yes."

"Well, I haven't."

Her words sink into me. I think of the scene I purposefully disrupted. The mint ice cream. The closeness between Roxie and Tim. The way Tim was leaning even closer.

I told myself I was rescuing her, protecting her. I never stopped to consider that I might be ruining a moment that was special from her point of view.

Roxie has just one more thing to say to me before she rushes off toward the ocean: "That was supposed to be my first kiss, Blair."

It's something I can't stop thinking about for the remainder of the day, even into the night. It chews at me, vexes me, makes my brain as melty as Tim's minty, drippy green ice cream.

But, the thing is, for some wacky reason, I know in my bones that if given another opportunity, I wouldn't change my actions at the Village Square. Even with the knowledge that it was supposed to be Roxie's first kiss—I know that I would still play the sabotage card, lobbing Nolan's ball their way all over again.

24

Roxie

The blackberries are getting closer. I'm in my wooded lot, talking to them, studying them.

There's nothing quite like seeing the way they evolve over the months, from delicate, white blossoms to perfect, sweetened fruit. Most of the berries have darkened now. They are small, firm, and shiny. Each drupelet glistens, a tiny, black sphere containing a world of its own. Now they just need time to grow larger, softer, and sweeter. Their natural sugars need to gradually develop within them. And I will wait until they're just ready; I will be patient with them. Just like Mama taught me.

I just wish I could be as patient with people as I am with berries. I guess people evolve kind of like the berries do, only they take so much longer, don't they? It takes more than just one summer. Sometimes, people take so long to develop, you can't even tell it's happening. I wonder if that's the case with Blair Porter. Or even with me.

Patience was something that always seemed to come naturally to Mama. I may have gotten my baking skills from her, but I wasn't granted her personality, her people skills. She had the calmest demeanor. An easy warmth radiated from every word, every smile.

There was only one time I can remember seeing her disposition really falter. It was one day in the middle of winter that I witnessed the temporary fracture.

∞

I was nine years old. The day was wet. Mama and I were in Tillamook that Sunday morning, delivering cakes, turnovers, and breads to a café not too far from the popular Tillamook Creamery.

We wore matching, cloud-patterned rain jackets and boots. Mama had her little ways of making winter fun, but I longed for summer, the sun on my skin, and school-free days. I'm sure she did, as well. But she was always set on making the best of each season.

"We can warm up with hot chocolate when we get back home, my rabbit. We can make shepherd's pie and watch a movie tonight, too. As long as we can come to a consensus."

I surrendered a smile in the rain, and we stepped out of the puddles and into the warmth and dryness of the café. Mama was transporting the last of the tiered, berry coffee cake, while I toted the final box of pastries and mini loaves. We made our way toward the back of the long, skinny building. The walls were dark in here, and the air smelled of earthy coffee and spicy cinnamon.

"What about . . . *Matilda*?" she asked. We had a list of our all-time favorite movies we saved only for rainy days such as this one.

"I don't think so," I answered. "How about *Forrest Gump*?"

"Hmmm. *Clueless*?"

I dragged out the negotiations: "*Little Women*."

"You're going a bit too sappy for me today," she laughed. "What about *The Princess Bri*—"

That's when it happened. The fracture. I heard Mama make a sound like she'd been stung by a bee. She dropped the coffee cake in its box. It hit the floor in a surprisingly loud *thump*. The lid flew open, and I could see the golden brown cake in crumbly, spattered ruins.

"Mama, what is it?"

Her face had blanched, her body stiffened. All her warmth and easiness had dissolved away. It was as if something had broken inside her. She stared across the way, and then I saw what had completely stolen her attention.

It wasn't a *what*—it was a *who*. A woman. Younger than Mama. Short hair, choppy and brassy-yellow. I thought her eyes were pretty, only they were rimmed in messy, purple eyeliner that made her look tired.

It took a minute for her to notice us. The woman. She was sitting at a corner table, picking at a muffin. But when she did see us, she sprung from her seat as though a puppet master had just yanked on her strings.

Mama was still frozen in place, and the look on the other woman's face made me think of a timid jack rabbit. She seemed to shrink in size, her uneasiness escalating, about to burst.

And then, in a flash—the woman pulled her jacket from her chair and dashed out the side door of the café, leaving her half-eaten muffin behind.

On the drive back home, the windshield wipers squeaked and whined like mad. The rain pelted the windows. Mama hadn't said a word since the odd incident in the café.

"Who was that?" I dared to ask over all the ruckus: the rain, the wipers, the noisy car vents blasting out warm air.

Maryanne stayed focused on the wet highway. She knew the *who* I was referring to.

"It doesn't matter."

"Then why did you drop the cake when you saw her?"

She didn't reply for a long time. Not until we were back in our driveway, after she killed the engine. We both stayed put in the car. The downpour persisted around us.

"She was just someone I used to know."

Her answer was the epitome of vague, but at least it was something. It was a start.

"What kind of someone?" I pressed, like I always did.

"Someone . . ." She sighed. "Someone I hadn't seen in a very long time. Someone who was important. Back then."

"Important how?"

"Roxie."

I realized then that slight tremors ran through Maryanne's arms. She said, "That was back then. But this is today. Today, she's just a person I saw in a café."

Mama opened the car door, and just like that, the conversation was over. We trudged through the muddy ground, up the porch steps, into the house. We had our hot chocolate. Made our shepherd's pie. We couldn't agree on a movie, so we worked on a puzzle instead.

While brushing my teeth that night, Mama stepped into the bathroom, and she looked at me carefully, quietly, pensively.

"I promise, Roxie, I'll explain everything better when you're older. Can you be patient with me until then?"

I spit out my toothpaste, dried my mouth with a towel. Then, I went to nestle my head right against her body, and she wrapped her arms around me.

"Of course, Mama. I can be patient."

But my patience was no good. We never got the chance to talk about any of those *when you're older* things. All we had was each present day, whether it was a rainy one or a sunny one, sappy or confusing or easy—but neither one of us understood that at the time.

Honestly, I still don't understand.

I don't think I ever will.

Noises shake me from my long-ago memories, snap me back to the present, to my secret blackberry haven. The rustling sounds grow louder, like an animal moving through brambles and underbrush behind me. I twist around, and I realize I'm hearing footsteps, one after the other, plodding right toward me. I stand up from my stump in alarm.

"Hey, there. Good morning. I found you."

It's Blair. Blair has emerged from all the trees and ferns and moss. He's wearing a shirt today that matches his eyes. And he looks strangely relieved to see me. Actually, to be fair, I feel relieved to see him, too.

"Blair. Good morning."

I think about everything that happened yesterday. The date with Tim. Which, to my total surprise, had been going pretty well. I wasn't having the worst time ever, if you can believe it. And I was just about to be kissed for the first time in my life. I was ready to experience it, to know what a kiss felt like, even if it was a kiss from Tim Redding.

But then, Blair came along and messed the whole thing up. I wouldn't have cared so much, except that he made the *older brother* remark. Once that happened, the teensy bit of patience I do have with others went out the window.

Blair approaches me by the towering blackberry bushes. But he does it slowly, cautiously.

"I can leave if you want. I know I wasn't invited today. I just wanted to find you and apologize again, for the millionth time this summer. I don't like the way it feels when things are off between us."

I think about patience again. I think about the berries' measured growth. I think about Maryanne and the days we never got together.

"It's okay, Blair. I know sometimes I can be short-fused."

He grins. "Maybe a little."

"But sometimes you can be pretty dumb."

His laugh flitters into the sweet air. Good natured. Easy.

"I can't argue with you there."

He comes closer to me, so close that I hold in my breath. He puts his arms around my shoulders, pulling me into a hug. A make-up hug, I guess. Whatever kind of hug it is, I'm not complaining. His chest and stomach are firm and warm, and I could stay like this for a very long time. But, a moment later, Blair is pulling away and going over to the brambles. I follow him.

"These babies still aren't ready for picking?" He pinches a dark berry between his fingers, giving it a small squeeze.

"Not yet. In August, they will be. You'll get to taste one then, if you want."

"I do want. We're going to pick them together, right? Whenever you give the word."

It sounds like heaven. Berry-picking with someone I care about, like I used to do with Mama. It sounds better than Christmas and my birthday and all the other holidays combined.

"So," Blair states. "Are you going on another date with Tim?"

"Not if I can help it."

"Ouch. Don't you sort of like him, though? Why'd you agree to go out with him in the first place?"

I start digging the toe of my shoe into the moist, dark earth, staining my already-worn sneakers. I'm not going to tell Blair the real, complete reason why I went out with Tim Redding. But I don't want to totally lie, either.

"I'm not really interested in Tim. Not like that. The date was more like an experiment for me."

"Oh. Okay." Blair almost sounds relieved. Or maybe it's just in my head. I'm trying to think of something else to say, something about how Tim isn't my type, but Blair speaks up again before I can:

"You've never kissed anyone."

He says it as though he's reciting a fact from a history book. Heat fans through my face, down my neck. Was it a mistake to admit that to him yesterday?

"Not yet. Is that weird?"

"Nah. I don't think so."

"How old were you when you had your first kiss?"

"Your age, I think." He angles an eyebrow in thought. "Maybe a year younger."

"Is it nice?" I ask.

Blair's eyes flicker over to mine. "It can be. You really were going to let Tim be your first?"

"You make it sound like I was about to rob a bank or something. Or get a dragon-turtle tattoo."

He smiles, shakes his head. "I *can* be pretty dumb, huh?"

"You have your moments. But . . . it wasn't that I wanted Tim specifically to be the one to kiss me. I just wanted to know what it

133

would be like. I think I'm tired of being a kissing virgin. Or whatever you call it."

Blair gently pinches another berry, then runs his fingers over a healthy, green leaf. Again and again, he pulls on the leaf, an unintentional rhythm while he seems to space out. Something's on his mind.

"What if," he says, "to make up for my stupidity yesterday—and just purely as a thing a friend would do for another friend —"

His voice trails off, and I stare at him, wondering if this is going where I think it's going.

"I could kiss you," he finally finishes. "If you want."

Warmth curls and twists in my stomach.

"You'd do that?"

When Blair takes a step toward me, I feel my chest tighten. He's looking at me the way Tim was yesterday, except it's so much more enticing this time, so much more colorful and dizzying, to the point my legs feel weak beneath me. Blair takes another step closer, and I really might lose my balance.

Then, all of a sudden:

"Ouch—dammit. I mean, dang it."

Blair swears while hopping away from the brambles, away from me, his head now angled down toward his foot. "Something bit me."

Shaking off that dizzying feeling, I go down to my knees to assess the damage. It's on his heel: a growing bead of blood. The size of a ladybug. It swells and starts to slide down his skin, a trail of dark scarlet. I can't help but think of another scene with my mother, and I mutter the two words we always used to say when this happened to us.

"What'd you say?" Blair asks, hearing my mumbling. "What got me?"

I stand back up and take in the amusing sight of his overly-worried expression. "A thorn, silly. From the vines. It's barely anything."

"Oh. Right. Man, those are some sharp suckers. Sharper than my out-of-tune piano, am I right?"

He laughs at his dumb joke while I roll my eyes. I understand what's happening: the previously exhilarating moment is gone now, and it won't be coming back. The thorny vine punctured what was probably too good to be true. I do my best to brush it off, to keep the disappointment from setting in.

"Blair, seriously. You're such a dork—"

Then, Blair takes me by the small of my back, drawing me right up against him, right into his body. Shock ripples through me as he bows his head, holds me steady, and he kisses me right on the lips.

My first kiss.

It's an amazing thing. More amazing than I could've imagined.

The sun is flickering through the leaves. The air is sweet. And Blair is holding me against him, his mouth pressing softly onto mine. Warmth, wetness—and a subtle hint of Trident. I can't seem to help it when I melt into him, and I feel him melt into me, gliding his lips over mine—and then, even though I'd rather he didn't, even though I want more, I want Blair to kiss me all day long—it's over. We break away, and Blair takes a step back.

At first, we're both quiet. A minute or so passes before one of us speaks.

"Was that okay?" Blair eyes me hesitantly. "I'm not sure—what you were hoping for."

My mind and heart are still reeling, but I try to keep myself grounded. I try to keep in mind this was just a one-time thing.

"I could've gone for some tongue."

The widening of Blair's eyes is priceless. I start laughing.

"I'm just messing with you, Blair. It was just what I was hoping for. Thank you."

He lets out an airy chuckle imbued with relief. "Well, I would say *my pleasure,* but in this context, doesn't seem quite appropriate."

We hang out amongst the brambles a few minutes longer before saying goodbye, before I sprint back to Christine's house for a day of wedding planning annoyances. I taste Trident on my lips throughout all those annoyances, though. And every time I taste the mint, I feel a prick at my chest. I know what Blair Porter did was just, as he put it, *purely a friend thing*, but that doesn't change the fact that it happened.

Before drifting off to sleep tonight, I replay the kiss in my head. The warmth of being in his arms. Feeling what it would be like to be his. I want to remember it for the rest of my life. I want to remember every little thing that made it so perfect.

25

Blair

There's a battle going on inside me.

I've been doing everything I can to ignore it this summer. I've been throwing myself into my music, taking Nolan to the beach two or three times a day, even spending time with my insufferable parents to seek out a distraction.

Still, this battle is something that's only grown worse with each passing day, the conflict raging at an all-time high.

I've never felt so at war with myself. How is it even possible to be this conflicted within one mind, one body? It's like there are two different versions of myself lately. Blair One and Blair Two.

Blair One thinks about Roxie Morah, and everything that makes her who she is. Her sharpness, of both tongue and mind. Her confidence, even when it seems practiced. Even when I know, deep down, she's as soft as that fluffy buttercream icing she can whip up in seconds flat.

Blair One envisions Roxie in the future. An amazing force of a woman, running her own bakery, wowing each and every customer with her pastries, cookies, pies. The fulfillment she would find from it all, the pride she'd feel in using the gift her mother gave her.

Blair One notices the smoothness of her bronze legs when we're sitting at the piano together. The firmness in her muscles from all the running she does. Her beautiful almond eyes that don't need any makeup, if you ask me. That first Blair imagines what it would be like to give into his desires, throw away his inhibitions and fears. Feel her waist between his hands, kiss her again, slowly, repeatedly this time, giving all of these feelings a chance to live and breathe.

But, then—there's Blair Two. And he's a pesky little son of a gun.

Blair Two reminds me of all those cold, hard facts. Just the plain, objective realities. Roxie's fifteen years old. She's just a kid. Not even a sophomore in high school yet, technically. And meanwhile, I'm about to start my sophomore year of college. My college that, by the way, is all the way across the country, in Ithaca, New York. Miles and miles away from Tangle Beach.

Blair Two points out all these very valid, very important dynamics that I *need* to keep in mind. Five years. That's the age gap between us. Isn't that too much? Maybe it's just because she's still in high school that it seems so drastic to me. But drastic it does seem, whenever Blair Two forces me to stop and really ruminate on it, which he does constantly. Like I said, pesky son of a gun, that other Blair.

Five years apart—I know it's not as much as my parents' nine-year chasm, yet that second Blair Porter can't seem to get over it. That *was* one of the first things I mentioned about myself, wasn't it? I said I couldn't stress it enough: I do not—ever—want to end up like my parents. Never ever *ever*. Rita and Philip are such a miserable pair. They drive each other crazy. They drive me crazy, too. They drove Graham away to another continent, for God's sake.

I know that Blair Two is right about all of that very valid, very important stuff. Five years. Fifteen years old. Ithaca. Tangle Beach.

Blair One is in the wrong. He's the guy who needs the wake-up call. Being with Roxie doesn't make any sense. Not for me, and not for her, either. It wouldn't be right, plain and simple. It would only lead to trouble, to confusion, imminent pain.

Wouldn't it?

Blair Two asserts that when I'm back at Cornell, I should consider looking for a girl who *does* make sense. A girl who's in college, like me. A girl who's much closer to myself in age. A girl who's not so volatile or blunt, passionate or stubborn. A girl I can control myself around.

A girl who doesn't split my being up into two different Blairs who quibble and bicker and just won't *shut up* for one split second to leave my torn, warring self in peace.

∞

July speeds away in a blur of foggy mornings, sunny afternoons, cloudy nights. Roxie and I hang out just about every day, whether we're working on the Sonata, taking Nolan on walks, or experiencing the ultimately classic music of The Beatles. (Turns out, Roxie approves of their *Sgt. Pepper* material but calls their older stuff *hokey*. Even *Revolver*, one of my personal favorite albums. Go figure.)

And regarding that first-kiss scenario that played out after her date with Tim—it seems that this pretty much, mostly worked out the way I'd hoped. It hasn't ruined our friendship, or whatever you call the relationship we have. It hasn't cast any awkwardness over our interactions. Yes, it *is* true that there are the two annoying-as-hell Blairs within me. And yes, it's also true that every now and then, from time to time, I wonder if Roxie is trying to test me, to push things a little further between us. Sometimes, I wonder if she's "experimenting" with me the way she says she was with Tim.

When we're on the piano bench together and I'm showing her the final part of Variation V, she'll casually rest her hand atop my thigh, as if it's simply meant to be there. Invariably, I react by gently sliding her hand away as soon as my fingers are freed up from the keyboard.

When we're watching a movie together, I've learned to keep a bowl of popcorn or candy or any kind of food-like substance positioned smack dab in between us. Otherwise, she will inch closer and closer toward me, ultimately leaning her head against my shoulder or even in my lap.

When we've finished baking something in the kitchen, Roxie occasionally tries to feed me a bite of the finished scone or tart or whatever the dessert may be. She'll hold it up to my mouth, asking me to give it a taste. And every time, I take the baked good from her grip before sampling it.

The worst incident of all was this one day we went to the beach without Nolan. We brought soda and chips, spread towels out on the pale sand, and made ourselves comfortable by the frigid, noisy tide.

I know, I know: I should've seen it coming. Roxie pulled her tank top over her head, revealing a blue swim top underneath. She proceeded to unearth a bottle of sunscreen from the tote she brought along and asked if I'd "get her back for her." About as cliché as can be.

When I responded by saying I don't believe in sunscreen, she gave me a look as though I were a caveman from another era. *Well, I do,* she told me, shoving the bottle into my hand. And so, I found myself lathering her up in lotion that day, as swiftly and platonically as I possibly could. Blair Two, meanwhile, was throwing a heck of a fit inside my brain.

But again, for the most part, there's not *much* weirdness. And now, suddenly, July is over. Things feel different. Summer feels vulnerable with August upon us. Roxie can now play Variation V of Sonata No. 11 in its entirety, no mistakes, no forgetting which part comes next. She's got it. She's done.

"Good job, Music Hermit. Your training is complete," I declare on this bright August day, sitting next to her at the Yamaha. I've just listened to her go through the whole song, and I'm feeling proud, accomplished. She turned out to be a fast learner, and I turned out to be a pretty damn good teacher, if you ask me.

Roxie gives me a knowing look. "Which means, now we're even."

"Even?"

"Yeah. Did you forget about the deal we made back in June? You agreed to teach me one song. Because you felt bad for hitting me in the head with a frisbee."

I point a finger in the air. "Riiiight. Wow. I actually did forget why we were doing all this. I guess I just stopped thinking about it at some point."

"Well, now, you can be free of me, Blair Porter. I got my song. You got your atonement. Or whatever you were wanting to get out of this."

I pop a piece of gum into my mouth, bob my head in consideration. "Atonement's nice and all. But, what was exponentially better was getting to expand your musical horizons. Act as your amazingly sage Oldies Shaman. Open your eyes to the endless wonders of the nifty sixties, the sexy seventies, the—"

"Blair. I get the point."

"Yes, Roxie. You *do* get the point. Because I taught it to you."

She scoffs, but there's amusement in the way her lips purse, her cheeks round into apricot shapes. Then, her countenance shifts into one that's more serious.

"Blair. Do you want to be free of me now?"

"No."

The word, strangely urgent, flies out before I even get a chance to think about it. I blow a bubble with my gum as a weird way of countering this. "No. We still have about four weeks left before I go back to New York. And, anyway, why would I want to be free of you? We're friends."

"That's not true," she says, and it makes me feel tense, edgy.

"It's not?"

"We're *kinda-sorta* friends. Remember?" She gives a playful nudge to my shoulder with her own before jumping off the bench and stretching her arms up toward the vaulted ceiling. "If you don't want to be free of me quite yet, then how about we get some food and watch one of your boring movies? To celebrate me finishing the Sonata."

I make sure to keep a bowl of M&Ms in its proper spot during our viewing of *Rear Window*, and it's nightfall by the time the movie ends. I walk Roxie to the front door to say goodnight, and just before she goes, she gives me a quick hug.

"Seriously, Blair. Thank you for teaching me that song. It's really important to me."

Roxie goes into the night, and in her absence, I realize I'm feeling good about everything in this moment. Really good. The two Blairs are actually being quiet, and the day feels complete, like I accomplished all I wanted to, like the upcoming days are all going to be just as good and accomplished and complete as this one.

That's when my dad suddenly swings open the front door, barging into the guest house, sapping all the good energy away with his stuffy, business-y aura.

"Dad. Hey. Whatchya doing here?"

It is the first time I've seen him step foot into my coastal quarters. He shuts the door behind him, dulling the sound of the ocean—which always seems louder at night for some reason.

Philip makes himself comfortable on the couch. He flips on the TV, finding a news channel like it's second nature to him, like it's something his body just does involuntarily. *Couch* plus *television remote* equals *obnoxious news channel.*

"Ah, Rita was snoring up a storm in our room. I couldn't find my damn earplugs. So I went to have a drink on the front deck, then thought I probably ought to come see what my son was up to."

"I see. Alrighty, then." I sit next to him on the couch.

He keeps his gaze on the TV when he says, "I saw Roxie leaving. While I was out on the deck. Saw her taking off out the door of your house here. At eleven o'clock at night."

So that's why he's here. Something to do with Roxie. I squirm around and clench my jaw, wishing I had a piece of gum on hand right now. I already know I'm not going to like this conversation. The really good feeling I had when Roxie departed is not going to last.

"Uh, yep," I say. "We watched a movie. It was longer than I remembered."

Philip narrows his eyes at the talking heads, wrinkling his forehead so he looks like a raisin. He's quiet.

"Roxie's just a pal, you know, Dad."

"Uh-huh."

The mindlessness of that reply makes me think he believes me, or that he simply doesn't care. Either option works for me. But then he has more to say:

"Blair, did I ever tell you about the summer flings I had before I met your mom?"

Oh, crap. Crappity-crap-*crap*. Not one of *these* conversations. Please, God, no. I'm squirming around again the way I would if an octopus were trying to entangle me in its gross, completely inappropriate and disturbing embrace.

"Nope, you haven't. And no offense, Dad, but I think I'd prefer if we kept it that way."

It's no use. I'm too much of a peacekeeper to actually stop him from elaborating:

"There was Natasha at first, the summer in Fiji. Then Cynthia, in Greece. I can't remember if Julie came next or if it was Pam — or was her name Deb? I always get those names mixed up."

"Don't we all?" I have to fight to keep myself from clamping my hands over my ears and humming a Billy Joel song to drown out this horrendously uncomfortable story-time session.

"Well, anyway. Summer flings. Your old man gets it."

"Dad, I'm not having a summer —"

"Those were some of the greatest times for me. Some fantastic memories."

Just when I think this conversation can't possibly get any worse, it does.

"To tell you the truth, sometimes I wonder if I should've settled for one of those girls."

I feel sick. Straight-up ill. Nauseated and clammy. Repulsed and flat-out depressed.

Did I mention that I do not, ever, ever, *ever* want to end up like my parents?

"Listen, Blair." Philip turns to face me. The TV is still on, but he's facing me. His eye contact is jarring, and it suddenly seems very serious. He looks almost . . . upset.

He says: "I had my flings, my fun. I get it. And this Roxie girl seems great and all—but she looks a little young—under eighteen? I'm not one to judge, you know that. But you've got big plans ahead of you, Blair. *I've* got big plans for you. It'd be awfully stupid of you to screw those plans up."

All I can do is stare at my dad, not knowing what to say.

"Anyway." Philip claps a hand over my knee as he stands up. He moseys back toward the front door. "I know you're not stupid, Blair. You're a smart kid. Whatever's going on with this girl, you won't take things too far."

He sends me a pointed look. "Right, Blair?"

My response is delayed.

"Right."

And he makes his exit, oblivious to the fact that he's left me feeling as if I've just been fed a plate of rancid seafood. Feeling low and weird, queasy and depleted and, most of all, confused.

26

Roxie

It's past eleven when I get home. The house is dark and hushed, and I have Mozart stuck in my head. The beautiful, tender song I know how to play now. The one that makes me picture a couple dancing in the rain. The one that Blair taught me, note by note. The one that really, truly is more important than he understands.

I tiptoe up the wooden stairs, swaying my upper body with the rhythm in my head. I'm so caught up in that internal melody and cadence, I don't notice that the light in Christine's room is on when I waltz by her doorway.

"Roxie?"

Mozart vanishes, and I come to a stop in the hallway.

"Roxie. I can see you. Come here."

Everything in my body resists as I force backwards steps until I'm standing at Christine's threshold. The door is cracked, and I stick my head in the opening, trying to act casual. Christine is sitting cross-legged in her bed, her satiny pajama set on, a magazine open on her lap.

"Can I help you?" I say.

"Yes, actually. You can. Come in here."

Again, my legs resist the movement of entering her lair, of propping myself on the edge of the bed when she instructs me to sit down.

"What is it you need help with, Christine?"

She shuts her magazine and sets it aside.

"Understanding what you're doing creeping back home at 11:30 at night."

I've done this two or three other times this summer—getting home close to midnight, I mean—but I guess Christine didn't pick up on it those other times. She's usually asleep by now.

"I don't have a curfew," I retort, quickly jumping to my own defense.

"You were at Blair's, weren't you?"

"Why does that matter?"

Christine is not happy. Her makeup-free face shows every ounce of her tension. Her judgment. Her control-freak nature. Because that's what this is about right now, I'm certain of it: Christine wants to control me, to keep me in my fifteen-year-old, quasi-child place.

"Are you having sex with him?"

Her question sends a flash of lightning cracking down my spine. I feel myself jerk backward from the shock.

"What? You can't be serious, Christine."

"I'm extremely serious. What else am I supposed to think when you're with this boy nonstop and getting home late at night?"

"You're being totally ridiculous right now."

But she's not about to let this go: "Roxie. Are you sleeping with Blair?"

"No!"

I'm absolutely fuming. This might be the angriest I've ever felt toward Christine, which, given all the contention we've shared over the past few years, is saying a lot. My anger is off the charts from her assumptions and accusations. From the way she used *Blair* and *sex* in the same, condemning sentence. From the way she's inserting herself into one of the only good parts of my life and trying to take control of it. Like she *always* tries to do.

Christine stays silent for a minute, performing some kind of calculation within that nitpicky mind of hers.

She says, "I thought we already talked about this. I said you should be careful with Blair. He's older than you. He's a *tourist*, Roxie. What do you think is going to happen? He's going to leave at the end of the month and forget all about Tangle Beach, and you'll be back to high school in September . . ."

"Oh my God, Christine. It's not like that. Blair's my friend."

"Really, Roxie? You're positive you don't have any feelings for him, at all? People have a way of lying to themselves about these things. Especially teenage girls."

I dig my fingernails into my palms, bite into my lower lip. The little thorn in my chest is tender, but I ignore it as best I can.

"Why are we even talking about this? Why does this have to be a *thing* with you?"

Christine's answer catches me off guard:

"Because I remember what it was like to have my heart broken."

I stop digging my nails into my skin. Stop biting into my lip. I force myself to take a deep breath, but it comes out shaky.

Christine doesn't understand a thing about me. She never has, and she never will. I hang my head and avoid eye contact with her. My anger has been replaced with sadness. A deep, vast ocean of it.

"My heart's already broken," I utter in a low tone. "It broke three years ago, the day my mother was ripped away from me. It'll never be repaired or whole again. It'll always stay broken."

I get off the bed with one more thing to say: "There's nothing you or anyone else can do about it. I don't need your help."

A week goes by. And then it's the day. The bad day. The very worst day of all.

I haven't seen Blair at all over the last week. That's intentional. That's my doing. Every year, as the bad day gets nearer and nearer, a heavy dread creeps upon me. Little by little, I sink down into a funk.

Last week, I left a note at Blair's door saying I'd be too busy with Lace & Tide stuff to hang out for a while. Which was kind of true, anyway. There were two weddings last weekend, and then Shelby Frasier was in town to make sure everything's still coming along well for her big day.

Now, it's a Thursday. A warm, summer morning. And I hate this day. I wish I could erase this day from the calendar, wish I could make it so nobody had ever heard of August eighth.

I'm sitting on the hard floor of my bedroom, folding my legs up into my chest. I can't go running today. I can't do anything today. All I can do is sit here and remember. Every piece of the memory cuts into me, but there's nothing to be done about this. My mind is careening back in time. Three years ago.

27

Roxie

I was twelve, and it was the very beginning of August. The start of the very best month of the year. Mama and I were out by the berries behind our home. I could smell their sugar in the air, and Mama had to remind me they needed just a little more time. She said when they were ready, we would pick them until our hands were as purple as could be, our fingers tender from the work and the thorns.

It made me think of a poem of hers I'd found once. It was written on the back of one of her charcoal drawings. I never quite knew what to think of it, but I loved it all the same:

Into my hands, the fruit, a child.
Out to the thicket, swollen, wild.
Scratches, berry blood and bruises. Comb
my fingers through your hair.
You are home.
You are mine, so says the vine.
Our hands among them,
copy me: pick the berries three-by-three.
We are the same now. We are where brambles
prick and give and bow.
Give us life. Black fruit. A single absolute.
At night, I hold you, small, unknowing.
At sun-up, we will be going
to the thicket, swollen, wild.
Into my hands, the fruit, a child.
Here, you are mine, so says the vine.
You are mine.

Mama told me that we'd freeze some of the blackberries this year. That way, she could make me a blackberry cake for my birthday come February. The thought of this set fireworks off inside me. She had always baked me a simple yellow cake for my birthdays, which I loved, of course—but a blackberry cake, in the middle of winter? I couldn't stop thinking about what the cake would look like, what it might taste like. I knew it would be the most beautiful, wonderful thing.

This August day, we stood together by the green briars, and I noticed a little, white butterfly flitting around above the vines. It made a soft landing atop one vine in particular, one that was brownish-gray and brittle. One that had died. It looked ugly to me. No color. No water. No fruit.

"I wish I understood death."

Maryanne looked up at me from where she was kneeling on the ground, uprooting dandelions.

"What do you mean, baby?"

I lowered myself to sit beside her, but I couldn't stop eyeing the lifeless vine.

"I mean . . . what happens after? Does *anything* happen?"

"After we die?"

I nodded my head.

"No one knows."

"No one?"

She gave the lightest little laugh, despite the darkness of this discussion.

"Well, not for certain," she said. "People have their ideas. But that's all they are, really. Just ideas."

I looked away from the dead vine and watched Maryanne pull on another dandelion, another, another.

I said, "What do you think happens?"

"I've wondered about different things. I guess we all do. But there is one idea I like the most."

"What is it?"

She seemed to meditate for a minute. No longer weeding. Just thinking.

"Here's a thought. Why don't we both write down our own ideas about what happens after? We can seal them in an envelope and read them together after we pick our first berries of the season."

Mama always had her ways of making things more interesting. The mystery of this envelope concept appealed to me, but at the same time, I wasn't sure exactly what the point of it was.

"You sure you don't want to just tell me?" I asked.

"I want to give you a chance to think about it for yourself. I'll set the envelope in the garden window. You can write down your idea and slip it inside whenever you're ready."

I thought about it for a few days. I thought about it each night before I fell asleep. I knew about ideas like heaven, of course, but what did *heaven* really mean? And was that idea even real?

It frustrated me, because all I could envision when I thought about *after* was the gray and brittle blackberry vine. Just that. Nothing else.

When it came down to it, the note I slipped into the envelope on the garden window contained three simple words:

I don't know.

But that was okay, I decided. Because soon enough, Mama and I would pick the first berries of the season. My favorite time of year would be here, and I would get to read her answer, waiting for me in the envelope.

August eighth. I slept in unusually late that morning, for some reason. I was having dreams about the white butterfly all night long, and it was so peaceful, so soothing, like my brain didn't want it to end.

Normally I was an early-early riser, so a thick and foreign grogginess weighed on me when I forced myself out of bed. My bedroom felt hot and stuffy with it being so late in the morning. I slid open my window to let the sweet, fresh air filter in through the screen.

I changed out of my pajamas and crouched down to the floor to peer beneath my metal bedframe. My journal was waiting for me down there, the one Mama had gotten for me for my twelfth birthday earlier this year. I'd been making little entries in it every day since.

8/8: I think the berries are finally ready. I think we're going to pick our first batch today. Mama said we'll pick 'til our hands are as purple as can be.

The journal went back under the bed, and I went over to the bedroom window to swallow one more gulp of air and steal a look at all the messy brambles and greenery that awaited me.

I saw the brambles, saw the greenery, and I saw something else: Mama was already out there. *Of course, she is,* I thought. *Because I woke up so late.*

She was at the edge of a berry bush, lying down right beside it. Cloud-watching, probably, or napping, or just letting the sun warm her skin.

Out to the thicket, swollen, wild.

I continued watching her a little longer, admiring how patient she was about me sleeping in late. Admiring the way her long, buttery dress fluttered about her legs in the breeze. She was so serene. So still. And that was when I felt it. A terrible shift. A sharp and sour feeling in my stomach. A gradual knowledge that wiped my smile away and stopped my breathing.

I bolted out of my room, to the back door of the house, and burst outside. I ran to the berry bushes and knelt beside her.

We are where brambles
prick and give and bow.

"Mama?"

She was beautiful. She was perfect. Her long hair, her bright eyes pointing up to the sky. She was nothing like that gray, brittle vine.

152

"Mama," I cried, setting trembling hands on her bare arm, her soft skin. I shook her. Her body moved. Her eyes remained fixed on the sun. The leaves of the bushes rustled against her arms and legs as I shook her, harder and harder, more and more. Frantic, desperate, afraid.

I sobbed: "Mama, I love you."

Scratches, berry blood and bruises.

I bowed over her body, pressing my head to her supple stomach, feeling the cottony smoothness of her dress upon my face. Trying to soak up as much of her warmth as was left. Feeling the sun's heat pressing down above me, pressing down onto both of us. My hot, endless tears drenched her dress, and I clung to her lifeless body until I couldn't feel any more warmth. It might have been minutes. It might have been hours.

Comb

my fingers through your hair.

"I love you," I heaved, and a breeze came through, rustling the leaves once again, almost as though they were trying to answer me.

I stood up. Detached from myself. Out-of-body. Looking at my Mama lying in the grass.

My entire world unraveled, then. *She* was my entire world. And suddenly, somehow, she was gone. *How can you be gone?*

Give us life. Black fruit.

I started running.

I wasn't sure why at first. Maybe to get away from the horrible scene. Maybe to pretend it wasn't happening, or to keep myself from passing out. I didn't have a plan. All I had was the urge to flee. I ran around the side of the house and down the driveway. I ran down the rural, loopy road. Tears blurred my vision, burned my eyes, and I wasn't even wearing shoes, but I ran as fast as my legs would let me. I sobbed and I gasped, and I sprinted until, all of a sudden, someone was calling my name out on the road—the local sheriff had spotted me, and he caught hold of me, forced me to stop my hysterical dash.

"What's going on?" he said. "Roxie? Where's Maryanne?"

∞

He drove me back to the house, let me stay in his car. An ambulance came. People I didn't know. They took Mama's body away from the berries. I tried to tell them what happened—even though I was at a loss as to what actually *had* happened. *How did this happen? How did you leave me, lying in the grass?*

Eventually, someone looked inside Mama's body—something I won't let myself think about—and they explained it to me. An aneurism. A ruptured aortic aneurism. The big blood vessel running from her wonderful, perfect heart, through her chest and down her abdomen—it grew weak in one spot, and it burst—and that was all it took.

She might have had something called Marfan syndrome, they said. It would explain why she was so tall and slender, and why this happened. They said I might have it, too, but they didn't know for sure. And I didn't care.

All I cared about was that she was gone.

You are mine, so says the vine.

I pictured her beautiful body nestled beside the green vines. It was all I could think about.

She was gone.

∞

Where did you go?

Where are you?

Everything changed. Everything was ruined.

I had to leave our home in Shoshone. I had to leave the berries that were finally ready to be picked.

I had to move to Tangle Beach. To Christine Lambert's house on Seawood Lane.

At first, I felt a little drop of hope, since I would be living with Maryanne Morah's cousin. Someone related to her. To me. But that single drop disintegrated as soon as I realized that Christine Lambert was nothing like my Mama. No one was like my Mama. And she was the only one I'd had. My only friend. The only person I'd loved.

It didn't take long before I got into my morning ritual: rising at the crack of dawn (I will never oversleep again), opening the window, making my daily journal entry:

I miss you.

They were the only words I wanted to write. The only words I believed in or understood.

And I started running, every day. I sprinted the way I had after I found her body. I ran because it numbed me. The faster I'd go, the number I became.

I found the unused parcel of land, and the secluded brambles. The closest thing I've been able to find to my real home.

My real home in Shoshone, my green house on Wild Road, was inherited by Christine. But Christine couldn't afford two homes. She wanted to stay in Tangle Beach, on Seawood Lane, where she felt life for the two of us made more sense. And so, she sold my old house. Mama's house. The place Mama said she bought shortly before I came along. The place she taught me how to bake. The place she gave me piano lessons, where the walls were covered in pretty wallpaper, where her charcoal drawings hung, where the rain left streaks on the garden window.

The wooded lot was the closest I felt I could get to all of that, and to her.

But every morning, I had to—I still have to—leave the blackberries. Return to reality.

Where are you?

Where did you go?

The world would surge by me as I ran, as I pushed my body as fast as I could. Trees, houses, sand, ocean, people, sky.

I've been looking for you everywhere, but you are simply nowhere to be found, and I don't understand where you've gone.

How can you be nowhere?

How can it be that you have altogether disappeared?

I never knew what happened to that envelope. So I never got to read my mother's answer.

Where did you go?

28

Blair

The weirdest thing has just happened. After getting dressed to "Sister Golden Hair," (a song I can't seem to get out of my head over the last week), a *ping* noise goes off on my phone, and when I take a look, the notification displayed on my screen shocks me.

I have a new email.

Subject: *Hey.*
Date: *Aug. 8.*
Sender: *Graham Porter.*

It takes a minute for this to sink in. I fall onto my bed and ogle his name.

I've heard from Graham just two other times since he fled the family and started working for his nonprofit. Both of those messages were brief and vague and, well, how else can one put it? Disappointing as hell. I try not to acknowledge my woundedness beneath all the Graham stuff, because I just want things to be easy and okay. I want to keep the peace. I am Blair—Peacekeeper Supreme—hear me *not* roar.

Still perched on the edge of my bed, I tap on Graham's name and feast my eyes on this rare bout of communication from my older brother.

Hey Blair-
Just checking in. Was in Ethiopia for a spell, now Uganda. Keeping busy. Feels really good.
Mom and Dad still royally pissed at me? At least you're not.
How's your summer? Keeping sane? What's the playlist like this year?

Don't let the Parental Units push you around. Do your own thing. Do what you want.

<u>Don't</u> tell them you heard from me.

Peace out, brother. Sending you a virtual fist bump from Africa.

-Graham

I read his message five, six, maybe even seven times through.

Do your own thing. Do what you want.

I read those words in particular over and over and over. That's what Graham did last year, what he's still doing this year: his own thing. What he wants.

Don't let the Parental Units push you around. Rita and Philip. Who, of course, are still and will always be royally pissed at Graham. I'm sure he knows that; he's not an idiot. I'm sure he only meant that as a rhetorical question.

Don't let them push you around. It's been a week since I last saw Roxie. She left me a note that said she was getting busy with wedding planning affairs. That was one-hundred percent fine by me. Because after my dad shared those highly disturbing and personal anecdotes with me the other night, after he gave me the warning he did—I didn't mind taking a step back from everything with Roxie. Getting some space. Some air. Focusing on other things. It seemed like a good idea. At the time, anyway.

Do your own thing.

Do what you want.

Graham always did have the best advice. And he still does. Even when he's on another continent, even when he doesn't know what's going on in my life in the slightest, and when I don't know what's going on in his—he still manages to say just the right thing. His advice is always just what I need to hear.

Do what you want. I know what I want. I want to hang out with my friend in Tangle Beach before summer's all dried up and gone forever.

I jump off my bed and head out the front door.

∞

I get to the blue house on Seawood Lane with a distinct spring in my step, an ethereal lightness about me, an easy smile on my face. I give the white door a quick rapping and hum to myself while I wait. It's still America's brilliant, intoxicating melody swimming around up in that crazy cranium of mine. I start singing it out loud, albeit quietly, and give the door another *tap-tap-tap*.

No one's coming. Maybe no one's here. Christine's Volkswagen is gone, but for whatever reason, I just had this feeling that Roxie would be here. That she'd be waiting for me, ready to see me again. I don't know why, but that feeling persists inside me as I'm standing here outside her door. It amplifies, even.

That's why I give the doorknob a twist. When I find that it's unlocked, I take a step inside.

"Knock-knock," I call out, but there's no response. I've never been inside this house before. It's clean and quiet. Smells like lemons and bleach. And everywhere I look, I see seashells or sand dollars or starfish or ocean waves. We get the point, Christine. You live on the coast.

"Roxie? You around?"

There comes a sound, then, from upstairs. It's her—I'm certain. The intuitive feeling sparks brighter. She's upstairs, and she's waiting for me. I go up the wooden staircase. I'm drawn down the hallway, and somehow, I just know where her room is. I know where to find her.

And there she is.

But something's not right.

Roxie is a hunched-over, curled-up ball on the floor. Her back is to me; she's facing a window whose curtain panel is ballooning from the breeze, then deflating, then filling up like a parachute again.

It's past six in the morning now, but she's not in her running clothes. She's still garbed in pajamas: butterfly-patterned shorts and a matching shirt. Her knees are tucked up to her chest, her head cradled atop them. Her long, brown hair spills down her back.

"Roxie?"

She lifts her head and turns around to see me. And I feel my face collapse into a frown.

"Hey. What's wrong?"

I go to her on the floor. Her face is wet. Eyelids swollen. Nose red. She looks back to the dancing curtain, and tears slide down her cheeks.

"Roxie," I say her name again, in my gentlest voice possible. I set a wary hand against her shoulder. I'm afraid to touch her right now. But it seems like the right thing to do.

"Blair." She doesn't bother to wipe away her tears or hide any of this anguish from me. "You're here."

"I'm here," I repeat, and next thing I know, she's burying her head into my chest, slinging her arms around my neck, and shaking terribly as she weeps into my T-shirt.

I'm scared and confused, but I take hold of her. I slide her up onto my lap, letting her pour all this pain out onto me, letting it bleed through my clothing, onto my skin. The tighter I hold her against me, the more soothed she seems to grow.

"What's going on?" I whisper above her head.

Her tears and convulsions subside, and she speaks into my shirt: "I miss my mom, Blair." Her words vibrate into my chest, sending a tremor through me. "I lost her today, three years ago. She had an aneurism in our backyard, and I found her out there, dead. Just lying there. Just gone."

Pain manifests in every part of me. A young girl happening upon her lifeless mother. *This* girl. I squeeze Roxie into me, and she squeezes me back.

"She was all I had," Roxie murmurs, her voice raspy and faint. I feel her lips move against me as she speaks. "I don't have anyone now."

"No. That's not true." I'm still whispering. "You have me."

When she pulls back to assess me, I see she is gravely serious. So am I. I don't know if I've ever felt so serious before in my life.

"Do you really mean that?" she asks me.

I stare into her reddened eyes. I nod my head.

Roxie scrutinizes me a minute longer before saying: "There's something I want to show you."

"Okay."

$$\infty$$

This shift in me is so . . . new. Unexpected. A tiny bit unnerving, if I'm being honest. I'm not used to feeling this somber. Focused. *Still.*

There's no music playing in my head now. No restlessness teasing at my muscles. No gum in my mouth. Just this moment, the somberness, the stillness.

Roxie's gone over to her closet, swinging open the door, stepping behind it. I realize she's changing out of her pajamas, so I avert my eyes, even though the closet door provides full privacy. I'm guessing she wants to take me somewhere, like she did that day we went to her blackberry spot together for the first time. I'm guessing we'll be leaving this house in just a few minutes' time.

"You can look now."

So I do, and I feel my jaw unhinge. Roxie is wearing a dress. A light purple dress—the kind that ties around the neck. It hugs her frame, her waist and hips, just barely flaring out at the midpoint of her thighs.

"What do you think?" she asks me. This is what she wanted to show me. Not a place—this dress.

"Oh." I blink and feel my mouth try to form words, but nothing's coming out. There's a tingling deep in my stomach now.

"Will you zip me up?"

Roxie moves in front of a mirror, and I come up behind her to slide the zipper up her bronze back. I look at her in the mirror as she smooths her hands down the soft-looking material. I feel myself swallow. There's something about the way she looks right now. Her face may be puffy and red from all the tears, but she just looks so . . .

"Blair. I need to know what you think of the dress. It's important."

What I think . . . What I think . . .

"Is it new?"

I'm being evasive, I know.

"No," Roxie says. "Not new. It's for this thing I'm doing tomorrow."

"A Lace & Tide thing?"

"No. Christine's gone for a couple days. She went to Portland for some big wedding expo thing. Thank God."

"Oh. So . . ." I've been keeping my tone soft and gentle this whole time. "What's the thing you're doing tomorrow?"

Roxie spins around so she's looking at me directly, rather than through the mirror.

"Don't make fun of me when I tell you," she says.

How could I make fun of her right now? I'm baffled that the notion could even cross her mind, but I simply reply, "I won't."

She takes in a big breath.

"Tangle Beach holds this big event every year. The Ocean Festival. It's kicking off tomorrow. They always start things off with this totally silly thing." She pauses. "A competition for high school girls."

I tilt my head. "Like—a pageant?"

Her cheeks go strawberry-red at the word.

"No. Well, maybe. Kind of. It's a talent show, basically. They don't make you answer dumb questions or parade around in a swimsuit or whatever. The winner is crowned the *Ocean Princess.*" A roll of her eyes. "It's stupid."

I absorb her in her lavender dress, her blushing skin.

"But . . ." I say, my words feeling trepidatious, "you're doing it. Tomorrow."

"*Don't* make fun of me, Blair."

"Hey." I place my hands atop her bare shoulders. I fix my eyes onto hers. "I'm *not* making fun of you. I'm surprised. I'm curious why you're doing it, especially since you *did* just call it stupid. But I'm not making fun of you."

She looks at me, looks at me. Then seems to accept my assertion.

"My mom did it," she says. "When she was in high school. It's open to girls across the whole county, not just Tangle Beach. She was crowned Princess her senior year. And . . ." Roxie pivots around, back to the mirror. She runs her hands down her waist. "This was the dress she wore."

I let this sink in. It must be the reason she looks so perfect right now. Why the dress fits her like a glove. I allow my eyes to scan her body in the mirror—her long legs—the spot where her hips curve out—where her waist curves in—even the spot where the neckline is lowest, and I can make out the shape of her chest.

Where is the nagging Blair Two when I need him? He seems to have vacated my brain for the moment. Meanwhile, the tingle in my stomach has transformed into heat.

I give my head a little shake. I make myself focus.

"What was your mother's talent? For the competition?"

"The same that mine will be," Roxie answers. She gives me a pointed look. "Piano."

"So that's why . . . That's why you wanted me to teach you a song? For this competition?"

"Mama taught me a few little things on the piano back in the day, but I don't remember them very well. The Mozart piece you taught me will be perfect, though. As long as I don't mess it up."

"You won't. You'll be amazing."

I don't know why, really—maybe it's the delicate smile Roxie gives me—but I find myself settling my hands against her sides and sliding them over the taut dress, around to her stomach. I ease her back against me, and blood is rushing through me, surging, hot and fast.

"Will you come watch me tomorrow?" Roxie's question is meek, uncertain. "It's right in the middle of town. At noon. They'll have a big stage set up. Would you come watch my performance?"

I keep myself focused on those catlike eyes, remembering the first time I saw them. That day on the beach, the frisbee, the moment she looked up at me.

"Yes. It's a promise. I'll be there."

29

Roxie

The way Blair's looking at me. The way he's holding me. Touching me. Things are different today between us. I can feel it: like little, tiny flames sparking, like music vibrating in my bones.

In the reflection of the mirror, Blair's caramel brows are scrunched together, and his hands are pressed into my middle. He's keeping me tucked against him, and I love the warmth of his chest and arms, his face so close to mine. I suck in air when he caresses my stomach slowly and meets my gaze.

Oh, God. That look he's giving me. Some of his hair has fallen over his forehead, and his eyes are so intense, so serious, it makes me ache inside. What's happening today? Today is August eighth. Today is the bad day, the very worst day. A day of emptiness and loneliness and despair.

But here is Blair Porter. Holding me before the mirror, gazing at me in my mother's dress, the one I've kept tucked inside my closet for three years.

And he's promised to come to my performance tomorrow. He's going to be there to watch me follow in Maryanne's footsteps and honor her with the tender, beautiful song he taught me. I'm trying to process the way this August eighth is unfolding. Wrap my head around it. Is it okay to feel the emptiness, the loneliness and despair, all fading away little by little, bit by bit, on a day like today?

Maybe it is okay.

Maybe Mama would want it to be like this.

Maybe it would make her smile, laugh the easy laugh that Blair sometimes does.

I don't get a chance to ponder my questions any further. Blair suddenly says, "I understand if you don't want to, if you need to be by yourself today—but. Is there any chance you'd want to spend the day with me? If you'd rather not, though, if you want to be alone—"

I cut him off before he can finish: "I don't."

∞

We go to the beach. I change into normal clothes first; I have to make sure the dress stays in perfect condition for tomorrow. For the competition.

Ever since Maryanne left me, I made the decision that I would one day sign up for The Ocean Festival. I finally got up the courage this year, back in May, just before the deadline. To be totally, completely frank, I'm terrified about it. Dressing up all frilly and girly, performing before a huge crowd, all of those eyes plastered on me, all of that attention . . .

I'd never in a million years consider it, if it weren't for her. She's the only reason I'm doing it.

Things are coming together surprisingly well now. Christine is out of town, so I'll be safe from her questions and judgment. Mama's old dress seems to fit me well enough. And, best of all, Blair will be there to cheer me on.

On the topic of Blair: he's acting *so* different today. It's seriously throwing me off. I'm not used to it. But I love it. I really, truly, absolutely love it.

Everything he does with me today is different. We run into the water together, wetting our feet, and he picks me up and spins me around. When he sets me down, he's slow and gentle, keeping my body molded to his for a minute, brushing hair out of my eyes.

He doesn't tease me. Doesn't call me "music hermit." Doesn't nudge me with a shoulder or laugh and turn away from me when I touch him. He doesn't put extra space between us like he usually does when I trespass into his bubble.

Is this all because he found me crying on my bedroom floor, because it's the anniversary of Maryanne's death? Maybe, but I wonder, I hope, it's something more.

The salt is thick in the air, the sun is high, summer is rich as can be. We go back to the shore and rest in the sand. There are people all around us, but they might as well be invisible to me. Blair startles me by taking my hand in his, sliding his fingers between mine, settling our hands atop his thigh. His touch excites me. His attention today is so tender, so new. I look at him closely, his bright eyes, his lips that once touched mine.

"Christine said something to me the other day."

Blair turns to me, curious. So, I go on.

"She thought—she was worried that—you and I were—"

"What?" Blair asks softly, so soft I almost don't hear him over the ocean.

"That we were having sex."

"Oh." His eyebrows jump a little and he glances off to the side. I feel my face heat up. Has the idea ever occurred to Blair? Has he ever imagined having sex with me? Dreamt about it at night? I would pay all the money I have to know the answer.

"Wow," he says. "She really thought that? What did you tell our deranged Queen Christine?"

"I told her to relax. Take a chill pill. I said we were only having sex after every *other* piano lesson."

Blair laughs, and this is normally when he would inch farther from me and change the subject. But he doesn't. He stays right where he is, keeps holding my hand.

"She drives me crazy," I say. "Christine. I swear, it's like her blatant mission in life to push all my buttons. Every single one."

"Maybe . . ." Blair hesitates; I give him a look to urge him on. "I know she's a tough cookie and all, that Christine of yours. I just wonder if maybe you should cut her a tiny bit more slack. Try to get along."

"Shouldn't *she* be the one trying to get along with me? She treats me like a child when it suits her, then blames things on me when they go wrong, as though suddenly I've transformed into the head of the household or something."

"Hmmm." Blair unweaves our fingers and starts grazing the palm of my hand. "I'm no relationship guru, but I think the fact of the matter is, you *are* the mature one in that relationship. So I think it is your responsibility to act like it and try to mend things when you can."

I don't much like his analysis. I feel myself squint as I take in the crisp horizon, where the deep blue water cuts the sky. I probably don't like his analysis because . . . it rings true.

"I don't think Christine and I will ever really get along. I can't imagine it."

"Well. I hope you do. I hope you guys figure things out. I hope she lets you bake all the wedding cakes next summer. And I hope you start up your own bakery one day."

"Do you?"

He only looks at me. An intent stare. Then, he stands up, pulling me to my feet. He walks along the shore with me, still holding my hand. It feels wonderful. Like I belong to him. Like we could be so much more.

"You know," I speak up. We step over pebbles and broken sand dollars. "I have my own hopes for you, Blair Porter."

"Oh? Do tell, Roxie Morah."

"I hope you do your own thing."

He swivels his neck around, practically gaping at me. It reminds me of the look he gave me when I said I didn't know who Michael Jackson was.

"Do my own thing?" he questions.

"Yeah. I mean, I hope you find your own path in life, Blair. You told me you don't want to go to Cornell. But it's where you go. It's obvious you're not even a little bit passionate about your family's company. But you go along with those plans, too. I guess you go along with all of it because it's easier that way, and because your brother made everyone lose their minds when he broke the family expectations."

Blair stops walking. He seems distracted by a seagull hopping over wet sand. But then he faces me.

"Wow. Well. That was creepy accurate. Have you been reading my imaginary diary? Or my emails?" His smile warms me inside.

I shrug. "That's what I mean when I say I hope you do your own thing. And I really mean it. You deserve to break away like your brother did. You owe it to yourself."

He proffers a crooked grin. "Owe it to myself. Why's that?"

"Because, Blair. You're amazing."

Blair bites his lip. His grin stretches higher up his face.

"So are you."

The next thing he does is one of those unexpected actions, the type of thing Blair would never do before today. He takes my temples into his warm hands and bows his forehead 'til it meets mine. I can sense his lips right in front of me, and I get lightheaded. Blair gives me the lightest kiss on the mouth, then kisses me on my cheek.

The ocean is within me right now: waves swelling, churning, breaking, sparkling, all inside me. My whole body, my heart, my soul, pulses with the rhythmic commotion.

Blair says, "Where to now?"

We go to his house. And we're both starving. He cranks up a song I've never heard before ("Oh, What a Night") and I get to baking in the kitchen.

Blair sings the funny high notes and takes my hands, dancing and spinning me around. I'm in the middle of trying to make us mini lemon pies; my stomach's growling and grumbling. Yet, I just laugh and savor Blair's big smile, his goofiness, the way he mimics the bass notes and forces me to jive to the beat with him.

After the pies are done and we've had our fill, Blair and I both flop on the couch. The fullness of my stomach is making me feel tired. Or maybe it's from all the crying I did this morning. I'm still trying to make sense of today and how much it's altered, transformed into something totally different.

Moving around on the couch, I get myself positioned so I'm lying down on Blair's lap, my back against his legs. It's something I occasionally try to get away with, though he usually doesn't let me. Today, of course, he does.

"Where's Nolan?" I ask, looking up at Blair from the armrest.

"Hmmm. Must be with either Rita or Philip."

"Not with both?"

Blair shakes his head. "No way. Nolan's basically a child of divorce. Split custody and all that. Bouncing from one parent to the other."

"So, when you guys go back to New York in a few weeks, Nolan goes with your parents, right? In the city."

"Yep, poor guy. I wish I could have him at school, but, nah. Against the rules. He'll be in our city townhouse. My mom will take him on walks here and there, since my dad's always busy with work."

I picture the sweet golden retriever trotting around congested sidewalks, being pent up in one of those skinny city houses I've seen in movies. It makes me a little sad when I compare it to the way he gets to bound and speed all over the beach here.

"I'm going to miss him," I say.

Blair's gazing down at me, not saying anything. Like he's contemplating something. Mindlessly, I tug on the hem of my shirt, and I'm amazed to see Blair's eyes flicker to my chest for an instant.

"Blair."

"Hmm?"

I'm thinking about Christine's accusation last week, the one that made me so angry at the time.

"Have you ever had sex?"

Blair doesn't answer. He looks . . . jolted.

I press on: "What's it like?"

Now he seems perplexed.

170

"You didn't give me a chance to answer the first question."

"Well, I guess I just figured, because you're almost twenty . . . and you've been in college a whole year . . . *and* you're a guy . . ."

"I've never had sex," he says before I can keep going. And he shrugs. "So I can't tell you what it's like."

"Oh." I grow quiet. The revelation surprises me. "Well. That's okay. I guess I'll just ask Tim Redding to teach me what it's like."

When Blair's eyes grow wide, laughter spills from my mouth.

"I'm kidding. I already said I'm done with him, didn't I?"

"Sheesh, I don't know. I never really know with you, Roxie. You were going to let the kid be your first kiss."

"That was just a kiss, though. That's different than . . . At least, I assume it's a lot different . . ." I pause. "Do you think it'll be nice?"

"Sex?"

I nod my head. Blair's eyes are wandering over my face. I like the way it feels. I like the way that word sounds when he says it. I like it even more when he slips his fingers through my hair, over and over.

"Yeah," he says. "I think so. Roxie?"

"Yeah?"

"Don't let Tim Bedding be your first. Okay? Don't rush into anything."

"Why not?"

"You deserve better."

Blair's fingers in my hair, his words, are almost too much. *Could I get away with kissing him right now?* I wonder. *What if I sat up, leaned in, and simply brought my lips to his?*

That doesn't happen, though. There comes a sudden, clamorous sound from the kitchen, causing us both to jump off the couch and look around for the source.

The metal mixing bowl. Somehow, it's toppled over onto the kitchen floor. Blair and I both stand there, soaking up the new silence.

"Should we . . . do you fancy a walk into town maybe?"

"Sure," I reply. Clear my throat. "A walk. Fresh air. That's probably a good idea."

∞

The day keeps going, just the two of us, this new and easy feeling emanating between one another. It's like there were all these walls previously standing between us, tall and mighty—and now Blair is letting them crumble. Things are raw and real. He's treating me like his peer, not like a little kid. It's what I've wanted this whole summer, whether I knew it or not.

We stroll into town and go to a chocolate shop, where Blair buys me a blackberry truffle. We go to the mini golf course and end up cheating and laughing at each other's pathetic skills. I feel myself growing tired again, and Blair can see it. It catches me off guard when he suggests we grab some real food for dinner and go back to *my* house to eat. We always hang out at his place. But Christine is gone, so I don't mind heading over to Seawood Lane.

Thai food is what we end up with. Blair opens all the take-out boxes on Christine's coffee table while I get an old movie going on her small TV. It feels odd being here together, but here we are— positioned side by side on the loveseat, eating out of the same containers, as though this is something we've been doing for years.

While today has been wonderful, I feel my mind slipping throughout our movie. Slipping back to the reality of this day. August eighth. Maryanne Morah. The hole in my heart. The brokenness that can never be repaired.

That fact that she is still gone. Nowhere. Vanished from my world.

The movie ends. I get another one going right away. I want the distraction, want Blair to stay here with me for as long as possible. He doesn't object to the second showing. He pops a piece of Trident into his mouth and curls his arm around my shoulders. I scoot closer to him, let myself go lax into the hollow of his arm.

This distraction helps. It works. It soothes my mind, and I don't mean to drift off, but I do.

∞

When I wake up, it's dark. The movie's over. I tilt my head back to find that Blair fell asleep, too.

"Hey." I give him a little shake. Then another, harder one. "Blair. Wake up."

He stirs, comes to life.

"Oh. Hey. Did I conk out?"

"We both did."

"What time is it?"

I twist around to find the clock by the front door. "Almost nine."

I figure he's going to say he ought to head home. But he doesn't.

"Hey, listen. I had an idea, before I fell asleep. What if, and hear me out: you took Nolan at the end of summer?"

I feel my face twist up in confusion.

"What? How? Why?"

"All three excellent questions. Well, the way I see it, you'd be a much better owner than my dysfunctional parents. And Nolan loves it here. He loves the beach. And you. I think he'd be a lot happier. And maybe you'd like it, too. You said you're going to miss him."

I turn this over in my mind. "You think your parents would be on board with it?"

"Oh, no way. Not even a little. But I wouldn't ask for their permission. I'd be 'doing my own thing.' For once in my life."

"You would steal your parents' dog for me? That's kind of insane, Blair."

"Yep, that's me. Kind of insane. What do you think, though, really? You like Nolan. He's a good pal."

173

"I do like Nolan."

"Then, it's settled. Nolan becomes your new best friend when I leave in a few weeks."

I laugh, not sure if he's being serious. I think about what it'd be like to take Nolan on walks and watch him dart around by the ocean.

The images don't last long, however. There's a flash of Mama's body by the brambles, and I try to shut it out.

Blair hasn't said anything for a while, so I fill the silence.

"Blair. I'm really tired. I keep thinking about my mom. Today's been amazing, having you with me. But I think it's time for August eighth to end. I think I want to go to bed."

"Oh." His voice travels through the darkness. "Okay. Let me help you."

He rises and finds my hand to help me up. He leads me up the staircase and into my bedroom. He switches on a lamp, and I lower myself to the foot of my mattress.

Blair looks as tired as I feel, like today has been new and strange for him, as well. I'm expecting him to tell me goodnight and leave, but he doesn't. He sits beside me on the bed.

Then he murmurs soft words: "Will you tell me about her? Your mom."

I take in a deep breath. I close my eyes.

"She was perfect. She was beautiful. Even-tempered and kind to everyone. She could draw. Of course, she could bake. She was going to make me a blackberry cake for my next birthday. We were going to pick berries that August until our hands were purple. We had so many more days and cakes and berries ahead of us. She was everything to me. Then I lost her. I lost everything. I had to leave our little green Shoshone house on Wild Road. Christine sold it. I don't even know what happened to it. I don't know what happened to her."

I open my eyes, and Blair is focused on me with that somberness he has about him today. He pulls his phone out of his pocket, an idea suddenly occurring to him.

174

"I want you to hear something."

"Blair. I'm not really in the mood for Elton John right now."

"Not a song." He holds a finger in the air. "Something else. Here we go, I found it."

It's a poem. He says it's by a woman named Mary Elizabeth Frye. I haven't been exposed to much poetry throughout my life, but this is the most beautiful composition of words I think I've ever heard.

Blair reads:

"*Do not stand at my grave and weep /*
I am not there. I do not sleep."

The speaker says she is "*a thousand winds that blow*" and the "*diamond glints on snow.*"

She says she is the "*swift uplifting rush*" of birds bursting into flight. She is the "*soft stars that shine at night.*"

And the last line—it cuts me deep as Blair reads it.

"*Do not stand at my grave and cry; /*
I am not there. I did not die."

Blair sets his phone aside.

Hundreds of thorns prick at my heart all at once. There is the pain, and somehow, a sugar-sweetness along with it. I look over at Blair, and that's when the bleeding commences inside me. This prickling in my chest has been escalating with each summer day spent with him, and now I feel full cuts, deep and scary and beautiful.

"Thank you, Blair," I whisper. I could say more, but I leave it at that.

He moves closer to me. My heart pounds madly. He takes my waist in his hands, draws his face down toward mine.

He mumbles, "We'll pick berries together this month. Okay?"

I nod my head, barely able to speak. "And you'll come watch me perform tomorrow?"

He nods his head. His eyes are boring into mine. I smell his sweet mint. See his wayward blonde locks hovering over his eyebrows. Eyebrows that are knitted in concentration. Tenderly, he places his hand just over my heart, causing me to inhale. My heart's going crazy, and he can feel it. I can see it in his blue fire eyes—he feels it.

"Blair?"

"Yes?"

He looks at me. Keeps his hand on my bleeding, pounding chest. My words pour from that very spot, out through my mouth, into the warm air between us.

"I love you."

He looks at me. Looks at me. My heart will soon burst from my body.

He closes the space between us, dips his head down to mine. Kisses me.

Blair keeps his hand on my chest as he wets my lips with his, carefully, gently. I'm floating, everything in me is pulsing, the feel of Blair's sweet attention, tender and raw, like the song he taught me.

Then things change. Blair changes. The sweetness, gentleness is gone. A fervency comes over him—Blair grips my sides and presses his body onto mine. He slides me farther up the bed, eases me all the way down onto my back.

Sparks go flashing. Breathing heavy. Blair comes over me, kissing me with an intense heat. I let him have his way, feeling so many pent-up emotions come free. His hands are hot against my skin. It's overwhelming, but I don't want it to stop. Blair's hand caresses my thigh. He slips his tongue into my mouth.

It stops, not long after that. It doesn't go further. It's like Blair has to force himself to pull away, and everything cools down once he does. Sparks die down. Breathing normalizes. We sit back up. Blair runs his hand through my hair. Says goodnight. That he'll see me tomorrow, at my performance.

I fall asleep, but I'm already in a dream. My heartbeat feels steady. My mind at ease.

And somehow, some way, it's like the holes inside me have all been filled.

It's like I'm no longer broken.

30

Blair

The next morning, I hinge upward in my bed. I look out the window, toward the ocean. I sit there and watch the whitecaps. Sit and watch. Sit and watch.

For the first time this summer, I don't get a song going on my phone. No dancing or grooving. No singing or lip syncing. I just stay put in my bed. Quietly. Until I identify the sensation that has gradually crept over me. It's a new one for me, for a guy who's spent his whole life wrapped neatly in luxury and comfort and a happy lack of unknowns.

It's fear.

I'm afraid.

Last night—with Roxie. The whole day, really, but mostly last night. And what happened. What I let myself do.

What she said to me.

Nervous energy urges me to take in a very long, very deep breath. I clasp a hand to my forehead as though I have a gnarly headache coming on. Perhaps I do.

I can't think about this right now. I force myself out of bed, get dressed in strange silence, and I head over to the main house. Why? I'm not sure. To find something that distracts me from the two damn Blairs in my head, probably.

Both my parents are in the house. Nolan's sleeping in his bed. My mom's on the sofa, drink in hand. My dad's on his laptop at the kitchen counter. Something feels different here. They both look oddly at peace, while simultaneously existing in each other's presence. What kind of witchcraft could this be?

Rita is first to notice me.

"Morning, Blair Bear," she croaks. I try not to cringe at the cheesy pet name. She only calls me that when she's really pleased about something.

"Top of the morning to you guys. What's up? Something going on?"

Rita says: "It'll just be you and me soon, turns out."

"Come again?" I stand in a spot halfway between my mother and father, clasping a hand to my forehead again.

"I'm heading to back to New York early." It's Philip who clarifies things for me. "I need to get back ASAP. Something's come up with the company."

"ASAP," I repeat. "How ASAP we talking?"

"Today," Rita announces, raising her drink in the air. Then she scowls at my dad. "It always goes this way, doesn't it, Blair? Only it stopped bothering me ten years ago. Give or take."

"Funny," my dad voices. "I seem to feel increasingly bothered over the years."

Ignore the toxic banter, ignore the toxic banter . . .

"Wait, so—really? Dad, you're leaving today?"

"Driving back to Portland this afternoon. Fly out of PDX at six. Get into JFK five hours later."

"But I told him," Mom chimes in, "I'm staying here. We have this place booked eighteen more nights. I'm not wasting that. I told him: you and I can just stay, Blair."

"Oh. Right. Alrighty."

Mom again: "And I think I'll treat myself to an afternoon at the spa today. I better call to make sure they can squeeze me in."

"Spa day. Right. Good. Great."

In a choppy, restless fashion, I move into the kitchen and find a bottle of ibuprofen. I swallow four of them without water. My dad is looking at me. Which feels weird. Usually his visual preference involves a screen.

"Something up, Pops?"

He stands up and comes round the counter so he's hovering above me. A rough hand claps my shoulder. His voice is hushed so my mom can't hear:

"I know you haven't been able to spend as much time in Manhattan as you'd like this last year, Blair. What with you going off to Cornell and all. I know that's been disappointing for you."

This is true. All facts. I cannot dispute them.

"Then, you've been trapped here in God-Knows-Where, Oregon all summer. Next thing you know, you'll be right back at Cornell."

Again, all true. All facts. I give a subtle nod to show I'm tracking.

"Well," he says. "I'm sure I could manage a second ticket on this flight. You could get some extra time in the City before school starts up."

I glance upward, to my father's sharp eyes, wondering if I'm understanding him right. There's the nasty biting at my skull, chiseled teeth that nip and gnaw.

"You could leave with me today." Philip states it plain and simple. I stand there, not responding, so he says, "Listen. You don't have to decide right away. I'll get you the ticket in case you want to tag along. I'm taking off at two this afternoon. But it's up to you. Whatever you decide."

Back in my guest house, I pace around the front room, and I can't stop. I pace and I pace and I fiddle my fingers together and I squeeze my head as hard as I can. I pull out my pack of gum but it's empty; I'm all out; I swear and toss the packet to the floor.

Roxie's performance is today. She's playing the song we spent hours working on together. Variation V. She's playing it in her deceased mother's dress.

I told her I would be there.

And she told me . . . Last night . . . She said she . . .

I can't think straight right now. I wasn't thinking straight last night, either. She said what she did, and I . . . kissed her. Not like I did before, at the blackberry bushes, or on the beach.

The blackberry bushes. We're supposed to pick berries together.

I don't know what to think right now. There's only one thing I know, and it's the fear, and it's making my head scream at me, the wail of a thousand off-key banshees.

Roxie told me she loves me.

Her performance.

The berries.

She loves me.

I release my grip on my skull. Deep inside me, I know what I'm going to do.

31

Roxie

Jitters shimmy up and down my insides. My legs feel like jelly, and my hands are clammy. At the same time, though, I'm confident. I know I can do this.

It's the big competition. Tangle Beach's annual Ocean Festival. I'm standing behind the stage they set up on the main drag in town. The crowd is enormous. How did Mama do this four years in a row? I'm fairly certain I'll only be able to do it this once.

A senior from my school named Kaylee Hicks is on stage right now. She's playing the piano, too, for her talent, so I'm scheduled to perform right after her. Really, it's a digital keyboard they have for us, since it was too impractical to get an actual piano.

Chelsea Bradshaw, the nasty queen bee from my grade, turned out to be in the competition, as well. She already performed. Her talent was singing "My Heart Will Go On," karaoke-style. Honestly, it was the hardest thing for me to keep myself from busting out laughing. I can't wait to make fun of it with Blair when this is all over.

Kaylee's performance concludes. There's a big wave of applause. My jitters get totally, off-the-charts wild. But I'm ready. I'm wearing Mama's lavender halter dress. I dabbed on some makeup, the way I did for my date with Tim. I even used Christine's curling iron, although my curls have relaxed now more than I'd like.

The event coordinator ushers me up to the side of the stage as Kaylee whisks past me, looking entirely relieved. I can't wait to feel that way myself.

Someone announces me over an echoey microphone: *Please welcome Roxanne Morah, an upcoming sophomore here at Tangle Beach High School.*

I can do this. I walk out onto the stage, into view of all these people, all these faces. I make it to the keyboard without tripping in my low heels, and I remind myself the two reasons I can, in fact, do this.

One: it's for her, to honor her beautiful soul, to strive to become more like her.

And two: Blair is out there in the crowd. He's watching me, and I'll get to see him once this is done.

The performance is a hazy blur, and all of a sudden, I realize I've finished. It's over. I did it. There's applause, and I leave the stage. I can't remember if I messed up at all, hit the wrong key or fumbled through the trills. But that's okay. It wasn't about being perfect, and I have never had expectations to win. It was just about *doing* it.

After the remaining girls perform, we're all summoned up to the stage at the same time. The final time. The Ocean Princess has been decided by the panel of judges. So have the first and second runners-up.

Three names are called. Kaylee Hicks, the senior from my school. Another senior, this one from Seaside, a girl named Anna Cho. And the third name makes my stomach drop. Because it's mine.

Now, I'm standing and sweating at the front of the stage next to Kaylee and Anna. This doesn't make any sense to me, but it's happening, and I wonder if Blair is laughing right now, able to perceive my total shock from down in the crowd.

Second runner-up. The announcer has just pronounced me second runner-up. Third place. There's a sash draped over me, and a bouquet of hydrangeas handed to me, and I'm hardly paying attention when Anna Cho is crowned this year's Ocean Princess, when celebratory music bursts out from the speakers.

Second runner-up. The competition is finally over and done with, and somehow, I was actually placed in the top three, amidst the whole county. I'm amazed. I'm in awe.

I know this would've made her proud.

As soon as the event people get pictures and say I'm free to go, I run around the stage and discover that the crowd has thinned out drastically. Almost everyone has cleared out to head one street over, where there are all kinds of booths and games and food. I run around the main drag in my sash, holding my hydrangeas, beaming as big as I ever have beamed.

I'm jumping out of my skin to find Blair. I can't wait to see him again. I can't wait to jump into his arms and hear his laugh. To have him kiss me again, here in the street. I want to kiss him all day long and not even talk about last night—just embrace the changes and roll with the tide.

Where is he? I stop and stand on my toes, pivot around to scour the remaining bodies still lingering about. There's no funny blonde hair that I can see. I keep looking, maneuvering around clusters of tourists who congratulate me on my way by. I'm no longer running. Just walking. Stumbling. More and more aimless. More and more rattled. More and more worried.

I call out his name into the sunny, windy street. The crowd keeps whittling down, thinning out, and I shield the sun from my eyes, calling his name another time.

My breathing has become labored. Faint moisture burns in my eyes. I'm standing there in the nearly empty road, my bouquet dangling by my hip, my sash loose over the lavender dress. My chest is growing tight and painful.

I drop my flowers to the asphalt. Something sickly swims in my stomach. It's like that feeling I got while watching Mama from my bedroom window. The knowledge that sinks in:

Something isn't right.

I cannot find him anywhere.

Blair is not here.

∞

I'm full-on panicked as I sprint down the road lined with beach-view vacation homes. I don't care that I'm wearing low-heeled sandals and a dress and a sash that threatens to fall off and blow away with the wind. I go as fast as I can, faster, faster, faster.

I'm rasping by the time I get to the driveway, up to the door of the guest house, and I don't bother knocking or ringing the bell. I burst inside and move through the front room, past the piano and kitchen, into the bedroom, the bathroom, back around to the front. Nothing. No one. And none of his stuff.

I run across the driveway and try the front door of the main house. It's locked. I go around the side and find the sliding glass door has been overlooked. I run inside and search every room. No one.

Back on the driveway, it hits me that the rental car, the silver Porsche, is missing. I stand there, feeling the sun beat down on me, the wind whip at me, hearing the ocean call behind me. I stare at the two empty houses.

My chest is heaving, burning. My throat swells and aches. I think I'm on the verge of hyperventilating. I wipe at my eyes and my hands come away black with mascara.

I take in the sight of the emptiness.

And then, suddenly, I can't stand it anymore—my mind is careening—my confusion is stabbing into me like a thousand tiny needles—and I can't stay here another second, beholding these empty houses, the way the guest house stands there with no one, not a soul, inside.

I back away and turn to run home.

∞

People see me on my way to Seawood Lane. They give me funny looks. I am the girl dressed up as small-town royalty, running through the streets, tears streaming down her face.

But I don't care if they see. I don't care what they think. I get into Christine's house. Slam the door behind me. And I sink to the floor.

My whole body convulses as I sob like a child. My mind is a mess. I can't make sense of anything. In a fit of flummoxed anger, I rip the stupid sash from my body and throw it across the room.

I want to transport myself to the wooded lot right now, to the blackberries, but my energy is all spent. Instead, I make myself get up and stagger through the house, out into the microscopic backyard.

What I find there makes me gasp. I feel the very largest, the very sharpest of thorns puncture deep into the center of my bruised and tender heart.

It's Nolan. Tied up to a fence post. A bowl of food and water sitting beside him.

The happy retriever springs up when he sees me, smiles as I slowly approach him. I collapse onto the grass and run a shaky hand over the dog's gorgeous, sunlit coat.

There's something else there on the ground: a handpicked bundle of wildflowers.

Nolan licks my hand. I look at the wildflowers. This is when I know, beyond the shadow of a doubt. I wrap my arms around Nolan's furry neck, and I cry. I feel disbelief hit me in waves, I feel pain bleeding all inside me. It hurts. It hurts so much I can hardly breathe.

Blair has left.

Blair is gone.

Where are you?

How can it be that you are nowhere to be found?

How can it be that you have altogether disappeared?

Where did you go?

Part Two

New York City

—TEN YEARS LATER—

32

Blair

Thanksgiving. Central Park outside the windows. Scent of cinnamon and turkey. Stiff conversation ricocheting about the table. People I don't know well. Except for one.

Not to sound un-American, but normally I despise Thanksgiving. That's because it tends to come with both my parents attached, despite the fact that Rita and Philip officially split up years and years ago. (No surprise there, right?) Yet, for some baffling reason, they insist on the three of us getting together for the holidays. As though we're still that happy, healthy family unit that never actually existed.

But, anyway. This year's different. Because this year, I'm spending Thanksgiving with a different family. Whose, you might ask? Allison Waterhouse's.

Now, I'm getting ahead of myself here, I know. Let me back things up, hit the rewind button, take some time explaining all that's happened over the last ten years.

The short answer is: Not much. Not much has happened.

Ten years is a long time, I know, but I honestly don't have oodles to report. Here's what went down:

I completed my MBA at Cornell, graduating at the age of twenty-four.

I made my return to the City—finally, after all those interminable, bland years trapped in Ithaca.

I went straight to work at Porter Publishing House. I've been busy performing a whole variety of different roles there over the past six years. All at the direction of my father, who is still eyeballs-deep in work as he ever was.

To top all that dull mumbo jumbo off, I turned thirty this year, just a couple months ago.

Can you believe it? I, Blair Porter, am now thirty years of age. The big 3-0. The *dirty thirty*. Or is it *flirty thirty*? You get the point.

I can hardly believe it myself. I don't *feel* thirty. I still feel like the same nineteen-verging-on-twenty-year-old I was when you first had the distinct pleasure of meeting me.

"Blair? Dark or white meat?"

"Blair only eats white meat, Dad," Allison answers for me.

Oh, yes. And Allison. How could I forget? Allison Waterhouse: my girlfriend. My girlfriend of six years.

"It doesn't have to be white meat," I speak up for myself. "I could take a leg, or a wing, or whatever nobody else cares for."

I take in the sight of Allison's bald father carving the huge, golden turkey. Her mother's also present at the table, as well as her sister and brother-in-law. Allison's parents dwell in an Upper East Side duplex, smack dab on Park Avenue. The view out the window keeps calling to me. I resist the urge to focus on that tantalizing glimpse of Central Park.

"Give him white meat," Allison says, and I have to smile at her. She knows me too well. That'll happen when you're in a relationship with someone as long as we've been.

Our Thanksgiving dinner with the Waterhouses proceeds nicely. But then, during dessert, Allison's father opts to stir things up a bit.

"Ally. You and White-Meat-Blair decide on a wedding date yet?"

Flakes of pie crust sneak down into my trachea. I cough to clear them, sip some water, cough again. Everyone at the table is looking at me.

"Quit it, Dad," is all Allison says.

It's always like this when we visit her folks. She's used to it; I, on the other hand, have never really adapted to such questions.

"Guess I'll ask again next year," he prods, but Allison simply shakes her head side to side.

Afterward, we are free to leave Park Avenue, and so we happily depart, exchanging hugs and handshakes with her family one last time. We both propel ourselves down the sidewalk, toward the subway.

Oh, man: New York in November. Is it even possible for me to fall deeper in love with this city? Evidently so, because it seems to happen every year.

Right now, the air is brisk, the trees are nearly bare, and everyone's bundled up in scarves and coats. Of course, I love this city in every bewitching season it provides, but today I'm convinced late fall is the finest, most bewitching season of them all.

"I hate it when Dad says shit like that."

Allison has her hands tucked away in coat pockets. Her black hair is tucked beneath a beret. Her lips are cherry-red, and I can't remember the last time I kissed them.

"I wouldn't sweat it. You handle him swell," I tell her.

I should clarify something really fast, before I get ahead of myself again: Allison Waterhouse and I are *not* engaged. There is no ring encircling her left finger. There is no "wedding date" upon the horizon, as her father implied. He just wishes there were. And he isn't the only one.

"He's not wrong, though, Blair."

Allison is not looking at me. She will not make eye contact, so I give up and admire an old cathedral as we pass it by.

"We've talked about this, Ally," I say, to which she just replies: "I know."

The subway delivers us to our neck of the woods, the West Village. It is the essence of charm, with all its brownstones and brick townhomes lined up in a medley of colors: clays and browns, creams and blacks. Trendy restaurants, coffee shops, music and comedy clubs are nestled into the cultured scene. Trees line the surprisingly calm roads; ivy climbs aged building walls and stair rails.

Allison wanted to live here, because, well, she's a writer. She fits right in with this crowd. I appreciate the Village's history with music (how could I not?), so I, too, moved into the neighborhood. Just—not into the same apartment as Allison.

I drop Allison off at the door to her building, beneath the ritzy-black awning. She's still upset, in her quiet, stoic way. That's been happening a lot lately. I can't say I blame her. When I go to kiss her red lips, she turns away, giving me her cheek instead.

Before I go, she says something.

"Will you ever be ready, Blair?"

I know what she's talking about. The same thing her dad was talking about at dinner. The same thing that keeps coming up more and more often, the longer we stay together.

"Of course, Ally. It's like I said—I just don't see the rush."

"Most people would say six years isn't rushing. I wish you'd just tell me the real reason you won't propose."

I undo the top button of my coat, suddenly too warm out in the freezing night air.

"Tell you what," I say. "We can go look at rings next week. If you want."

"Again?" She sounds annoyed. "What's the point if you're not going to buy one?"

I sigh. I don't like this tension. I want everything to simply be okay between us. I'll do what I have to in order to make it so.

"I mean it, Ally. Let's go look at rings together. We can get you sized, too."

She holds my stare—holds it—holds it—then breaks into a little almost-grin.

"Next week?" she says.

"Next week," I confirm.

And I head back to my own apartment a few blocks up, knowing I've slapped a Band-Aid on things.

For now.

I know what you're thinking. I know what you're wondering about.

I've gotten you mostly caught up on the gist of my present life—but there's one topic I've been conveniently avoiding.

Don't worry. I'll get to it eventually. Just . . . not quite yet.

Back home at my own apartment, the first thing I do is get some music going. I have a record player nowadays, and there's just no beating the real, analogue deal. Tonight, I select a Carole King album, and I flop on my bed that's situated against a brick wall.

Here's one thing that's changed about me over the years: I don't listen to music in the mornings anymore. I don't wake up and get dressed to ELO or Paul Simon or Elton John.

There's no time for that, for one thing, with my job. But more than that . . . I just stopped feeling the urge, the drive, the beat, in that exhilarating way I used to.

Nowadays, I listen to music at night. Like I'm doing right now. And I don't dance to it. I don't change my clothes. I just lie in bed, still and quiet, not even singing along. I close my eyes. I let my mind wander to the past.

And I remember her.

I remember that summer. Ten years ago (how is that even possible?) in little Tangle Beach.

Flashes of it come back to me.

The frisbee. The girl.

The piano lessons. The baking sessions.

The thorn whipping at my heel; the feel of blood slipping down my skin.

The sound of her voice saying my name.

The feel of the ocean around my legs. Her hand in mine. Roxie's hand.

It's overwhelming, every time I do this to myself. Every time I remember. It brings me joy, at first, reliving that long-ago summer. But eventually, I come down from the high. And there's always a nasty little emotional crash waiting for me at the bottom. Always.

So, this is what you want to know, right? This is what you've been wondering about. Her. Roxie. And what I did.

This is the part of my night where I switch the record over to a different one. One that plays Sonata No. 11, as performed by Mitsuko Uchida. I listen to the whole thing but pay close attention to Variation V.

I left Tangle Beach, the day of her performance. I jumped ship that fateful day ten years ago. And I understand if you hate me now. Because, the thing is, I rather hate myself.

I wish I could go back to that summer. God, I wish I could go back. It is the very epitome of nostalgia for me, of longing, of pining, of regret. I didn't appreciate it while I had it, and now that it's gone, I'd give anything to wake up by the Pacific Ocean again and teach Roxie Morah some Mozart at the baby grand.

If only I'd understood to hang on to each and every moment of those days. If only I'd been brave enough to stay put even one day longer.

When the Sonata is over, I open my eyes, and I come back to the present. To reality.

The reality is, I left Tangle Beach—I left *Roxie*—and that was the end of that story. Countless times, I considered trying to contact her, to apologize, to hear her voice one more time. Even now—especially now—I dream up plans as to how I might find her and contact her. Yet, no matter how much I daydream, I can never get up the courage. I am simply too scared. I am sure she hates me, just as I hate myself, through and through.

That summer is gone. Roxie is gone. I closed that book and burned it. I moved on with my life.

And, in my final year of college, I met Allison.

Allison Waterhouse. Back when we met, she was finishing up an MFA program at Cornell, while I was wrapping up my MBA. She was nice and cute and wanted to get a cup of coffee with me one morning. She was from Manhattan. Of a similar background and family (aka: wealthy parents). She played the cello. And, she was the same age as me.

It was easy with Allison from the start. I would say it still *is* easy, only, I have to admit, the road has finally grown a bit rocky for the two of us.

It's normal for people to get married at our age. I get that. It's normal for people to get married when they've been together for six straight years. I get that, too. At the very minimum, it's normal for people like us to be living together by this stage in the relationship.

Yet—no matter how normal all of that is—I seem to exhibit a severe case of abnormality. And Allison can tell. She's no dummy. She's a published author and hosts writing workshops at NYU every Saturday. She wants to get married, move forward, and she can see something is holding me back.

She doesn't know what that something is. But, to be honest, I'm not sure I really know, either.

I lie in bed, and I think about all this. I promised her we'd go ring-browsing next week. I said it to relieve tension, to keep the peace. But, maybe I shouldn't view it that way. Maybe I should be serious about it. Maybe I shouldn't merely browse, like we've done in the past.

Maybe I ought to finally pull the trigger. Buy a damn ring. Pop the damn question.

I get up to brush my teeth and properly hit the hay. I had today off from work, with it being a holiday and all, but tomorrow I'll be back at the Publishing House. No rest for the wicked, as they say. No rest for a Porter man, as I've learned on a firsthand basis (unless your first name is Graham, who is still AWOL most of the time, in case you were curious).

Back in bed, under my covers, I think about that summer just one last time before drifting off.

With a backdrop of the crashing ocean, I see her glowing face.

33

Roxie

Growing up, I couldn't wait to be older. To break out of my adolescent limbo, the highly annoying *in-between* stage. To become a fully legitimate, no-doubt-about-it adult.

Well, now I am one. And, it turns out, being twenty-five isn't all that different than being fifteen.

It's still seriously annoying.

I thought it'd be different. Worlds different. But, as I've learned, people still treat you with that same inconsistency I remember from being a teenager. One minute, people say you're still just a kid. Just an irresponsible millennial flailing through their twenties, making mistake after silly mistake, too young and inexperienced to be trusted and relied upon.

The next minute—you're only a stone's throw from thirty, practically a middle-aged adult, and you really ought to have your life figured out by now, shouldn't you?

So, yes. Me at twenty-five. I'm as responsible as I was at fifteen, though mistakes are admittedly made here and there. I am undeniably approaching thirty years old (which only scares me a little bit). And as for my life? Do I have it *figured out*?

That's the one question I can never quite seem to figure out.

∞

My alarm goes off at 5 a.m. sharp. I'm still an early riser. But the rest of my morning routine has changed over the years.

I don't open my bedroom window. The air outside is the furthest thing from fresh, and there's not a drop of peace and quiet to be found out there.

I don't make an entry in my journal. I stopped doing that ten years ago. Truthfully, I don't even know where that journal is anymore.

And, lastly, I don't go running. I just don't see the point in it these days. I have nowhere to run to, and it stopped giving me that sense of control I used to find in it.

I gave all these things up, my morning rituals, because they were childish. Naive. Pointless. It was something I realized back at fifteen. My eyes were opened. Lightning flashed, and suddenly I could see just how childish and naive and pointless all that silly ritual-stuff was.

Me at fifteen . . . I never could've predicted the way my life would turn out. I never in a million years would've thought I'd end up where I am today. Or with the person I am today.

He tosses around in bed beside me. I push at his shoulder and he moans.

"Hey," I say. "We gotta get up. Come on."

"Must sleep," he groans back at me.

"No. Must work. It's our first day on set. You're always saying first impressions are everything."

That gets him to sit up and rub around his eyes.

"All right. I'm up. I'll get the smoothies made if you want to get our clothes picked out?"

I wince. "Other way around. Your fashion sense is always a notch above mine. You know that."

"I won't tell anyone on set you said that," he laughs.

Thirty minutes later, we're dressed and groomed and fueled from our green protein smoothies. We lock the apartment door behind us, clamber down the stairs, and burst out into the frigid, noisy, rushing world.

On the way up the block, he says: "Are you nervous for your first day?" I can see wispy tendrils of his breath in the air.

"No," I lie.

"Maybe we should check out Washington Square Park tonight. We haven't been yet. What do you think? Roxie?"

I haven't been listening very well, but I snap my attention over to him at the sound of my name. I try to go by *Roxanne* these days, but he gets a pass. He's known me too long to call me anything else.

"Yeah. Sure," I say. "Fine by me."

We descend into the urban underworld of the subway station. It will bullet us toward Central Park.

Fifteen-year-old Roxie would be shocked, all right.

She'd be shocked to know that ten years into the future, she would find herself living in New York City.

With Tim Redding.

How did it happen?

It's a question I ask myself nearly every day of my adult life. How did I end up here—what decisions did I make to get myself on this unexpected path—*how* did this happen?

Actually, I know all the answers to these questions. I am constantly and extremely aware of the way everything has unfolded for me over the last decade. And I have my reasons for all of it.

All of it. All of it goes back to that August. The August I was fifteen years old. The August my world fell apart for the second time around, an event I thought was only supposed to happen just the once, back when I was twelve. But I'd been wrong, and the second collapse was, in some ways, worse than the first.

I started up school that September, my sophomore year of high school. And Tim was there. He found me on our very first day back. He caught up with me in the parking lot, trying to ask me about my summer, wanting to inform me he'd gotten his driver's license last month.

Naturally, my first instinct was to blow him off. I'd had my fill of boy drama for the year—for a whole lifetime and then some. But Tim Redding persisted in chatting me up in the parking lot, eventually concluding with:

"I had a really nice time with you at the pizza parlor this summer. Maybe I'm way off base, but I thought it seemed like you had a nice time, too." He paused. Then, "I'm having a party this Friday at my house. If you want to come . . . well, it'd be cool to see you."

He left me alone after that, for the remainder of the week.

At first, of course, I had scoffed at the idea of going to Tim's party. But as the week went on, I kept thinking about it. I kept thinking about how complicated things had been this summer (with *him*—The Tourist Who Shall *Not* Be Named). I kept thinking about how angry I was about everything that happened back in August. How everything I thought I knew had collapsed on me.

So, that Friday, I went to the party.

I went to Tim's house, and I found him inside. It was my anger, my confusion and wounds that had driven me there. And there Tim Redding was. Waiting for me in the corner of a room. Happy to see me. I knew because of the way he smiled at me, and because he told me so.

"Hey, Roxie," he said at one point. "You know that New York tourist guy you were hanging around with this summer? What was his name again?"

My stomach soured, churned. My chest ached.

"Doesn't matter," I responded.

"Not to pry, but," Tim said, "I could never really tell. You guys were just friends, right?"

I did my best to ignore the oily-swimmy feeling in my gut, the pain that persisted deep in my chest.

"No," I said. Tim looked confused. I elaborated: "We weren't even that."

And I kissed Tim Redding on the mouth.

My fate was sealed that night, with that kiss. Tim and I became a thing. A couple. We've been together ever since.

Well—more or less. On and off. There have been times over the years we mutually chose to "take a break," "get some space," have some "time apart." There have even been times I swore I was done with the relationship for good.

But, at the end of the day, Tim was—Tim *is*—always there. Waiting for me. Happy to see me. And so I've always fallen back into that safety net, the familiarity, the simplicity of him, of *us*.

We went to college together after graduating from Tangle Beach High. He wanted to go to Pacific University in Forest Grove, about an hour's drive inland. I had never given college much thought up until that point, never had any preconceived notions about it, so I simply jumped on board. Ethan ended up going to Pacific with us, too. *Costco Ethan,* as he had been referred to back in our high school days. So, it was the three of us struggling to figure out college life together.

And struggle we did. It took each of us a long time to figure things out. I kept changing my major just about every semester, because I was directionless and felt totally alien inside the academic world.

College hadn't been part of my plan, originally. My plan, growing up, had always been to open a bakery. But that one, wretched August had derailed everything. After that, I became clueless and lost. Nothing was the same for me; nothing made sense anymore.

I stopped baking. I stopped dreaming about a *someday* bakery. I even stopped trying to get Christine to let me do the Lace & Tide wedding cakes—but that's a story for another time.

Anyway. It took me six long years to finish a degree. And at the end of it all, I had majored in psychology, and I was as directionless and clueless as I'd been at the start.

Tim completed his theatre degree shortly before I finished my bachelor's in psychology. Ethan never actually completed a degree and decided to call the whole thing quits, *finito*, "enough is fricking enough," as he so eloquently put it.

After that, we all worked random jobs in Forest Grove for about a year, trying to pay off college debt. It turned out, when Christine sold my old house in Shoshone, she had put the humble proceeds into a college savings account for me. It hadn't covered all of my tuition, but combined with grants and scholarships, it had helped me steer mostly clear of student loans. Still, there were plenty of bills to pay, and that final year in Forest Grove flew by.

And then, just five months ago, Tim asked me a question.

Tim had always dreamed of being an actor one day. He'd been actively engaged in the local theatre community over the past six years. He would drive into Portland from time to time, hoping to make connections and find his break in the city.

Finally, he realized it wasn't going to be enough. The city of Portland wasn't going to cut it, and the small town of Forest Grove certainly wasn't. Tim asked me if I would be willing to move somewhere else with him, somewhere he could really have a shot at living out his dream.

And so, in May this year, at twenty-five years old, I moved across the country, turned a very new leaf, and began my life in New York, New York.

Oh—and Ethan, of course, third-wheeled it like always, making the move with me and Tim.

So, that's how all of this happened. I mean, I *am* leaving out some details. There is more to the story. But for now, this account will suffice. Right now, on this cold morning at the tail-end of November, I'm about to start my first day at a new job. A new job that Tim helped me secure.

I need to be in the present, need to stay focused and sharp and ready. Because I've learned to accept what Tim always says, just like I've learned to accept a lot of his takes on life: first impressions are everything.

∞

Okay. So. It's not lost on me that I'm residing in *his* city. The land of The Tourist Who Shall Not Be Named. Voldemort's very birthplace; Satan's very realm.

I refuse to say his name. I refuse to even think it. I've worked hard, I've done my best, to bury him away, to bury every song and look and touch. Every fluttering heartbeat, each pang of heartbreak.

Yet, here I am, in his homeland. He always talked about how much he loved this place. He wouldn't shut up about it, sometimes. And now I'm here, seeing it for myself, and although I've never considered myself a city person, this place does have its upsides.

When I first arrived five months ago, I felt like the tiniest, most miniscule, little bug. The city was so much bigger than my brain ever could have conceived of. I couldn't believe the vastness of it, the density of it, and I thought I might get swallowed up forever. Or just plain squashed.

Now, I've had some time to adjust. Once work is done for the day, Tim and I go check out a vegan restaurant and visit Washington Square Park. I've seen this arch, this fountain, in movies growing up, and now, I'm meeting them in the flesh.

Part of me knows I will always be a small-town girl at heart, but I'm trying to wear this city like a new pair of fancy, stiff high heels. They always hurt at first, these stupid shoes—they provoke blisters upon your skin—they may even draw blood—but eventually, if you stick with them long enough, you *will* break them in.

I *will* break in this city. I *will* push through the blisters and the blood. I will make this work.

We go back home after a while, me and Tim. We live in Hell's Kitchen, because it's one of the only neighborhoods we can afford. We climb up to the fifth floor, entering into our two-bedroom, seven-hundred-and-fifty square-foot apartment. Tim and I have one of the bedrooms for ourselves, while Ethan shares the other with his new-ish girlfriend, Mischa.

Ethan and Mischa are both lounging in the front room when Tim and I shuffle into the warmth of our crammed home. Ethan looks over his shoulder at us.

"You're home late," he states.

Tim says, "Yeah, we grabbed some dinner. Did some exploring." We shed our coats, scarves, hats. Mischa is reading a book and has barely registered our presence as far as I can tell, but Ethan perks up at what Tim just said.

"Dinner? Any chance you brought some back for us?"

"No, you leech." Tim throws his beanie at Ethan's face; Ethan successfully dodges it.

"Hey, come on now, buddy. I'm legit starving over here."

Tim says, "Then move your ass down to one of the eight restaurants on our block. And anyway, Roxie and I ate at a vegan place. You wouldn't have liked it."

Ethan makes a face.

Tim turns to me, saying: "I'm spent. I think I'm just going to crash out. Want to join?"

"In a bit," I say. Tim kisses me on the head, then makes sure to give Ethan a shove on the shoulder before disappearing into our bedroom.

"All right, then, dammit." Ethan stands from the couch, stretches his lower back. "I'll go venture out for some food. Mischa, what sounds good?"

Mischa doesn't look up from her book but arches an eyebrow in thought.

"Cheese," she voices.

"Cheese." Ethan considers this. "Yeah, cheese does sound good. Crazy vegans and their lack of cheese. I'll go see what I can find."

On his way past me toward the door, he ruffles the top of my head. I bat his hand away. It's our little routine I've gotten used to over the years.

"Roxie. Did your first day go all right?"

205

"Um, yeah. Good enough."

"Good, good. Our little Timmy's going to light up the whole city, isn't he? Guess that's why they call it The City of Lights."

"That's Paris, Ethan," I correct him.

"Paris Shmaris." And he heads out the door.

I'm tired. My feet ache. So do my hips. But I don't want to go to bed quite yet. Everything's been so busy and crazy lately, I just want a moment of peace while I'm still conscious. I tread across the faded oak floors and drop into a chair beside the old, closed-off fireplace. Mischa, surprisingly, sets her book down and eyes me. She does so for a while, not saying anything. Just looking at me. Assessing me.

Then, she says:

"You don't like it here, do you?"

Her question jars me, causes me to scrutinize her more carefully. She's sitting cross-legged in her chair. Her outfit: a dark sweater with a big, yellow smiley face on it (ironic, because I've never witnessed her smile in real life) and a long, green, snake print skirt.

Mischa, I've learned from experience, rides the line between offbeat and off-putting. Personally, I really like that about her. She's grown on me a surprising amount over the past couple months that she's been living with us. I don't know how Ethan met her or managed to catch her interest—I really don't. She was born in Russia and has the faintest accent remaining. She dyes her hair silver and doesn't seem to care what anyone thinks of her. In some ways, she reminds me of my younger self.

"The apartment?" I respond. "I like it okay. I don't think we could do any better for the money."

"You don't like it *here*." Mischa points out the window, indicating the city, now cloaked in darkness but ever as restless.

I stiffen in my chair. "That's not true."

"I think you miss Oregon," Mischa goes on.

"I do *not* miss Oregon," I push back. "Not even a little."

"I think you do."

"I don't." And I mean it. I left that place behind, and I have no intentions of ever going back.

Mischa looks at me with her intense eyes—they are the eyes of a wild, keen creature.

"Okay," she chirps, and she picks up her book again, dissolving away from our conversation.

I get up. I really should get a head start on my sleep, like Tim's doing. This new job is kind of ruthless, and I can't make Tim look bad, since he's the one who got me this spot.

"Enjoy your cheese with Ethan," I say to my off-putting roommate. "See you tomorrow."

"*Spoki,* Roxie."

That's her way of saying goodnight in Russian. I like the sound of it, but something about her foreign words always reminds me how far away from Tangle Beach, Oregon I really am.

I linger in the front room a moment longer.

"*Spoki,* Mischa."

34

Roxie

It was the second worst day of my life. The day *he* left without a trace.

I guess it's not accurate to say *without a trace*. Because there was Nolan. And the wildflowers he presumably had picked for me, leaving them behind in my backyard, messy and tangled and dry.

I had stayed out there in the backyard with Nolan for a long time. I'm not sure how long it was. Hours. I had fallen asleep at one point, only to wake up and find myself hurting all over again.

At some point, I went into the house. I brought Nolan and his food and water with me. My stomach grumbled; I hadn't eaten all day, but the thought of forcing food into my body sounded like too much work.

I climbed the stairs and got into bed. I let Nolan jump up and rest beside me. I cried into my pillow until nightfall and then some.

All I could think about was my pain. My shock. Him. Our previous night together, on the anniversary of Maryanne's death.

I had truly believed that night was going to be the start of something real between us. I'd thought the very last wall keeping us apart had suddenly toppled down—no more boundaries—just a new beginning—after I opened my heart up to him that night. After he kissed me the way he did.

But it hadn't been the start to anything. It had been the end. Everything good and valuable in my life—it seemed such things were always bound to come to a sharp and painful ending. I was meant to be unhappy. I was meant to be alone.

"Roxie?"

I snapped my head up from my soaked pillow. Nolan craned his head, too. It was Christine. She was back home from the wedding expo in Portland. Standing in my doorway. Beholding me in my disastrous state.

"Go away," I said, burying my face back into the wet pillowcase.

But she didn't. She rushed to my side at the bed. She didn't even ask what the golden retriever was doing in her house, in my bed.

"What happened?" she said.

"Nothing."

"Something happened."

"Leave me alone," I mumbled into the bed.

"Cut it out, Roxie. I haven't seen you this upset since . . . Just tell me what's wrong."

"No."

"Roxie."

"You were right, okay?" I rolled over in order to spit the words out. I saw the concern lining Christine's pretty features. "You were right about Blair. He's gone. I never should've gotten involved with him. You were *right*."

I hated admitting it. I was certain the next words I'd be hearing from her were something along the lines of, *I told you so*. But that's not what I heard.

"I'm sorry."

I looked at her. And I could see: she meant it. She wasn't working to spin this into something against me. Wasn't using it to feel self-righteous or vindicated. She really was just . . . sorry.

And then—she hugged me. I let her hug me. It was the strangest thing. I tucked my arms beneath hers, and I let myself cry on her shoulder. Next thing I knew, I was telling Christine everything that happened. It just spilled out of me, like I needed to get it out of my mind, out of my body, so that maybe it wouldn't hurt me so much.

That didn't happen. The pain didn't stop. Not for a long, long time.

It was funny, though. Ironic, maybe. Blair had told me, just the day before, that he hoped Christine and I could work things out between us. And shortly after that, because of what Blair had done, Christine and I did just that. We worked things out. After that evening, after she let me cry my eyes out on her fancy blouse, our relationship was permanently changed. It was better. Smoother. More civil. I realized Christine Lambert did care about me. When it came down to it, she was on my side.

We talked about things for the first time ever—about our relationship, and the way the world had thrown the two of us together. It turned out, Christine didn't resent me for disrupting her life. She'd never had any plans of getting married or having a family, like I assumed she did. In fact, she said that she never really *wanted* to be a mother. She really just enjoyed working and growing her business, doing her own thing.

Still, Christine wasn't angry at me for coming into her little, coastal world. She was simply overwhelmed when, all of a sudden, she found herself responsible for a twelve-year-old girl. She didn't know how to handle me. And I think it goes without saying that I didn't know how to handle her, either.

But then, things changed for us. We learned how to handle each other.

She let me keep Nolan. She complained about him endlessly, about his fur getting everywhere, the dirt he tracked into her sterile house. But she never asked me to get rid of him. She knew that was simply out of the question.

Later that week, she made dinner for the two of us, and I ate it quietly, not mentioning the lack of flavor in the chicken or the overcooked sogginess of the pasta. I tried to be nicer to Christine, because she was finally trying to be nicer to me.

"The Frasier-Isaac wedding is next weekend," she'd remarked as we ate. "I was thinking about the whole wedding cake thing. You wanting to take on that responsibility. I know I said we'd wait and see how you do with Shelby's wedding, but . . . I think I was just being paranoid. Lace & Tide means a lot to me. I can't afford to make any mistakes. But I know you can handle it. I know how great a baker you are."

She paused, waiting for a reaction from me. I only took another bite of food.

"Let's just plan on you baking all the cakes next summer. Okay? Provided the clients are on board, of course."

I looked up at her. I wanted to feel victorious, after months of wishing for this, fighting for it, quarreling over it. Yet I couldn't feel the victory. I was numb. I nodded my head to let Christine know I was in agreement. It wasn't until later that I changed my mind completely, stopped baking altogether.

After dinner, I was washing the dishes while Christine put leftovers away and reorganized the fridge. There at the sink, I started thinking about him. I tried not to. I tried to block it all out, forget his fire eyes, his music, his Trident breath. Forget the fact that we were supposed to have three more weeks together. We were supposed to pick blackberries together.

Just then, a soapy dinner plate slipped from my fingers. It collided with the floor, shattered into jagged pieces.

I dropped to my knees, stupidly trying to gather the fragments up with my hands. I was already crying before I felt the sharp, ceramic edge slice through the skin of my palm.

"Roxie, what are you *doing*?"

Christine had gone to get the broom as soon as she heard the accident. Now, she was ogling me there on the kitchen floor: a pathetic girl, crying harder and harder at the sight of her blood.

"Sugar thorns." My voice crumbled in the tears. It was the same thing I uttered when Blair got cut by the blackberry vine.

"What?" Christine grabbed a paper towel for my cut and knelt next to me.

"I hate him," I said. I pressed the towel into my palm and watched the blood soak through. "I *hate* him."

"I know. I'm not the biggest fan myself."

"Why couldn't he just say goodbye? Why couldn't he tell me how he felt about me? He should've been honest. Upfront. Even if he thought it would hurt me. Because this hurts me more." I paused. "Why can't people just be *real*? I wish they'd just be real."

Christine crouched there, looking at the broken mess, looking at me. Her jaw had gone slack. She was oddly deep in thought.

"Do you really mean that, Roxie?" Her forehead was creased, and she almost looked ill.

"I mean everything I say, Christine."

"But—you wish *everyone* would be honest and real with you. And upfront. Even if it would hurt you?"

I stared at her. Something weird was happening right then. I could feel the significance of this moment. Being on the brink of something I'd never forget.

"This," I said, holding up my sliced hand, "hurts more."

Christine inhaled. Closed her eyes. When she exhaled, her breath was shaky. Her pale eyes flickered back open.

"Okay. Then there's something I have to tell you."

That August has never left me. I carry it with me everywhere I go. I wish I could get rid of it. I wish I could get rid of *him*, get rid of the loneliness I feel all the time, every single day—despite being in a ten-year-long relationship, despite living with three other people in a tiny apartment, despite residing in a city packed tight with eight million souls.

Still, I am lonely. I have too many holes in my heart. I just try my best not to think about them. Try my best to never remember *him*.

I may be in *his* city, but I will make it *mine*.

And hopefully—although I know it's unlikely—although the chances are slim to none—hopefully, fingers crossed, he never even returned to New York City after college. Hopefully, out of all those eight million souls, *he* isn't one of them.

35

Blair

It's weird to think that I've been working at Porter Publishing for six years now. What's even weirder is how my father has gone about "training" me over the course of these six years.

As I think I may have already mentioned, Philip's had me dip my toes in all kinds of roles within the company. He says it's to make me "well-rounded" and develop a "thorough understanding" of the business. Really, I get the sense it's more of a way to keep me occupied while he clings to running the show.

But that's fine with me. Seriously. It's completely A-okay. Honestly, I'm hoping it's not for another decade or two until Philip decides he wants to turn things over to little-old-me. It was always meant to be Graham, and the selfish part of me wishes it could still be him.

Anyway. Nowadays, Philip has appointed me "Publicity Assistant." Initially there'd been talk of me becoming the company's Associate Director of Publicity, in more of a long-term capacity. But all that responsibility? And being so high-up? It made my ultimate destiny all too real for me, so I managed to negotiate myself into a lower spot on the totem pole. At least for now.

That's just my style, I guess. Temporary fixes. Diplomatic compromises. Like the way I've been handling things with Allison—only now, I think that's finally going to change.

It's been six days since that night I promised we'd go ring-shopping. Tomorrow, we're doing it. It's really happening. Just as I'm heading out of my office for the day, my phone starts buzzing with a call from her.

"Ally. What's cracking?"

"My editor's driving me mad. I don't think she *gets* what I'm going for in these chapters. She wants me to change every single word that's poignant and worth a damn."

I breeze down the street, going the same direction as all the taxis and cars. I zigzag from one side to the other so I don't have to wait for the lights. Jaywalking is a way of life here in Manhattan.

"I suppose that's what you get for signing contracts with someone else," I tease.

It would've made sense, Allison being one of Porter Publishing's authors. She's a writer—I'm basically a publisher. But her family had plenty of connections all their own, so it just didn't work out that way.

"I'll figure it out," her voice bleeds through the phone. "Are we still going shopping tomorrow?"

An edgy wave hits me. A man on the sidewalk hollers out, *Ladies and gentlemen . . .* and starts performing with his accordion. I get past him, past the confused tourists, as fast as I can.

"You bet we are," I respond. "I can take a long lunch to squeeze it in, if that works for you? Eleven o'clock. We'll meet up wherever you want."

The other side of the phone stays quiet for a beat.

Then Allison says, "Yeah, that works," and I can hear her smile. "There's this place in SoHo. I'll text you the name of it."

"Sounds nifty."

"Do you want to come over later tonight? I could show you their website, give you a better idea what I'm looking for. We could open a bottle of wine . . ."

"Ah, can't." I grit my teeth. "I've got this party thing tonight. For work. You're welcome to join, though, if you don't have anything better going on. I could use the backup."

I can tell she's mulling it over. Allison usually loves these kinds of things. Work parties. Networking. Schmoozing.

Her sigh transfers into my ear. "I really should work on my chapters tonight. Sorry, Blair. But I'll see you tomorrow. Right?"

The uncertainty in her voice is obvious. She's having a hard time accepting that I'm serious about things this time. Which, I am.

"Eleven o'clock," I say in my most reassuring tone. "SoHo. Can't wait."

We hang up, and I squeeze into a subway car in the nick of time. A million thoughts race through my mind. Tomorrow is going to be hectic. Overwhelming. A lot of big stuff going on for my noncommittal, simplicity-loving brain.

But first, before I can get through the craziness of tomorrow, I have to get through tonight.

∞

I lucked out that tonight's event is being held just around the block from where I live, in someone's skinny, four-story, Village townhome. Honestly, I have no idea whose townhome it is. I'm not even quite sure what the exact reasoning is behind this event, except that it's connected to our latest bigshot author, Clarence Reeves.

The other specifics don't really matter. I'm here. I'm all shaved-up and suaved-up, ready to play my part. And my part is pretty simple: I'm just here to act as the face of Porter Publishing. To make sure everyone here remembers who first discovered this author and helped him become what he now is: an especially cocky caterpillar-turned-butterfly.

The first thing I do inside the townhouse is go up and down its many stairs in search of said butterfly, Clarence. Turns out, he's on the lowest level, and it's a relief to find him. He's chatting with some actress (I can tell she's an actress from one quick glance—it's always that way, isn't it?). She appears very enthused to be in the presence of the author himself, meanwhile Clarence is trying not to appear equally enthused that such a glamorous creature has taken interest in him.

"There's my guy," I raise my voice as I interject myself into their bubble, clap a hand to Clarence's shoulder. He and the actress both look a tad surprised.

"Hi," Clarence intones. "Who are you? I know I'm supposed to know you."

Ah, Clarence Reeves. The young, newly successful writer. The type who lets it all go straight to his head.

"I'm Blair." I force a smile. "Blair *Porter*." I make sure to emphasize my surname.

"Oh, shit," Clarence laughs as the connection is formed. "Yeah, I forgot you were coming tonight. This dude's like my babysitter at these shindigs," he says to the actress. She doesn't seem all that interested.

"Just here to represent the Publishing House," I clarify, snagging a flute of alcohol from a passing waiter. "Plus, while I have you here, Clarence, I'm supposed to run some new book signing dates by you."

"Maybe later, Blair."

The actress chimes in with a thought: "Let's go back upstairs. The vibes were way better up there."

"Upstairs," Clarence seconds. "Come on, babysitter. We're going back upstairs."

I force out a laugh, praying this night will go by as quickly and painlessly as possible.

∞

It doesn't. The place gets more packed. The music gets worse (it must be something modern, because I don't recognize it). And Clarence is just . . . being Clarence. Bless his soul.

We end up staying clustered in the ultra-modern kitchen for most of the evening. The scenery includes blue, handle-less cabinets, a white brick fireplace, and a huge black-and-white portrait of a sad-looking woman above the mantel.

I can relate to this sad-looking woman tonight. I nod in her direction from time to time. The imaginary solidarity keeps me going.

Now, you might think I'd be one to enjoy these bustling events. The socializing, the people-watching, the mingling. And I *did* enjoy them—at first. When I was fresh out of college and back in Manhattan, I felt completely jazzed to be part of these scenes. The thing is, though, after six years of all these parties, they have this tendency to just . . . bleed together. They're all too alike. They have all become mundane.

Just one more hour, I remind myself. One more hour, and I can safely make a socially-acceptable exit. I can bid Clarence farewell and walk back to my apartment, play some decent music on my record player, sprawl out in bed and have a moment or two of peace.

Through the open doorway of the kitchen, I notice a young-ish guy pass by—something about him is vaguely familiar to me, but I can't place him. A second later, he's gone, and I turn my focus back to Clarence Reeves while grabbing another drink.

Clarence has just about forgotten I'm here. I still haven't been able to ask him about the signing dates like I'm supposed to. Whenever I try, he gives me that exceedingly polite, two-word reply: "Later, Blair." Now, he's jabbering on with a fresh cluster of socialites, and I think I've had enough. Screw one more hour. I've done as much as I can. I'll report back to my dad tomorrow morning that Mr. Reeves' latest project is proceeding well.

I'm about to snag one last champagne flute and let Clarence know I'm going off babysitting duty. But that's when something weird happens. Something really, super, crazy, *mad* weird.

My attention is drawn back to the open doorway, the one that leads into the foyer, where the front door is.

There's a woman standing there. I look at her. There have been a lot of women here tonight, of course—but then, this one, in the doorway. Her back is to me. Her hair is short and sleek. Her shoulders, draped in a rosy-hued dress. A sudden buzzing comes to life in my head, drowning out other sounds. I don't know what it is about this doorway-woman that captivates me so. An impossible answer flitters through my head. Is that a freckle, just behind her ear? No. I'm seeing things. This has happened to me before, more than once. I brush it off, about to look away, but then—she pivots—just enough to reveal her face.

My glass flute crashes to the floor.

Did I call this party mundane?

I take it back.

36

Roxie

Tim and I are on our way to a party tonight. It's for work, and even though I'm dreading it, I tell myself it'll be nice. Fun, even. I have to get used to this stuff now that Tim's finally, maybe, hopefully made his big break.

After months of auditioning and getting nowhere, Tim finally got a real acting job. It's for a TV mini-series being filmed in Manhattan, based on one of those bestselling books you see in all the bookshop windows.

It's not a huge role Tim got for himself: a side character who shows up in maybe one scene per episode. Still, it's something, and it seems like it could lead to so much more. It could be the gateway to what Tim has always dreamed of.

And as for me, how I got involved in all this . . . Somehow, Tim convinced the wardrobe department to bring me on as an assistant. I couldn't think of a reason to turn it down. I need to pay my share of the rent somehow, and working at the corner bodega was barely cutting it.

Really, I'm kind of a glorified gopher at this new job, if there is such a thing. The costume designer orders me around to get coffee and food, but sometimes, she'll send me out to pick up clothes from expensive boutiques or funky thrift shops.

The party tonight is in Greenwich Village, not too far from where we live, although a hundred times nicer. We could never, ever afford it here, unless Tim Redding becomes the next Tom Cruise. Once we get to the townhouse, I follow Tim up the stoop, into the mayhem, reminding myself to smile, willing my feet not to hurt in these patent heels.

Tonight's soiree is apparently just to celebrate the fact that we've officially started filming the mini-series. Tim says there will be parties for all sorts of reasons throughout the filming process. I secretly wonder how many I can get out of.

Tim heads upstairs, so I follow behind him. At the top, I tell him I'm going to find a restroom, that I'll be right back. But when I'm done checking my hair and pointlessly washing my hands, I can't see where Tim went. I don't see him anywhere.

This place is crowded. I spot the costume designer, Bianca, across the room, but there's no way I'm going to approach her tonight. Not out of my own free will, anyway.

I go up another floor, but still, no Tim. I go back down a flight, and there's just no sign of him.

That's okay. I'm sure he'll turn up eventually. In the meantime, I can handle myself. Down one more flight of stairs, I return to the main level of the townhouse, the floor we entered in on. I look at the oversized art hanging on the walls, the bold light fixtures that dangle from the high ceilings. In the foyer, one of the art pieces is a framed photograph of the ocean. I move in front of a doorway to study it better. It's probably the Atlantic, but it gets me thinking about the ocean I'm acquainted with. The one I grew up beside. The one I left behind and have hardly thought of since.

"Roxie?"

Instantly, I am frozen. Unmoving. Paralyzed.

"Roxie?"

The raised voice comes again—from somewhere behind me. My heart begins to pummel into my chest, a sledgehammer clobbering me from within.

"Roxie, is that you?"

Almost no one calls me Roxie these days. Tim does, but this voice isn't Tim's. I manage to break out of my paralysis, though it frightens me, terrifies me, to do so. Stiffly, I turn around in a one-eighty, peer through the doorway I've been standing in.

And there he is.

Him.

It's *him.*

My heart hammers even harder. I feel it throb up in my skull. He's here. In the back of the crowd. Standing on the other end of the kitchen. A nightmare come to life. It is the one thing I hoped would never happen since moving to this place. But it's happening.

Our eyes lock. Linger. My chest and head are about to explode.

"Roxie!"

He moves. Toward me. Right in my direction. He's pushing against people, urgently trying to get around them, keeping his wide eyes locked on mine the whole time.

"It's really you!" he calls through the crowd, and I'm shaking, I can feel the cold blood rippling and surging, up and down within me, and I have to get away. He is getting nearer and nearer, and I have—to—get—away.

I bolt out the front door. Try my best to run down the stoop, but my legs are shaking and quivering; I can't move them as fast as I need to. I'm breathing rapidly, shallowly. My mind feels clouded. I have to get away. *Now.* I cross over the sidewalk, step out into the street, tell my legs they *have to* start running—

—and there's a sound of a blaring horn—a pair of headlights are suddenly there, right in my face, blinding me, about to mow me down—I feel something grab my arm and wrench me backward, out of the way—back onto the sidewalk.

I look up. The car goes on honking, but I don't care; I am horrified by what I see.

Blonde hair. Fire eyes. Those creases right below.

He has ahold of me. He stares down at me.

And he says:

"Hi?"

A weakness, a nausea, spirals through my body, climbs all the way up to my brain.

One moment I see Blair Porter. The next, I don't see anything at all.

37

Roxie

I wake up to the sound of Carole King. Somehow, I know this can't be good.

I'm in a bedroom. A twinkling skyline presents itself outside the windows. A deep blue night. A record player whirls around opposite the bed, the source of this music I recognize. The intimate piano chords. The husky voice. The only reason I know this music is because of . . .

Him.

I sit up and push myself off the bed, to my feet. The sudden movement summons a lightheadedness. But I push through it. I hurry out of the bedroom, around a corner. Find myself in a kitchen. And find him.

He has his head ducked in the open fridge, until he pulls back, and our eyes meet.

I stand there, staring at him. He stands there, staring at me. This can't be happening. This *can't* be happening. I will it to un-happen. Make him disappear. Erase all of this.

He closes the fridge, then, and walks closer to me. And I see *Blair.* I allow myself to really look at him. Blair Porter. Ten years older.

"Roxie," he says my name, gets closer still.

Abruptly, everything in me aches. Sutures pop open. Fearfully, dubiously, I continue taking in the sight this new, aged version of a boy I used to know. The eyes are the same, burning blue. But his face is more hollowed out. Faint lines dash across his forehead. The hair is the same caramel blonde, only much shorter, more tamed. His stature seems taller, trimmer, and he looks so neat, so *grown-up*, in a gingham plaid shirt beneath a dove gray suit jacket.

"I can't believe it," he says and comes right up to me. He brings his hand up toward my cheek, not quite touching it. He laughs. That sound. "It's you."

I gawk at him. I see him on the beach. At the piano. Before the brambles. Inside my old bedroom.

Just as Blair Porter sets his hand onto my face, I push him away. Hard.

"What the hell is happening?" I erupt. I back away from him. Carole King is still playing in the other room. I'm trying to keep myself from yelling, but it's not working very well. "Where am I? What did you do to me?"

I see the widening of his eyes, like he's been snapped out of a pleasant dream. Well, good. Blair Porter doesn't deserve pleasant dreams.

"You passed out," he says. His arms have gone limp at his sides. I can't believe I'm looking at him right now. I hate how . . . *dapper* he looks. How well he wears his extra years. I hate that there's a clear hint of happiness, elation, within his eyes as he looks at me.

"This is my apartment," he goes on, daring to take a step forward. "I carried you here. It was just around the block, and I didn't know what else to do. You were like a stoned-out zombie or something, half awake, half asleep."

He hazards another step toward me. And then a smile curls up the side of his face.

"Roxie. You're here." Endless awe resides in his gaze. "Seriously, not to sound obnoxiously trite, but am I dreaming?" He laughs—it hurts me—it infuriates me. "You're here. You're in New York. Why are you in New York?"

"I live here, Blair."

I regret it as soon as I say it. He doesn't need to know that. He doesn't need to know anything. I run my fingers up and down my temples. Blair may think he's dreaming, but I know this to be a nightmare.

His face becomes more awestruck at my slip of information. He steps forward yet again.

"You live here? In New York City? That's amazing. That's incredible. Roxie, I know it's been a long time—like, a really, insanely long time—but I've never stopped thinking about—"

"Don't," I raise my voice along with my hand. I'm shaking again, like I was back at the party. "Don't say that. Don't say anything."

He doesn't. He looks at me, words begging to be let out, but no, I won't let them. I look to the floor, keeping my hand out between us, fingers trembling.

"I don't want to hear anything you have to say, Blair. It doesn't matter. *This* doesn't matter. In fact, it never even happened. I'm leaving now, and this will just . . . go away."

With that, I locate the door and rush in that direction. But Blair is following me.

"Look, Roxie, I understand why you're not so pumped to see me, but I think we should talk. I want to explain what happened that day—"

"Stop it!" I whirl around to face him. "Blair! I don't care what you have to say!"

I breathe hard. I take a moment to regain my cool. "I'm leaving now. Forever. I'd say goodbye, but I know that word is totally foreign to you."

He has become desperate and tortured in his expression, in that newly sculpted face.

"But—Roxie—you live in New York."

"No," I say.

"We were at the same party."

"No."

"No?"

I lean forward, drawing my eyes nearer to his. Sutures in my chest pop, pop, pop.

"I should slap you, Blair Porter. I should sock you right in your face."

He waits, but it doesn't happen. All that happens is I twist the doorknob, and I make my escape, hoping I don't pass out again, knowing I have to keep my wits about me, enough to get myself back home.

Before I make it to the elevator, I hear his voice resonating from the doorway:

"I can't explain how good it is to see you, Roxie Morah. I really, really can't."

That's when I know: this nightmare isn't over yet.

38

Blair

My eyelids flutter open, and everything is different today. Everything is great. Awesome. Superb. The bee's knees. The cat's meow.

For the first time in a long time, I allow myself the luxury of getting dressed to some dance-worthy music ("Sister Golden Hair," that perfectly produced song I haven't let myself enjoy in years). I had forgotten how energizing the tradition is, the way that song invades me, its mix of melancholy, hope, and jubilation filling up every nook and cranny of my being.

My clothes fit better today. My coffee and bagel taste of Nirvana itself. The December chill doesn't bite—it invigorates. The aroma of the subway has magically vanished, and my office doesn't feel like a bland, spiritless prison.

She's back in my world. I sit at my desk, put my head in my hands, and laugh. I can't stop smiling. Roxie Morah lives in New York City. Roxie Morah was in my apartment last night. Roxie is *here*.

Okay, so I know our reunion last night didn't play out all that smoothly. I know she wasn't as pleased as I was to be in each other's presence after all these years. And I know—believe me, I know—she hasn't retained the highest opinion of me after everything that happened. After what I did.

But—she's here. For the past ten years, I have been reliving that summer over and over, evening after evening, wishing I could go back, yearning for those unreachable days, knowing I should've done things differently, picturing her face . . .

This turn of events can't be a coincidence. Coincidence is a myth. And you can be sure I'm not going to squander this non-coincidence. This *anti*-coincidence.

I don't have a game plan yet. For now, all I can think about is the fact that I saw her last night, the reality that she's running around inside my own city. I think about it all morning, as I make my phone calls and pay a visit to my dad's office and send out a hundred different emails. It's constantly humming in the back of my mind, a song of its own, happily stuck in my head.

I'm still thinking about it when a notification goes off on my phone at twenty 'til eleven. A text that reads:

See you soon B. I'm so happy we're doing this!?

The long-lasting smile falls from my face. The welcomed melody dissolves from my mind.

Allison.

Crap.

Shit.

∞

Where are you right now? was the text I sent back to Allison at my office, and now I'm in a café, sitting across from her at a small, round table. Watching her sip on a latte. Watching her watching me.

"Ally," I say. "Allison."

My hands are writhing around together on the tabletop. Out of habit, one of them dives into my pocket for a pack of gum, but there's nothing. I had to stop with all the gum-chewing a while back—my dentist said I was overworking my jaw.

"Blairy. Blairison."

Allison Waterhouse looks at me over her mug. Her black hair is in a braid over her shoulder. Her jacket is a camel-colored suede. While she is generally of stoic countenance, it's clear right now that she is not happy. She knows something is wrong. She's known for years.

"Ally," I say again, trying to find the words.

"Just tell me what's going on, Blair. What is it this time? Why aren't we in SoHo right now?"

The words suddenly shoot out in one spurt: "*I-have-to-break-up-with-you.*"

I'm sweating. I'm actually sweating. I feel the beads forming at my hairline. I've been with Allison for six years. We were going to buy a diamond ring this morning.

Allison sets her mug down. Her red lips part. Her eyes begin to dart around. Processing. Processing.

"I'm sorry," I sputter. My head falls into my hands. "God, Allison, I'm so sorry. I know this is, like, maximally shitty of me. I know it's messed up—I mean, six years—and it's upsetting—"

"No."

Her voice is steady. She's not looking at me, but her eyes remain very active, flitting this way and that.

"No," she says. "It's not upsetting."

"It's not? I really feel like it is."

"I mean, yes, it is, but . . ." She sighs and finally meets my gaze. "Come on, Blair. There's a reason we haven't even moved in together yet. There's a reason you don't want to marry me."

I grimace; it sounds so bad out loud. Because it's true. I don't want to marry Allison Waterhouse.

She pulls the strap of her tote bag over her shoulder. "I am upset. But . . . at least you've made a real decision, Blair. Put me out of my misery. At least I can stop wondering what's been going on with us and maybe just—" she makes a sad scoff, "—move on with my life."

She stands up; I stay seated. I should've done this years ago. I should never have put Allison through this.

"I'm sorry, Ally."

"It's okay, Blair. I hope you figure your shit out." Allison buttons up her jacket, readjusts her scarf. "Honestly. Whatever it is. Figure it out."

She touches a hand to my shoulder on her way out, and just like that, we're done.

∞

It's undeniable: I am one hell of a mess when it comes to relationships. Always have been. What would Graham think of what I've just done? What would he say to me right now?

I didn't want to hurt Allison, even though I know that's what I've done. That's what I *was doing* the whole time we were together.

This weighs on me the rest of the day, back at work and back at home.

Yet, I have to be real—in the midst of that weight, there's still the beautiful, glorious, miraculous truth imbuing itself in everything I see, hear, and feel today.

Roxie Morah is here.

I have never stopped thinking about Roxie Morah. Now that she's popped back up into my life—well, it's as if John Lennon and George Harrison have both been resurrected, as if The Beatles are miraculously reuniting. In the face of such an event, I feel I am obligated to take this second chance I've so graciously been given.

Yes, the Allison stuff sucks. Majorly. I can only hope she finds someone who's worthy of her, right for her, someone who's not dreaming of another person when he's with her.

But I do not believe in coincidences. I surely don't. In my bedroom tonight, I catch sight of something on the floor, at the edge of my bedframe. I stoop to investigate and see that it's a black clutch. And inside: a cell phone.

The smile that creeps upon me is impossible to prevent. Fate is working a game plan out for me, all on its own. I think of a resurrected Beatles and switch out the record on my player. "Got to Get You Into My Life" becomes the lively, rhythmic outro for my crazy, anti-coincidence day.

39

Roxie

Stupid, stupid, stupid.

I hate myself so much right now. I am the dumbest person alive. The Village is oddly hushed as I traipse through this brisk morning, reminding myself of my sheer stupidity on repeat. I'm returning to the place I should totally not be returning to. And it's my own, stupid fault.

I slip into the building at the same time an elderly man comes ambling out the doors. I ride up the elevator to the top floor, and I mentally chant my reminder when I knock upon the door:

Stupid, stupid, stupid.

The door swings open, and my breath gets stuck in my throat at the sight of him.

Blair Porter: why must I come face-to-face with you again? Why does your stupid, slim, wrinkle-free dress shirt match your stupid eyes so perfectly? Why did I forget my stupid phone in your stupid apartment two nights ago?

He grins a lopsided grin.

"So, we meet again. Good morning. You're up bright and early."

It's 6 a.m. Yesterday, I managed to get through the entire day without my phone. I got by using the smartwatch Tim got me for Christmas last year, but I simply cannot go another day like that. I need my phone. So I had no choice but to come back to this cursed place.

"I'm only here for one thing." I break eye contact with Blair, wrap my arms around my chest. "And I'm guessing you know what that is. So don't bother playing any games with me."

"No games." Blair puts his hands in the air. "You're here for your clutch. Which you just so happened to leave in my bedroom. Which I'm sure wasn't at all intentional on any level."

"It wasn't," I snip. "Just give it to me, Blair."

"It's still in my bedroom. Come on in."

"No. You bring it to me."

He hesitates, ultimately giving in to my demand. A minute later, he's handing over the clutch, and I check that my phone is still inside.

"You didn't try to unlock it, did you?" I tap in my password to see if I missed any important calls or emails.

"No. I left it alone."

I look up at him. In his eyes, I see the ocean. I see everything that once was. Bad idea. I tear my gaze away—and something catches my eye on the wall behind him. A photograph framed in silver. In the picture is Blair (this older version of him, with whom I'm not so acquainted) and a woman.

He has her in his arms: Dark hair. Pointed nose. Big smile. Cherry lipstick. She tilts her head up at him, laughing.

"She's pretty," I comment. Blair looks confused, until he realizes what I'm referring to. "It's good you have someone, Blair."

I turn around to leave, but I'm not getting off that easy. He is following me, calling out: "Wait, wait, wait . . ."

I take the stairs instead of the elevator, and he hurries down after me.

"Roxie, please, just wait a minute."

Out onto the quaint street, he persists, but I'm not here to listen to whatever Blair Porter has to say to me. I keep moving.

"I'm not with anybody, Roxie. I'm not with her. Not anymore. I ended it. Yesterday."

That makes me stop in my tracks. Blair takes advantage of this by jogging up in front of me.

"As soon as I saw you the other night . . . I had to end things with her."

His words are highly distressing. Alarms go off within me.

"Well," I say. "That was a really stupid thing to do." I swerve around him and keep walking.

"It was the only thing to do. Roxie. Will you tell me why you're living in New York? How long have you been here? What were you doing at that party? I'm dying to know—anything you're willing to share. Just one sentence. One word. A series of hand signals and grunts. Anything."

I ignore each of his questions, his pleas. I march forward.

"You shouldn't have broken up with your girlfriend, Blair."

"Why not?"

He gets up in front of me again, so I stop.

I look him in the eyes and say: "Did you just assume I'm single? And that, what, I would come running into your arms the moment I saw you, crying tears of joy?"

The creases in his forehead deepen. I remember this look. I remember all of his looks. I hate that I do.

"You're seeing someone," he states. Runs a hand through his hair. He sighs. He thinks. "Okay. Not ideal. But—okay. Who's the guy? What's his deal? What's his name?"

I bite into my lip. Look off to the side. There's this feeling that has suddenly risen up within me. I can't quite identify it, but it's something verging on . . . embarrassment? Shame?

"It doesn't matter who it is, Blair."

"Please, Roxie, just tell me *anything*. Is it serious? Has it been going on a long time? Is he—"

"It's Tim," I hear myself blurt out.

Blair looks at me.

"It's Tim, Blair. Tim Redding."

His forehead crinkles even deeper. His mouth opens. And then—he starts laughing.

"Funny," he says. "Good one. Really, Roxie, who is it?"

I don't say anything. I only look at him until understanding sweeps through his face. My cheeks are burning, that strange, shameful feeling amplified by the incredulous expression Blair now wears.

"You're serious?" he breathes. "Oh my God, you're serious. That kid from the bonfire? With the brand-name surf clothes? Tim *Bedding*?"

Time to get back to walking. I veer around Blair and move fast. Blood rushes through my face. I'm not sure why. Why should I feel embarrassed? What do I have to be ashamed of?

Blair keeps up with me. "Not Tim. Roxie. What happened? You said you were done with him. You went on that one pizza date with him and said you were done."

"Well, I guess I wasn't."

"But you didn't even like him. You said — remember? And we were in my guest house, and I asked you not to . . . I said you deserved better . . ."

"I don't really care what you said, Blair. You said a lot of stupid, bullshit stuff. And it's none of your business, anyway. No part of my life is any of your business. Now, if you'll kindly stop harassing and delaying me, I have to get to work."

"Wait, please, just wait. Just one more minute, please."

He puts a hand on my shoulder. And he utters possibly the only word that has the power to grant his wish, that makes me pause right then and there upon the sidewalk.

"Nolan."

I turn around. I see the corners of Blair's mouth fall.

He says: "I'm sure he's . . . By now . . . Is he?"

My throat swells. A hard lump forms in there. I look into Blair's earnest eyes.

"Seven years ago," I say.

I think of all the beach days the sweet retriever and I shared, just the two of us. All the tears he let me shed into his comforting coat. Nolan was there for me. Nolan became my best, my only friend.

"I was eighteen. He wasn't — he stopped eating, and . . . he was selfless and loving right up to the end."

Blair lets out a breath. A watery gleam lingers above his lashes. I order the lump in my throat to go away. But it won't.

Blair speaks after a minute: "Nolan was the best. He deserved to be with you those last few years."

I stand there, feeling a sharp, winter wind penetrate my clothes. Nolan. I remember the moment I found him in my backyard. The moment I knew for sure what Blair had done.

"Roxie. I know you hate my guts. You've made that crystal clear, and I don't blame you for it. I can't. To be honest, I feel like a monster. Worse than that. I feel like the villain in one of those fairytales, with the gnarly, scarred face, and the wart on the nose, and the hair growing out of the wart, and the evil laugh and—"

"Blair. Get to the point."

"Right. Okay. The point is: despite all that, I would really, really, really love it if you'd give me another chance. If you could find it within yourself to hang out with me . . ." his eyes go up toward the white sky, as though he's doing math in his head, ". . . just three times."

I scoff. Sneer. "Right. Sounds like a blast. Plus, I'm sure Tim would really like that."

"Just as friends," Blair exclaims. "Just in a platonic way. Three . . . *outings*. So I can make things up to you. Like with the frisbee incident. I have to even things out. I can show you around my city." He breaks into a careful smile, extends his arms at his sides. "The most amazing, snazziest place on the globe. I'll make it worth your while."

I can't believe I'm listening to this. Absorbing what he's proposing. Considering it, even.

"Three outings," Blair perseveres. "And after that, if you decide you still hate my guts, I'll leave you alone. For good."

He sticks his hand out between us. I examine it. It must be the memory of Nolan that has softened my heart, weakened me to this point. It's the only explanation.

"Fine. Whatever. Three outings." I meet Blair's hand, and we shake. When he grins, I add, "Rest assured, I'll still hate you at the end of all this."

"Maybe so. But a lot can happen in three outings."

"I doubt it," I say, and I march past him, feeling as stupid as I did when I knocked on his door.

∞

A distracted mind plagues me all day at work. I deliver a set of clothes to the wrong actor. I accidently order Bianca a regular matcha latte instead of soy (I give it to her anyway, and she doesn't notice the difference). I even struggle with the "wear-and-tear" Bianca delegates to me, the simple act of roughing up a few sets of jeans so they adequately match the scene. All of these tasks prove to be too much for my cluttered condition.

And then, of course, Bianca asks me to work late. It is the day that never ends. When I finally get back to the apartment, I find that Tim's already asleep, closed up in our room. It looks like Ethan and Mischa have turned in, too. So I'm by myself. But that's fine. I'm good at being by myself.

In the bathroom, my plan is to quickly jump in the shower and wash off the messy day—but I notice myself in the mirror first. I approach this mirror-self, leaning over the sink, the ceramic pressing into my stomach. I stare. I take a good, hard look at what, who, is there.

At fifteen, I was the girl with long, plain hair. A face clean of makeup. I wouldn't touch the stuff, with a few exceptions.

I was the girl in old, comfortable outfits and running shoes. Christine could barely get me to set eyes on a dress or let my practical ponytail down.

I was the girl who loved being outside, sprinting down the gravel road, the beach, looking after the berries . . .

Now, today, I am confronted with someone different. In the mirror, I see cropped hair. Styled, with a curling iron. Makeup I've trained myself to perfect. Brows that get professionally waxed and tinted, something I never even thought of growing up.

My outfit is a chunky, black turtleneck, a brown leather jacket, plaid pants. Pointed-toe heels. Earrings dangle on either side of my face. Bracelets circle around my left wrist.

I turn away from the mirror. I try to brush off the uneasiness that's come upon me. I proceed with my shower, tying a robe around my waist when I'm finished. When I step out into the front room, I know I should be going to bed, but something in me wants to disobey. Something in me wants to sit down in my chair and replay the whole scene this morning, with Blair Porter: the words we exchanged, the looks, the body language. The plan I agreed to, out of foolish weakness.

Could I have agreed to it out of more than just weakness? Could it have been . . . curiosity? I can accept this. I can accept my curiosity about Blair Porter, wanting to see who he is now that he's thirty years old, witness what his life has become.

What I can't accept is a notion that darts through my consciousness, like a dragonfly zooming through a windy sky: Old feelings. Feelings that have the potential to be resuscitated. I won't accept this dragonfly notion, because my old feelings cannot be brought back to life. They are dead and gone, buried deep in a grave in Tangle Beach, fully decomposed, all one with the dirt, not even a dried, petrified bone to be found.

My purse is on the floor next to me. I pick it up and grab the black clutch I stashed away in there after retrieving it from *him*, after securing my phone. Undoing the clasp, I peek inside the clutch, see lipstick and mints. And something else.

There's a business card. It's from Porter Publishing House. A scoff escapes me, yet I bring it up to my face and flip it over. There's handwriting on the back. A note. For me.

Outing #1
Meet me at 72nd/Central Park West
Saturday 10 a.m.
Or whenever you have your next day off.

His phone number is scribbled at the bottom. As if I would actually call him, communicate with him more than is necessary.

Then, something hits me. I realize what this note means, and my anger flickers brighter. He must have written this note *before* I showed up at his apartment. He had formulated the "three outings" plan *ahead of time*, slipping this business card inside my clutch, knowing I'd be back for my phone. Assuming I would say yes to his scheme.

"What are you looking at?"

I give a start at the sound of Mischa's soft voice. She's standing outside the closed door of her and Ethan's bedroom. It seems that even Mischa's sleep attire is odd. Fuzzy, fleece leggings. A cropped hoodie speckled in mini peaches.

"Nothing," I say, slipping the business card back into the clutch. "Did I wake you up?"

"No." She looks at me. "Just my thimble-sized bladder."

She retreats into the bathroom, and when she comes back out, she takes a spot in the chair across from me. Leaning in. Eyeing me.

"Something about you . . ." She squints her eyes. "You're different. Tell me."

"I'm just really tired, Mischa."

"No B.S., Roxie. Tell me."

"Why do you want to know?"

"I want to be a therapist one day. I'll practice on you. Tell me."

I realize I'm clenching one hand into a tight ball. The other is squeezing the black clutch against my stomach.

"I ran into someone I used to know," I divulge. "Someone from a really long time ago. I didn't want to run into him. It's been upsetting."

Mischa leans back in her chair. "Why upsetting?"

"Well, because . . . I hate him." I laugh as I say it.

"So what were you looking at when I came out? Something to do with him? Your face was scrunched like the neighbor's Shar-Pei."

I sigh. "He left me this little note. He wants me to meet up with him soon. Three different times."

"Are you going to?" Mischa asks.

"Yes."

"But you hate him?"

"Yes."

"But you're still going to meet up with him?"

I hesitate. "Yes."

Mischa stares at me in the darkened room. She doesn't nod her head or ask any further questions. She simply gets up and floats back to her bedroom door.

"*Spoki*, Roxie."

"*Spoki*, Mischa."

40

Blair

"Don't look so pleased with yourself."

The first outing. It's happening. Unfolding right before my eyes. The game plan that Fate is orchestrating for me. There's no possible way I *can't* look pleased with myself, because I am. Very much so.

Roxie has just emerged from a mass of pedestrians, approaching me at the 72nd Street entrance to Central Park. She wears a deep green coat. A white cap tops her shiny, chocolate hair.

"What can I say?" I respond to her, feeling perfectly warm despite the thirty-six-degree weather. "I'm just happy you showed up."

"We made a deal. So I'm here. But seriously, Blair. Lose the goofy grin. It's already too much of a struggle not punching you in the face as is."

"Alrighty, then. Shall we?"

We begin our stroll into the park. Her thorny words remind me: this is not going to be easy. She is not going to warm up to me as quickly as she did ten years ago. She may not warm up to me ever again. Nevertheless, I need to try.

"I never thought this would happen," I remark. "You being here. I'm still trying to wrap my head around it. It's crazy, right?"

Roxie doesn't say anything. We wind through the pathways, and I see her observe the park. The naked trees. A lake that is lacking its summer boats in December. The tall buildings that pop up on the edges around us, towering above the trees. Central Park is a magical realm, its very own galaxy within an urban universe. It doesn't matter how many times I've experienced this park—it never ceases to charm me, always ensures I get pleasantly lost within its whimsy.

Roxie still hasn't said anything.

"Any chance you'll tell me what brought you to New York?" I say. "I don't know if I made this clear or not, but I'm itching to know."

"Itch away," she utters. We get to the Alice in Wonderland statue, but she keeps walking. She doesn't seem all that interested in our scenery thus far.

How can I get her to talk to me? I need to find a way.

"You look different," I try, and it causes her to shoot me a glance. "Quite a bit different, honestly."

"Well, yes. I'm twenty-five now, Blair. I wasn't going to stay fifteen forever."

Twenty-five. I remember that fifteen-year-old girl well. But today, I don't see a girl; I see a woman walking beside me. The way she carries herself is different. The makeup around her cat eyes. Her physique that seems to have filled out.

"It's not just the extra ten years," I say. "You seem . . ."

"What?" Her tone is crisper than the air.

"I don't know, like you're dressed up in someone else's clothes."

She doesn't like that answer. I shouldn't have said it. Even if it's true.

We pass a busker—a man grooving "Winter Wonderland" on his saxophone. A clump of folks has stopped to watch and listen, but Roxie keeps moving, all disinterest. Or, at least, feigning disinterest.

Then she mutters: "You look different, too, you know."

"Do I? How so?"

With an appraising sweep of the eyes, she says, "Well, look at you, in your button-up coat and shiny shoes and ironed pants. No more bright swim trunks and T-shirts. I guess I'm just seeing you in your natural environment. What I saw in Tangle Beach wasn't real."

"That's not true, Roxie." But she doesn't have anything else to add on the topic. I want to talk about Tangle Beach. I want to discuss that summer. It's too soon, though. I can tell, it's too soon.

We make it to the Bethesda Terrace, which pulses with crowds, alive as anything can be, even in the midst of a cold December. A woman is creating huge bubbles with a wand near the fountain, attracting children. Roxie and I walk through the lower passage, where we find a wedding party posing for photographs: another tourist magnet. On the other end of the passage, a violinist and a cellist are recreating "Eine Kleine Nachtmusik," the art of their strings reverberating in larger-than-life sounds against the stonework and tiled ceiling.

I chuckle. Roxie looks at me.

"Mozart," I say, pointing to the talented street performers. Roxie looks away, concentrating on the grand staircase we are now ascending.

At the top, she finally stops. Looks around, takes in the view. I can only look at her.

"Does Tim know you're here?"

A cold slash of a glance. "Yes," she says.

"Really?"

"Yes, Blair. I told him this morning before I left."

"And he was okay with it?" I press.

"What's not to be okay with? I told him I ran into you at that party. He remembered that you and I—that we hung out together in Tangle Beach that one summer. As friends. So I said you wanted to do some catching up is all."

"Oh." I think about this. I'm surprised she told Tim. But that's good. Probably. Is it good? Does Tim Bedding really not mind?

"I *would* like to catch up," I say. "But you're making it a teensy bit hard on me."

"Good. You should just be grateful I came at all. Because I really shouldn't have."

"Yet, here you are."

Her lips roll together tightly. Then: "And this is what you have to show me? Central Park? The most obvious, cliché thing in New York City? You know, I've already been here about a hundred times. Hard to miss when you've lived here for five months."

"Five months," I repeat, clinging to this bit of data. "Good to know."

Roxie ignores my comment, saying: "I just thought, you being the Prince of the City or whatever, you'd have something a little more unique up your sleeve. Something less expected to show me."

"Wow. Okay. You're not impressed. I can see that. Well, then . . ." I tilt my head side-to-side as I brainstorm. "Okay, I can show you something more unique. Less expected. But first, are you hungry?"

My favorite food market has moved indoors for the winter, up on the top floor of a long, brick building. It's not the same as the colorful, humming summer experience, but it'll have to do.

I maneuver us among the different vendors, ordering up a collection of foods to take away with us. And all the while, Roxie remains unimpressed. In my imagination, I had pictured her smiling through this first outing, surrendering to the vibrance of Manhattan, relinquishing a laugh here and there, a look of surprise.

Shows how great a fool I am, I suppose. Roxie follows me past the big windows overlooking Saturday streets, through the mouth-watering aromas of the market, not saying a word until we arrive at our next and final destination for the day.

I've taken her to Socrates Sculpture Park in Queens. She said she expected something unique—well, I'm fairly sure this fits the bill. The waterfront park acts as a museum of sorts for large-scale sculptures. Sculptures that lean a bit on the avant-garde side. A pink pyramid covered in painted lips. A word sculpture constructed of twigs, spelling: *LAND*. A brownstone stoop leading nowhere. A yellow lion toting stacked bicycle wheels upon his back. All of this bizarre art set against the backdrop of the East River and Manhattan skyline.

We locate a bench to sit on, and I start opening up our many food containers from the market.

"What do you think?" I ask, referencing the park. She keeps two feet between us on the bench. "Unique enough for you?"

Roxie scans the area.

"This is just weird, Blair."

I can't help but laugh. "Man, tough audience. I don't remember you being this picky. But, to be fair, I remember you once telling me you weren't much of a city person."

"I'm not *not* a city person," she retorts. "People change."

"Do they?"

She eyes me. "Some people change."

We dine on the eclectic lunch I have scrounged up: Hot dumplings. Something called *pizza pastries*. Loaded sweet potato fries. Kobe beef skewers. It all tastes spectacular, especially in the cold weather. If Roxie is enjoying it, she betrays no signs.

When we're finished, I open up the last item. It's a humungous cookie, one from the bakery I once told Roxie about. The bakery that I used to believe had the best cookies on the planet, until I tried hers. I break the cookie in two, hand her half of it. She is skeptical as she examines it and takes a bite.

I take a bite myself. "I still think yours are better. I still remember how amazing they were."

"You're right," Roxie says. "Mine were better."

"You were going to open a bakery. Did you ever do that?"

"Nope."

"Are you going to?"

"Nope."

"Why not?"

"I don't bake anymore, Blair."

The news jolts me. "Not at all?"

She shakes her head side to side.

"But you loved baking."

Roxie twists away from me, gazing across the river.

"I wish you'd talk to me." I pause. "But maybe we can just . . . listen."

I dig into my pocket, pulling out my phone and wireless earbuds. It's my backup plan, and it seems I'm in need of it today. I say, "Did you know, the very *Simon* Paul himself lived here in Queens?"

She looks at me, and I think I can make out the faintest hint of a smile along her lips. Maybe. It gives me the confidence to reach out and gently offer one of the earbuds. To my surprise, she accepts it. I put the other earbud in my own ear, and it isn't long before those bright horns of "You Can Call Me Al" commence.

I watch her as she listens. The corner of her mouth curls up at the funny lyrics. It makes something in me burst into colors of hope. I start lip syncing, bouncing my head around, catching her attention. As she watches, I get more and more ridiculous with it, more exaggerated, clapping my hands like I'm at church.

Just then, two teenage girls happen to be moseying by our bench. I clap more aggressively and start singing out loud, which causes the girls to look over their shoulders at me. They make concerned faces between each other before skittering away.

Roxie laughs. She actually laughs. It's the best thing I've ever heard. I look at her, and her youthful, golden glow suddenly returns, a warm sun in the middle of this chilly winter. When the song fades out, I ask, "Another?" but she shakes her head no and gives the earbud back to me.

I slip them away, back into my pocket, and wait. I wait a little longer, a little longer, until she finally speaks.

She says, "So, here's the deal. To answer the many obnoxious questions you've asked: I moved to New York because of Tim. He wanted to live somewhere he could be an actor. He got a role on a TV mini-series here. I'm working as an assistant in the wardrobe department. We were both at that party in the Village for work."

I nod my head at this beautiful onslaught of information. Well, I say *beautiful*, but really, there are details about it I don't love.

"Wow. Okay. So, wardrobe assistant. How did that happen? Is *wardrobe* your new passion in life?"

She gives a light scoff. "No. It's just a job Tim helped me get. It'll probably lead to something more if I stick it out awhile."

"And that's what you want to do?" I question. "The entertainment industry. No bakery."

The look she aims at me—it's the same one I saw when we sat at the baby grand together and she struggled with Mozart's lightning-quick trills.

"I'm just saying," I go on, "it sounds more like, I don't know. What Tim wants to do?"

"It's what we both want."

"And you and Tim . . . you've been together . . . how long?" I keep myself from wincing. Part of me wants to know; part of me doesn't.

"Ten years."

The wince gets out. "Well, damn."

"On and off."

"On and off?" A little flicker of hope ignites. "What does that mean exactly—on and off?"

"Blair . . . It doesn't mean anything."

"And the two of you—do you—live together?"

"Yes, Blair, we live together."

I wince yet again. Tim *Bedding*. In *bed* with Roxie. That's not even funny; I can't laugh at that.

"We live with Ethan, too. Do you remember Ethan? From the bonfire."

Searching my memory, I recall the mischievous girl at that event, Chelsea. Of course, Tim was there, on the other side of Roxie. And then . . .

"Costco Ethan?" I ask.

Roxie laughs. "Yeah. That's him."

"Does he realize Manhattan isn't exactly a Costco-friendly environment? I mean, there is one in East Harlem, but he doesn't actually go there, does he?"

"Don't worry, Blair. It was just a phase." She rolls her eyes. "Now he's all about Trader Joe's."

"Oh. Phew. So, can I ask, what's Tim like, really? What's *he* all about?"

What I really want to ask is: *Why in the hell are you still with a boring, fame-seeking kid from your high school, a kid you didn't even like? What the hell is up with this "ten years, on and off" business?*

Roxie stands up, so I do the same. I toss our empty food containers into a trash can. We walk atop the dying grass while people around us take photos of the eccentric sculptures.

Roxie says, "Tim's nice."

I laugh. I don't mean to, but it happens, and Roxie raises her eyebrows at me.

"He's nice?" I shake my head. "That's all you have to say about him? That's the best you can come up with?"

"Okay, if that's how you're going to be, then I think we've dissected my life plenty for one day. Let's talk about you, Blair. Your life. Bring your case before the judge."

"My case. Okay. Well. I finished business school at Cornell six years ago. Moved back to the City, naturally. Been working for the Publishing House ever since. Right now, I'm a Publicity Assistant. I was at that party because Clarence Reeves is one of our authors."

She gives me a blank stare.

"Clarence Reeves wrote the book that the TV show is based on," I clarify.

"Oh. Right," she says. "So, then. One of us took an unexpected path. And the other did exactly what was expected."

A judgment most certainly lies beneath those words. I feel it. It actually hurts.

"And you were dating someone?" Roxie asks. "The girl in the picture."

Allison. More pain seeps into me.

"I was dating her, yes."

"For how long?"

"Six years."

Roxie stops and looks at me.

"And you seriously broke up with her the day after that party? You really did that?"

"Roxie . . . Yes."

Her lips part. I wish I could touch her. I know I can't. It is different now, though—now that she's not fifteen anymore. Now that I've gone a decade without her in my life, thinking I'd never see her again. That changes things.

"I try to go by Roxanne now," she changes the subject rather abruptly.

"Why?"

A shrug. "Just something different."

"What's wrong with what used to be?"

"A lot," she answers. "You should know."

We are by the icy river. Pigeons waddle on the bank. I want to tell her. I need to tell her. Cautiously, I set my hands atop her shoulders.

"Roxie, the day that I left Tangle Beach. I was—"

She pulls back, flames flickering to life in her oblique eyes.

"I don't want to hear it, Blair."

"If you could just let me—"

"No." She takes another step back. Then another. Like a spooked animal. One I have wounded.

"I think . . ." she says, letting out a breath. "I think that's enough for today. Don't you?"

She goes off past the lion, the pyramid, the twig sculpture. The stoop that leads nowhere.

41

Blair

I have three secrets:
   1. ██████████
   2. ██████████
   3. ██████████

You'll notice they have been redacted. That's because I'm not ready to reveal them. Well, one of them, I am ready to reveal, I am actually very eager to make known.

Except Roxie won't let me tell her. Twice, I have tried: the first time being the night she passed out and I brought her to my apartment; the second time occurring at the end of Outing #1, in the Sculpture Park.

I'm back home now after our outing. Lying in bed. Listening to Sonata No. 11. Wondering what she's doing right now. Hoping it's not something with Tim Bedding.

And I'm thinking of my secrets. My three secrets I've been keeping for so long.

And one of them is this:

1. I was there.

Ten years ago, before leaving town, before ditching Roxie without a goodbye—I was at The Ocean Festival in Tangle Beach.

I was there.

∞

That August day. When my father presented me with two options. Option one: Stay in Oregon another eighteen days. Option two: Leave with him early. In my guest house, I made my decision. I threw my empty pack of gum to the floor and knew what I would do. Instantly, I hated myself for it.

I was going to leave.

But I must not have been a complete monster. My conscience must have been sounding off alarms. Because I realized there was still time to go to the Festival. And I had promised her the night before: I would be there. To watch her perform.

So I went. I was there. I stood as far away as I could from the stage. Holding a cluster of fragile flowers I had picked on my way into town, breathing in that briny air, I watched her from afar.

She was amazing. She was perfect. Her mother would have been proud. In that lavender dress, I could see the woman she was meant to grow into. As she played the Sonata before the crowd, I was entranced.

But I was a coward. A child. I had been telling myself I was more grown-up than Roxie, that our five-year gap, her youth, was a problem. The truth was: *I* was the problem. I was brimming with fears. Those fears were rising in me, a swelling tide, the longer I stood in the crowd, watching Roxie perform. Remembering what had happened the previous night, what she had told me.

I waited to see the results. Laughed at the shock on her face as she was called up with two other girls and pronounced third place. The sash draped around her. The hydrangea bouquet. All so deserved. A rare moment in time when everything was as it should be.

That's when I snapped back to reality. To my cowardly heart.

I left then, while the crowd still lingered, while Roxie was still up on stage. Hastily, I went back to the vacation house. Then over to Seawood Lane. I got Nolan set up in the backyard of Christine's house. I hugged him, told him how much I loved him, how good of a pal he'd been to me. Explained he would be happier here, which I believed with all my heart. He would be better appreciated, so much more loved. Nolan nestled down into the grass at my words, as though he understood them, as though he agreed.

I lowered the mixed flowers beside him. And away I went.

I was the scum of the earth. I was a selfish, scared boy. I don't deserve to have her pop back into my life again, to have these three outings, to see her face again and hear her voice.

But, if it counts for anything at all, if there's any drop of redemption in it: I went to her performance, as promised. I witnessed her play Variation V, the song we spent weeks preparing. I watched and listened, mesmerized and terrified, hanging on to each and every note.

I was there.

42

Roxie

Two weeks have gone by since I spent that Saturday with Blair Porter. And I can't express how pissed I am at myself now — because I can't stop thinking about him.

Sadly, I'm not exaggerating. It's gotten to the point that I'm now wearing a rubber band around my wrist, and whenever I realize he's on my mind, I give myself a good, sharp snap. Throughout the course of a day, I snap myself more times than I can count.

When I got back to the apartment that Saturday, after spending the day with Blair, Tim asked me how it had gone, to which I replied that it had gone just fine. Not a totally true statement. I just don't want Tim worrying about the Blair stuff. Because — other than my disobedient thoughts — which I will get under control soon enough — there is nothing to worry about.

My days at work somehow drag and race by at the same time. Bianca is as demanding as always. Tim always goes to bed before I do at night, leaving me sitting in my chair, snapping away at my wrist. Mischa sometimes joins me there in the front room, either quietly reading a book or pointedly asking me personal questions.

"When will you see him again?" she posed to me one night. And by him, of course, she meant *him*.

"No idea," I responded. Blair hadn't mentioned anything about our second "outing" that Saturday. I still don't know how he plans on getting in touch with me again, and I tell myself I don't care.

"Why did I hear Tim call him your friend when you say you hate him?"

Oh, Mischa and her loaded inquiries. I didn't know how to answer that one, so I just said, "I don't know." Then I got up and went to my bedroom, uttering to Mischa our Russian goodnight.

Today is another Saturday. A week before Christmas. Ethan and Mischa will be spending the holiday with her family in Long Island. Tim's mom is flying all the way from Oregon to have Christmas with us in the big city. So today, before we scatter, the four of us have agreed to enjoy a pre-Christmas dinner together in the apartment.

Ethan and Tim go out that morning to purchase the food. While they're gone, Mischa and I scoot all the furniture in the front room against the walls and prop up a folding table-and-chairs set we found on Craigslist the other day.

After that, the fun stuff begins. I cover the ugly, plastic table in a tablecloth Mischa scored at a flea market. It's a soft, black material, with holly and ivy embroidery dancing around the edges. We arrange gold dinner plates and clear wine glasses on each side of the table. In the middle, I lay out evergreen sprigs, nestling white pillar candles into their emerald embrace.

For our final adjustments, Mischa makes sure our miniature fake tree by the fireplace is twinkling away, and I queue up some warm holiday music.

By the time Ethan and Tim return, our little dwelling has been festively transformed, like a princess for her ball. I'm not surprised to see that the guys went to Trader Joe's to supply us with this evening's feast. Ethan rants and raves about their great prices and selection, showing us the glazed ham, the butter-herb rolls, the spinach-cranberry salad kit, the boxed white-cheddar scalloped potatoes.

Ethan and Tim insist on preparing everything themselves, so I leave them be. Just as the sun is beginning to set, they declare our supper ready. I follow Mischa to the tiny kitchen, inspecting it all, feeling that, for a handful of twenty-somethings, we've done pretty well for ourselves tonight.

Tim's phone goes off while Ethan is saying, "You just *can't* beat the quality . . ." and Tim cuts in: "I'll be right back, you guys." He's looking down at his phone, smiling. Then he heads to the door.

"Where are you going exactly?" I call from behind him, but Tim just repeats, "I'll be right back!" and disappears from the apartment.

A few minutes later, there comes a rapping at the door. I go to open it and see Tim, flashing those pearly teeth of his. But Tim is not alone. He has brought someone up with him. Someone who's also flashing a smile, foxlike, my way.

"Look who I found outside, Roxie," Tim exclaims. "It's your old buddy!"

Blair.

As both men squeeze inside, I try to glare at "old buddy" Blair, but the only expression I can seem to manage is a taken-aback gawp.

"What—what's he—" I stutter. Blair is shedding his coat, revealing a black sweater over a collared shirt.

"How's the night treating you, Roxie?" He winks at me, and that urge to punch his lean, sculpted face comes to me at full force.

"Costco Ethan, is that you? Who's this lovely lady at your side?" Blair, ever the diplomat, immediately strikes up a conversation with Ethan and Mischa in the kitchen. Meanwhile, Tim wraps an arm around my waist and explains:

"He was on set yesterday. I guess he works with Clarence Reeves, has something to do with our show? Anyway, we bumped into each other. He had to remind me who he was, but then it all snapped into place. So I thought, why not invite him to our dinner? Surprise you with your old friend?"

I force a weak smile Tim's way. He was only trying to do something nice for me. He has no idea that Blair manipulated him, that the last thing I want is for Voldemort to partake in the intimate, pre-Christmas dinner at my apartment.

"Let's eat while everything's hot, huh guys?" Tim raises his voice to address everyone.

"I'll get an extra plate for Tourist Blair," Ethan agrees. Blair points out that Ethan is more of the tourist nowadays, and Mischa sends me a raised-eyebrow signal from across the room. As if to say, *This is the guy?*

Blair and I are last to fill up our plates in the kitchen. The others are over at the table, digging in. I take advantage of the opportunity and say, "So, this is how it's going to be." I speak in a low voice as Blair serves himself salad, still grinning like an idiot.

I go on: "You're going to go creeping around at my work, 'accidentally' bumping into Tim. Sabotaging my plans. Forcing these outings on me when I least expect them."

"Whoa." Blair scrutinizes the dinner rolls. "That's a lot of accusations. I'll have you know, I was looking for you, actually, when I came to your set. Instead, I came across Tim. He invited me here, not the other way around. Plus," he continues, grabbing a roll and pointing it at me, "this doesn't count as an outing."

"Are you serious right now?"

"We're not *out*, are we?" Blair gestures toward the walls and ceiling. "Think of this as some bonus, holiday time together. Two legitimate outings still remain."

He heads for the table, leaving me with an impulse to scream and storm out of the apartment. Of course, I don't do that. I swallow the fiery impulse, snap the rubber band on my wrist, and calmly head in to take my place at the overcrowded table.

∞

"I thought Blair was a girl's name."

It's the first thing Mischa has said since we began dining on the Trader Joe's extravaganza.

Blair smiles at her, twirling a fork in his hand. "I thought Mischa was a boy's name."

She considers this, staring at him for a minute, then goes back to stabbing at her salad.

Ethan reaches over to Blair, setting a hand on his shoulder, potatoes in his mouth as he speaks. "Listen. Dude. May I call you dude? Tell me, where do you do your grocery shopping these days?"

Ethan goes on nattering about groceries for the hundredth time today, and we all listen politely until he's done. And that's when Blair takes control of the conversation.

"Tim, I have to say, I'm impressed you got a spot on Clarence's cast. How's the acting world been treating you so far?"

"It's been amazing." Tim sips his wine. "It is, by far, the coolest thing that's ever happened to me. No doubt."

"Wow, coolest thing ever. By far." Blair sends me a quick glance; I look away. "Can I ask, where do you see yourself going in the entertainment industry? I mean, ultimately. What's the big dream?"

It sounds as if Blair is interviewing Tim for a job. But I know what he's really up to.

Tim seems to swirl these questions around within his wine glass. "The big dream is to get as big as I can. I want to do movies. I want to be a household name. Like Robert Downey Jr. He's pretty much my role model."

"Ah, yes. RDJ. Isn't he everyone's role model?" From the corner of my eye, I see Blair smirking. "And you want to stay in New York for your acting career, Tim?"

He shrugs. "Hoping I can convince Roxie to go to LA with me, sometime down the road."

"LA," Blair echoes, excess interest oozing from his tone. "You're more of an LA guy, Tim? Roxie, what would you think about becoming an Angeleno?"

I haven't said one word throughout all of this. As I open my mouth, Tim answers for me.

"Well, she's the one who picked New York over LA this year."

Blair's obnoxious smiling slips into a totally different expression. His eyes widen. Mouth falls ajar. He looks at me from the end of the table, crossing his arms over his chest.

"Is that so?" he speaks.

"Yep," Tim continues, oblivious as can be. "Earlier this year, still in Oregon, I was telling Roxie, '*It's gotta be either New York or LA.*' I made it clear my preference was Cali. You know, the beaches, the nice weather. And the acting opportunities are just plain better. But Roxie's pick was the big apple. So here we are."

"Interesting." Blair points his body my way. "I did not know that."

"Are we ready for dessert?" I suddenly chirp before this discussion can go on any longer. My cheeks burn under Blair's gaze. I wish I could rewind everything and hit the mute button on Tim's big mouth.

Mischa stands up and boldly declares: "I'm making the dessert." She then goes to the kitchen.

Blair is still looking at me. "You're not baking something for us?"

"Roxie doesn't cook," Tim chuckles, finishing the rest of his wine. Where is his mute button? Why must he say all the wrong things tonight?

Before Blair can make a snide comment, Mischa is groaning in the kitchen, and wafts of burnt sweetness drift around the table.

"I think I messed up," she calls.

I need an excuse to get out of the front room anyway, so I'm there in a flash to see what's wrong. On the stovetop, I find myself looking at a disaster of a sheet cake.

"I put it in the oven when they took the ham out. But I think I turned the temperature up too high."

Mischa is visibly upset for the first time that I've known her, biting her nails, frowning at the cake, as though it has dishonored her with its very existence. It's burnt all around the edges, as well as in splotchy areas across the top. Suddenly, Blair is standing there with us, seeing for himself what the fuss is all about.

"Roxie can fix it," he says. Like it's a fact as simple as *one plus one equals two.*

"She can?" Mischa regards me.

"I don't know." I am dubious. "What was it supposed to be exactly?"

Mischa points to a tub of store-bought frosting on the counter. "A Christmas cake. Vanilla on top." She points to a jar of cranberry reduction next. "Drizzle with cranberries."

Blair says again, "Roxie can definitely fix it."

"Okay, okay," I give in. "Mischa, I'll take care of it. Go hang out with Ethan."

She leaves.

Blair stays.

"You can go away, too," I tell him.

"I want to help. Put me to work."

I sigh, thinking about what I need in order to repair this. "Fine. Get the wine glasses from the table. Wash and dry all of them. Then open the Moscato from the fridge.

He gets going on his appointed tasks, and so do I. First, I forage in the fridge, happy to find some ripe pears awaiting me. I grab eggs, heavy cream. Brown sugar and honey from the cabinet. Two saucepans. Blair opens the Moscato and starts washing the wine glasses. I do my best to ignore his presence as I work.

It feels good, actually. Really good. Being in the kitchen like this. I tend to the egg yolks and cream in one saucepan, rendering a custard. In the other, I simmer the Moscato, honey, brown sugar, and add sliced pears.

Blair, having finished his tasks, comes up beside me at the stove, watching me stir and whisk. I feel so strangely serene right now. As though a sweet ocean tide has rushed over my feet, foaming and running back to where it came. A salty wind combing through my hair, down my back, tickling my skin.

I say to Blair: "Salvage what's not burnt of the cake and cut it into cubes."

"Yes, ma'am."

I glance at him and see the pleasure sitting in his eyes. It doesn't bother me in this moment. My serenity rushes and flows, foams and combs.

It would be better if I could take my time with the custard and poached pears, but I don't want to keep everyone waiting much longer. I open the cranberry reduction, set the wine glasses in a row, and proceed to create five individual trifles—dainty layers of the cake, the cream, the sweet pears, and the cranberries.

Blair leans in toward me when I'm done, whispering into my ear: "She's back."

Ignoring him, I say, "Will you get some spoons from that drawer?"

In an awkward blunder, we both move into the same spot of the tiny kitchen, bumping into one another, so that I end up right between the counter and Blair. It's tight quarters in here. It's tight quarters between us. My heartbeat quickens. Blair doesn't move. Neither do I.

I peer into the front room. Tim isn't there. Maybe in the bathroom. Ethan and Mischa are looking out a window. Nobody is looking at us in the kitchen. Nobody is seeing the way Blair is so close to me right now, the way I'm so close to him. I can feel Blair's proximity, a warmth that emanates from his body. I dare to look up and meet his gaze.

"You really are something in the kitchen," he says. "I can't believe you stopped baking."

"I'm not that great."

"Yes. You are."

Blair inches closer to me, so that our stomachs, our chests almost touch. My skin tingles. I look at him in his neat, black sweater, a brilliant contrast to his blonde hair, blue eyes. Blue eyes that search mine. It scares me. The searching. The blueness. It scares me because of that thorn in my heart, the one I thought was gone, the way it pulses just as it did when I was younger.

"Roxie," Blair mumbles, and he lets our bodies press together as he cups my face in his warm hands.

"Blair, stop," I whisper.

He doesn't listen. Instead, he combs my hair behind my neck, becoming the ocean breeze. He leans down and presses the gentlest of kisses behind my ear. So soft it is barely anything. A whisper, a ghost of a kiss.

Shivers move through me; I hear myself breathe. The feeling of his torso warming mine. Suddenly I'm back in my old bedroom, back to that night, when I told this boy I loved him. When I showed him my heart, spilled my truth, and he kissed me, never telling me how he felt in turn.

I yank backward, but Blair's already pulling away, too. He steps back.

"Sorry," he says. "I shouldn't have done that."

I look at him. Then grab two of the trifles, hoping he'll get the hint to grab the other ones.

"No. You shouldn't have."

$$\infty$$

Dessert is well-received. Everyone is impressed. Tim says, "I didn't know you could cook like that," and Blair doesn't bother making one of his remarks this time.

He does, however, take it upon himself to change the music that's been purring from the speakers this whole time. I recognize both the song and the singer he selects. "Have Yourself a Merry Little Christmas." Billy Joel.

The formality of our holiday feast has petered out by now. Tim and Ethan are lounging on the couch that's against the wall, watching YouTube videos on a phone, laughing. Mischa has gotten herself a second trifle and eats at the table alone. I've meandered to a window, peering down at the winter street below me.

"First snow."

It's Blair. Again. He stands at my side but keeps his hands behind his back. What he's just said is correct—the first snow of the season has fallen tonight, gathered softly on the city ground, glistening in the streetlights.

"It always looks so pristine at first," Blair goes on. "For about one day. Then it gets all muddied up and half-melted. But this part is nice, while it lasts."

"I don't think I like it." The words slip out of me.

"No?"

"It never snowed in Tangle Beach." I almost laugh at the thought of it. "And it wasn't so dry like this in the winter. The air was softer. Things were greener. I think I'm just ready for this winter to be over."

"Already?" Blair chortles. Then he gets quiet, seems to turn something over in his mind. "Why did you leave Oregon, Roxie?" His voice has become gentle, like the kiss behind my ear. "What happened? I thought you wanted to stay close to home, to your mother's house? I thought you wanted to use the gift she gave you. Baking. You were so proud of it. So talented."

I shut my eyes for a moment. "No, Blair. Things change."

"But why?"

I look over at him, at this dapper man I once knew as a less-than-refined boy. Here he is, tall and trim, groomed and handsome. It's horrible, but in this instant, I envision what it would be like if he were to suddenly sweep me up, hold me, kiss me. Quickly, I snap my wrist.

"Um. What was that about?" Blair arches a brow. "Is that a rubber band?"

"It's nothing," I dismiss, and we stand there, taking in the crystal blanket outside.

"I'll go now," he says all of a sudden. "Sorry I barged in on you like this. Honestly. It seemed like a good idea at the time, but . . ."

I wait for him to finish.

"I'm just—sorry." He bites his lip. "I was hoping to meet up with you on New Year's Day, if that's all right. For our second outing. Here."

From behind his back, he reveals something in his grasp: a gift wrapped in green paper, tied in a ribbon, the whole thing about the size of my black clutch. Before handing it to me, he unearths a pen from his pants pocket and scribbles away at something on the gift. Then, he hands it over.

I take a look. There's a slip of paper secured beneath the ribbon. It's what Blair was just writing on. I read it:

Outing #2
Jan. 1st 12 p.m. . . .

Directions are crossed out and rewritten below, something about which trains to take to what stations. I hold the green gift up between us.

"What's this?"

"Just a Christmas present," he says. "I truly hope you have the most splendid of holidays. You and Tim Bedding both. Goodnight, Roxie."

I shake my head but smile for some reason. "Goodnight, city boy."

Blair leaves. Everything gets cleaned up, the front room restored to its normal condition. Later that night, when Tim's asleep, I sneak out into the front room. Make sure Mischa isn't lurking in the shadows. The Christmas tree lights remain twinkling in the silence.

I unwrap Blair's Christmas present, carefully, slowly. I'm scared to see what it is. And when I do, when I realize what I'm holding, my heart bleeds.

It is the poem. Framed behind glass. Surrounded in an antique-gold perimeter. The poem Blair read to me that night, the moment I could no longer deny how I felt about him. "Do Not Stand at My Grave and Weep" by Mary Elizabeth Frye.

I read each word by the light of the Christmas tree. I press it against my chest, and everything in me hurts.

43

Roxie

It's New Year's Eve. I wake up from a dream. Not a dream exactly. A memory. One that came to me while I was asleep. One I haven't thought about in years.

I was a child, and I was with her. Maryanne. We were sitting at the piano. She was showing me a new melody. But my mind was elsewhere. I was thinking of Lavender Man again for some reason. It must have been that same summer, when he bought one of our blackberry pies at the farmers' market.

I'm not sure why Lavender Man made such an impression on me. I guess because it was the first time I realized Maryanne could be in a relationship with someone, if she wanted to be. She could possibly even be in love with someone.

"Have you ever loved a boy before?" I asked her on the bench.

She stopped playing, and I sensed tension in her body.

"I'm not sure I ever have. Why do you ask, my rabbit?"

"Will you love someone one day?"

"I love you right now," she said.

I looked down at my bare toes, her bare toes, by the brass pedals.

"That's not what I meant," I said, but she didn't offer a reply.

Later, while the sun was sinking, casting golden rays upon our walls, I walked down our hallway. Looking at the framed charcoal drawings. The way the sun's filtered radiance shimmied across them, bringing them to life. There was one drawing that caught my eye in that moment. Most of the pieces depicted wildlife, but this one was a portrait of a woman. Not Maryanne, but someone I didn't recognize. Her eyes were beautifully shaped, though her mouth seemed sad.

I looked and looked and looked at it. And she found me in the hallway, saw me studying the art.

I asked her: "Mama. Will I be in love one day?"

She answered, "Oh, baby, I'm sure you will. It happens to most everyone at some point. You just can't help when it is. Or who it is. You don't get to choose who you fall in love with, Roxie."

I looked at the portrait of the woman on the wall. I looked down at our bare toes again. I didn't like what she'd said. The idea that I couldn't be in control of such a thing.

"I want to choose," I said.

I thought to myself: *I am going to choose.*

That same day, New Year's Eve, after having my memory-dream, I go back to Greenwich Village. I go back to Blair Porter's building. I climb up the stoop, search for his buzzer. My finger hovers over the button once I see it. I let one finger rest against it, not yet depressing.

I'm here to call it off. Everything. The remaining outings. All contact. I want to be done with this—with Blair. It's something about his Christmas gift that's triggered my reaction. The way it made me hurt. The memory it brought back to life this morning:

I'm going to choose.

I *am* going to choose—Tim.

Just about to push the button, I'm startled by a voice coming from right behind me, a little: *"Oh."* A woman's voice.

I turn around and come face-to-face with the woman standing there on the stoop. I feel I know this woman. She's achingly familiar, with her black hair, pointed nose, wide, red lips. Then, I realize—she's the woman from the picture on Blair's wall. The one he had been with for six years.

She looks at me, jarred. Just as I look at her, jarred. She sees my finger over Blair's buzzer. I take it off.

"Here to see Blair?" she asks me. Her gaze is investigative. "I am, too. I left some stuff here that I need to get back."

Stuff. I can imagine. T-shirts, lipstick, jewelry. Mementos. Pictures.

"How do you know him?" she goes on. She doesn't seem offended by my muteness, nor by my being here. She is just curious, I can tell. Harmlessly curious.

"I don't really know him," I blurt, finding my voice. "Well, I do, but mostly from a long time ago. A really long time ago. I hadn't seen him in years until recently."

I include the last part as an attempt to downplay my relationship with Blair. But, it has the opposite effect.

"Years," the woman repeats, and then a sadness pulls at her features. An understanding blooms in her eyes.

"I better leave." I move away from the building, get down three of the steps before she says something else:

"You're lucky."

I look up at her.

"Lucky?" I ask.

"I wish someone would hold me in their heart the way he's held onto you."

Her statement rattles me. I look into her eyes, not knowing what to say. And then, I don't say anything. I go, giving up on my plan to call things off, just needing to get out of there, away from what she said, needing just to leave.

44

Blair

She called me city boy. The last time I saw her, that evening in her apartment, she said, *Goodnight, city boy.*

I've been feeling light, confident, optimistic, ever since. City boy. It's what she used to call me that summer. It's the brightest, shiniest sliver of hope to me. It's what's keeps me pushing through my busy workdays, pushing through the holidays spent with Philip and Rita. It's what boosts my confidence on New Year's Day, as I wait for her on the street, ELO's "Can't Get it Out of My Head" playing in my ears.

Outing #2 is set to begin. All systems go. Ready for takeoff. And then she arrives. I pop out my earbuds, offer Roxie a warm smile in the midst of the snow-speckled day. She only raises her eyebrows in return and says, "What are we doing in the Bronx?"

"Follow me and you'll see."

I want to hold out a bent arm for her to take, for us to stroll into the New York Botanical Garden as an old fashioned, Victorian couple might. This is just a fantasy, though. In reality, Roxie and I walk side by side, hands stowed in our respective pockets, no physical contact, hardly any eye contact. I buy us tickets, and we proceed, swerving around snow patches, breathing in frost.

"Seems like a better place to visit in the spring or summer," Roxie comments. A little smirk makes my mouth twitch.

Then we come to it: the Haupt Conservatory Greenhouse. It's a magnificent, huge, sprawling, Victorian glasshouse comprised of several ornamented pavilions—a breathtaking sight, even from the outside. Of course, it's what's inside that we're really here for.

Roxie and I walk up the steps leading to the central, ninety-foot dome of elaborate white steel and glazed windows. She gives me a skeptical glance when I open the door for her. And inside we go.

It's like stepping into another world. This is the Palm Dome. As its name suggests, this part of the greenhouse shelters a lush and various collection of palm trees, all reaching toward that ever-so-high-and-magnificent glass ceiling up above.

"Blair." Roxie circles her head around, stepping slowly, trying to take in the overwhelming, green splendor. "What's this about?"

"Glad you asked." I rub my hands together excitedly. "You said the New York City winter was bumming you out. The snow, the dryness. Sounded like you needed a little escape from it. So, here it is." I roll my hands outward with a flourish. "Your escape."

She looks wonderstruck. She walks around the reflecting pool, eyeing everything carefully, intentionally. I trail behind her, admiring the awe in her face.

Coming here was the right idea. No doubt about it. It's like I can see the weight lifting from Roxie's shoulders, disintegrating into vapors and floating away through the glass. She heads into a rainforest section of the greenhouse and becomes even more entranced. The air is humid in here, warm and easy—so warm that we both slide off our coats and hold them in our arms while continuing on beneath the umbrella of foliage.

I keep quiet as we meander down the wet walkways, around the gargantuan leaves and curving branches. I let Roxie enjoy this place in peace and quiet. I let her recede into her escape.

We come into another rainforest section, and finally she says: "I needed this."

I dare to respond, "I thought so."

Her eyes are fixed on a rubber tree. In this lighting, her hair and skin seem to glow from within.

"It's kind of like being back home," she says. "At least, the closest thing I've found."

"Do you get homesick often?"

"No. Not homesick. I haven't totally adjusted to the East Coast yet, but I have no desire to go back to the West."

I ask, "Why not?" but she just goes on regarding the rubber tree. "Is it true what Tim said at your apartment? You chose New York over LA?"

That gets her to look at me.

"It had nothing to do with you, Blair."

"Not even a little?"

A shake of her head. "You're really self-centered, you know that?"

She moves on, away from the rubber tree, into the desert section, a pavilion filled with unusual cacti. We don't stay in here very long, though—too dry, I figure—and next up are the aquatic plants and vines. There's a bench in here, and I take a seat, expecting Roxie to explore on her own for a while. Instead, she lowers herself beside me.

"Did you open my gift?" I ask.

"Yes." Her voice gets quiet. "Thank you."

"And what did ole Timmy get you for Christmas?"

"Blair."

I aim to be gentle while still speaking my mind: "I just wish I understood what you're doing with him. Why you're with him."

"Tim's a nice guy."

"Right," I say, "so you've mentioned. He *is* nice, but he's just so . . . *typical*, isn't he? He wants fame and fortune. A big, fancy house, probably. Big, fancy car. A flashy life."

"And you're so different, Blair?"

"*You* are."

She's quiet. I take a beat, hoping I haven't pushed her too hard. That's what I've come to understand over these past few weeks: I need to go easy with her. I need to restrain myself, give her room to think and breathe. But then, Roxie twists around to look me right in the eyes; I realize she's waiting for me to say more.

"You don't want to live someone else's life, Roxie."

She sits up straighter, tenser. "Well, what about you, Blair? Your life? I thought you were going to take control, break away from your parents, find your own path. Do what you wanted. What happened to all that? You stayed at Cornell. You became some random employee at your dad's company. What gives you the right to judge me when you're not living the life *you* want?"

It stings. Having such truths flung at me from Roxie Morah's mouth.

"I guess we both have our faults," I admit. I've almost forgotten where we are right now, the greenhouse, our serene surroundings. All I see is her. "I'm just trying to understand what got you here, why you left Tangle Beach, came to the City, why you—"

"Please. Blair. I'm not in the mood to get into all of this with you."

I pipe down. Recalibrate. Then say, "Okay. What *are* you in the mood for?"

After a few minutes of contemplation, she surprises me when she gives me a meek kind of gaze and replies, "How about some music?"

I smile. "I'm always down with that."

I pull out my earbuds, scroll through my phone, and get a special song ready for us. My first thought is Sonata No. 11, but it feels too soon for that. Too heavy. Instead, I go with "Sister Golden Hair," and we sit on our bench, the way we did at Socrates Sculpture Park, sharing this song that's always made me think of her.

As the music goes on, though, Roxie's face warps, frowns. I wonder if the lyrics are too apt for our circumstances. Actually, I *know* that they are, because I want to burst out singing during the chorus—I want to make these pleas to her—I want to win back her heart—or at least make it so she doesn't hate me through and through.

We both make it to the end of the song. "Another?" I ask. And my hope grows when she nods her head yes.

This time, I pick a song that I vividly remember sharing with her back in the day, in my guest house on the beach. Elton John's "I Guess That's Why They Call It the Blues." Roxie gives the smallest smile when the piano starts up. She remembers it, too. My past musical efforts with her weren't all for naught. She was my Music Hermit back in those days, and I, her Shaman. Now, Sir Elton's piano chords roll and tumble, pull me back in time, and suddenly a strong desire comes over me, and I wonder . . .

"What are you doing?" Roxie looks at me questioningly. I've risen from the bench, turned to face her. I offer her my hand.

"Dance with me?"

It happens easily, smoothly; she surprises me once again, standing and taking my hand. I walk us closer to the trickling, tiered fountain, the pool that holds bobbing water lilies. We are curtained by lush vines up above, arching across the ceiling, dangling chains of leaves, strands of blossoms. Cautiously, I wrap my arms around Roxie and settle them to the small of her back. With equal caution, she moves her hands to the back of my neck. And we dance.

It's a long song. I can't express how grateful I am for that in this moment. We move timidly at first, but the swinging rhythm prompts us onward, loosens us up. I give us an exaggerated sway here and there with the beat, and Roxie laughs, which makes me beam right back at her. This feels so right, smiling with her, making her laugh. Holding her in my arms. I'm on another level right now.

At first all of this is lighthearted, dancing here beneath the glass, among the vines. Until, suddenly, it isn't. Suddenly, a seriousness falls over me, a deep longing, and I pull her close, I hold her body against mine.

She lets me. She holds me back. This song is one of nostalgia. Of romance. I lean down and press my forehead to hers, feeling like we are on the coast again. I feel her breasts rise and fall against me, faster, faster. We dance with our foreheads touching. Our noses. When the song is coming to its close, I hear myself murmur, "I've never stopped thinking about you, Roxie. Not even for one day."

Roxie breathes heavily, her head tilts up, and I take it as an invitation. Her breath runs over my face as I bow lower, close the gap, and bring my mouth to hers.

I kiss her, for the first time in ten years. We're pressed against each other, and I cling to her, she clings to me. I kiss her gently, slowly, again and again—the way I always wanted to when we were younger—the way I never did. That night in her bedroom was too impassioned, inflamed, juvenile. This, right now, is tempered, seasoned, pure. Her mouth softens, harmonizes with mine, and it's like all the greatest songs rolled into one perfect symphony. Until . . .

Roxie breaks away. I feel her shove at my chest. Again—another hard, forceful shove into my sternum, making my breath catch in my throat.

Roxie backs away from me, tears shining in her eyes, that wounded animal beholding me in anguish and confusion.

"What's wrong with you?" Her words shake in her throat.

I gape at her. No one else is around. It's just the two of us. Which is better than the alternative, because she's louder this time:

"What's wrong with you, Blair?"

Eyes filled with pain. Pain that transfers into me.

"Is all of this because I'm older now? Huh, Blair? Because I'm all grown-up and age-appropriate, now you want to be with me?"

"No, Roxie."

"You told me I was too young that summer. You made me feel like a child."

"You *were* young, Roxie. You were *fifteen*. What was I supposed to do—" I cut myself off, because this isn't even what I want to be saying right now. This isn't what I want to convey.

"I knew what I felt," she rasps. "I knew that I loved you. Like I hadn't loved anyone since my . . . And you left me, Blair." She tries to raise her voice, but it's gone hoarse. "You left me."

I stand there, frantically searching for words. Not one comes to me. I force myself to look at Roxie, even though it pains me to do so.

"You went without a word, Blair. I told you I loved you, and you got what you needed from me that night. You satisfied your itch, your curiosity. You promised you'd come to my performance,

270

and you were nowhere to be found. I ran around looking for you, everywhere, out in the street. I ran to your house, and it was empty. You were gone. You *left*. I was alone, all over again. Like when she died. Except *you* went willingly, Blair. *You* chose to leave me."

Roxie, her tears, her tirade—they are blades to my skin, my chest, my soul. I knew I was the monster, the villain in this story, but I hadn't understood how deep it really went. How severely I hurt her. Even so, my secret (one of my secrets) is there in my throat, burning, searing me, screaming to get out.

Roxie turns away from me. I watch her pivot and start to walk away.

"I was there," I release the words. She stops. "I was there, Roxie," I say again, and she turns back around. She looks at me.

"I was at the Festival." My eyes are stinging with tears, but I hold them in. "In the back of the crowd. I watched your performance. I watched the whole thing. You wore the lavender dress. You sat at the keyboard, and you played our song without a hitch. It was perfect. And you couldn't believe it when they called you up into the top three. When they made you second runner-up and gave you that sash. The hydrangeas."

I take a breath. I stare at Roxie, who goes on staring at me.

"I was there, Roxie," I say one more time, and I take a step forward.

Roxie keeps her eyes locked with mine. Her face is wet. The fountain trickles. Now *she* is the one taking a step closer to me, closer and closer. Hope twinges inside me. Roxie comes up to me and sets one hand on my chest, over my heart. My heart that is waiting to burst into flight. Then, I feel as she digs her fingernails into me, through my clothes. She brings her mouth to my ear, and she says:

"You think that changes anything?"

And she leaves me there alone, with the water, glass and vines.

45

Roxie

Three weeks go by. No word from him. No surprise drop-ins at my apartment. No slips of paper with directions for Outing #3.

I give up on the rubber band around my wrist. I still think of him. I think of our kiss in the greenhouse, the way I wanted to melt into him, the way I nearly forgot my anger, almost let my bitterness slip away. The way his body comforted me, the feeling of being back home, being back in his arms again.

But then, I remind myself the way our time in the greenhouse ended. And that brings on a painful, sharp rubber band snap of its own kind.

At work, I feel as though some kind of hazy curtain has been pulled down over my eyes. I'm foggy. Fuzzy. It makes it hard to run all of Bianca's errands, carry out every tedious wardrobe task. I drink extra caffeine throughout the day, trying to keep sharp, focused.

When I'm not working, I try to spend time with Tim. But we're out of sync. Whenever I have free time, he's taking a nap, or at the gym, or out doing something with Ethan. Whenever he has free time, I'm either out getting food, clearing my mind with a walk, or doing something with Mischa.

One night, when everyone else is asleep, Mischa and I are in the front room, sitting across from each other in our respective chairs. Her outfit: a sweatshirt with The Rolling Stones' tongue and lips logo, and a pair of tie-dye sweatpants. She asks me:

"What happened to Blair? Aren't you supposed to see him again?"

"I'm not sure, Mischa. I think all that might be done now."

"Why? What happened last time you saw him?"

My brain wrestles with her question, seeking the vaguest of answers. Then I realize I don't want to lie to her.

"We kissed, and I yelled at him," I sum it up.

And he told me he was at my performance. He was there in the crowd, cheering me on after all.

But that doesn't matter. Does it?

No. It doesn't. He still left me.

Mischa shows no visible reaction in her face. "Why would you kiss someone you hate?"

"I don't know."

"Are you going to tell Tim?"

It's a good question.

"I should tell him. Shouldn't I?"

Mischa doesn't answer. Tonight, it is her turn to get up first and head to her room. "*Spoki*, Roxie."

"*Spoki*, Mischa."

∞

"Tim?"

The next morning, before our alarms go off, I lie in bed completely awake. Dawn pushes through the blinds. I have been awake for hours. I can't take it anymore. I need to talk to the man on the other side of my bed.

"Tim," I whisper, rolling over to face him. Gently, I shake him on the shoulder, and then he groans and opens his eyes, his face a half-moon, partially obscured by the navy pillow.

"What's going on?" His voice is more like a croak. He sits up and gets a drink of water from the nightstand. "Something wrong?"

I think to myself, *Yes, something is very wrong.*

I say: "Do you ever feel . . . like we're living parallel lives?"

He slouches back into the mattress. His face slouches into confusion.

"What?"

"Like," I go on, "we just happen to be on the same train or something. Or like . . . we don't even know where we're really going."

Tim pinches the bridge of his nose, as if a frontal headache is coming on.

"I have no idea what you're talking about, Roxie. I know where we're going."

"You do? Where?"

"Well, we're going to stay in New York for the time being. I'm going to finish this show, see what comes next. And then, like we've talked about, we'll get to LA eventually."

Now I think I might have a headache coming on myself. "That's not really what I meant," I say.

Although, when I think about it, his literal answer is pretty telling. Revealing. Is that where I want my life to go? Am I *"living someone else's life,"* as Blair asserted?

"Tim. Do you ever question—why we're together?"

He sucks in a long breath.

"Ah, not this again. Roxie. Do we have to go through this every single year?"

Every single year. I think about this. I realize he's right. The on-and-off nature of our relationship over these last ten years. It's always been *me* who wants to press the pause button. Always *me* coming up with some vague reason for needing space, time. What is this crazy loop I have gotten myself into? Why can't I break free of it?

"I kissed someone."

The words tumble out of me fast and hard. My face burns as I check Tim's reaction.

He doesn't look mad. He looks—confused.

"I'm sorry, Tim. I think I'm—I think I'm really confused right now. I think maybe . . ."

"Do you love me?" he asks, wheels turning in his head. Daylight persists, shoving its way into the room, onto the sheets.

I consider the question.

"I don't know. Do you love me?"

He gives a little recoil, as if it is totally ridiculous for me to pose the same question to him. But then he hesitates. His eyes go off to the side, looking at nothing.

"I just wonder sometimes," my voice cracks, "if we're together because it's easy. Familiar. Have you ever thought that?"

He flips the covers off him, stands up. Thinks. He changes into a pair of jeans, saying:

"So, we'll take a break. Like we do. Hit the off switch. For a couple weeks, months, however long. I can stay with a friend of mine from work."

"Tim. Maybe we should just talk some more. Right now."

"We'll take some time to think," he doubles down. "When you figure out what you want, Roxie . . . Just, be honest with me, okay? Be honest with yourself. Because I don't know if I can do this anymore. I don't know how many more times I can . . . I just don't know."

He goes toward the door, and I should probably protest as he does so, should probably be crying and saying his name, asking him to stay. I should be. But I'm not.

46

Blair

Now is the time, here is the place, for sad songs. And I'm not talking about Sir Elton's tune of that same name (which, let's face it, is as cheery and upbeat as sweet Nolan was at the beach).

I'm talking about *real* sad songs. "Yesterday" by The Beatles. "Fire and Rain" by James Taylor. "Landslide" by Fleetwood Mac. You catch my drift.

One of my secrets is out. I told Roxie I was at her performance. But in her words, this revelation, this truth, doesn't "change anything." And she's right.

I let the days go by without bothering her. Not one peep from me. Not one peep from her, either. I wonder if I've completely screwed this whole anti-coincidence up. See, the thing is, I still have those two other secrets stashed away. Part of me hopes that these secrets, once revealed, *will* be enough to change things. Yet, the other part of me (another Blair One and Two situation) keeps wondering as these days go by—these days of "Yesterday," "Fire and Rain," "Landslide"—wondering if maybe . . .

Maybe I should give up on the game plan entirely.

Maybe it's a lost cause.

Maybe Fate was only taunting me with the shimmery, golden illusion that I could be worthy of this girl.

Days pass in the office. Nights pass with my record player. And I wonder.

∞

It's late January, another day at Porter Publishing House, another upcoming meeting with my dad. I've just gotten off the phone with about a million different bookstores, still trying to sort out Clarence Reeves' signing tour details. Exhilarating stuff, I know.

Over to Philip Porter's office I go, wondering what Roxie's doing right now, wondering if she thinks of me at all. Then, when I step foot into my father's office, all of these thoughts are vacuumed right out of my skull.

Philip is standing in front of his desk with another man. A man who is taller than me. Bearded. Well-dressed, yet understated. A face I know well, yet somehow not at all.

"Graham?"

My older brother breaks into a familiar smile when he sees me, and then we're hugging, clapping each other's backs, drinking in the sight of the other person's eyes. The gleam of brotherhood, of deep, genetic connection.

"Blair," he croons. "Man, it's good to see you."

"Blair," now speaks my dad. "Look who finally decided to show up to his real job."

Graham laughs it off. "I'm only here visiting. Then back to Africa in a few days."

"Uganda still?" My question comes out earnest, impatient, like I'm begging for a pat on the head.

"Ghana now."

"Ghana now," I repeat, clinging to this knowledge, embedding it into my brain matter.

Graham says, "Listen, I was thinking, if you're not too busy, maybe we could grab some lunch?"

"I'm always too busy," Philip replies, moving back behind his desk, settling into his throne.

But Graham just smiles. He slings an arm around my shoulders and says, "That's okay, Dad. I wasn't talking to you."

Graham is here. The elusive brother. The unseen sibling for over a decade. What does this mean, that he *and* Roxie would appear in my city like this, within just a couple months of each other?

Graham and I get hot dogs out on the street. Like we did when we were kids. We eat and talk and walk, and it's like we were never separated. We just snap right back into the way things were.

Somehow, while I got blonde hair and blue eyes from our parents, Graham got brown and hazel. Somehow, he got six feet, five inches in height from them, while I received six feet, two. By some mystery, Graham got the genes that provided him the guts to break away from Rita and Philip. And as you know, of course, I did not.

We talk about our respective lives. Graham's magnanimous work overseas. His love of the simpler lifestyles he's encountered, the connection he feels to the people, the satisfaction all of it brings him. I tell him about working for Dad, and that's really about all I have to bring to the conversational table. Until he says:

"How's Allison?"

Allison . . .

Did I mention that on New Year's Eve, she stopped by my apartment to retrieve some of the old stuff she'd left behind? She seemed okay, honestly. Possibly even lighter somehow. Less burdened. Graham knows about Allison Waterhouse because of the occasional emails he and I have exchanged over the years.

"I kind of broke up with her, actually," I say on the sidewalk.

"Oh?" Graham sounds aptly surprised. "Why'd you go and do that?"

"There's . . . someone else."

"Blair. You cheated?"

"No! God, no. But thank you for immediately jumping to such a low assumption of me."

"So, then, what's the story?"

I tell him. I tell him the whole thing. I start at the beginning, in Tangle Beach. I try to describe the way my relationship with Roxie shifted and burgeoned over the course of that summer. The conflict I felt, the two Blairs. Worrying about her age, the five-year gap, falling into the footsteps of our dysfunctional parents. I explain how I left after we kissed in her bedroom, my cowardice. How I never stopped thinking about her. How she stumbled into my life last December (fainted, really). I tell him all three of my secrets, but how I'm afraid everything's too spoiled now.

Graham listens to me the whole way through. Considers. Ponders. The January day is clear — cold but sunny. The skyscrapers glisten. Graham and I keep walking

"I don't think anything's ever too ruined to be redeemed, Blair."

My wise, poetic brother. He goes on:

"You know, I think I understand you now. Better than I did."

"Am I such an enigma to you, Graham?"

A small smile. "I guess what I mean is, I've always wondered what your drive was in life. I figured out what I really wanted and made it happen, but you never seemed to figure it out for yourself. Now I think I understand what you want."

"What's that?"

"Her. And for what it's worth, I think you need to get her. You *need* to make this right. Because, let's face it, from everything you just said — you wrecked this girl's life. You hurt her, Blair — bad." Graham stops walking, then, and sets both hands on my shoulders. "Look, Blair. As far as I can tell, there's nothing optional about this. It's not a game. You need to fix things for her, and for you. If you've really been stuck on this girl for the last ten years — you think that's ever going to change? It's time to stop going through the motions, brother. Stop playing it safe. Forget about all the noise in your life: the Parental Units, the Publishing House, even the City. I say focus on your drive — Roxie — and give it your all. Do what you have planned for her. Tell her everything. Better yet, show her."

Show her.

His monologue reverberates in me, like a fizzy soda pop, like tiny, carbonated bubbles. I feel awake, for the first time in a long time. I feel every single drop of all the pain and havoc I have caused. Graham goes back to walking, so I do the same, turning to admire this man beside me.

"Graham. Is it disgustingly selfish of me to say I wish you never left?"

He sucks in a tempered breath. "No. It's not. I'm sorry, Blair. I guess you know what it feels like to be abandoned, too." He regards the skyscrapers as though they are the walls of a prison. "I should've at least invited you to come with me, back when I made my decision."

I can't help but smirk at that. "We both know I would've turned you down. I've never had your *drive,* as you call it."

We've wandered back to the Publishing House now. By the way he hugs me, I realize he's not coming back inside.

"You have drive, Blair," he says. "It's just time to put it to good use."

Back in my office, I take a seat. I frown, rubbing my hand along my jaw.

Show her.

I pull open the top drawer of my desk. I reach all the way back inside, rummage around among sticky-notes and paperclips, until my fingers find what I'm looking for.

A pack of gum. Original Trident, to be exact. This stuff always helped clear my head, helped me think. Sorry, dentist—sorry, overworked jaw—but I have some serious clearing and thinking to do. Some serious planning.

Show her. The game plan is back on. We'll see whether Fate is on my side or not. For now, I have some arrangements to make. First things first, I need to make a call to my very best buddy, Mr. Cocky Butterfly himself, Clarence Reeves.

He answers the phone with a concise: "This is Clarence."

"Hey, bigshot. It's your babysitter here. I've got a favor to ask you."

47

Roxie

It's been six days since Tim left. Six days without him. What's strange about it is how *not* strange it's felt.

I don't feel any more alone than normal. The bed feels just as empty as ever. My days are spent just the same. My nights by the defunct fireplace, as well, aren't any different. I don't feel the loss of him. That's not right, is it? I should feel the loss.

This evening, I'm in the apartment kitchen, staring into the fridge. I squint at the eggs in there. The butter. I try to remember what it was like to be fifteen and throw myself into the passion of baking. So effortlessly. Unquestioningly. Completely.

Then comes a knock at the door. Unsettling for ten o'clock at night. But when I check the peephole, I see that I'm in no danger. Well, technically, that could be debated.

I open up, stand there, look at Blair Porter. I'm in my sweats and a floppy sweater, my hair in a bun. He's bundled in a suave coat, clean shaven as always.

We look at each other; we stand on either side of the threshold; I feel the weight between us after what happened the last time we were together.

"Hey," he says. Hangs his head a little.

"Hi," I say, my voice hollow.

I hear him inhale through his nose. Clear his throat.

"Well." Blair looks tired. His typical enthusiasm isn't present tonight.

"Well?" I say.

"We do have one last outing."

He looks up at me, a flicker of worried hope, a question floating on the surface of his eyes.

I give him my answer: "So we do."

With that, he reaches into his pocket and hands me a slip of paper. I see a time and place—the airport—and then he says, "Tomorrow. You'll have to pack a bag."

I don't know why, but all I do is look at him. A slew of questions ripples through me, a parade of concerns goes marching across my consciousness. But I just look at Blair. And I give him one little shrug.

"Okay."

After closing the door, I don't move. I read his writing (*Outing #3 . . .*) and wonder where I'm going with him tomorrow. Where I'm going with my life in general.

"Roxie."

Mischa pops up behind me, poking her silver head around a corner. She sports mustard leggings and an oversized T-shirt printed with the obscure message: *COOKIE.*

"Mischa. How long have you been there?"

She arches a dark brow. Says:

"I'll help you pack."

48

Roxie

We land in Portland.

Pick up a rental car.

Blair drives us the hour and half it takes to get to the edge of the continent.

Just like that, despite leaving this place behind me, despite never planning to return, never wanting to return . . .

I'm back in Tangle Beach.

∞

On the flight over, Blair explained how he'd managed to get me a mini-vacation of four days off from work. It was a bit alarming to me that I hadn't even considered my job, hadn't given it a second thought when I met Blair at JFK and boarded the plane with him.

Apparently, he had called Clarence Reeves, the author of the TV mini-series. Through some convoluted sequence of connections and favors, I had been granted some time off. Bianca, I imagined, was probably pissed at losing her trusty gopher. Or maybe not. Maybe she'd be glad to be rid of me for a little while.

"Not gonna lie," Blair had remarked on the plane. "I thought Clarence was just a self-absorbed tool. Seems I was wrong, though. The guy came through for me."

That was the only conversation we shared on the journey to Oregon. I wasn't in the mood to talk, and Blair respected my quiet detachment the whole way to our destination.

Tangle Beach. I'm back on the Oregon Coast.

The brown-shingled buildings.

The quaint little roads.

The bushes and brambles and trees, all lush and green in the middle of winter. After being in New York for seven months, it's like stumbling upon a different planet. None of this feels real. Being back here, with Blair, doesn't feel real.

Blair drives us through the little roads, up to a rental house by the ocean.

"I thought about trying to book the old guest house with the Yamaha," he explains. "But I was afraid that might be . . . you know. Too much."

"This is fine," I reply. I'm glad he didn't bring us to that other house. All the memories there. The piano lessons and confused feelings. It *would* have been too much.

After getting our suitcases inside and inspecting the simple, cozy rental, I go stand before the west-facing windows. The ocean is out there. My old friend. Slate gray in February. I try not to look at it too closely. I try to fight the pull I feel to it. Blair comes up beside me, and I cross my arms around my chest. I finally give voice to some of the questions running through my mind.

"Blair. What are we doing here? Why are you doing this?"

The ocean swells with white foam, ghostly waves below the foggy sky.

"I want to show you something," Blair says. "Tomorrow. When we have more time."

With the time changes and traveling, it's about 4 p.m. now. The sun will set in around an hour.

"I don't like being back here."

Blair glances at me after I say it. "Why?"

I don't answer.

"Because of me? What I did?"

"Not exactly."

The ocean begs me to make eye contact with it. I give in, and I can taste its salt just by seeing the way it curls and surges and breaks.

"Wanna go out there?" Blair nudges me with his shoulder, the way he would when we were younger.

"It's not August, Blair. Do you know how cold the beach gets in the winter?"

His mischievous smile is daring, childlike.

"So?"

∞

He lets me go out ahead of him, says he'll follow me in a few minutes. So I go. I make the chilly, windswept walk, feeling my cheeks tingle, my core shiver.

A storm is coming. I can feel it. It's nearly here. I trudge over the smooth ripples in the sand until finally, I'm face to face with it. The ocean.

Just to be near it is enough. It's as if I can feel it tickling my ankles, tugging against my balance with the strong undertow. The air is thick with soft, humid salt. Salty and sweet, the way I remember. I can feel my heart pounding as though I'm sprinting up the shore in my old sneakers, headed for my wooded lot, the blackberries. I spread out my hands by my sides and let my fingers grow numb, let my hair whip around my neck, feel the soft ground beneath my feet.

It takes a while before I realize Blair is standing next to me. I am so entranced by all of this: My reunion with these waters. Eventually Blair speaks up over the steady roar. He pulls something out from behind his back, brandishes it into the air.

"Might I interest you in some frisbee?"

I actually laugh. It sounds so strange after being nothing but serious for days, weeks, on end.

"On one condition," I say.

"What's that?"

"Don't whack me in the head again."

He grins. "I have to be honest, Roxie. Whacking you in the head was probably the best thing that ever happened to me."

∞

It's crazy. I'm flinging a frisbee back and forth with Blair. On our old beach. On an evening that is much too cold and windy to be engaging in such an activity.

And, craziest of all, I'm laughing. He's laughing. The wind takes the frisbee on wild paths of its own. Blair and I struggle to catch it and send it back the right way. It's totally ridiculous how much fun I'm having, almost like I'd forgotten what the word *fun* even meant.

But the storm is still brewing, the wind is growing stronger, so we call it quits, out of breath and surprisingly warmed up. Blair suggests a trip to the market so we can make some food before the day concludes. I'm starving, so I don't protest. We go to the same market where we first ran into Tim. Back when Blair Porter was *The Tourist* and Tim was just *Tim Redding*: the annoying boy at school who kept pestering me at my locker when I didn't want him to.

I ponder on this while Blair and I weave through the aisles, making our selections. I've spent ten years with that boy from my high school, and I've known the whole time that my heart was never truly in it.

We walk back toward the house with our groceries. Tangle Beach has not changed at all, stuck in a timeless realm. The storm continues to bolster. It twists the trees. Leaves are whipped from them, thrown across the sky—others dive down toward the sidewalks. Up above, seagulls are pushed this way and that as pewter clouds billow closer and closer.

It's strange, seeing this storm. The way everything bends in unison with it. The wind connects every branch and weed and bird so they are not alone. I want to bend with them. I want the wind to bring me into its fold and connect me to everything else.

Then the rain comes: a quiet, dense drizzle. Thunder cracks. Blair and I start running. I hear him laughing. I'm laughing, too, because he is, because I'm letting myself. Because deep down, when I see his smile and hear that good-hearted laugh, I want nothing more than to be part of it.

The rain soaks us by the time we get back. We breathe heavily inside the house, cold and in need of some towels.

Was I wrong to leave this place?

Or is the mistake in coming back?

49

Blair

Current report: So far, so good.

She's here with me. Roxie came all the way back to the place it started. The beginning of our story. And while we are here, I'm going to reveal my two remaining secrets. As Graham advised me, I'm going to *tell* her, and I'm going to *show* her.

Tomorrow is the big day. The final steps of the game plan. For now, tonight, I'm just trying to take things easy, find the right balance, not push Roxie too hard. I can tell it's difficult for her to be back in Tangle Beach. I know the memories here are not all sweet and sunny for her. But I'm hoping that, while we're here, I can help remind her of some of the good ones.

We make a simple pasta primavera for dinner, with bread and wine. We sit at a little table on one end of the kitchen, where we can see the wild weather outside. It never stormed like this when I was here that summer. Actually, it never stormed at all. I'm hoping tonight's storm is, somehow, a good sign. A portent of things changing. A breaking point.

"I should see Christine while I'm here," Roxie says as we eat.

"Wow, Queen Christine," I comment. "I kind of forgot about her." That blonde wedding planner who was constantly clashing with my Music Hermit. "Have you stayed in touch? How did everything end up between the two of you, anyway?"

"You'd be surprised." Roxie twirls pasta around her fork. "We made things work together. Found peace, like you wanted. She was really there for me after you . . . you know."

I nod, bite my lip.

She goes on: "We send each other the occasional email or text. She's never left Tangle Beach. Still in the same house, too, on Seawood Lane. She started making enough money with Lace &

Tide that she could quit her other job. And I guess she recently started dating this guy from Pacific Pastries who always used to be terrified of her. Probably still *is* terrified of her."

That makes me laugh. "The woman did have an intimidating air about her. Remember that one wedding on the beach you helped her with?"

"Blair. Every wedding was on the beach."

"Well, yes. But that one with the seashell ceremony. Christine threatened to essentially devour your very soul if you didn't find a vase and a billion shells in time for the wedding."

Roxie smiles, rolls her eyes. "She made me so mad."

"But we figured things out just in time."

Peering at me from across the table, her smile falls slightly, becomes rueful.

She says, "You figured it out for me." Her fingers run up and down the stem of her glass. "That was the moment I first realized . . ."

"What?" I ask, softly, carefully. I'm dying to hear the end of her sentence.

Cat eyes grow cloudy; she looks away.

"That I was beginning to fall in love with you."

I stay quiet. It's not the right time to say anything. I wish she could fall in love with me again. I wish I hadn't been an idiot, a wishy-washy coward of a boy.

Roxie stands up. Wind whistles against the windows, and the glass trembles in turn.

"I'm exhausted," Roxie states. "I think I'm going to go to bed."

"Okay."

This isn't what I had hoped for this evening. In my overly-optimistic imagination, I was going to ask Roxie if we could bake dessert together. Specifically, those first cookies she made for me, the ones that rocked my world so long ago. In my head, she'd say yes. I would get some great music going, and we'd end our day acting young and silly together like we did on the beach, with the frisbee.

But all that's just me being selfish. And this trip, I need to remind myself, isn't all about me. I need to give Roxie room to breathe, time to process. It's good she's going to bed so early, anyway.

I suspect she will need her rest for tomorrow.

∞

The next morning, breakfast consists of bagels and coffee in the kitchen. The bagels are nothing compared to the ones in New York, but I'm trying not to compare-and-contrast in that obnoxious way of mine. More than that, I'm trying not to even think about New York at all. Because today is a big day. It's *the* day. I want to be in the moment as much as humanly possible.

"Did you really have to fly me all the way across the country for whatever this is?"

We're in the rental car. Roxie doesn't look at me when she speaks. It's like she's talking to the window.

"Yes," I respond. "I really did."

"Is it the wooded lot with the blackberries? Are you trying to remind me of all the great times we had? To manipulate me into forgiving you?"

I steer the vehicle through town. Every fiber of every muscle is humming in me right now. I'm somewhere between excited and terrified. Restless, maybe, is the right term. Pins and needles.

"I would love for you to forgive me one day," I say to Roxie. "But that's not what this is about. And no, it's not the wooded lot."

I just hope I've made the right decision in all this. It's a bit insane. But I guess that's just who I am. And if I understand Roxie well—which, I think I do—then I *have* made the right call, and what I'm about to show her in a matter of minutes will be exactly what she needs.

I drive, and then, I pull up to it. We're here.

My second secret.

50

Roxie

I had another memory-dream last night, while sleeping in a room by the ocean. A memory-dream of her, of course. Of Maryanne, and me.

I don't know how old I was. But it was summer, and we were picking berries together behind our house. There were so many to choose from, all ripe and fragrant, dark and full. One in particular caught my eye: the perfect berry. Bigger than all the rest. Perfectly matte, indicating its readiness. Its beautiful sweetness I imagined on my tongue.

Eagerly, greedily, I went for it. But in the process, I got something else instead. A hidden thorn pricked me, tore at me, so fine and sharp, a sting and a snag down my thumb.

The berry, heavy on its vine, disturbed by my incident, dropped to the earth, disappearing into the web of vines below. I pulled my hand away and saw the blood running down my thumb, mixing with the berry juices. My hand still stinging. Purple and red.

"Mama." I showed her my wound, and she took a napkin from the pocket of her dress, pressed it to the side of my thumb. She was always prepared for this. Unperturbed. But on this day, I wasn't. I was not prepared to lose that perfect berry and get pricked. I was perturbed.

"We'll get you a bandage when we're back inside," she said calmly, going back to picking fruit.

I didn't go back to picking.

"Mama. Why do there have to be thorns? Why can't there just be the berries?"

She took her time mulling this over, which made me impatient. Then she answered.

"It's just the way it is, my rabbit. You can't have one without the other. The sweetness doesn't come without the pain."

As always, I let her words turn and spin in my head. I looked at those little knives twisting up and down among the sweet berries. They were everywhere.

"Sugar thorns," I said.

She looked at me with a soft smile.

"Sugar thorns. Exactly. I like that."

I wasn't so sure I did. It was just the best my young mind could cope.

I behold the place Blair has brought me to. It feels like my dream come to life. It *is* my dream come to life.

It's the house.

It's my home.

I get out of the car, and I'm standing before green walls in the lush woods of Shoshone. The world is damp and calm after last night's storm. Blair gets out of the car, too, not speaking, letting me adjust to what I'm seeing, where I am.

My heart seeps hundreds of emotions as I stand there, dumbfounded. This was my haven as a child, before life got in the way, before I knew what real pain felt like.

This was my home. And hers.

I take cautious steps forward, over soggy leaves. Birds are trilling, water is dripping. The house looks exactly as I remember. Small and beautiful. Humble and welcoming.

"You can go in, if you want."

I twist around at Blair's voice. My own voice is barely working.

"No one—" I glance at the metal-framed windows, look for movement behind them. "No one's here? Isn't that breaking in?"

Blair just shakes his head back and forth. Gestures toward the front door.

My body trembles as I step up the tiny porch with Blair behind me. As I spin the cold doorknob. As the door squeaks in that plaintive way it always did.

And then I'm inside. And it's surreal. Unbelievable. Impossible.

It's the same.

Nothing has changed. How is that possible?

Emotions beat at my chest, well up in my eyes. I'm a child again within these walls. I see the pretty wallpaper. I run my hand along it. It is rough, it peels at the corners, but it's the same.

Down the hall. A creaky floor. And the charcoal drawings. Somehow, they still hang upon the walls. Her signature there in each corner. *Maryanne.*

I curve into the kitchen. It still smells of yeast. I see the little rabbits on the tile backsplash. The garden window, even streaks of rain sliding down it. I can see her moving from the oven to the counter, rolling out dough, rinsing a bowl of berries, cracking an egg with one hand. In my mind, I can see the dried flowers she used to hang upside down from the ceiling.

Then, the sitting room in the back. Blair trails me with every step I take, staying silent. I can hear myself breathing. Heavy, shaky breaths.

The old, upright piano. It's still here. Chipped, yellowed keys. Worn wood. Nothing atop it (an instrument, not a shelf for décor). All of the furniture is the same, too. I don't understand. How can this be? It's been thirteen years. She's been gone thirteen years. And so have I. Why hasn't any of this changed?

I go to the piano. Sit on the sturdy bench. Blair comes up beside me.

"A retired couple bought the estate thirteen years ago. The house and everything in it." He is answering the questions I can't even voice. "They used it as a vacation home. They liked everything about it, just the way it was."

"Where are they now?" I manage to ask.

Blair, steady and serious: "The man passed away last year. The woman didn't want to come out here by herself. Didn't see the point in holding onto it. So. She put it up for sale."

I look from the piano to Blair.

"I bought it," he says.

My heart pounds. My forehead creases so much it hurts, and my eyes burn with wetness.

"You . . ."

"I found the address a long time ago. I remembered you calling it your *'little green Shoshone house on Wild Road.'* I wondered what had happened to it, after you had to leave and go live with Christine. I kept tabs on it over the years, and then it came on the market last year. And I didn't even think. I just snatched it up. I knew I had to get it back to you somehow, and then last December, I ran into you at that party." He smiles, but it's small and mindful. "Talk about an anti-coincidence."

"Blair." Tremors have taken hold of my arms and legs. I don't know what to say. How can I express what this means to me . . . There are no words . . .

"Sit," I say, scooting over on the bench. He does, and we are in that old position: me on the right, him on the left.

I start to play. C sharp. The first note. It only takes a moment for Blair to know what I'm doing, and timidly, hopefully, he joins in. Together, we play the Sonata. The fifth variation. The one that still makes me think of a couple dancing in the rain. The tender, warm, unhurried feeling of falling in love.

It would be a good note to end on: me and Blair playing that song again. Yet there's more to be done here. More to be said. When the song concludes, I give a minute for the music to sink in. I give Blair a minute for it to sink in. Then I get up, and I go to the hallway. Gingerly, I pull a framed drawing off the wall. I head to the back door, and Blair follows me out behind the house.

Out to the thicket, swollen, wild. The blackberries. They twist and curl and sprawl and climb. Just like always. They are dormant for now, but they are thick and ever-present, and I know I have to go to them. I stand at their edge, remembering that awful day. *We are where brambles prick and give and bow.*

This was where I found her. She died here, where she belonged, in her favorite place, in her butter-yellow dress. The brambles took her gracefully, left me empty and alone.

"I still remember getting cut by one of these things." Blair, also, studies the vines. "It got my heel bleeding pretty bad, right before I kissed you."

"Sugar thorns," I hear myself say.

Blair raises his brows in question.

"It's what she and I always said, whenever one of us got pricked while berry-picking."

"Oh. Your mother."

The air is damp. The brambles surround us. I almost want them to take me. To curl their vines around me, twist up my arms and legs, hold me tight, even if it were to hurt, even if I were to bleed. A bruised sorrow spreads throughout me.

"She wasn't my mother."

Blair's head swivels my way. The words have fallen out of me, handed down to winter vines.

"What?" Blair says. Confused. Unsure. I know the feeling. Yes. I know it well.

"Maryanne. She wasn't my—" and I break down. I nearly collapse, and Blair catches me, holds me while I cry into his chest. We are two people pressed into one. I feel his hand in my hair, the worry emanating from inside as he holds me tighter, as I bleed my tears into him.

This is what Christine told me ten years ago. The August night I broke the soapy plate. This is why I stopped baking. Stopped journaling. Stopped running. Why I left Tangle Beach when I had the chance, with no plans of ever coming back.

With Blair's arms around me, I tell him the story.

51

Roxie

Maryanne Morah was many things, but she was not my biological mother.

Christine Lambert, conflicted and concerned, told me this truth that August night and gave me a sheet of paper she'd been keeping in her closet.

It was covered in Mama's handwriting. Maryanne had been planning on giving it to me when I turned eighteen. When she died, it made its way into Christine's hands, along with that intent to wait until I was an adult to share it with me. But that night of the shattered plate, I was given the chance to read it early. And I did, front and back.

It was the story of what happened. Where I really came from.

Maryanne Morah, in her late twenties, was living her peaceful life in Shoshone, alone. Just her and her baking. Her berry-picking. Catering. Selling pies and cakes to local restaurants. Farmers' markets.

That was where she first interacted with her. My real mother. It was at one of the indoor farmers' markets in Shoshone. It wasn't the first time Maryanne Morah had seen her, though. Evidently, Maryanne had spotted the woman in town before, here and there, briefly, like cloudy wisps of a ghost in a room. Each time it happened, the woman seemed to be eyeing Maryanne. Curious about her, for some reason.

I say *woman*, but I shouldn't. *Girl* is really the correct word. Because she was young. Anywhere from seventeen to nineteen, Maryanne estimated. Always a frightened look in her eyes. Tired, scared. And pregnant.

Maryanne was at the winter farmers' market, selling her blackberry pies and jams on a February day. The market was held in the high school gym that time of year, and Maryanne had used frozen berries from last season to concoct her beloved treats. The gym was only moderately busy, and most shoppers that day were primarily interested in the heart-shaped cookies for Valentine's Day, the chocolate-coated marshmallows and cherries. Not the summer-berry pies.

But then there came an interested patron, slowly wandering up to Maryanne's table. The girl. She kept a shy distance, looked at all the golden, flaky crusts. Looked at Maryanne, but only for a fleeting instant. Her eyes were almond-shaped and beautiful, but they didn't seem to think they were worthy of holding the pie baker's gaze.

"How far along are you?" Maryanne bestowed warmth upon the girl, that sunny, caring way she always had with people.

The girl didn't answer. She looked away, embarrassed. Her stomach was full. Her clothes didn't fit right. She must have been in her third trimester.

The girl lingered at the table, her focus beginning to wander over the pies again. There were free samples being offered in paper cups, but she didn't take one. Still, Maryanne could sense the girl's hunger.

"Take one," Maryanne said, to which the pregnant girl shot her a pair of wide eyes. Maryanne wasn't referring to the samples. She slid one of the large, full pies across the table, all the way to the edge.

The girl spoke finally, cluttered words. "I can't—I don't have any—"

"It's free," Maryanne said. "Take it." She leaned over to tie the container in ribbon, a sprig of dried flowers and her business card tucked underneath, just like she did for all the other customers. The girl stood there awhile, staring at Maryanne with her frightened-animal eyes. Finally, she took the pie in her arms, over her swollen belly, rasping, *Thank you,* and whisking away.

Maryanne didn't see the girl again. Not exactly. It was a week later. Maryanne was home, baking in the green house on Wild

Road. It was only a couple months earlier she had bought the house. Had gotten it set up with her secondhand furniture and dried flowers. Had gotten new business cards with her updated address printed on them.

The day was cold and dry when she heard a frantic knocking at the door. A moment later, there was the sound of acceleration down the driveway. By the time she made it to the door and opened up, the car was nearly gone—but Maryanne saw who was in the driver's seat just before the girl turned onto Wild Road and sped away.

And then Maryanne saw what was sitting down by her feet, on the small porch. A cardboard box. With a baby inside. Swaddled in a stained blanket, little rabbits circling about the worn fleece. The baby squirmed and cooed, oblivious—Maryanne stooped and examined her, shocked.

There was a business card tucked in the box. Maryanne's. On the back, a brief note:

You are better.

Maryanne never even knew the girl's name. She knew nothing about her. But she took her baby inside the house. She named her Roxanne Morah and raised her as her own. Taught her to bake. To play the piano, to pick berries. Answered all her curious questions as best she could.

People in town always said Maryanne Morah had her share of secrets.

I had just believed they were referring to her cakes and pies, her breads and pastries, her ways in the kitchen, and in the kitchen alone.

∞

Blair holds me throughout the story. Doesn't say a word. I'm warm in his arms, and I bleed and I bleed, I let every detail out, every pent-up tear I've tried to deny under the guise of being strong.

Finally, I pull back, just a little. I still have something in my grip, clutched against my stomach. The framed charcoal drawing. I look at it, and I show Blair.

It is the portrait of a woman I didn't recognize growing up. Now, I know it is the same woman Maryanne and I came upon in Tillamook. That rainy day, the café delivery. The moment Maryanne saw her sitting in the corner and dropped the cake to the floor. The way the woman became so scared when she saw us, before she rushed away.

I understand now. That woman, that scared girl, the one behind this sheet of glass, is my mother. And what has always felt infinitely more important and gutting:

Maryanne Morah was not.

I tuck the drawing back against my stomach. Three thorns have wounded me in my life. Three events that each left me in more pain than the one before. The first ripped straight through my heart, when my sweet, beautiful Maryanne died, leaving a permanent, infinite hole. Blair's thorn was the second, a thorn that punctured me, stuck itself inside my chest and never left—I still feel it in there, throbbing with each and every pump.

But the last one got me differently. As a keen knife. A sickly blade. Dragged and ripped through the middle of all my tissues and matter, the last thorn severed me in two, leaving me with no ground beneath my feet, no peace within my soul.

"I don't know who I am anymore," I say into the tender air. "I'm so lost, Blair. I'm lost, and I'm hurt. Everyone leaves me and lies to me. I'm terrified I'll always be alone."

Blair takes my face in his hands. His blue fire eyes are saturated in concern, compassion, regret. He pulls me back in his embrace and squeezes me, as though he might squeeze every last drop of grief and confusion from my body.

He whispers into my ear: "You're not alone, Roxie."

His words replay in my head.

I think, maybe, just maybe, I might believe him.

52

Blair

I, Blair Porter, have been an outright fool. A small-minded idiot camouflaged in a big city. I've misjudged what feels like so many things. Believed *I* was the one with all the secrets. Been asinine and selfish in so many ways.

Although I tried to tell myself differently, the truth is, I really had believed this was all about me. And in some ways, it was about me—that is, I've had my part to play—but only on the periphery, never at the very heart of it all.

When I said Roxie and I had come back to the beginning of our story here on the Oregon Coast, I was wrong. It is so much more than that. Roxie has come back to the beginning of *her* story.

Everything makes sense to me now. All the changes I've seen in Roxie since last December, the glow she's seemed to have lost—at the very heart of it was not me, but her mother. Her adoptive mother.

She's exhausted. She's had too much of this for one day. When I ask her if we should go back to the rental house on the beach, she simply nods her head.

Back at the house, I go to make some tea in the kitchen. Roxie sits on a couch and stares at the ocean, wordless, quiet. The kettle whistles, and I bring out a cup of chamomile, set it before her, and take a cautious seat beside her. Roxie stares at the ocean, stares and stares.

"This doesn't change who you are, Roxie."

She looks at me. She's crying again, and I can't stand it. I don't want to overstep, to push too hard, but after learning everything I just have, I can't contain myself any longer. I move closer to her and rub the tears from her cheeks. I dare to speak the truth, to say the words she needs to hear. I keep her face in my hands and ramble on and on in a low tone.

"It doesn't have to change who you are. You don't have to live somewhere else. You don't have stop baking. You don't have to force your way into someone else's life. Maryanne was still your mother, the one who raised you and gave you all her love, gave you the talent you have now. She never wanted to leave you. And I—I was confused and selfish and immature. Let's be real, I'm still trying to mature at thirty years old. I've hated myself these last ten years for what I did to you. Now I see the full extent of it all, and I'm sorry, I'm so sorry, Roxie. I can't say it enough. I'm sorry."

She shuts her eyes as I'm speaking. Squeezes them tight as tears keep coming. She lets me go on to the end. But then her eyes open. And she pulls away. She gets off the couch and walks up to the windows. She lingers there, dazed and drained.

I decide to get up and move behind her.

I move a little closer. A little closer.

"Roxie. I know that you hate me and everything. You have every right to. And I know I should have said this ten years sooner, but . . ."

I wait a moment. She turns to view me, and I feel her cat eyes lock with mine. This is my third secret. The last one. Though I'm not so sure how secretive it really is. And so all my secrets are as follows:

1. I was at Roxie's Ocean Festival performance.

2. I bought her childhood house in Shoshone.

And, 3. . .

"I love you." My voice wavers. "I've loved you since I was nineteen. Since that day I saw you on the beach."

She looks at me and looks at me. It feels like hours pass. I feel my declaration out there in the open, hanging between us. I feel how *she* must have felt that night she uttered the same words to me. I should have said them back. Now, the tables have turned. I try speaking again:

"Like I said, I know you hate me, I know you don't feel the same way anymore—"

"Blair."

Roxie comes up to me. She leaves no space between us. And she smiles. She actually smiles—small and careful, but real.

"I don't hate you, you weirdo city boy." She cups my face, and her touch sparks life within me. "I love you like crazy, Blair Porter. As much as I loved Maryanne. I love you as much as I did ten years ago. I've tried not to—God, I've tried. Because I love you so much, Blair, it hurts."

I kiss her, then.

And she kisses me back.

I feel joy cascade around me. I hold her in my arms, knowing this is how it always should have been. Not the silly first kiss in the forest. Not the confused, fervent kiss in her old room—nor the confused, premature kiss in the greenhouse.

This. This is right. *This* is every amazing song put together, every perfect note and chord and beat and lyric. Who even needs music when you have this?

I take Roxie's waist in my hands, kiss her lips the way that is right: unrushed, tender, careful yet passionate, sensual but true.

"I never want to leave you again," I say in between the soft melding of our mouths. Roxie goes on kissing me as I talk, not ready to stop, like I'm a baked creation she's been longing to consume for a long time. When she is ready, I finish my thought. Not that I want to put the brakes on what's happening, but this other thing is important, too.

"If I could have my way, Roxie, we would be together, and I would love you and always stay with you. You'd never be alone. But I know you have to make your own decision. You have to choose what you want in life. And who you want to be."

She slides her hands down my arms, stopping at my wrists.

"You know we can't go back to being kids again, Blair," she says, a hesitancy lurking in her tone.

"I know. I don't want to."

"I'm not sure I can ever be that fifteen-year-old girl again."

"I'm not asking you to. I loved you then. I love you now."

She's quiet.

"It just depends on what you want," I say. "You have to decide."

Still quiet.

"Roxie. What do you want?"

53

Roxie

The phone is ringing. It's nine o'clock at night here. Midnight over there. I'm in my bedroom of the beach rental house, cell phone pressed to my ear.

After everything that's happened today, my mind is somehow whirling yet perfectly still at the same time. I think about my Shoshone home. The fact that Blair bought it for me, that he took me there, that it was exactly the same as I remembered. I think about the berries and my confession to Blair, a secret I've been bottling up within me for an entire decade. Now, I've released it. Blair knows. And there is peace in that. I think of everything he told me today. I think of this boy who's had my heart since the beginning. I think of the question he posed to me, the decision I must make.

I know my decision. I've known since he uttered those words: *I love you.* The only thing now is a quick phone call. The phone rings one more time, then I hear a click and a pause.

"Roxie?"

"Mischa. Did I wake you?"

"Yes. I was dreaming." Her slight accent filters into my ear from across the country. I wonder what her outfit is like right now.

"Sorry. I can call tomorrow."

"No. Tell me. How is it going? Where are you?"

I press my hand to my chest. As though I can feel my wounds healing in there.

"I'm in Oregon. It's going . . . well, actually. It's good."

"I thought so."

"Mischa. I just wanted to say. Thanks for all the late night talks these past few months. You'll make a great therapist one day."

"I don't want to be a therapist."

"Didn't you say . . ."

"I just wanted to be your friend," she says.

I smile. "In that case, you're a great friend. Thank you."

"Okay. Well. Anything else?" She yawns.

"No. Get back to your dream."

"*Spoki*, Roxie."

The smile lingers on my face, my hand over my heart. I let out a breath.

"*Spoki*, Mischa."

Part Three

Tangle Beach, Oregon

—SIX MONTHS LATER—

54

Roxie

Berry season.

It's August. The days have been warm in Shoshone. There isn't much ocean breeze this far inland, but what trickles through is enough. I wear a light, airy dress. My hair is long again, down to my shoulder blades. I'm in the kitchen, in my element, with the side panels of the garden window cranked open.

I start with butter. Sugar. Cream them together. Eggs, cracked precisely, expertly. I'm making cookies today, at Blair's request. Soon, I hope to be whipping something up with a fresh batch of berries from the backyard. Blackberry cobbler. Blackberry scones. I might even try homemade blackberry ice cream.

For now, I get lost in the simple cookie dough. I smell sweet vanilla and brown sugar. I smell dried lavender hanging from the ceiling. All of it mixes with the fresh air from outside.

I'm back where I belong.

This summer has been blissful. Suddenly, it's like everything makes sense again. Everything feels right. Snapped back into place. Realigned. There were a lot of changes to be made in my life, but with each one, I began to feel more and more like myself.

I parted ways with Tim Redding back in February. It was civil and peaceful. It was right. Word is, he ended up moving to LA when his mini-series wrapped up. He got a role on another TV show and happily returned to the West Coast. Of course, Ethan tagged along for the move—Ethan *and* Mischa both became Californians along with Tim. I talk to Mischa every so often on video chats, that way I can stay up to date on her life, as well as her outfits. I guess Ethan got a job at Trader Joe's, and he swears he saw Robert Downey Jr. shopping there one day. Mischa suspects he might just be saying it to make Tim jealous, but who knows?

But back to me—it was six months ago I made my return to Oregon. To Shoshone, to this house that's always been home. This place that has no true substitute, no matter how much I appreciated my old wooded lot in Tangle Beach.

Blair gifted the estate to me, so that this green house, everything in it, the piano, the art, the blackberry bushes out back—everything is officially mine. I hung dried flowers from the ceiling and the Mary Elizabeth Frye poem on the wall above the piano. I got a copy of the sheet music for Sonata No. 11, which rests in the music stand, ready for Variation V to be played whenever the fancy strikes me.

The changes didn't stop there. A truly momentous event took place, also in February. A certain city boy named Blair Porter left his beloved New York, New York. What's more, he told me he didn't mind one bit, had no second thoughts. Blair left Porter Publishing House. Left his parents, his brownstones, his skyscrapers, Central Park. He moved all the way to Oregon and started renting a house in Tangle Beach.

He said he wanted to give me time to live in the Shoshone house by myself, to get reacquainted with it. To get reacquainted with Maryanne, and absorb all the memories she and I shared within these walls.

He wanted to find a place to rent in Shoshone, but the nearest he could find was in Tangle Beach. It works out well, anyway, having Blair live over that way. Because there is a little project we have in the works there. Blair has been helping me realize the dream I had when I was fifteen: to open my own bakery. Technically, it will be *our* bakery. He will take care of all the business details, the money, the marketing—stuff he seems to have a knack for. And naturally, I will take care of all the baking.

We should be opening by the end of the year. Sugar Thorn Bakery. We have a building leased right in downtown Tangle Beach, and Blair has been busy getting the place remodeled and furnished. It's a little bit of a drive for me, but not too bad, and we'll have more business there with all the beach tourism.

In the meantime, I'm keeping myself plenty busy. I'm running again, every morning. Not because I'm empty, not because I'm trying to sprint away from my pain—I run because it enhances my peace, because it reminds me of who I really am. I'm journaling again, too, because I never want to forget, because I want my beautiful Mama to know, wherever she is: *I miss you.*

Of course, I'm baking again. This summer, I am officially the dessert caterer for Lace & Tide. I get together with Christine on a regular basis to plan all of the beautiful wedding cakes and treats for her clients. She says that once Sugar Thorn Bakery is up and running, it'll be her number-one, "expert" recommendation. When I asked how her Pacific Pastries boyfriend would feel about that, she asserted that she didn't care—if he didn't like it, he could get lost. Secretly, I think the guy will be kind of relieved that he won't have to work for his intimidating girlfriend anymore.

Things are good. I can hardly believe it sometimes. Right now, my cookie dough is turning out just as thick and well-balanced as I hoped—*every bit of sweetness needs its salt.* Blair will be coming over later today. And then the next day. And the next day. The day after that.

I send an avalanche of butterscotch chips into my bowl—but I get messy—I spill some on the counter, down onto the floor. Fetching my broom and dustpan, I crouch down to clean up the mess. And while I'm down there, something catches my eye. Something hiding below the fridge.

I slide it out: it's a cookbook. Not one you would buy at Barnes & Noble. This is a handmade cookbook.

Breath gets trapped inside my lungs. A strange feeling comes over me. I crack the spine—and I am confronted with familiar handwriting.

Maryanne's. Mama's.

There are tens of recipes in here. I'm in shock as I flip through them. I thought she never used recipes. I thought she had been an intuitive baker, making things up as she went along.

I take my time perusing each recipe card, each ingredient she listed, each stroke of the pen. Then, I get to the very back of the binder, and my surprise escalates even further.

Two things wait for me there, tucked inside a plastic sheathing. Two things I never thought I'd see. One is a recipe. It's called: Roxie's Birthday Cake.

I scour the list of ingredients. Eggs, sugar, buttermilk. Blackberries.

This was the cake she was going to make for my thirteenth birthday, the one we never got to share together. I always wondered what that creation would have been like, how she would have formed and married the batter, icing, fruit. And now it's all here in front of me, on a recipe card, ready for me to bring it to life. My eyes are wet. My heart beats strong. Then, I take note of the other item.

It's an envelope.

I slip it out from the plastic. Open the flap. My knees dig into the hard kitchen floor. I hover over my discovery. Timidly, almost nervously, I let two slips of paper flutter down into my palm.

What happens after? I had asked my Mama. I'd been so eager to read her answer, and I never got the chance.

The first paper scrap is mine. *I don't know*, it reads.

Anticipation boils within me as I go to read the second. The one she wrote. My heart flitters about wildly.

And when I read it, a smile, a fragile laugh, lifts from me, rises up through the ceiling, up into the sky. Tears blur my vision. I laugh, and I feel free, light. Whole.

I think it is like perfect music that never ends.

A feeling of harmony pulses in the air around me. *She* is in the air around me. She is the sound of Blair's laughter. The taste of sun-sweetened, finger-bruising fruit. The rhythm of the crashing ocean. She isn't *nowhere to be found*, as once I thought. She is everywhere. She's inside me.

I look at the slip of paper again, press it to my chest, over my healing heart.

I can't wait to show Blair when he gets here.

I have this funny feeling he will strongly agree.

55

Blair

I've always fancied myself a city person, sure, but things change, don't they? One day you can feel deeply entwined with the scintillating streets of New York City—the next, you can feel inexpressibly content on the quiet back roads of the Oregon Coast.

I can't stop smiling today. I have some things planned. Ever since I got all three of my secrets out in the open, Fate has made a smooth ride for me. But it turns out I'm still making game plans, whether it's for the bakery, or for the surprises I have in store today.

I'm driving over to Roxie's house to pick blackberries with her. Finally. We were meant to do it together years ago, when I was nineteen and she fifteen. But it's happening now. "Sister Golden Hair" plays on the car's stereo system, and I sing along, feeling the joy that is present in this song, much more than the melancholy.

I have two different gifts for Roxie, when I get to her house, when we are set up in the backyard before the blackberries. I can't wait to give them to her. I can't wait to collect the berries and start making even more game plans—together. Strangely enough, we might even be recruiting Queen Christine for some planning-related help, sooner rather than later.

One of Roxie's gifts, in case you were wondering, is tucked away within my pocket. It's a ring. Yellow gold. An oval diamond. Nothing gaudy, nothing over the top. It is simple, elegant, perfect. Just like her.

A little yelp comes from behind me, over the sound of the music. Oh, yeah. That's the other gift, tucked safely in the backseat.

A puppy. One month old. Cute as they come. He's a golden retriever.

I was thinking we could name him Simon Paul Butterscotch Nolan Jr.

Or something like that.

∞

My name is Blair (not-just-a-girl's-name) Porter, and there are really only three things you need to know about me:

1. I no longer wish I'd been born in the sixties, seventies, or eighties. *Now*, I fancy, is a fine, a truly dandy time to be alive.

2. I still love music more than a chubby kid loves cherry cheesecake, more than a vampire loves a supple neck, more than a fluffy puppy loves romping up and down a sunny, sandy beach.

And:

3. Somehow—and I cannot stress this enough—I love a girl named Roxie Morah even more passionately and fully and deeply than any music in the world.

Blair's Playlist

1. "New York State of Mind – *Billy Joel*
2. "Have You Ever Seen the Rain?"– *Creedence Clearwater Revival*
3. "Me and Julio Down by the Schoolyard" — *Paul Simon*
4. "You Can Call Me Al" — *Paul Simon*
5. "The Boys of Summer" — *Don Henley*
6. "Dancing in the Moonlight" — *King Harvest*
7. "Sister Golden Hair"– *America*
8. "Livin' Thing" – *Electric Light Orchestra*
9. "Build Me Up Buttercup"– *The Foundations*
10. "I Guess That's Why They Call It the Blues"– *Elton John*
11. "Rich Girl" – *Hall & Oates*
12. "Starman"– *David Bowie*
13. "What Is Life" — *George Harrison*
14. "If Not for You" — *George Harrison*
15. "Make Your Own Kind of Music" — *Cass Elliot*
16. "So Far Away" — *Carole King*
17. "I Feel the Earth Move" – *Carole King*
18. "Got to Get You into My Life" – *The Beatles*
19. "December, 1963 (Oh, What a Night)" – *Frankie Valli & The Four Seasons*
20. "Sonata No. 11" – *Wolfgang Amadeus Mozart*

Author's Note & Acknowledgments

This story lived and developed inside my mind for about eighteen months before I began writing it. I had so many high hopes for it, and I endured a wild emotional roller coaster while chiseling away at each chapter, trying to get out of my own way so I could focus on Roxie and Blair. Now, I feel I've done this story justice, and I hope others will feel the same way.

First, I'd like to *un*-thank the year 2020 (the year I wrote this book) for making my writing process much rockier than normal, and for shaking up everyone's lives in general.

As always, I must thank my parents for reading each of my books and providing me with feedback. My dad deserves a little additional "credit" here, for exposing me to some great, Blair-approved music over the years.

A few extra shout-outs: My father-in-law, Rick, has read every one of my books, and I'm filled with gratitude for his support. My Auntie Di, also, has read all of my stories and always encourages me to keep going. There's also my Aunt Sandy who supports me and has plugged me on her blog, Reluctant Entertainer (thank you!).

To my readers: *Thank you, thank you, thank you.* I can't say it enough. You've helped fill my life with purpose. Your support blows me away. Thank you to each and every person who has taken the time to read this book, giving me a chance and a voice.

Lastly, to my husband: Thank you for being my #1 supporter. Thank you for constantly lifting me up, rooting for me, believing in me. Your partnership is the most profound thing I know of, and I wouldn't be able to keep writing these stories without you.

-Kayla

About the Author

❖ KAYLA ROSE is a self-published author in her twenties with no impressive credentials to tell you about. The only credential that really matters, in this context, is the one she possesses: a deep love of writing. Additionally, she loves the rain and thinks llamas are pretty great, too. Kayla lives in Washington state with her husband and fluffy Norwegian Forest cat, Sugar. She has written four novels: *The Apple Tree, The Rain in Sapphire, The Hallowed Hideaway,* and *The Sugar Thorns.* Kayla hopes to write and share as many stories as she can throughout her life.

❖ To learn more, read Kayla's blog, or send her a message, please visit kaylarosebooks.com

❖ Find Kayla (and Sugar) on Instagram: @kaylarosebooks

❖ For now, Kayla's entire corpus consists of the following books: *The Apple Tree, The Rain in Sapphire, The Hallowed Hideaway,* and *The Sugar Thorns.* You may come across other works on Amazon under the name Kayla Rose; please know these are different authors who happen to share her name.

❖ Please enjoy my short story entitled *The Ocean's Kiss* on the following pages, and thank you for your support!

The Ocean's Kiss

I was standing at the cliff's edge when I saw her. I was gazing down over the shoreline, tracking each wave as it crashed onto the land. It was the break of dawn, the sky a dusty rose color, the darkness of night still trying to cling on.

Given the time of day and the fact that this stretch of beach was not a tourist-friendly spot—large rocks were scattered across the sand, preventing children from running free and wild—I had not been expecting to see anyone from my place on the cliff. That was why I was there. To be alone.

Yet I wasn't. Not exactly. She was down there, right where the water met the earth. She was sitting, her knees drawn up to her chest, her arms wrapped around her legs. Her hair matched the color of the sand. She wore a deep blue dress and nothing else, despite the chill of the early morning. I could not see her face, because she was looking out toward the water.

As I studied her from afar, a sense of mystery came over me, followed by a sense of alignment. I knew something then, a fact as deep and true as the ocean's floor.

I was going to see her face. I needed to.

I did not approach her that first day. I had developed a list of rationalizations in my head as to why I didn't, but the truth was simple: I was afraid to. I was still afraid the next morning, when I returned to the cliff and saw that she was down there again. Sitting. Watching the water. Wearing the same blue dress.

I battled with myself atop the cliff. I should go to her. *No.* Maybe she is lonely. *Maybe she wants to be left alone.* But I am lonely. *But you come to the cliff to be alone.*

One side of me lost the battle. By the time I had descended the cliff and made it to the sand, the sun was just a little higher over the horizon, the world just a little lighter. The woman was still there, crouched down at the shoreline.

When I reached her, she did not seem to notice. She did not move. I still could not see her face, with her sand-like hair being

I

blustered around from the wind. Her dress was getting wet, rhythmically touched by the remnants of waves. I did not know what to do; I did not want to startle her. I was going to give up. I began turning away, but then she spoke.

"Sit with me."

Her voice was a higher pitch than I would have expected. Almost like that of a young girl's, but not quite. There was also an aged element to it, somehow.

"I'm sorry to bother you," I said. "I just noticed you here by yourself. I wanted to make sure you were okay."

This was not the real reason I was there, but I didn't know how else to explain myself.

"Please," she spoke. "Sit with me. Won't you?"

I did. I did it hesitantly, bending my knees slowly, arranging myself atop the wet sand. I flinched when the tide rushed up underneath me, soaking my pants.

"Thank you," the woman said. The ocean was roaring around us, but her voice came through clearly.

"Why are you sitting here?" I asked. "Are you waiting for someone?"

"I was. Now, someone is here." Finally, she craned her neck toward me, revealing her face. It was pale, free of makeup. Long, blonde lashes encircled the eyes that matched her dress. Her lips were the lightest pink, akin to the dusty rose color of dawn. She was beautiful in a way I'd never encountered before. She was raw. I was drawn to her.

"What's your name? I'm Marvin."

"Marvin." Repeating my name seemed to bring her some kind of pleasure or amusement. The corners of her smooth lips curled upward, just barely. "Marvin. Yes."

"And your name?"

"I have many names," she said. Then she became very serious. "People have tried breaking me into pieces, and naming each one. Has that ever happened to you, Marvin?"

"I don't know. I don't think so."

"Coward."

"What?"

II

"That's one, isn't it? That's one of the pieces of you that people have tried to name."

She was correct, I realized. It was my father who had used that exact word, years ago, the last time he had spoken to me.

"Failure," the woman said. It brought to mind an image of my mother, staring at me in a way that did not require speech to convey her thoughts.

"Shallow. Selfish. Weak." The woman on the shoreline spoke the words as though they constituted a strange poem. But to me, they felt like knives against my skin. Each one conjured up a memory, some that were decades old, some only months old. I turned my head away from the woman, focused on the ocean that lay beyond us.

"*Liar.*"

My head swiveled back around to face her. She was staring at the waves. I realized I was crying.

"That's the worst one of all, isn't it?"

It was. She was right. It was something I had never known until then.

"Lies." She uncurled her arms from around her legs and lowered her fingers, letting the water graze their tips. "So many lies. How do we expect to live when we have built our lives upon so many lies?"

I did not respond to that.

"It is not easy to reverse all the lies. When we are younger, perhaps. But as we grow older, it becomes difficult. At a certain point, there are far more lies than truths, and one cannot tell the difference anymore."

"It becomes difficult," I repeated.

"Yes. Or, perhaps, impossible. For some."

Neither one of us spoke for some time. The sun had not risen up over the horizon any further since I had taken my spot next to the woman. It appeared to be stuck there, only slightly visible above the ocean.

"Do you see everything you have done?" The woman addressed me with direct eye contact. Her irises seemed to contain movement within them.

III

My tears had dried up, but my sorrow was still with me. "Yes," I answered. "I see."

"You can come with me," she said. "You can follow me out there." She looked toward the ocean. "I am not broken pieces, as people would like to think. I am connected. I am one."

I tried to imagine what lie beneath the waters. Dim shapes. A murky unknown. Darkness.

"But this is not your only option, Marvin. I can go alone. I do not mind being alone. This is my truth, but it is your lie."

"I know," I said.

"It's not too late for you. It becomes difficult, but already, you can see the lies. You can tell the difference. Can't you?"

"Yes."

"Then you will make your decision. You can come with me, because of your lies. Or, you can let me go alone, because you will begin finding the truth. The first option will be simple. It will feel like sweetness in your mouth, at first. The second option will be difficult. It will feel like these knives I've been telling you, cutting through your tissues. At first."

We were both quiet again. We watched the water. The sun was still stuck. Then, I felt something on my arm. It was cold and smooth. I peered down and saw that she was touching me with her hand. I looked into her deep blue eyes.

"Marvin."

"I will stay." My answer hurt in my throat. A wave of pain coursed through my body, stabbing, biting, fierce.

"Very well."

When she kissed me, the pain in my muscles relinquished. When she stood up, a looseness found its way inside me. When she walked out into the waves, I kept my eyes on her billowy dress, her sandy hair. When she disappeared into the water, the sun rose higher above the horizon. The world grew steadily brighter. I left the rocky beach. I never returned to it, nor to the cliff that overlooked it. I did not need to return. Even if I did, I knew I would not find her there again.

∞

IV

Made in the USA
Las Vegas, NV
16 April 2022

47560400R00184